MARY JO

JILL BARNETT

AND

JUSTINE DARE

SUSAN KING

$6.99
**SPECIAL
HOLIDAY
PRICE
$4.99**

A
STOCKINGFUL
OF JOY

SIGNET

SIGNET

$4.99 U.S.

ISBN: 978-0-451-22348-7

9 780451 223487

50499

EAN

A
Stockingful
of Joy

MARY JO PUTNEY
JILL BARNETT
JUSTINE DARE
SUSAN KING

A SIGNET BOOK

SIGNET
Published by New American Library, a division of
Penguin Group (USA) Inc., 375 Hudson Street,
New York, New York 10014, USA
Penguin Group (Canada), 90 Eglinton Avenue East, Suite 700, Toronto,
Ontario M4P 2Y3, Canada (a division of Pearson Penguin Canada Inc.)
Penguin Books Ltd., 80 Strand, London WC2R 0RL, England
Penguin Ireland, 25 St. Stephen's Green, Dublin 2,
Ireland (a division of Penguin Books Ltd.)
Penguin Group (Australia), 250 Camberwell Road, Camberwell, Victoria 3124,
Australia (a division of Pearson Australia Group Pty. Ltd.)
Penguin Books India Pvt. Ltd., 11 Community Centre, Panchsheel Park,
New Delhi - 110 017, India
Penguin Group (NZ), 67 Apollo Drive, Rosedale, North Shore 0632,
New Zealand (a division of Pearson New Zealand Ltd.)
Penguin Books (South Africa) (Pty.) Ltd., 24 Sturdee Avenue,
Rosebank, Johannesburg 2196, South Africa

Penguin Books Ltd., Registered Offices:
80 Strand, London WC2R 0RL, England

Published by Signet, an imprint of New American Library, a division of Penguin Group (USA) Inc. Previously published in an Onyx edition.

First Signet Printing, October 2005
First Signet Printing ($4.99 Edition), November 2007
10 9 8 7 6 5 4 3 2 1

"The Snow Rose" by Susan King copyright © Susan King, 1997
"The Best Husband Money Can Buy" by Mary Jo Putney copyright © Mary Jo Putney, 1997
"A Light in the Window" by Justine Dare copyright © Janice Davis Smith, 1997
"Boxing Day" by Jill Barnett copyright © Jill Barnett Stadler, 1997

Contents

The Snow Rose

_~∞~_

BY SUSAN KING

Prologue

❧

Christmas Day, 1573
The Highlands

"I am Catriona MacDonald of Kilernan, and I need your help." Her soft Gaelic echoed in the silence. Catriona held her breath, and waited for a response from several men gathered near the hearth in the great hall at Glenran Castle. She lifted her chin slightly, determined to show no fear, though these were Frasers, and enemies of her clan.

No one spoke. Although she stood in the center of a hall filled with men, women, and children, amid the Yuletide scents of pine and juniper, of spices and cakes and roasted meats, she felt utterly alone in that instant. Still, she could not blame the Frasers for staring at her so warily. She had broken the peace of their Christmas by coming to their castle.

As the silence continued, Catriona lifted trembling fingers to the red plaid she wore draped over her frayed green gown, and unfastened the silver brooch that she had owned since infancy. She held it out toward Callum Fraser, the laird of Glenran.

"This brooch marks an honorable pledge, made on Christmas Eve twenty years past, by your father," she said. "I have treasured the snow rose all my life."

"Snow rose?" Callum asked as he accepted the brooch.

She nodded. "I called it that when I was a child, because of the silver setting, and the rose quartz stone."

He examined the piece thoughtfully. "I remember seeing it when I was a child."

"Lachlann Fraser gave it to me on Christmas Eve, when I was but a few days old. He pinned it to my swaddling and told my mother that it marked his pledge of protection for me. He said that if I ever was in need, my mother or I should come to him."

"And you are in need now?" Callum asked.

"I am," she said quietly. "Though I am a Mac-Donald, and you are Frasers, and our clans have feuded for generations, I must call upon this pledge. I know that Lachlann of Glenran died several years ago, but I hope that his son will honor his promise, in the spirit of the Yuletide season."

Callum watched her somberly, then leaned over to murmur to the man seated beside him; that man had dark hair and brilliantly blue eyes, and seemed older than the others. Callum listened to him carefully.

The other Frasers murmured among themselves, most of them standing with their backs to the yellow light that spilled from the stone fireplace. While Catriona could not see their faces clearly, she saw that they were tall and well made, blond, dark, and red-headed, wearing plaids of deep green and midnight blue, colors favored by the Glenran Frasers.

Another dark-haired man watched her intently from

where he stood in a shadowed corner near the hearth. He leaned against the wall and folded his arms over his wrapped plaid, crossing his long, muscular legs, cased in deer-skin boots. His gaze never wavered from her face.

Although her heart thumped, Catriona looked at him boldly. He inclined his head in acknowledgment; Catriona soon lowered her eyes, her cheeks heated.

She waited, ignoring the sting of her chilled fingers and toes as they warmed after hours of riding in the cold. She ignored, too, the rumbling of her empty stomach, roused by the scents of the Frasers' Christmas feast. She stood straight and held her head high, feeling the weight of her black hair as it spilled down her back, and curling her toes inside her worn leather boots. Her knees shook, her heart pounded, but on the outside, she remained quiet and still.

Finally the laird leaned forward, his strong, handsome face lined with a frown. "My father told us the story of a Christmas Eve when the widow of Iain Mac-Donald of Kilernan saved his life."

Catriona nodded. "My mother took Lachlann Fraser in during a blizzard. He had been hunting and stopped at Kilernan, unable to make it back to Glenran because of the storm. My mother was still in childbed, and could have directed her men not to admit him," she continued. "He was a Fraser, and she had been recently widowed by the hand of a Fraser. But she honored the custom of Highland hospitality, which is offered to any visitor, friend or foe. Lachlann gave me the brooch and the pledge in return."

"My father was deeply touched by your mother's generosity," Callum said. "I recall that he mentioned a babe, whom he promised to protect. But the Mac-Donald widow never contacted him again." He glanced at the other men. "My father would expect his kinsmen to honor this vow." A few of them nodded agreement. Callum turned to her. "What is it you need?"

Catriona sighed in relief, and gathered boldness in her next breath. "My uncle, Hugh MacDonald, holds Kilernan Castle. I am the Maid of Kilernan, my father's only heir. My uncle will not acknowledge my claim unless I wed the man he has chosen for me." She paused. "I want you to take the castle from Hugh MacDonald."

Callum stared at her. His kinsmen stared at her, too. From across the room, she sensed the gazes of the women as well.

The laird cleared his throat. "Take it?"

"Take it," she said, "and give it into my keeping. I have loyal kinsmen living at Kilernan who will help me hold it."

"Let them take it for you," a red-haired Fraser said.

"My kinsmen are afraid to go against my uncle, although they disapprove of his actions."

"Hugh MacDonald is a drunken fool," the redheaded Fraser said. "Surely when he sobers, he will honor your claim."

"He refuses to do that unless I wed Parlan Mac-Donald, my third cousin." She drew a breath. "The Glenran Frasers are well known for fearlessness and clever raiding. You can take the castle and give it into my keeping."

"We will not take Kilernan by force," Callum said. "Surely you are aware of our signed pledge to end the feud with Clan Donald." He handed the brooch back to her. Catriona pinned it to her plaid. "Let us help you some other way," Callum said.

"Lachlann Fraser promised whatever I needed," she said.

"Lachlann did not promise to kill MacDonalds for you," someone said in a precise, deep tone; she noticed that the dark-haired man standing in the shadows spoke. His frowning gaze pierced hers.

"Kenneth is right." The man beside Callum leaned forward. "The Frasers signed a bond years ago that forbids them to fight MacDonalds. Your clansmen signed the same pledge, though they have not kept it. The Frasers honor it."

"Are you not a Glenran Fraser?" she asked the man.

"I am Duncan Macrae of Dulsie, kin by marriage to the Frasers. And I am a lawyer for the Privy Council. What is the dispute with your uncle? There may be another way to solve it."

She shook her head. "My uncle took over Kilernan when I was a babe. My mother never wed again, and died a few years ago. Now my uncle insists that I marry Parlan. I fear that I will lose Kilernan if I agree."

"Hugh is within his rights as your guardian to choose a husband for you," Macrae said. "But I will look into your legal position when I go to Edinburgh in the spring, if you like."

"By then I will be wed, unless you help me," she said.

"This is no affair for Frasers," Callum said. "Go home, girl, and listen to your uncle."

"I cannot. I fled Kilernan a few months past, to stay in a shieling hut in the hills above Loch Garry. Parlan and my uncle want me to return to Kilernan, but I have refused, until the castle has been promised into my keeping."

"Take your troubles to your clan chief," Kenneth

Fraser said. "We cannot solve this for you." Catriona glanced toward the shadows again. His deep voice had a soothing quality, despite his harsh words.

"I sent word to the MacDonald," she said. "He refused to take Kilernan from Hugh, and promised to send a silver spoon to my firstborn."

"Then you have his blessing to marry Parlan," Kenneth said. "Do that, and you will have Kilernan. You have no choice."

"I do," she pointed out. "I came to you."

His dark eyes gleamed in the firelight. "Stubborn girl," he said softly. "Let us add to your sheepfold, or give you oats and barley to see you through the winter. We cannot attack a MacDonald castle for you."

"Then you must take the castle without bloodshed," she said impulsively. "The Glenran Frasers are said to be very clever."

"Without bloodshed? That," Kenneth said, "is impossible."

"We will gladly help you some other way," Callum said.

Hopelessness wrenched through her. "I must have Kilernan," she whispered. She had not told them the whole truth. Now that they had rejected her plea, her throat tightened over the words.

She doubted they would care to learn that she needed to provide a home for eight children, her cousins. Hugh MacDonald had not cared, either; he had told her that she was a fool to take on the responsibility. The Frasers might say the same.

She saw the dark Fraser frown deeply, watching her. His eyes seemed kind, and his gaze warmed her like a hearth fire. But he offered her no real aid, no solace. None of them did.

"Catriona," Callum said. "Please stay and share our feast."

Food would not solve her dilemma, though her stomach clenched in hunger; she had eaten little that day. Catriona glanced at the tables, which were loaded with dishes, greenery, and blazing candlelight, and looked away again. Her pride urged her to accept nothing from the Frasers now.

But eight hungry children awaited her visit later today. She could not deny them this chance for a Christmas feast.

"I cannot stay," she finally said. "But I will accept a gift of food for my cousins, who have no fine Christmas meal."

Callum nodded. "And for yourself?"

"I want nothing from you," she said proudly. "Farewell, and blessings of the season to you." She turned away.

A woman stepped away from the tables and came toward her, carrying a sturdy blond toddler in her arms. The mother was delicately beautiful, with copper gold hair and wide gray eyes. A boy with dark hair stood behind her, and two young children clung to her skirts, a boy and a girl who shared their mother's striking gray eyes. The children watched her curiously, and the babe sucked a finger and babbled, grinning. Catriona smiled at him.

"I am Elspeth Fraser, wife to Macrae of Dulsie, the lawyer," the woman said. "The Frasers here are my cousins. We were all fostered by Lachlann of Glenran. We do not mean to dishonor his vow to you, but please understand our position. I will urge my husband and my kin to look into the matter for you."

Catriona nodded. "Thank you. Farewell—"

"You look cold and tired," Elspeth said. "Warm yourself by our fire. Eat with us, and share songs and dances with us. It is Christmas, Catriona MacDonald. Be of good cheer this day."

Catriona hesitated, urged by her empty stomach, her cold feet, her lonely heart. She looked into Elspeth's silver eyes, and smiled at her beautiful children. She glanced at the tantalizing burden of cakes, meats, and cheeses on the table, and inhaled the scents of beeswax candles and fragrant greenery.

She glanced at the other women and children who watched her. They were all handsome, keen-eyed, looking at her with interest, and without suspicion. No one seemed anxious for her to be gone.

She sensed the warmth and love among these Frasers, as tangible as the aromas of ginger cakes and evergreens. Suddenly Catriona wanted to share in what they had. The desire and the need nearly buckled her knees. She starved for more than food.

But she could not endure pity or charity in place of the real help she desperately needed. When Christmas was done, the Frasers would still be enemies of the MacDonalds. The pledge marked by her silver brooch could not change that.

"I must go," she murmured. "Others wait for me."

Elspeth touched her arm gently. "Take this, then," she said. The older boy held a cloth bundle toward her.

"Cheese, cakes, and roasted meat," Elspeth explained. "The cheese has holes in it. Look through a slice, and you will see what will come to you in the new year. And there are candles to bring the blessing of light in the coming year. I added a flask of *uisge beatha,* too. May it warm you well."

Catriona took the bundle, blinking away the tears that

pooled in her eyes. "Thank you," she whispered. "A happy Christmas and luck in the new year to all of you." She moved toward the door. Behind her, she heard a strong tread as a man strode the length of the hall.

"Catriona MacDonald." The voice of the dark Fraser, deep and mellow, sounded. She turned to see Kenneth Fraser walking toward her. "Stay. We will escort you home later."

She gazed up into his strong, lean face, into heavily lashed eyes of brilliant, warm brown, like firelight shot through polished, dark cairngorm. Somehow all the tempting, wondrous comforts of this place seemed to gather in those deep, rich eyes.

She shook her head. "I must go. A good new year to you."

"Bliadhna Sona," he said. "A lucky new year to you."

"Luck," she said softly, "is what I need most." She hurried toward the door, knowing he watched her.

Although they had refused to help her in the way that she needed, the Frasers' kindness made her ache inside, down deep where she had felt empty for so long. Their charity reminded her keenly that she lacked what existed in such abundance here. Loving kin, comfort, safety, and companionship were commonplace to them—and as rare as gold to her.

She shoved open the door and ran down the stone steps. During Yuletide, charity always flowed like wine, she told herself. They would gladly share with her now. Later, after the new year, the Frasers would once again be her enemies. Fraser pledges would prove false after all, just as her uncle had often said whenever he saw the snow rose brooch pinned to her plaid.

She ran through the yard, fighting back a sob. Then

she tore the silver brooch from her plaid and tossed it
into the ice-crusted mud.

Kenneth Fraser walked through the yard as the girl
cantered away on her garron pony. He watched her
until she was a dark speck moving over the snow-
coated hills. He sighed and turned.

Something sparkled in the mud beside his boot, and
he bent down to pick up the silver brooch. The snow
rose, she had called it. Silver tracery, curved like
flower petals, circled a round, pale pink stone. He
imagined Catriona as a little girl, naming the brooch,
cherishing the pledge it represented. But he knew that
the Frasers had disappointed her.

Gripping the brooch, he walked toward the tower
entrance, and looked up to see Duncan Macrae
standing in the doorway.

"You want to help the girl," Duncan observed
calmly.

Kenneth shrugged. "Someone should help her."

"If blood is spilled in feud between Frasers and Mac-
Donalds, the crown will send fire and sword upon your
heads. The Regent will not hesitate this time."

"I know." Kenneth frowned as he studied the
sparkling brooch. He thought of the MacDonald girl,
shining like a Christmas angel come to earth: gentle,
graceful, and yet filled with a marvelous strength.

She stood proudly, but he had noticed the worn hem
of her green woolen gown, and the peeled edges of her
leather boots. He had seen the haunted look in her brilliant blue eyes, and the quick touch of her tongue to her
lips when she had looked at the food heaped upon the
tables. The girl had many needs, yet asked for only one
favor, nearly impossible to meet.

"Lachlann pledged protection to her," Kenneth said. "We owe her something for that."

Duncan nodded. "We do. But we all signed that bond, Kenneth. We cannot do what she asks of us."

"True." Kenneth frowned. "Perhaps I should ride out to her shieling hut in a few days, just to be certain she is well. I do not like to think of her alone during the Yuletide season. She reminds me—" He stopped.

Duncan watched him evenly. "The girl does have a little of the look of Anna."

Kenneth nodded curtly. Anna, his betrothed, had died of an illness three years ago on New Year's Day. Since then, the Yuletide season had proved hard for him to endure.

Like Anna, Catriona MacDonald was slim and black-haired, graceful and strong. But Anna had always glimmered with humor and joy, her rosy cheeks dimpling often. Catriona MacDonald was somber and sad, her skin as pale and delicate as the rose quartz stone in her brooch.

She was not Anna; no one could be like Anna, ever. But he did not like the thought of Catriona fearful and alone on Christmas, or on New Year's, the day that Anna had died.

"You could ride out in a few days," Duncan agreed. "Make certain that the girl is well, and bring her provisions. We can at least see that she is safe through the winter. By spring, she will likely marry this Parlan MacDonald."

Kenneth smoothed his thumb over the cold surface of the brooch. "And I will return this to her," he said. "She should know that it does have some meaning, after all."

Chapter Two

❦

Juniper smoke billowed up from the central fire pit in a gray, stinging cloud. The tears that wet her lashes were the first she had allowed herself to shed in a long while. Catriona blinked hard, wiped her eyes, and grasped an iron poker to prod the high pile of evergreen branches that smoldered over glowing peat bricks.

Coughing, she waved her hands to spread the smoke to every corner of the little shieling hut to cleanse and purify and protect, just as her mother had done on every *Oidhche Challuinn*, New Year's Eve, when she had been a child. Such memories, bringing back her mother's kindness and loving companionship, had sustained her during these months of living alone here, without hope for her future.

The hut was hardly a fine fortress, but it was her home. Castle Kilernan was lost to her now. The memory of Christmas Day, and the Frasers' refusal to help her, stung as harshly as the smoke in her eyes. New Year's Eve was a time to gather blessings and attract luck to the household; she would honor her little home with the proper traditions, and hopefully turn her luck for the better.

She waved at the billowing juniper smoke. When she could scarcely breathe—her mother had taught her that the smoke must be thick enough to drive everyone from the room—she went to the door and pulled it open. Cold air and swirling snowflakes rushed inside.

She coughed and pulled her plaid snugly over her frayed gown as she watched the storm. Bitter chill snapped at her cheeks, and she ducked deeper into the plaid, keeping the door open while the smoke dispersed.

A small, solid body rubbed against her leg. She glanced down at the black cat who blinked up at her with pale green eyes. "*Ach,* pardon the smoke, Cù," Catriona said. "But you and I will have some wonderful luck after the juniper is burned," she said with forced brightness. She reached down and scooped up the cat, and watched the snow pile wild and thick over the hills. The darkness had a soft blue tint, and the air felt gentle somehow, filled with promise and hope.

But she knew the dangerous reality of such a storm. Behind her the dim hut offered shelter and warmth. Tonight she would not set foot beyond the wedge of light that spilled into the flurrying snow.

No one else would venture outside tonight, either, although it was New Year's Eve, and likely near midnight by now. No one would come up to her hut for a traditional visit after midnight, bringing small gifts of food or drink or coin as tokens of good luck. The storm and the distance would keep visitors away. She was disappointed, but relieved to know that Parlan MacDonald would not ride out to see her.

"Little Mairead MacGhille told me a wonderful

surprise would come to me this New Year's, Cù," she whispered to the cat. "She spoke of it when I visited the children earlier today. Perhaps she felt the approaching storm, though. All that snow is like a gift, wondrous and peaceful. Ah, Cù—I hope the children are not alarmed by the storm. The snow had not begun when I left them."

Cù mewled and poured out of her arms. Thumping down to the rushed-coated earthen floor, he stretched beside the warm stones that encircled the fire. Catriona began to close the door, but a faint, steady sound caught her attention. She peered out, seeing little beyond the fluttering, lacy whiteness.

But she could hear the drums of the *gillean Callaig,* the lads of New Year's Eve, as they marched around the *clachan,* a cluster of a few farms and kale-yards. Even a blizzard would not stop them, although she doubted they would walk far with their torches and drums and songs. The young lads, with a few young men among them, would pound intense, driving rhythms on hide-stretched drums, and chant loudly; from this distance, only the strong beat penetrated the drifting curtains of snow.

She smiled, imagining their antics. They would be disguised in robes and animal hides, some wearing horns and acting like oxen, while others chased them, carrying blazing torches. Chanting and beating drums, they would circle each house to frighten away evil spirits, sending out the old year to make room for the new. They were given wine, *uisge beatha,* and sweet bannock cakes in return for bringing luck for the new year.

"Just as well no one will come up here in this weather," Catriona told the cat. "I have little food or drink to offer. Another poor omen for the new year."

She sighed. "Who will set first-foot in my home after midnight, to bless it for the year?"

When she had been young, the adults at Kilernan had laughed and celebrated with midnight visitors, singing and drinking fine drams until the small hours. Whoever set foot first in the hall after midnight would determine good or ill fortune for that year. Tall, dark-haired men with pleasant natures, bearing small gifts, were the luckiest New Year's visitors of all. Blond men were quite unfavorable, and women might be lucky or not, according to their hair color and disposition.

But Catriona would have no midnight visitors at all, surely an unfavorable portent. She sighed, and watched the cat stretch on the floor. "You may not be tall, Cù, but you are a dark-haired male. You will have to set first-foot in the door. We have to make our own luck this year." The cat only looked at her with disinterest.

Closing the door, she went to the table and picked up a flaming beeswax candle, part of the Frasers' Christmas bundle, and placed it on the narrow window-sill. The glow would attract lucky spirits toward her home and help to bless the coming year.

She had given the other candles and most of the food to the MacGhille children, keeping a little cheese and oatmeal for herself, along with the flask of *uisge beatha,* which she doubted the children should have.

Remembering the Frasers' gifts, she went to the cupboard and sliced off a bit of the cheese, which was pierced with round holes. As she passed the circle of hearthstones, the fire blazed brightly for an instant. Catriona frowned, aware that a sudden burst of flame could foretell the coming of a stranger. A chill slid through her, but she dismissed the unsettled feeling.

She opened the door, then held the cheese slice up to

one eye. Elspeth Fraser had told her that looking through a hole in the cheese would show her what would come in the new year. She peered through the hole, partly dreading whatever omen she might see, convinced that good fortune had forgotten her existence.

Seeing only fluttering snow and darkness, she wondered dismally if the view portended a cold, lonely year for her.

Then she gasped. Through the small hole, something moved out in the falling snow. She narrowed her eyes, and saw a man and a horse coming slowly along the ridge of the hill. Lowering the cheese, staring in disbelief, she watched the horse advance with high, labored steps through the deep drifts. The man was enveloped in a thick plaid, unrecognizable through the darkness, though he was a tall, large man.

Parlan, she thought. Surely Parlan rode toward her house for a New Year's visit. Catriona stepped backward to slam the door shut, and leaned against it.

Regardless of his thick blond hair, Parlan MacDonald was a poor omen indeed. She would not let him into her house.

He was thoroughly lost, and his head ached fiercely. Not an auspicious end to the old year, nor a lucky start to the next, Kenneth thought in irritation. Icy, slanting snow stung his face and hands, and he shivered in the bitter cold. He drew his plaid higher over his head and peered through swirling veils of white.

Snow smothered the hillsides and filled the air. He had little sense of his location anymore. A few hours ago, when the snowfall had been a mild, pretty flutter, he had approached Loch Garry and turned toward the hills that edged its northern side, certain that the Mac-Donald girl's shieling hut would be there.

Riding upward, he had met three MacDonalds, who had ridden toward him with suspicious glances, no doubt recognizing the Fraser badge, a sprig of fresh yew stuck in his woolen bonnet, and the Glenran pattern of his plaid. In turn, he knew the distinctive red and green design that they wore: Kilernan Mac-Donalds. Kenneth had nodded politely as he passed.

"Fraser! A Fraser!" The MacDonalds turned to chase him. Leaning forward, he urged his garron to a canter, but his mount slipped on the icy slope. The Mac-Donalds caught up to him, shouting threats. One swiped an unstrung bow at him, another swung a sword, and the third kicked at him. Struggling to dodge their blows, wary of fighting them, Kenneth noticed that they wavered and laughed drunkenly; they had already begun to celebrate the New Year, and saw him as some sport.

His garron stumbled and went down, pitching Kenneth from the saddle. He rolled to avoid the Mac-Donalds, who landed on him in a brawling, hooting cluster. The force of their attack drove his head against a rock. As he faded from awareness, he heard them swearing and running back to their horses.

When he awoke, the snow gathered silently around him in the growing darkness. Groggy and shivering, grateful that two thick plaids had saved him from freezing, he struggled to his feet, found his garron, and managed to ride onward.

Now he touched his fingers to the painful lump on the back of his head and felt the swelling there, then felt his bruised and cut lip. The horse walked ahead slowly, impeded by heavy snow and dim light.

Kenneth did his utmost to stay warm, and to stay upright in the saddle as dizziness swamped him.

"What a pair we are," Kenneth muttered. "Ambushed and wounded, and now caught in a blizzard. Luck is not following us into the new year." He glanced around, certain that the hour must be close to midnight. The Mac-Donald girl's shieling hut was somewhere in these hills, but he would not find it this night.

He would take shelter wherever he could, in a stranger's home, an empty shieling, even a cave. Tomorrow would be time enough to find the girl and deliver the pack of food and household items that was tied to the saddle behind him.

He shivered with cold, despite the protection of two plaids, a leather doublet, woolen trews, and deer-skin boots. He patted the horse's neck with a note of encouragement he did not feel; riding through Mac-Donald territory was dangerous enough for a Fraser, but exposure and death were a far more real threat now.

He remembered the tale Lachlann Fraser had told of traveling one Christmas Eve through a fierce snow-storm. No wonder Lachlann had promised protection to the newborn child of the woman who gave him hospitality. Just now Kenneth would give anything he had for the barest sort of welcome.

He peered through the snowy veil that obscured his surroundings. A moment later he saw a faint sparkle of golden light ahead. He narrowed his eyes, wondering if the light was a trick of the blow to his head, but the glow flickered and held.

Riding forward, he saw a small house, a single candle glowing in the window. Grateful for his good fortune, Kenneth dismounted stiffly. When his dizziness abated, he untied the bundle from the saddle, wanting to offer something in return for the hospitality he hoped to gain. He waded through the deep snow to knock at the door. Silence followed. He knocked again.

"Be gone from here!" a woman's voice called out.

"I am in need of shelter for the night," he called.

"Go away, Parlan MacDonald!" she returned.

Hearing that name, and the woman's soft voice, he realized that he had found the MacDonald girl's shieling after all, through sheer luck. "Catriona Mac-Donald," he called, knocking again. "I am a Glenran Fraser. Let me in." A long silence followed his statement. He pounded on the door. "I am in need of shelter for myself and my horse."

She opened the door a crack and peered at him. "A Glenran Fraser! What are you doing here on such a night?"

"Let me in, if you will, and I will tell you," he said. The firelight that haloed her form darkened oddly as he looked at her. He leaned against the door frame. "Let me in, girl," he said wearily. "I have come far."

"Which Fraser are you? Are you the blond man? If so, I must let black Cù go out and come in again before you enter."

Confused, he realized that she referred to the midnight tradition of first-foot. If only for the color of his hair, he would be welcome. He lowered the plaid that covered his head.

"I am the dark-haired one," he answered. "Kenneth Fraser. May I come in?" His legs felt strangely weak. He willed the sensation to pass. It did not.

The girl opened the door, and Kenneth stepped across the threshold. He heard her speak faintly, as if from a distance. Then darkness gathered around him like a thundercloud.

Chapter Three

∽◦∾

He went down at her feet like a felled oak. Catriona dropped to her knees and slipped her hand under his head. His tall, muscular body took up much of the space in her tiny home: his feet were on the threshold, his head lay near the hearth. The cat, who had leaped upward when the man fell, now sniffed gingerly at him.

"Kenneth Fraser!" Catriona said anxiously. "Kenneth!" After a few moments, he groaned and moved slowly, then raised himself to his knees. Catriona helped him to stand, but he leaned so heavily against her that his weight and height threatened to topple her to the floor.

She half dragged him the few feet toward the bed, a narrow mattress boxed in the wall by wooden panels and a heavy curtain. Shoving the curtain aside, she let the man drop to the bed. He sank, face downward.

"You may have dark hair," she said as she lifted one of his legs, then the other, to the mattress, "but a drunken, staggering first-foot must be a poor omen, and I do not thank you for it."

"I am not drunk," he said. His voice was slurred. "I

came to bring you blessings of the new year. Am I your first-foot?" He put a hand to his head and rolled to his back, groaning.

"You are," she said, "and an unlucky one, I am sure." She scowled down at him. She had thought him a handsome man when she had seen him at Glenran, but now he was bedraggled, bruised, and near frozen; his lip was cut and swollen, and his expression was stupefied. She had seen men in this condition at Kilernan, men who drank and brawled on New Year's Eve, and indeed celebrated heavily from Christmas through Twelfth Night. Her uncle was the worst of the lot.

"Tcha," she muttered. "This sort of blessing I do not need. You are drunk, wet, and frozen."

"I am not drunk," he said again, sitting up. *"Ach,* my horse is outside. I must—" He stood, swayed, and grabbed the frame of the box-bed for support.

Catriona slipped beneath his arm to keep him from falling over. He laid an arm over her shoulders, and walked, unsteady and stumbling, toward the door.

"Lie down," Catriona said, turning with him. "I will see to your horse." She led him back to the bed, and pulled the fur covers over him.

She threw her spare plaid over her shoulders, and went to the door and opened it, nearly tripping over the cat, who pawed tentatively at the snow piled on the doorstep.

"Ach, Cù!" Catriona pushed the cat aside. "Stay in here. Both of you," she ordered, glancing at the man on the bed, who mumbled indistinctly.

Catriona trudged through icy winds and hazy snow-fall, took the garron by the bridle, and led him to the small byre, where her own horse and a cow, lent her by a neighbor, were stabled. She murmured reassuringly to the animals, filled their manger with oats, and hurried back to the hut.

Kenneth had removed his damp plaid and sat on the bed in trews and doublet, a blanket pulled high around his shoulders. His face appeared grayish, and he sagged against the bed frame. Catriona glanced at him as she stamped her feet and shook the snow from her skirt, then undid her plaid. "However did you find my house, as drunk as you are?" she asked.

"I am not drunk, girl," he growled. "And it was pure luck that I found you."

"Luck? I have little of that, and your arrival like this, on New Year's, is certain proof." She hammocked their plaids between the table and the bed to dry, leaving scant room to edge her way past Kenneth Fraser as she approached the central hearth. "Are you hungry? I can offer you oats and hot *uisge beatha* to warm you—but perhaps you have had enough of that."

He glowered at her. "Porridge would be kind," he said curtly. "I nearly forgot—that sack by the door is for you, with blessings of the New Year from the Frasers."

Catriona looked at him in surprise, and retrieved the bundle that he had dropped inside the door when he fell at her feet. She took it to the table and opened it. Inside, she found an abundance of goods: wrapped cheeses and roasted meat, more candles, milled oats and barley in cloth sacks, a flask of claret, a packet of currants, parchment papers holding spices, and even a small sack of white sugar. Catriona dipped a finger in the sugar to taste its sweetness, then glanced at Kenneth.

His dark eyes gleamed warm in the amber light.

"Luck in the New Year to you, Catriona MacDonald," he said softly.

"Thank you," she whispered, her throat tightening. This man, a Fraser, had ridden a long way in foul weather to bring her a New Year's blessing. No one had ever done such a thing for her. She glanced away from his steady gaze uncertainly. "I will make you some food. It will cleanse the drink from your head."

He sighed, a half laugh. "No need. But I am hungry," he said. Catriona cooked oats and water in a kettle over the fire, stirred in thin slices of the roasted beef he had brought, and ladled the food into a wooden bowl, handing it to him with a wooden spoon.

"Will you not eat, too?" he asked. When she shook her head, he frowned. "When was the last time you ate a meal?" he asked. She shrugged; she wanted to bring his new gift of food to the children when the weather cleared, just as she had done with the other goods the Frasers had given her.

Kenneth scooped up a spoonful of porridge and offered it to her. She shook her head again. "*Ach,* girl, you cannot refuse my New Year's gift. You will offend me and bring ill luck to us both. Here, eat."

She leaned forward, and Kenneth touched the spoon to her lips, slipping the warm, salty oats inside. She swallowed, knowing he watched her, and felt a hot blush seep into her cheeks, and an intimate swirl ripple through her body. He offered her more. She shook her head, but he insisted, until she took the spoon from him and ate some. Kenneth finished the rest.

"There," he said. "That should bring us both some luck."

"I hope so," she said softly. "I need some luck."

"Believe me, girl, after being lost in that snowstorm,

I am glad for the chance to bring some to you." He smiled a little.

She smiled, too, feeling oddly safe and peaceful then, as if he was not a stranger, or an enemy of her clan. She liked his smile, liked the quiet lilt in his voice, his gentle, teasing manner, and the bronze lights in his hair and his eyes. She liked the comforting weight of Fraser beef and oats in her stomach. Most of all, she was glad to have her loneliness eased on the first night of the year.

Kenneth looked toward the shuttered window, which trembled as the wind shoved it. "I cannot leave until the weather clears. May I sleep by your fire?"

"You are too weak to go anywhere. You may stay as long as you need. Cù sleeps by the fire, but he will make room for you."

"Cù? Dog? Where is it?" He glanced around the room.

She laughed. "Cù is my cat. A little girl I know saw him as a kitten, and mistook him for a black puppy, so 'Dog' became his name. Mairead is nearly blind," she added.

"Ah. A cat named Dog," he drawled. "I am sure he protects you well." He smiled, and the boyish quirk of his lips charmed a quick, shy smile from her.

He stood slowly, his weakness evident, and picked up his plaid, wavering unsteadily as Cù shot between his feet to snatch at the cloth. Kenneth spun to avoid stepping on the cat, and sat heavily on the bed.

Catriona picked up Cù. "The house is small, I know," she told Kenneth. "It is just a shieling, meant for use by the men who bring their herds into the hills to graze in the springtime. It lacks the comforts of a true home."

"Some of the comforts are here," he said, watching

her steadily. "It only has to house two of us—and your cat named Dog—for one night. I will leave in the morning." He cradled the back of his head and grimaced as he took his hand away.

She frowned, seeing blood on his fingers. "You are hurt! What happened? Were you in a drunken New Year's brawl?"

"My horse and I went down on the ice. I am fine," he said shortly, when she leaned forward to part his hair.

Catriona winced in sympathy as she looked at the wound. The swollen, bloody lump looked painful. "Fine? Hardly. And these bruises on your jaw and your lip—" Leaning close to look, she did not smell strong drink on his breath. "You are not drunk," she said. "My pardon for thinking you were. What happened? Were you attacked as you came here? *Ach,* it was MacDonalds!"

"I went down on the ice," he repeated sharply.

She narrowed her eyes. "And just who took you down?" He was silent. Catriona shook her head. Here was trouble indeed, if her kin had attacked a Fraser and tracked him here. She went to a shelf, fetched a folded cloth and a bowl of water, and went back to the bed. "Now, let me tend to your head," she ordered.

He turned obediently. She cleansed his wounds carefully, then combed her fingers through his dark hair to ease his headache. His tangled hair felt like heavy silk. He groaned softly as she worked.

"I did not mean to hurt you," she said, lifting her hands.

"Such gentle hands could never deal out hurt," he murmured. "My thanks. I know you are not fond of Frasers." He opened his doublet, took it off and set it aside, then unpinned a small brooch from his linen shirt. He held it out. "This is yours."

The snow rose brooch winked in the low light. She began to reach out, then closed her hand tightly. "I—I do not want it."

"Take it, Catriona," he said. "Let it continue to serve as a token of the Frasers' goodwill. We wish you no harm."

She glanced at him. "Have you come here to take Kilernan from Hugh MacDonald?"

"You know I have not."

"Then the snow rose means nothing to me." She spoke firmly to hide the fact that she had always treasured the brooch, and stood. "You keep it. Good night." She snatched up her plaid and spread it on the floor like a pallet.

"What are you doing?" he asked.

"I will sleep here," she said as she sat on the plaid and began to remove her boots. "You are injured, and need the bed."

"I will not take your bed, girl." He stood. In the dim light of the peat fire, she saw his face go suddenly pale.

"Lie down. Will you refuse my hospitality and bring us both ill luck?" She echoed his own words. "The hearth fire cannot be allowed to go out on this night of the year, as anyone knows. I need to watch over it. Go to sleep, now." She stretched out and pulled the plaid over her.

After a moment she thought she heard him swear a low oath. Soon she heard his boots thud to the floor, and heard the bed creak as he lay down.

The peat fire crackled, the wind howled cold and bleak outside, and the man sighed in her bed. Catriona tossed on the flat, hard pallet, and wondered just what this odd evening portended for the new year.

* * *

Kenneth opened his eyes again. Restless for a while now, he had lain in the bed listening as the girl shifted and sighed, huddled in the plaid on the cold floor. He peered toward her. The light from the glowing embers revealed that she curled tightly, shivering.

"Catriona," he said softly.

"Kenneth? What is it? Are you ill?" She sat up.

He flung back the plaid and the furs. "Get in the bed."

"I will not!" She turned away abruptly.

He sighed in exasperation. "I will sleep by the hearth. Get in and get warm," he ordered, sitting up. "Your knocking teeth have kept me awake all the night."

She sighed, then got up and came toward him. "It is freezing on the floor. We can share the bed. But if you touch me, I will use the poker." She lay down and deliberately stuffed part of the fur robe between them.

"You can always call out your Dog on me," he muttered, and shifted to his side, his back to the cold wall. The box-bed was narrow, and they were jammed together as if in a snug nest. Kenneth felt the tension in her shoulders as she lay stiffly against him. "Relax," he said, adjusting his position. "I must rest my arm somewhere. If I lay it just here, will you attack me with your poker?" He balanced his forearm gently on her hip.

"I might," she said. He smiled at her wry tone. He settled, inhaling the sweet smell of her hair and enjoying the feel of her, close and warm on a cold night. Their bodies fit comfortably together—far too comfortably, he thought, and stirred slightly away from her.

He thought of Anna, for it was New Year's and the third anniversary of her death. But he was deeply exhausted, and her image seemed distant. He sighed, feeling strangely content, almost peaceful. Listening to Catriona's even breathing, he slipped into a heavy, dreamless sleep.

Catriona opened her eyes once again, wanting to be certain that the banked fire still burned. She lay half awake and heard the wind shove at the outer walls, and heard Kenneth snore.

Snuggling against his solid warmth, she felt safe and comfortable, although he was a Fraser, and largely unknown to her. In the morning daylight would bring a new year, and cold reality. But now, while darkness spun a bridge from the old year to the new, she felt a brief respite from loneliness.

Turning, she felt his arm, heavy with sleep, fall across her abdomen. His breath stirred her hair. Lured by his warmth and strength, hungry for the reassurance of simple touch, she rested her head against his chest. He sighed in his sleep and wrapped his arms around her.

Drawn into that shelter, Catriona suddenly felt tears sting her eyes. Kenneth did not awaken, but pulled her closer, as if he sensed her need for solace even in his sleep.

Curled into the curve of his body, listening to the deep, even beat of his heart, she sniffled and wiped her eyes. Finally growing drowsy, she knew that, this once, she could sleep peacefully and without fear.

Chapter Four

❦

Kenneth awoke to silence, but for the low crackle in the hearth, and sat up to see that Catriona was gone. Shoving his fingers through his hair, he felt a throbbing reminder of his injury, and still felt the grogginess of total exhaustion. Judging by the light, he must have slept late into the morning. He crossed the room and pulled open the window shutter, then blinked at the brightness.

Snow blanketed the hills and piled high in drifts of down. After a few moments he saw Catriona wading through the yard. She entered the house on a draft of bitter wind, shaking the snow from her clothing and setting down a small bucket of fresh milk. Her cheeks were a high, clear pink as she unwound her plaid.

"Blessings of the New Year to you, Kenneth Fraser," she said. "I have been out to see to the animals. The snow is quite deep. I could hardly walk from the hut to the byre." She sat on the bench to remove her boots.

"Luck of the New Year," he returned. "You should have asked me to see to the animals."

"You were asleep," she said. "And why should I ask you?"

"Because I owe you for sheltering me."

"You are injured and fatigued, and you brought gifts to me. I will repay you with hospitality," she said. "After that, we owe each other nothing. Our clans are at feud, after all."

"Catriona." He glanced at her somberly. "We are not at feud, you and I. I know a promise was made to you when you were born. I came here to honor Lachlann's pledge as best I could."

She sent him a swift glance. "With food and candles, or with men at your back and a sword in your hand?"

"I came here to see that you were well," he said firmly. "I came here to protect you, if you need that."

She looked away. "I need nothing from a Fraser."

He sighed, watching her profile, delicate but precisely made, as if stubbornness began in her core, in her bones. "I know you want us to reconsider, but we cannot. We signed a bond given us by the Privy Council," he explained. "If we fight with MacDonalds, the man who serves as pledge for our bond can be imprisoned and even executed. That man is Duncan Macrae, my cousin Elspeth's husband."

"The lawyer?" she asked.

He nodded. "I owe Duncan my life. He once saved me from a beheading." She glanced at him, her eyes wide. "We all owe him," he continued, "and we will not endanger him. The MacDonalds do not honor this bond as cautiously as we do, but no Glenran Fraser will willingly shed MacDonald blood ever again."

"I understand," she said, and sighed. "But my uncle has done me a great wrong, and I need help to right it. I may never be able to go back to my home again." She bit at her lower lip.

He undid the silver brooch, which he had repinned to

his shirt, and held it out to her. "Take the snow rose, Catriona," he said. "Take it, and let me help you some other way."

She did not touch the brooch. "Oats and candles are kind gifts, and brooches are pretty. But none of those help me."

"Kilernan cannot be taken without starting a blood feud."

"Then take it without bloodshed," she said simply.

He shook his head. "That cannot be done."

"I need only that. All else I can do for myself."

He bowed his head in exasperation. He wanted to help her, but she would accept only what he could not give her.

"Do it without blood, Kenneth," she said. "If you want to help me, find some way to take Kilernan. Please." He heard the pleading in her soft voice, and heard a tremble of fear there.

He frowned, and grabbed up the brooch. Standing, he went to the door and yanked it open. He stared out over the hills, white and vast and endlessly pure. Behind him, Catriona knelt by the hearth. He heard a wooden spoon stir inside an iron kettle, heard the splash of liquid as she began to prepare a meal.

"You will have to stay another night, because of the snow," she said as she worked. "And with that head wound, you need rest before you can travel. When you return to Glenran, please thank your kin for the New Year's gifts."

He said nothing. The cross pin of the snow rose pierced his skin as he grasped it. He looked down, and saw a bright drop of blood on his fingertip.

* * *

They ate a hot meal of barley and beef, and oatcakes made with a hole in the center, traditionally shaped New Year's bannocks. Kenneth noticed that Catriona did not add the sugar and currants he had brought, as would have been customary. She made a spiced, watered wine with the claret, but sipped only a little herself.

After the meal, Kenneth slept heavily, as if he had not rested for days, and awoke to find that his headache had lessened a good deal. He looked around. Near the door, Catriona wound a thick plaid around her head and shoulders, over her gown and another plaid. Her hands were covered in heavy stockings. She picked up the cloth bundle that he had brought, opened the door quietly, and stepped outside.

Frowning, he sat up and dressed, wrapping and belting his plaid over his leather doublet and long trews. Yanking on his deer-skin boots, he followed her outside.

She rode her garron away from the yard, through deep drifts. Kenneth ran to the byre and saddled his own horse to follow Catriona. He rode after her steadily, his breath frosting in small clouds, his eyes narrowed against the glare of sun on snow.

"Catriona! Go back!" Kenneth called as he neared her. "These drifts are too deep."

She turned. "You go back! You need to rest. I am not going far."

He rode alongside of her, determined to watch over her. If her garron became stranded, at least she would not be alone. She rode ahead of him while their ponies struggled through the drifts. They crossed a long ridge and waded down a hill.

"It is but a short way now," she said after a while.

She urged her garron over a moor. Kenneth followed, his garron, like hers, plowing through deep snow. Cold nipped through his boots and plaid. Finally he saw a small stone house set in the lee of a hill. Gray smoke twisted up from the roof hole. In the yard, a snow fortress, piled high with snowballs, was flanked by crudely shaped snowmen, wearing flat Highland bonnets.

Catriona dismounted and led her horse into a small, crowded byre, which already contained a goat, four sheep, two cows, and two dark garrons. She motioned for Kenneth to stable his horse as well. Then she handed him the bundle she had brought, and knocked on a small door in the wall.

"You must enter as the first-foot," she told Kenneth. "A dark-haired man, holding gifts, will bring them good luck. And besides, they will adore you for it."

Kenneth gave her a puzzled look and stepped through. He stared in amazement as a swarm of children rushed past him, shouting and laughing, to throw themselves at Catriona. She hugged them, each in turn, from a tall, dark-haired boy to a tiny blond boy—and every size in between, Kenneth thought, stunned. Finally she embraced a little red-haired girl, kissed her soundly, and turned to Kenneth.

"These," she said, "are my children."

He blinked at her, while the children laughed loudly, and Catriona smiled. He looked around, hardly able to take in the din, the laughter, and the jostling and giggling of six, seven, eight children in all, seven boys and one girl.

"Your children?" he asked uncertainly.

She laughed sweetly, like a small bell. "Well," she said. "I wish they were mine. But they are my cousins, and ... they have been orphaned. This is Kenneth Fraser," she told the children. Kenneth nodded, and received sober stares in return.

"This is Patrick MacGhille," she said, touching the tallest boy's arm. Kenneth saw Patrick frown, his beard-wisped cheeks flushed, as if he disapproved of a Fraser in his home. Those of the name MacGhille, Kenneth knew, were loyal to Clan Donald.

"And here are Angus, Malcolm, David"—she touched each lower head as she spoke, like going down a stair— "and Donald, Edan, and Tomas. And their sister, Mairead." Kenneth nodded hesitantly to each; the little girl, he observed, was only a bit older than the two youngest boys, Edan and Tomas.

"Triona, Triona!" Edan tugged at her hand and pointed to Kenneth. "What does he have in that sack?"

"Wonderful things, but you must be patient," she said.

"*Bliadhna Sona,* Triona," the little girl piped.

"And a lucky New Year to you, my Mairead," Catriona said, smoothing her hair. Kenneth saw then that the child's left eye was milky-blue and wandered to the side. This, then, must be the little half-blind girl who had named the cat "Dog."

"Tell me, how did you fare in the storm?" Catriona asked them. The children began to chatter of their adventures as she crossed the dim, smoky room and sat on a bench beside the table, lifting Tomas to her lap. The boys sat, too, on the bench, on stools, on the earthen floor. Kenneth stood while Catriona and the children spoke about the storm.

As he listened, he realized that Patrick and his brother Angus, who seemed to be proud, capable lads, had taken responsibility for their younger siblings. The children clearly loved Catriona, and Kenneth saw that they depended on her for support and friendship.

He glanced around the house. Snug and well made of stone, earth, and thatch, the crofter's hut had one room with a central hearth; the furnishings were simple and few, and he saw two box-beds in the wall. Overhead was a dark, narrow loft, likely with more beds. Behind him, he heard—and smelled—the animals in the byre, separated from the house by a wattle and daub wall.

He looked at Catriona, who gathered the children close to tell them about her New Year's adventure. They gasped as she told them about her first-foot, and turned to stare at Kenneth.

"But he is a Fraser!" one boy said. "He is not lucky!"

"He has dark hair," Mairead said in his defense.

"Why would a Fraser come to see you?" Patrick asked.

"I came as Catriona's friend," Kenneth answered.

"He brought gifts," Catriona said. "I will show you."

"He is the one," Mairead said, nodding. "The lucky one."

The smaller boys tugged at Catriona's skirt. She smiled at them and looked at Kenneth. He handed the bundle he still held to an older boy, Angus, who untied it on the floor.

The younger children exclaimed over the packets of food and spices and goods. Mairead sat on the floor to examine the contents eagerly, while Patrick and Angus watched, frowning, as if too old to be excited by simple things.

Mairead, Edan, and Tomas, the blond toddler, dug their fingers into the sugar sack until Catriona whisked it away. Malcolm, David, and Donald began swordplay with the candles, which Patrick grabbed from them with a fatherly growl.

Ah, Kenneth thought as he watched; he recognized the items as the Frasers' New Year's gifts to Catriona. So the children were the reason that she had not used the sugar and spices at home, and the reason why she made use of one candle, when she had been given several. She gave whatever she could spare, and more, to them.

"The Fraser brought these things?" Malcolm asked Catriona.

"I did," Kenneth said. "My kin and I are friends to Catriona." The children looked at him in amazement.

"Kenneth and his kin know all about my children," Catriona said. "They wanted to share their wealth and good fortune with you on New Year's Day." She slid a keen glance toward Kenneth.

"That we did." He nodded. "Your good luck is ours."

"This Fraser is a good omen," Mairead said. "He is Triona's New Year's surprise."

"Triona's what?" Kenneth asked her.

Mairead licked sugar from her fingers and nodded. Her left, milk-blue eye appeared totally blind, while her right was vivid blue; she gazed at him in an oddly wise manner. "I told Triona that New Year's Eve would bring her something wonderful. You are her New Year's gift. We can have the other things," she added brightly.

Kenneth raised his brows in astonishment. Catriona blushed and gave him a faltering smile. "Mairead did say that New Year's would bring me a lucky omen. She has the Sight."

"My cousin Elspeth has the Sight," he told Mairead.

"She sees visions that come true. You must meet her one day."

"Is she a Fraser, too?" Mairead asked.

"She is," Catriona said, "and a very nice woman, too. Come here to the hearth, Mairead, Patrick, Angus—I will show you how to make New Year's bannocks with oats, sugar, and spices. But you must promise not to let Tomas eat sugar from the sack. Store it up high, where he cannot get to it."

They gathered around Catriona as she knelt by the hearth and made several sweet cakes, which she cooked on a flat griddle over the fire. Then she made a thick soup with onions and beef, and prepared a hot, watered, spicy wine. When the meal was ready, the children helped Catriona serve the food in wooden bowls.

Kenneth shared their New Year's meal, eating as lightly as Catriona did while the children ate with enthusiasm. He answered the boys' curious questions about the feud between Frasers and MacDonalds, and about hunting, herding, and winter care of livestock. The older boys soaked in whatever Kenneth told them, nodding and asking more, as if thirsty for the knowledge and guidance he offered.

Later, while they gathered near the peat fire, David, Donald, and Malcolm began to sing Gaelic songs traditional to the New Year. Their voices were high and pure, and filled the room with peace and serenity. Kenneth watched their faces shining in the warm light, and thought of his own childhood.

Lachlann Fraser had fostered fifteen Fraser children after their fathers had died in a battle between Frasers and MacDonalds. Although Kenneth had been an orphan, he had never felt isolated or unwanted under Lachlann's generous care.

He looked at Catriona, who held Mairead and Tomas in her lap. She glanced around the room at each child while the boys sang, her blue eyes full of kindness, pride, love. Kenneth was fascinated by the depth of spirit that he saw in her.

When she dipped her head to kiss Tomas's sleepy head, he felt some lost, forlorn part of his soul stir. In that moment he felt the strength of her love for these children, and felt as if she included him, too, in the warm circle created by her gaze.

But he was sure that wine and firelight and good cheer created that sense. In truth, she regarded him as a Fraser who did not keep promises. The rare privilege of Catriona MacDonald's love was not meant for him. The thought made him infinitely sad.

He shook his head to clear it, and listened to the song.

Later, he watched as Catriona said farewell to each child with a soft word and an embrace. Kenneth bid them good fortune and peace in the new year, and he and Catriona led their rested garrons outside to ride back to her shieling hut.

"How long have the MacGhille children been alone?" he asked as the horses waded through snowdrifts.

"Their mother died when Tomas was born three years ago," Catriona said. "She was my second cousin. Their father was a farmer. He died a few months past, when he went out on a cattle raid with my uncle Hugh."

"And you alone are helping them?"

"I am their only kin here, except for Uncle Hugh.

But when I asked him to see to their welfare, he refused—he said that they would be far too much trouble, and someone else should do it." She sighed, shook her head. "Patrick is fifteen, and he and Angus think themselves old enough to watch over the younger ones. They have hunted and fished for their food and protected the children, and they have done well so far, but—" She shrugged.

"But the winter will be hard for them," Kenneth said.

She nodded. "I have offered to take the youngest ones to live with me, but none of them want to be separated."

"Your little house is not much bigger than theirs."

"Nor do I have the means to care for several children." She looked directly at him, her eyes snapping blue. "I want to bring them to Kilernan to live. Hugh will not allow it."

"Ah. So that is why you want your castle so desperately." He gazed at her thoughtfully, realizing that she considered the children's welfare more important than her own.

"It is my rightful home, after all." They rode in silence until the shieling hut appeared on the next hill.

In the yard they dismounted, and Catriona looked up at him. "Thank you for coming with me," she said. "Perhaps your first-foot into the children's house will bring them good luck."

He moved closer to her, his breath misting the air between them. "And will it bring luck for you?" he asked. "You said Mairead predicted a good omen for you this New Year's Eve."

She looked up at him, holding her horse's bridle. "That I do not know," she said. "Tell me, Fraser, was it good fortune that you set first-foot in my house, hurt and bleeding and in need of shelter? Or will the whole year be shadowed by that moment?" She turned away.

Kenneth stepped after her, ready to reply. But Catriona stopped so quickly that he nearly knocked into her, laying a hand on her shoulder.

"The poor luck may have already begun for the year," she said grimly. "Look." She pointed toward the front door.

Kenneth saw the flattened, trampled snow near the doorway, saw the troughs made by large feet and deep hoofprints. "We did not make those marks," he said slowly.

"Parlan MacDonald has been here, I think." She sent him a worried glance. "He may come back."

Kenneth shrugged. "If he does, I am here with you."

"If he finds a Fraser here, there will be trouble. You are forbidden to fight with MacDonalds."

"We are forbidden to *begin* a fight with Mac-Donalds," he explained. "But if they start a dispute, we certainly can defend ourselves."

She reached up, her fingers muffled in a thick stocking, and brushed his tender lower lip. "Who took you down on the ice?"

He could not hold back the truth when he looked into her deep blue eyes; her gaze was too serious, too perceptive. "Three men," he said. "MacDonalds. One of them was a huge blond man."

"That," she said, pulling on her horse's bridle, "was Parlan. Your fight with MacDonalds has already begun, Fraser."

Chapter Five

❦

Catriona peered out the window often, and listened for the thud of hoofbeats, but heard only the whip of the rising wind. She tried to ignore her apprehension by attending to simple tasks: sweeping the floor, repairing frayed woolen stockings, and stirring a thick soup in a kettle suspended over the hearth fire.

She and Kenneth talked, softly and leisurely, of snow, and sun, and the Highland hills, which they both loved in any sort of weather; they spoke of food, and hunting, and the best weave for a good plaid, and went on to share events from their childhoods. Neither mentioned feuding clans, or the disputes and pledges that lay unsolved between them.

Kenneth told her some amusing adventures he had experienced with his cousins, while she shared a few comments about her childhood, spent with her mother as her closest friend, isolated in Kilernan Castle from Hugh MacDonald's masculine world of raids, drink, and hunting.

Finally, seeing Kenneth yawn, his beard-shadowed cheeks pale, she told him to rest for a while. When the last of the daylight faded to blue dusk, she lit the beeswax candle.

"New Year's Day is not yet over," she said when he sat up from his rest and looked at her. "Candlelight attracts good spirits to a house."

"Ah," he said. "That must be why I came here last night."

She turned to scowl at him, but he grinned at her, boyish and charming, and she laughed. Setting the candle on the windowsill, she turned back and caught his somber gaze.

His brown eyes gleamed deep, dark, and rich. She remembered the warmth and comfort of his arms last night when they had shared the narrow bed. Blushing at the thought, she reminded herself sharply that he was a Fraser. He and his kin had denied her what she most needed. Any comfort she sensed in him was surely false.

A week ago, even a day ago, she would have believed that easily. Now she found it harder to hold on to the hurt and anger that the Frasers' refusal had roused in her. He was more than a Fraser to her; she had come to consider him a friend.

After supper, Kenneth sat on the floor with Cù, dangling a woolen stocking for the cat to snatch, and rubbing the cat's head and stomach. Catriona laughed when Kenneth dropped to his hands and knees and faced the cat, making growling sounds.

Kenneth glanced at her. "If he is determined to carry a proud name like 'Dog,' " he drawled, "he should learn to behave like one." The cat batted at him gently, and tangled his claws in Kenneth's long hair. When Kenneth's playful growl turned to a howl of genuine pain, Catriona sank to her knees to rescue him, chuckling softly as she freed the glossy strands.

"Ah, but some dogs have claws, I think," she said.

Kenneth slid her a look of chagrin. The cat leaped away as Catriona sat close to Kenneth, her fingers wound in his warm, soft hair. She sensed the heat of his body, and could smell an intriguing blend of smoke and leather and maleness about him. Looking up, she met his brown eyes directly.

"Triona—" he murmured. Her gaze dropped to the dusky curve of his mouth, to his chin, sanded with black whiskers. She was keenly aware of small, fascinating details—the sooty thickness of his lashes, the spicy scent of wine on his breath, his strong, warm fingers resting beside hers on the floor.

"What?" she asked him. Inside, her heart pounded like a drum. She lowered her fingers from his hair.

"Triona." He sat up and leaned close. "Come to Glenran."

She shook her head. "I cannot do that."

"You can hardly stay here for the winter."

"It is comfortable enough here," she said defensively.

"You need food, fuel—"

"I will manage. Patrick and Angus will help me to hunt and fish and find fuel."

"We can support you at Glenran," he said. She shook her head again and looked away. "It is dangerous for you to stay here. Even if you had enough supplies, you are alone."

Alone. She had begun to discover how very much she craved his solace and companionship. She rose briskly to her feet and turned toward the window. "I will be fine here."

"Catriona." He stood and touched her shoulder. His soft voice and the heat of his hand made her want to turn toward him. She stayed still. "Come with me," he said.

"I need to be here," she said. "The children need me."

Behind her, he heaved an exasperated breath. "I am sure your cousins can come as well. Callum will not turn them away. His father took in many orphans for fostering, all cousins, by the way. I was one of them," he added.

She tilted her head. "You were orphaned?"

He nodded. "By MacDonalds."

She turned then. His somber gaze and the muscle that thumped in his cheek told her that he knew the pain of growing up without a natural father, as she had done, as the MacGhille children would have to do.

She sighed. "I had heard that Lachlann fostered several fatherless babes. You were one of those, then."

"Fortunately, I was. He was a good man."

"He was generous to me, too, when I was born." She paused. "A Fraser killed my father, a MacDonald killed yours. And Lachlann of Glenran helped us both."

"Then let his kindness be our bond," he murmured. "Lachlann would not want us to continue the bitter feud between our kin. Come to Glenran with me."

She shook her head. "That will not gain back Kilernan."

"It will not," he agreed. "But you will be protected."

"I do not need protection. I need my home. The children are the only kin I have, other than my uncle. Help me gain a home for them." She looked up at him, and felt the rising sting of tears. She blinked them back.

He tilted her chin with his fingers. "I wish I could tell you what you want to hear. I cannot."

"There must be a way," she said. His hand on her chin, his warm, steady gaze, held her pinioned as she stared up at him. When his thumb brushed over her lower lip, she felt a flood of need rush through her. He lowered his head.

"Stubborn girl," he whispered. His gaze moved down to her mouth, traced up again. His fingers were warm and firm as they slid to cup her cheek, and his breath was soft on her skin. "Let me help you. Let me protect you."

Her heart quickened. Frasers and MacDonalds, Kilernan and promises, seemed far distant suddenly. She watched his lips, his eyes, and moved closer to him by a breath, tilting her head in silent answer. Her body, her heart, surged toward him, seeking.

His mouth covered hers then, gently, poignantly. Joy curled sudden and deep within her, and rose like a wave of the sea. She let out a little moan as he pulled her into the circle of his arms and slanted his lips over hers, drinking there, his hands warm and strong on her back.

Beside her, Cù leaped to the windowsill, nearly upsetting the candle. Startled, Catriona broke away from Kenneth, her cheeks hot, heart slamming. The cat mewled and jumped down, striding to the front door and meowing there.

"Cù wants to go out, I think," she breathed.

Kenneth leaned past her, his hand at her waist, and peered through the crack in the shutter. "That cat is more of a watchdog than I thought," he said grimly. "Look."

Catriona did, and saw three horsemen riding into the

yard. "Parlan, and his kin!" she gasped, and pushed at Kenneth's chest. "Hide, quickly—get into the box-bed!"

"Hide? I owe them a beating, and I have the right to deliver it."

"I will not have bloodshed and fighting in my home on New Year's Day! You might be hurt! And it is hardly a good omen!"

He sighed. "Talk to Parlan through the door, then, and do not let him in. That should keep your house free of poor omens."

She slid him a sharp look, bit back a remark about wounded first-footers, and went to the door.

Kenneth folded his arms over his chest and waited, watching Catriona. She pressed her hands against the door and sent him a nervous glance. When the first knock sounded, she jumped.

"Who's there?" she called quickly.

"Parlan MacDonald." His voice, through the door, was thick and deep. Kenneth peered stealthily through the shutter crack; he saw a blond, huge young man, wrapped in a red plaid that added more bulk to his heavy build. Surely Parlan was the same man who had attacked him on New Year's Eve; the other Mac-Donalds looked familiar, too. Kenneth scowled, feeling a gut-centered urge to go outside and settle a debt. But he had promised Catriona that no violence would mar her New Year's Day.

"What do you want, Parlan?" Catriona asked. "It is after dark. You should be at home on such a cold night."

"I came to wish you well for the New Year," Parlan

answered. "I came earlier with my cousins, but you were not here, and your horse was gone. So we came back."

"I went to see the MacGhille children," she said. "Thank you for thinking of me. Good night."

"Catriona," Parlan said, knocking again. "Let me come in."

"I will not," she said. "It is late."

"Hugh told me to come here and see that you were well. Let me in, Catriona. Let me in, girl." His voice sounded slurred.

Kenneth moved toward Catriona and leaned a shoulder firmly against the door. He glanced down at her pale face.

"He's drunk," she whispered. "He is often so."

Parlan knocked again. "The wind is strong, and the air is cold. Will you not offer me a dram?"

"You have had your share of drams tonight," she said primly. "And you must not be my first-foot of the New Year. You are blond-headed."

"Then let my cousin Niall in first. He is dark-haired."

"He is a gloomy man, and is surely unlucky, too," she said.

"No one lets me inside first on New Year's," Parlan grumbled. "Hugh would not let me in the hall this morning until someone else set foot in there before me."

"Go back to Kilernan," she said firmly. "I am tired, and I want no visitors just now. Good night."

"Catriona, your uncle sends a message," Parlan said. "He wants you to stop this nonsense and come home."

"Nonsense!" she exclaimed.

"We both think this hiding in the hills is silliness.

Come home, and wed me. Hugh expects you to be the queen at his Twelfth Night feast in three days."

"Tell him I have no mood for revelry," she said.

"If you are not at Kilernan by Twelfth Night Eve, Hugh says he will ride here himself and carry you back."

Catriona sighed wearily. "I will think about his invitation. Go home, now."

"Catriona—we saw a Fraser in these hills yesterday. We knocked him from his horse. Have you seen any strangers?"

She glanced swiftly at Kenneth. "None at all. But I will be careful."

"If you are anxious, I could stay with you," Parlan said.

"I will be fine. Good night, Parlan."

"Catriona, I do not like to leave you alone here."

"Good night!" She faced Kenneth, waiting silently with him. When hoofbeats finally thudded out of the yard, Catriona sighed and looked up. "He will come back tomorrow. If he finds you here—"

"I will be gone by then. Come with me." Kenneth brushed back a lock of her hair. When he touched her, the memory of the kiss they had shared rushed through him like lightning.

She turned away abruptly. "Every man I know wants me to do what pleases him," she said. "None of you care what pleases me." Grabbing a folded plaid, she shook it out vigorously and laid it on the floor near the hearthstones.

"You do not have to sleep on the floor," he said.

"I know," she said. "This pallet is for you. I want my

own bed tonight." She knelt by the hearth to stir the soup that simmered in the kettle.

Kenneth accepted the bowl she handed him with quiet thanks. They ate in silence, and afterward Catriona stacked the bowls and spoons. "I will clean them tomorrow," she said. "It is poor luck to clean dishes on New Year's Day."

"You are careful of such things," Kenneth said.

"I need to be, to improve my luck," she said.

"Good fortune will come to you this year, Catriona," he said. "I promise." He reached out and took her hand, pulling her down to sit beside him on the bench.

She slid him a wary look. "I do not trust Fraser promises."

He smoothed his thumb over the back of her hand. "Trust this one," he said. "Good luck will be yours this year."

Her look was still doubtful. "You sound like a soothsayer."

"My cousin is one. And she would tell you that you need a strong good-luck charm to cleanse away the old year and seal the luck of the new."

"The best omen I have had so far this year was a beaten and bleeding first-foot." She scowled at him, but he smiled in return. "It would take a strong omen to balance that out."

"True. Did you know," he murmured, "that the most powerful charm of all for New Year's Day . . . is a kiss?"

A blush colored her cheek. "I know. We have done that."

"We could bless the year again. If you like," he added.

She watched him, her eyes deep blue wells, filled with

uncertainty, and a hint of yearning. Slowly she closed her eyes and lifted her face. He leaned toward her.

She tasted salty, like the broth, and sweet, like warm honey. Kenneth sank his fingers in her hair, cupping the back of her head as he kissed her deeply, gently, touching his lips to hers, lifting, touching again. She sighed and raised a trembling hand to his cheek. Sliding her fingers through his hair, she tilted her mouth beneath his, her lips opening tentatively.

His body surged. He had not touched a woman in a long while, but the need that made him quaver now, that stirred through him like a flame in the dark, was far deeper than physical. He wanted her profoundly, in his heart, in his blood.

He remembered, distantly, vaguely, as if it had happened decades ago, that he had felt a shadow of this for Anna. But what swept through him now was more powerful, soul-deep. He could not explain it, but knew its strength was great.

Wanting her fiercely, he held back, sensing that her willful nature had a fragile side, too. He kissed her gently, pressing a hand against the sweet curve in her lower back, but no more than that. She sighed and broke the kiss, tipping her brow against his shoulder.

"Enough blessing," she said breathlessly.

He smiled, his cheek against her hair. "That should bring us both some luck." He drew a breath and waited for the thudding in his heart to calm.

Catriona laughed, a breathy gulp, and sat up, her cheeks flushed and velvety. She stood and picked up her plaid, throwing it around her shoulders.

He stood, too. "I will see to the animals," he said, guessing what she intended to do. "You stay here, by the fire. Stay warm. That wind sounds wickedly strong." He fetched his spare plaid and wrapped it over his head and shoulders. Catriona opened the door for him, and he stepped into a rough, icy wind.

By the time he returned, Catriona had gone to bed. The curtains of the box-bed were closed. Kenneth took off his plaid and moved toward the window, where the candle still burned.

"Do not blow it out," she said from behind the curtain. "The light will attract good spirits. And please watch the fire, to see that it does not go out on the first day of the year."

"I will. Good night, then." He stretched out by the hearth. The cat jumped up on him, and Kenneth made room for both of them. He watched the glowing fire and listened to the wind howl and push past the little house; he thought about luck, and promises, and the unknown year.

Catriona had enjoyed too little luck, he knew. He wished he knew a charm to grant whatever she wanted—safety for her and the children, home, happiness. He thought of Anna, who had never known lack or struggle until her brief illness. Kenneth had been her betrothed, her lover; but she had not truly needed him until the last days of her life. Her death had left him lacking.

Catriona needed him. He knew that, even if she did not. He would leave tomorrow, but he would return to bring her food and goods, and to watch over her. Lachlann would have wanted someone at Glenran to fulfill his promise. And Kenneth had made his own pledge to improve Catriona's luck. He felt an odd sense of obligation; the Frasers owed her something—and he had been her first-foot of the year.

As he drifted to sleep, he wondered if Kilernan could be taken without attack. Then he sighed, for that deed was impossible. He realized, too, that once he left here, Catriona might not accept further visits or gifts from him. He was a Fraser, after all. She was not fond of Frasers.

He wished, suddenly, that she was.

Chapter Six

❦

Sleet hurtled downward on shrieking winds, rattling against the walls and the roof. Catriona slid out of bed in a murky gray light, and wondered if it was morning yet. She pulled her plaid over her linen chemise and went to the door, cracking it open.

Icicles hung crystalline from the doorway, the byre, and the trees. Frozen rain poured down in fine sheets from a dark sky. Catriona shivered as the wind cut past her, and stepped back, bumping into Kenneth, who now stood just behind her.

He peered out. "Poor weather," he commented dryly. "I had better go see to the horses and the cow. They could freeze to death in this." He shut the door and turned. "Even with a hearth fire, it will be hard to stay warm inside today."

"You cannot ride to Glenran in this," she said.

"I cannot. Will you mind if I stay a bit longer?" He smiled and shoved a hand through his tangled hair. She noticed the sleepy creases around his brown eyes, and the heavier beard shadowing his firm jaw. He looked tousled and comfortable, standing beside her in his

rumpled shirt and trews. Suddenly she did not want
him to leave, regardless of the weather.

"Please stay," she said. "I would like the company."

He nodded and turned to gather his plaid and boots,
pulling them on to go outside. When he was gone,
Catriona dressed quickly and warmly, built up the
smoldering fire with peat, and then made a thick, salty
porridge in a kettle over the hearth.

Her thoughts turned to the children. Although she
trusted Patrick and Angus to watch over the younger
ones, she was deeply concerned for them in such a dangerous storm. She would go there as soon as travel was
possible.

After a while Kenneth returned, his face red with
cold. He blew on his hands to warm them, and ate
quickly. "Thick ice has formed on this roof, and the
byre," he told her. "I have to clear it off, or the thatch
could collapse."

"I will help you," she said. He protested, but she
grabbed her spare plaid and soon followed him outside.

The wind shoved at her, and the raw, bitter chill
stung her hands and feet while she and Kenneth used
broken tree limbs to prod at the ice on the low thatched
roof of the shieling. When they turned toward the byre,
they saw that the sloped, low-slung roof sagged under a
burden of ice.

Fighting the keening wind, Kenneth opened the door
of the byre, and held her back with his arm. "Stay
here," he told her. "The roof could fall. We will have to
move the animals to safety. There is no choice but to
bring them inside the hut."

"I know," she said. "We will make room for them
somehow." He led the two garrons and the cow out of

the byre, and she helped him guide the animals through the doorway of the hut.

Cù hid under a bench when they came inside, although Catriona got down on her knees to speak reassuringly to him. She turned to the agitated horses, patting their broad necks while Kenneth tipped the table, bench, and stools to build a makeshift stable area. Going back outside, he returned with oats for feed, and straw to spread on the floor.

Catriona perched on the bed, the only remaining seat, and watched while Kenneth soothed the horses with gentle hands. He spoke calmly to the cow, a small, shaggy black creature who stared at him with limpid eyes. Then he stepped over the barrier and skirted the hearth to come toward her.

"The animals will be warm and safe," he said, "though it will be crowded in here."

"We will manage," she said brightly.

He unwound his damp plaid and hung it over the table to dry, then sat beside her to unlace his boots. "When the weather improves, I will repair the byre roof. I suppose"—he looked at her—"you would not consider coming to Glenran."

"With my cow and my horse, and eight children?" she asked.

He shrugged. "Lachlann and his wife raised fifteen fosterlings and their own son at Glenran. There is room." He stripped down to his shirt, trews, and bare feet as he spoke, and began to rub his pale, blotched toes with a blanket from the bed.

"Your feet look frostbitten!" Kneeling, she took his foot in her hands and rubbed gently for a while, then warmed some water and sluiced it over his feet.

She felt the power and grace in his long bones and

lean muscles. Even when his feet looked improved, she continued to stroke his ankles and knotted calf muscles. The rhythm and warmth was as soothing to her as she hoped it was to him.

"Thank you," he murmured, watching her.

She nodded, and turned away to fetch the flask of *uisge beatha* that the Fraser women had given her. Heating some of the liquid in an iron pot, she added cream, ground oats, and pinches of spices and sugar from Kenneth's New Year's gift. She poured it into a bowl and handed it to him.

"Drink this brose. It will warm you inside and out."

He sipped. "Ah. This is good. Thank you. I thought you gave the sugar and spices to the MacGhille children."

"I kept some for you," she admitted shyly.

He raised an eyebrow. "Girl dear, you are generous with your guest, but not with yourself. Come here." He patted the mattress. She sat beside him, and he held the bowl to her lips. "Drink," he said. "I am not the only one who is cold."

She sipped, feeling the hot, sweet burn of the brose slide down her throat. They shared more between them, and then Kenneth reached out to remove the outer plaid that she still wore.

The cow lowed morosely as Kenneth draped her damp plaid beside his to dry. He patted the animal's head affectionately and murmured to her. She nuzzled after him for a moment when he left her side to return to the bed, kneeling beside it.

"Let me warm your feet now," he told Catriona. She allowed him to unlace her damp leather boots and pull them off; then he reached under her skirt to peel off her knee stockings as if she were a child. He kneaded her bare feet between his strong hands, then bathed them in the water that remained in the bowl.

His touch sent subtle shivers of pleasure throughout her body. She sighed, and watched his dark head and wide shoulders as he gently stroked her feet, coaxing warmth into her toes. No one, since her mother's death, had taken care of her like this man did now. No one had shown concern about her comfort.

And no one, other than the children, had touched her with gentleness or affection. She blinked back tears and closed her eyes, relaxing under his languid touch. Her feet and ankles seemed to glow with luscious warmth. When he set her foot down, she curled her toes and made a playful little moan, as if begging for more.

He smiled. "Enough, I think. Who knows what kind of an omen this might be."

"What do you mean?" she asked, frowning.

He raised a brow. "Do you not know about the ritual of foot washing for a bride and groom, the night before they marry?"

A hot blush flooded her face. "I forgot about that," she said hastily, and drew her feet up to pull on thick, dry woolen stockings, folding her legs beneath her.

He sat on the bed again, his weight shifting her against him slightly. He sipped brose and offered her more. "The MacGhille children," he said as they listened to the steady torrent of sleet. "How will they fare in this storm?"

"I have been thinking about them, too," she said. "Patrick and Angus are clever lads, and they will do their best to keep the others safe. But if ice collects on their roof, as it did here, or if one of them gets hurt or sick—" she sighed. "I wish we could go there."

"I will ride there as soon as the weather allows. Patrick will take care of them. He's a smart lad, and nearly a man."

She nodded and sipped the brose. The thick, sweet stuff slipped down her throat like fire and honey, warming her despite the pervasive chill in the hut. The wind shrieked past the house, but the blazing hearth and the presence of the man beside her were vastly comforting.

Kenneth stood to toss a few sticks of kindling over the peat chunks, and used the iron poker to coax a bright, leaping fire.

"Do you see those little blue flames?" she asked. "Those are the spirits of the hearth."

"Good omens, I hope," he said as he sat beside her again.

"Quite good. That square bit of peat, there, foretells wealth coming into a house. And that long, round shape means a stranger will come into the house."

"Ah," he said. "I told you I was lucky for you."

She rolled her eyes. "That remains to be seen."

He smiled. "You will be surrounded with luck, Catriona MacDonald. A dark-haired man fell across your doorstep, loaded down with good fortune and goodwill." She laughed softly at his gentle teasing. "Ah, look," he said. "More square chunks in the fire. They predict much wealth for you this year. What does that fat little chunk of peat mean?"

"That?" She frowned. "A birth within the year, I think."

"Ah. Well," he said, "perhaps your cow will calf."

"Perhaps." She wrinkled her nose. "It is beginning to smell like a stable in here."

He chuckled. "I will have to shovel out the straw

sooner than I thought, if we are to share this place with them."

"This will help." Catriona grabbed a slender juniper branch from the kindling pile, and tossed it on the fire. Soon the smoky evergreen fragrance of the juniper began to counter some of the animals' pungency. She climbed back into the warm nest of the bed and sat beside Kenneth; they both welcomed Cù there when he slid out from his hiding place to curl between them.

Kenneth smoothed his hand over the cat's sleekness, as did Catriona, and their fingers touched. His hand moved past hers slowly. She shivered, but knew it was not from the chill, and remained silent, as he did, both of them stroking the cat.

She listened to the thrust and whine of the storm, and the purring cat, watched the fire and sensed the peacefulness of Kenneth's silence. Delicious currents of heat and contentment poured through her, and she sighed. She felt truly sheltered, while bitterness raged outside.

"The storm is fierce. The cold and the ice could last for days," Kenneth murmured.

"It could," she agreed. Then this heaven of peace would continue, she thought dreamily.

"I should leave soon," he said.

"But you planned to stay," she said, looking up at him.

"Tomorrow my horse should be able to manage the hills, and I will ride out to see the children. Then I must return to Glenran. My cousins will be wondering what happened to me." He smiled at her. "But I am not leaving just yet."

"I am glad," she whispered.

"Are you?" His gaze was steady and deep.

She nodded. "And I am glad you set first-foot in my

house. You have brought me good fortune after all. You saved the animals from the cold, and cleared the ice on the roof. It was good luck that brought you here in that storm. I might have been alone here, to deal with the ice."

His fingers covered hers over the cat's back. "Perhaps I shall be your first-foot next year," he murmured, "if you like."

"I would like that," she whispered. He leaned closer, and she tilted her head toward him, hoping suddenly.

The first touch of his lips was soft and tentative, but the next kiss, deep and full, swept her breath away. She circled her arms around his neck, pulling him closer. Kenneth pushed the cat gently out of the way and wrapped her in his arms.

His mouth delved over hers with such strength and heat that she seemed to melt, like butter in hot brose. She felt the light caress of his tongue across the seam of her lips, and she sighed, loving the strange new intimacy of it.

She leaned back and let him take her down to the pile of pillows and furs on the narrow bed. His lean, hard body fit against her curves, even through layered wool, and his lips moved over hers in a breathless rhythm. What rushed through her was more heady, more dizzying than the strong drink that still coursed, hot and languid, through her blood.

He drifted his fingers over her cheek, along her neck and shoulder, touching her as if she were fragile. His fingers grazed over her breast and moved downward, pulling her hips toward his. She gasped and tightened her arms around his neck, pressing the length of her body to his. Her heart beat in a fierce cadence, and she sensed the heavy pounding of his heart, too, when her fingers skimmed over his chest.

He traced his lips over her cheek, her ear, along her jaw. Shivers cascaded through her, and she moaned softly, turning to find his lips with her own. She moved against him, craving more of his grazing touches and deep, luscious kisses. She had not known this kind of tenderness existed. All she wanted was to float in its luxury, in its slow, effortless current; no matter where it took her, she knew she would be safe.

Once, Parlan had kissed her in a dark corridor at Kilernan, swift, sour wine kisses followed by the heavy thrust of his tongue. She had arched away from him, and slapped him when his large hands rounded boldly over her behind, pulling her hips against the hard swelling beneath his plaid. He had claimed drunkenness; but she had known that, drunk or not, Parlan would never be a tender husband.

But this Fraser, a stranger who had no reason to care about her, touched her as if she were made of silk and roses. His kisses were kind and yet strong, surging through her like bursts of flame. No threat, no sense of wrongness spun awry in her gut, as she had felt with Parlan. She felt herself relax and sink into the warm ocean of pleasure Kenneth provided with his lips, his hands, his breath.

His hand soothed over her breasts, rousing a shiver of need that spooled deep within her. She felt as if she had found the heart of a fire, and never wanted to leave its comfort.

When he hesitated, as if offering her a chance to stop what grew between them, she let her silence, and the kiss she returned, answer his unspoken question. When he drew the lacings of her bodice loose, when his fingers found her breast, she pulled in a breath. Slipping her hands over his wide, tightly muscled shoulders and chest, she sighed.

His touch, his kisses, roused a sudden swell of joy in her, and she smiled to herself, loving this—loving him. The thought stunned her, and she paused, wrapped in his arms, knowing, in a strange, complete, wordless way, that she was where she belonged.

She sank into the cocoon he provided, and wanted more, anything, all, from him. He glided his lips to her breast, and a deep, thunderous tremor rippled through her, as if strong enough to shake the bed, shake the room—

Kenneth sat up quickly, bolting from the bed with a muttered oath. "The roof! It's close to collapsing!" he yelled. He leaped past the hearth toward the animals.

Bewildered for a moment, Catriona scrambled out of the bed. The walls trembled, and noise and chaos flooded the room. She swept the anxious cat into her arms and watched as the ceiling over the stable area sagged and groaned. The horses and the cow shifted, bumped, and kicked out at the furniture and the walls.

The cow stumbled against the upturned table, which crashed to the ground. Kenneth struggled to pull and push and cajole the three animals to safety across the room. Then the thatched roof above the abandoned corner emitted an unearthly groan, and shivered down in a heap of ice, snow, and straw.

Chapter Seven

~∞∞~

"Argh," Kenneth said, leaning back into the recess of the box-bed, "she seems to like me." He held up an arm to protect his face and turned his head, trying to avoid the cow's hot breath as she snuffled sloppily at his hair. Beside him, Catriona laughed with delight. He shot her a wry look.

"She adores you," Catriona agreed, and shoved helpfully at the cow's massive shoulder. The animal turned and swatted her tail at Catriona as she moved away, only to bump into one of the horses. Sidestepping, the cow knocked over a stool.

"She'll step in the hearth fire! Here, move!" Catriona said. "You'll burn yourself—*ach*, silly cow, go that way!"

"What's her name?" Kenneth asked as he reached out and guided the cow's hindquarters away from the hearth.

"I do not know," she said. "A neighbor stabled her here so that I could have milk over the winter. What shall we call her?'

"Well, the cat is called Dog"—he frowned in a pretense of concentration—"how about Pig?"

Catriona laughed again, a bell-like sound that Kenneth had grown to love over the last few hours. Ever since the roof caved in, their shared laughter over the mishap had made the work of cleaning and repairing the damage seem easier. Now she bounced off the bed and danced quickly around the hearth, intent on keeping a horse from knocking over the remains of the ruined table, which Kenneth had set up as a crude fire screen.

"You are giddy as a lark in spring," Kenneth said, watching her. She moved lightly, with a kind of joy he had not seen in her before. "Your little house is in shambles, and yet you are happy as a child."

She chuckled sweetly as she patted one of the garrons. Kenneth smiled, and glanced past her toward the dark corner of the house where the roof had fallen. He stretched his shoulders, weary from a day spent clearing the wreckage and repairing the roof. He and Catriona had worked together to drag out chunks of ice, shovel dirty snow and straw, and haul timber and fresh straw from the collapsed byre to shore up the ceiling of the hut. The repairs had sealed out the sleet and the wind for now, but he was not sure how long the roof would hold, particularly if the ice storm continued.

Another onslaught of wind and sleet battered the outer walls, but soup steamed, fragrant and savory, in the hanging kettle, and the crackling flames in the hearth warmed the snug, overcrowded hut. Kenneth felt oddly content; Catriona's smile, directed toward him, told him she felt the same.

"What makes you so happy now, Catriona MacDonald?" he asked softly. "Surely a fallen roof is a poor omen, and yet you smile."

She sat beside him on the bed. "I do not know," she said. "I feel good, safe, somehow, in here, with the storm outside." She grinned, quick and charming. "And you made me laugh all through the day, just watching you try to repair the damage, with the cow licking your face and the horses bumping into you." Kenneth chuckled. "But a fallen roof must be a very unfavorable sign, as you say," she added somberly.

"It would be favorable enough, if it forced you to find a better place to live," he said. "You cannot stay here now. Come to Glenran with me."

She shook her head. "You know I will not do that."

"I am concerned for your welfare," he said. "Come with me. Please. Will you make me get down on my knees and beg?"

"I might," she said saucily. "Would you do it?"

"Tcha." He smothered a grin. "I will more likely toss you in my plaid and carry you off. No Fraser will beg for a favor."

"Abducting the Maid of Kilernan is probably grounds for a feud," she said. "My uncle would be after you, then."

Kenneth watched her sparkling blue eyes, and his heart swelled within him. He realized, with a sudden, powerful clarity, that he had begun to love her. He drew a long breath, relishing the feeling, and an idea burst into his mind, stunning him with its strength, and its undeniable truth.

"Catriona," he said, "what if the Maid of Kilernan wed a Fraser?" He spoke slowly, wondering, his heart pounding.

She stared at him, her cheeks flushing high pink. "That—that would surely start a feud between Kilernan and Glenran."

The bold step he was about to take felt wholly right. "A marriage can sometimes end a feud," he said.

She lowered her head, her cheeks gone pale, as if all the joy drained out of her. "Go back to your kin in safety, Kenneth Fraser," she said, so softly that he barely heard her.

"I will not go back without you," he said.

"My uncle and Parlan might kill you if we—if we wed."

"I have faced death before," he said. "A sure death, with the white cloth already about my eyes, and the executioner's ax a swing away from my neck. Yet I am here beside you now." She glanced at him, frowning in concern. "That happened years ago, when I was wrongly accused of breaking the signed bond with the MacDonalds," he explained. "My kin stood by me then, as I will stand by you now, Catriona. Your uncle might approve of a marriage between us. Surely he knows that any attempt to heal this feud will please the Council."

She twisted her hands in her lap. "He would not like it."

"Shall we find out?" He watched her steadily.

She began to speak, then shook her head.

Kenneth leaned toward her. "Am I such a poor omen?"

"You are not a poor omen," she said. Her voice quavered. "But Parlan and my uncle would seek you out, bond or none."

"*Ach,* my girl," he said, touching her shoulder. "Who would you rather take to husband—me or Parlan?"

"You," she breathed out, without hesitation. "But I will not do it." She turned away, curling up to lie on the bed, her back to him. He heard her sniffle, as if she fought tears.

He sighed and shoved a hand through his hair, regretting that his impulsive words had upset her. But he knew his mind, and his heart; the past few years, with Anna and then without her, had taught him much about himself, and about what he needed.

In the space of a few days, Catriona had blessed his lonely existence fully, kindly, like candlelight dispels shadow. Still, he had spoken his thoughts far too fast—not for him, but for her. Stretching out beside her, he circled his arms around her.

"All I ask is that you consider it," he murmured.

"It would never work," she answered. "Go back to Glenran, and remember your bond. Keep your distance from the MacDonalds."

"Remember the brooch, Catriona," he said softly. "The Frasers have a pledge to fulfill to you."

She shook her head, curled away. "I fear that misfortune would befall both of us this way. Forget the brooch." She drew a shaky breath. "I should never have come to Glenran asking for payment of Lachlann's pledge. I always hoped that the snow rose would bring me luck. Marriage between us would"—she paused—"would only invite danger for the Frasers, and the MacDonalds."

"The snow rose will bring you luck, if you let it," he said. "If not for the brooch, I would never have set foot across your threshold. I will be your luck, Catriona," he whispered. "I *am* your luck. Depend on it."

She caught back a sob and grasped his hand tightly. He held her, but she did not turn, did not speak. He felt her cry silently, and knew she kept her fears and her thoughts within. After a while, her breaths grew more even, and she slept, exhausted, in his arms.

He kissed her damp cheek, then sighed and sat up, aware that he must keep watch over the animals, so that none of them stepped into the open hearth, or knocked something into the fire.

He leaned against the bed frame. The cow wandered toward the bed and nuzzled at his chest. Kenneth patted her huge head gently, distracted by his thoughts: he meant to find a way to fulfill a promise made twenty years ago.

The ruined shieling sat on the hill like a pile of broken dreams. Catriona sighed, looking at it as she stood outside in the yard. The thatched roof sagged sadly at one end, its hole filled with straw and timber scraps; the small byre beside the house resembled a large pile of kindling.

She turned away to watch the cow and horses, who wandered close to the house, where the snow was packed flat. She had brought them outside after milking the cow, to let the garrons walk a bit; she would guide them inside again soon, for the air was still frigid, although the sleet had stopped. Cù had stepped out briefly, and had gone inside, making his preference clear.

Ice slicked the hills to milky smoothness, and turned the trees to bare, delicate sculptures. Catriona walked carefully over the slippery, crusted snow, her boots sinking with each step, and glanced back at the house.

Kenneth still slept, although it was well into the day. She knew that he had been awake much of the night. Just after dawn, when Catriona had awoken and got out of bed, he had been sitting beside her. They had said little to each other beyond a somber morning greeting, and he had lain down and drifted to sleep quickly. She was not sure what she would tell him when he awoke.

She sighed and began to crush the snow around her with her boot, making idle patterns while she thought. She had to convince Kenneth to go back to Glenran. If he stayed with her, if he wed her, the risks to him, and to the Glenran Frasers and Kilernan MacDonalds, frightened her. If she wed him, she feared that she would be widowed too soon, as her mother had been.

But the thought of being wed to him spun through her like a whirlwind, stealing her breath. To have him near her always, strong and calm, kind and comforting—but that was a dream, a wish. No matter how much she desired it, that could not happen.

Gazing at the broken, sad little house, she sighed. She had no choice now but to return to Kilernan. Twelfth Night Eve, when her uncle expected her, was two days away; by then the weather would allow travel. Kenneth would leave, and so would she.

She pressed her foot down again and again, turning in a slow circle as she thought. Before Christmas, all she had wanted was a rescue from her dilemma, and better luck in the future. But since Kenneth had fallen through her door at midnight on New Year's Eve, as if fate had guided him there, all had changed.

Somehow, fate had swept through her life like snow and ice, covering all that she thought existed, leaving a new, pure vista, filled with possibility and risk. But she would not risk Kenneth's life to grasp at joy.

I am your luck, he had said. She wished it could be true. His words had been filled with devotion and love; they were a pledge in themselves. Tears stung her eyes, and she wiped them away. She rarely allowed herself to cry, but last night she had been flooded by bitter joy.

Desperate to turn into his arms, knowing he wanted her, too, she had not; she feared what would happen if she let herself love him as she wanted to do.

Kenneth was more than her luck. He was her life, the soul of what she needed and desired. The heart-wrenching choice she faced was no choice at all: she wanted him to live, wanted peace for him and their clans. If she had to return to Kilernan to ensure that—if she had to marry Parlan—then she would do it.

She stepped back, and looked down at the design she had made. Spreading around her like an opened flower, her footprints formed a rose in the snow.

Chapter Eight

〜∞〜

Kenneth looked up from lacing his boots to see Catriona open the door and guide the cow into the house ahead of her. She shut the door against a blast of frigid air, and turned toward him. Her pinkened cheeks grew even brighter.

"You are awake," she said. "Have you eaten?" She took off her outer plaid and folded it as she spoke.

"Not yet." He stood. "How is the weather?"

She knelt by the low fire and poured water from a bucket into a kettle, swinging it over the fire to heat while she scooped ground oats from a sack. "Bitterly cold, but the sleet has stopped. Walking is difficult, and riding might be nearly impossible on some of the hills. You may have to stay another day or so." She seemed to be avoiding his gaze.

He watched her add the oats. "Catriona, I—" He stopped, having much to say, and unsure where to begin.

"I will not wed you, Kenneth," she said quietly, stirring the porridge. "But thank you for wanting to help me."

He walked over to stand beside her. She did not look

up. "I did not suggest it as a way to help you," he said, "although I think it would solve your situation. I suggested it because I want to wed you, Catriona MacDonald. Just that."

She stirred silently. The cow lowed and shoved gently at him, and the cat slid over his feet to sit by the warm hearthstones. Kenneth did not move. He studied the dark sheen of Catriona's braided hair, and noted the proud, tense set of her slender neck and shoulders.

"I will not wed you," she repeated, adding salt.

He sighed in exasperation, annoyed with himself for bumbling through this matter impulsively and foolishly, and distressing her. He would have to begin again.

Catriona knew little about him beyond what he had mentioned of his childhood and his cousins. He wanted to tell her about the last few lost years of his life. Perhaps then she would understand him better; perhaps then she would believe that he knew what he wanted in his life.

He sighed, rubbed at his jaw, wondered where to begin. "I was betrothed just over three years ago," he said finally.

She frowned, tilted her head. "I did not know," she said.

"I loved Anna very much," he said quietly. "She was a sweet, happy girl, and easy for anyone to love. But she died three years ago of a quick, fierce illness, on New Year's Day."

Catriona glanced up at him, her blue eyes wide and sympathetic. "New Year's? Dear God."

He tensed his jaw, looked away. As much as he trusted Catriona, he found it difficult to reveal the hidden corners of his heart to anyone. "Since her death,

I have dreaded the Yuletide season, every day of it, from Christmas to Twelfth Night," he said. "I thought only about what I had lost. I did not want to be happy if she was not there."

She lowered her lashes, bit her lip, and said nothing as she circled the spoon in the thick porridge.

"I had set my mind to loneliness," he said. "I was content, in a bitter way, to be discontent. Then you walked into Castle Glenran on Christmas Day." She glanced quickly at him. "At first, I thought how much you resembled Anna," he told her.

"Oh." She looked away. "Now I see—"

"You do not see," he said firmly. "Listen to me well. I know that you are different from Anna," he said. "Black-haired, blue-eyed, kindhearted, that much is true of both of you. But now, though I fell through your doorway only days ago, I feel as if I know you well, as if I have known you for years."

She sucked in a little breath. "I—I feel the same," she said. "But we have spent much time together, shut in here." She sighed as she stirred the porridge. "I am sorry about Anna, Kenneth. It must be hard to lose the one you love."

"It is," he murmured. "Do not make me endure it again." He met her gaze evenly, though his heart thumped like a wild thing.

"You do not know me well enough to . . . love me," she whispered, looking down.

"Do I not?" He knelt beside her. "I know that you are strong and determined," he murmured, watching her. "You are keen-witted, and beautiful, and hopelessly willful."

She frowned, but her cheeks blushed brightly. He smiled. "You laugh like a child, and make me want to laugh, too. And you have the heart of an angel where others are concerned," he continued. "I think you might do anything for those you love." His fingers curled over hers while she continued to stir the porridge. "And I know that you are scared just now," he added.

"I am not," she said stiffly, knocking the spoon against the side of the kettle, and lifting the pot away from the fire.

"Are you not? Well, I am," he said. He tugged at the spoon, but she would not give it up. She stirred resolutely, though her cheeks bloomed with color and her breath quickened. "Catriona," he said patiently. "Let go of the damned spoon."

"Why?" she asked. "Are you hungry?"

"I am that," he growled, and flung the spoon away, turning her in his arms. He pulled her close, kneeling with her beside the hearthstones, and kissed her profoundly.

For a moment she hesitated. Then she sighed, and her lips softened beneath his, as if she had struggled within herself, and found the strength to surrender.

She circled her arms around his neck and tilted her head beneath his, framing his jaw with her slender hands, kissing him with a trembling joyfulness that made him want to weep suddenly, not for what he had lost, but for what he had found.

He slanted his mouth over hers and kissed her deep and certain, and let his hands skim the curving contours of her body. A wealth of thick wool separated them, but he felt her graceful, willing undulations against him. That silent eloquence poured through him like fire, and the hardening strength in his body urged him onward.

She slid her fingers through his hair, returning his kiss with a fervency that took his breath. He circled his hands around her waist, beneath the drape of her plaid, and moved upward to find the slope of her breasts. He caught her little glad cry between his lips, and knew that she shared his need.

He hoped, ardently, desperately, that she also shared the love he felt. Like sunlight bursting through clouds, the feelings that burgeoned inside of him streamed through his blood and being, adding fire to his touch as he held her.

If he let go of her, then and there—if he walked out into the cold and let the lust that flamed in his body cool to ice—he would still feel this fiery yearning that fueled his desire. She charmed him, nurtured him, filled the emptiness within him like light poured over shadow. Kin and feuds and promises aside, he loved her, simply, deeply. He could not do without her now.

Kneeling with her as they kissed, he wanted more of her, more of this. He touched the incredible softness of her breast, warm and hidden beneath wool and linen, felt his own breath and blood pulse through him like wind-driven waves. He stood, lifting her as if she were made of no more than silk and a soul.

Setting her down on the fur-covered, rumpled bed, he looked into her eyes, questioning, waiting. Silently she reached past him and drew the curtain shut. Her fingers closed around his arm, pulling him toward her in the darkness. He knelt, leaning over her, hands to either side of her, and kissed her gently.

"Catriona," he whispered, "listen to me, now. I love you." He kissed her again, letting his mouth, his breath, linger and blend with hers. "Whether we have been together for days or years is not important. What has begun will only grow stronger."

She closed her eyes, sighed, lifted her mouth to his. He caressed her lips, then lifted his head to gaze at her through the shadows. "I may be a Fraser, but I will be your luck, the whole soul of it," he murmured, "if you want me."

She made a small sound, half sob, half laugh, and drew him down to lie beside her. He wrapped his arms around her, his heart pounding against the rhythm of hers.

"I do want you," she answered. "Good omen or poor, you fell at my feet on New Year's Eve, and I want you for my own, so much," she whispered. "But you must not ask me to wed you."

He opened his mouth to speak, to protest, but she laid a silencing finger against his lips. He felt a poignant tug of deep emotion in his chest, and sank his fingers into the silk of her hair as he kissed her gently. The hunger of her returned kiss surprised him, fired his craving for more. Meeting her lips again, he thought he tasted the salt of tears. But she smiled when he looked at her.

He savored her mouth, and his hands traced over the graceful shape of her, impeded by wool and linen. She caressed his arms, his waist, and tugged at his plaid; he shifted, letting her divest him, while he pulled at her laces, slid wool gently away from her, until they lay bare together. The curves of her body were luscious in shadow, touched by tiny stars of daylight that fell through the curtain weave.

He was aware that they hurtled fast toward a brink that would carry them forward, and change them both forever. Heart pounding, he kissed her mouth and slowed, giving her time to think, to stop him. She sighed and traced her fingers down his arm, a welcoming, loving gesture.

He kissed her throat, the soft, globed sides of her breasts, her velvet-firm nipples, until desire rendered him breathless. When he smoothed his hand over her flat abdomen, she gasped and shifted closer, settling her hips to his so sweetly, so intently, that he groaned and tilted himself away from her.

"Hold," he whispered. "Hold, love. You must be certain."

"I am," she said. "Did you not say yourself that I am quick to decide, and hopelessly willful?"

"Hopelessly," he murmured, and kissed her again. He slid his fingers gently along her waist, over her abdomen and down; he found the small, soft seam and parted it delicately. She sighed, and swayed against his caressing fingertips, showing him the cadence with her breath and motion. Her seeking, tender fingers explored the hard map of his torso until he gasped and groaned low and rolled to his back, pulling her over him.

His heart thundered, his blood and breath pulsed heavily, and he could hardly hold back. She moved over him with gentle, inexorable power, like a wave of the sea, sweeping him into her current. He held her, kissed her, shifted toward her; she opened over him in a graceful arching motion, and he was lost.

He sucked in a long, full breath and slipped inside the warm haven of her body, rocking beneath her with a lingering, aching, heartfelt rhythm. Her body thrilled him, nurtured him, gave him solace. He felt her love then, genuine and deep, flowing over his heart like warm, restoring rain. And he knew, as if these exquisite moments worked subtle magic, that now he was forever blended to her, body and soul.

He held her in his arms while the shared rhythm of their breathing slowed, while their bodies parted reluctantly. She curled beside him under the warm fur covers, while wind whistled against the outer walls. After a long while, she looked up.

"I love you well, Kenneth Fraser," she murmured. "I want you to know that." Her voice was soft and sad. "But I will not wed you. I will not risk that for you."

"*Ach*, stubborn girl," he said gruffly. "It is my risk, and I will take it."

"I will not have you die at the hands of the Mac-Donalds for loving me." She sat up, grabbing her clothing, pulling her shift and her gown over her head. He reached for her, but she slipped out of the enclosed bed. He snatched up his shirt and trews and yanked them on, then moved toward her, where she stood by the window.

He touched her shoulder. "Surely you have changed your mind now," he murmured, tracing a finger over her cheek.

She shook her head, sadly, firmly, and looked through a crack in the shutter. "The sky is clearing," she said. Her voice sounded faraway, as if she had withdrawn to some place where he could not follow. "You will be able to ride out soon. I hope you will go to the children. I am concerned about them."

"Did I not promise that already? Come with me."

"The cow would trample this house to bits if I left her alone," she answered. "If the children are fine, I want you to go on to Glenran from there."

He sucked in a breath, his heart pounding, aching. "What of the pledge the Frasers owe you?" he asked.

She stared out the window. "You have honored that," she said. "You helped me when I was ... in need." He heard the tremor in her voice. "Now you are free. Go back."

"Not without you." He reached out for her.

She stepped away to gather oatcakes and cheese and wrap them in a cloth. She took up his plaid and handed it to him.

"You must go," she said. "Parlan and Hugh will come here, for it is the eve of Twelfth Night. You must leave, Kenneth."

"Catriona," he said softly. "What if a child comes of this between us?"

She lowered her head. "Then I would be glad," she said.

He stepped toward her, but she turned away. He sighed, sensing that she would not waver in this, not now. He knew her well enough to know that she needed time alone to think; he hoped that she would realize that her love was stronger than her fear.

"I will ride to see the MacGhille children," he said. "And then I will be back." She began to protest, and he held up a hand. "This is not over between us. I owe you a pledge, and I will fulfill it."

"I think Lachlann's pledge has been met."

"Perhaps." He watched her slender back, her proud head. "The snow rose brooch is but silver and stone, and its promise is easily met," he said. "But my pledge to you is priceless, endless. Do not render it worthless." He snatched up his plaid and led his horse toward the door.

Chapter Nine

❧

Crisp smacking sounds and the high trill of children laughing soared through the air. Kenneth guided his garron carefully along the ridge of an icy hill, and looked down.

Below, on a small, frozen pond amid leafless trees, the eight MacGhille children slid and laughed and yelled. They brandished long sticks in their mittened hands, and batted a rock back and forth across the pond surface, then ran, skidded, and slipped in pursuit of the missile.

Kenneth smiled, recognizing the game as one he and his cousins played often in the winter. He urged his horse down the slope. As he approached, one of the younger boys saw him and yelled to the others, pointing. The children dropped their sticks and ran toward him.

"Kenneth Fraser!" Angus called as he ran at the head of the pack. "Where is Triona?"

"At the shieling," he said as he dismounted. "She sent me to see how you fared in the storm." Soon all eight of them, from Patrick to little Tomas, gathered near his horse.

"We did well enough," Angus said. "Patrick and I watched after everyone. Edan and Donald were scared, but—"

"We were not!" Donald protested, pouting.

"I'm proud of all of you," Kenneth said, smiling. "Catriona will be, too."

Edan pulled at his sleeve. "Did you bring gifts?"

"Cheese, and some oatcakes." Kenneth patted the bundled that hung on his saddle.

"We could not open the door of our house yesterday," Mairead said. She smiled up at him, her milky, glazed left eye drifted to the side. "Patrick and Angus had to push and push. It was frozen shut, but we were warm inside. And Tomas got a burn."

Kenneth frowned, and bent toward Tomas, who stood with his hand in Mairead's. "Let me see, lad," he said.

Tomas held up a blistered finger. "Fire hurts," he said.

"It does that," Kenneth said, sighing as he thought of the dangers these children faced without an adult to watch over them. He patted the child's head and stood. "How is the game of *sinteag* going?"

"We have no wooden ball to play the shinty properly," Angus said. "But we found a round smooth rock. Patrick's team is winning, because my team is smaller, and we have Tomas."

"I can do it," Tomas insisted.

"I will be on your team, if I may," Kenneth said. With enthusiastic hoots, Angus and Malcolm ran off and returned with a broken tree limb. "Ah, this will do for a *caman*," Kenneth said, hefting the stick as he walked with the children toward the pond.

The game was lively and fast-paced. They slid over

the ice in their boots, laughing and falling, and sweeping the smooth stone back and forth across the ice between their goals. Kenneth helped Tomas to skim the rock over the ice several times, raising cheers from everyone, none louder than Tomas. Kenneth made certain that each of the little ones managed to slide the stone past the opposite team's goal; he had rarely laughed so hard, or enjoyed a game so much, in his life.

When their cheeks were red with cold and their toes were numb, they left the pond and walked carefully over an icy hill. Kenneth perched Mairead, Tomas, and Edan on the horse, and led the pack, walking beside Patrick.

He smiled, hearing their chatter, and thought of his own childhood. He and his cousins, most of them orphans, had been as close as siblings, playing, teasing, laughing, and competing, though always fiercely loyal to each other. But Lachlann had always been there to guide the young Glenran Frasers. Beyond Catriona's loving concern for them, the MacGhille children were guiding themselves through life for now.

He sighed, glancing at the children, and realized that they had stolen into his heart, easily and completely, just as if they had always been there—and just as their beautiful cousin had done. With a strangely certain sense of rightness, he felt as if he had acquired a family of his own. He could not leave these children to fend for themselves, just as he could not return to Glenran and leave Catriona alone.

As they approached the house, Kenneth laughed aloud. A garden of snowmen filled the yard, tall and short, fat and fallen over, decked with bonnets and plaids. Beyond them, the snow fortress was partly collapsed and clearly well used. "You have all been busy," he remarked to Patrick.

The boy grinned. "We built most of them after you and Catriona left the other day," he said. "But after the ice storm, I would not let the younger ones outside until this afternoon."

"You take good care of them, lad," Kenneth observed.

Patrick raised his head proudly. "I promised my parents that I would. A Highland man never breaks a pledge."

Kenneth nodded silently, thinking of the pledges he owed to Catriona. If he could have taken Kilernan Castle from Hugh MacDonald alone, without bloodshed, he would have already done it. He wanted Catriona to be content, but he could not perform the impossible. He sighed heavily, wondering if he could ever convince her and the children to come to Glenran with him.

Later, while the children sat by the fire and ate cheese and oatcakes, Kenneth looked up to see Mairead, Malcolm, and David take long white robes from a chest; they pulled them over their heads and pranced around the room while their siblings chuckled.

"We are practicing for our Twelfth Night feast tomorrow," Mairead announced. She tripped, her poor vision further obscured by a large white hood, and Kenneth righted her. "Will you and Catriona come? We shall have singing and dancing, and we shall all be guisers," she said. She spread her arms wide, long sleeves hanging limp. "My mother made these guising robes for my father and my older brothers to use at Yuletide. There are more things in a chest in the loft.

They used to go about the hills with the other lads and men. Have you ever been a guiser?"

"I have been out with my cousins," he said, "on New Year's Eve and on Twelfth Night, wearing robes and animal hides and horns. We marched around singing, and beating drums and making merry while we frightened away the bad spirits." He grinned.

"Will you come to our feast?" Mairead asked. "Though we shall have only porridge and not a roasted beef. But Patrick said we could make a large oatcake to hide the bean, so that we could have a King of the Revels. Or a queen," she added. She reached past Kenneth and picked up a slice of cheese full of holes, and held it to her right eye. "I wonder if this will show me who will get the bean this year." She squinted playfully through a hole in the cheese and looked toward the fire.

Kenneth smiled. "I'm sure your brothers will let you be the queen of the feast," he said. "And I will ride back to the shieling and fetch Catriona for your Twelfth Night revels."

Mairead frowned as she peered at the fire. "*Ach,* Kenneth Fraser," she murmured. "Triona will not come. She does not want you to ride back for her. She wants you to ride home."

A chill ran along his neck and arms. He remembered that the child had the Sight, and he respected the natural ability of seers like his cousin Elspeth, whose visions often proved true.

"Mairead," he said quietly. "What do you see?"

"Triona cannot come to our feast, because she is not at home," she answered. Behind them, her brothers turned to listen. "She has gone to Kilernan." She turned, her eyes wide, her cheeks pale. "I saw Parlan MacDonald and Catriona in the fire just now, through the hole in the cheese. They were holding hands, as if they were about to be married." Mairead leaned toward Kenneth. "But she would rather wed you," she whispered. "Even though you are a Fraser."

He drew in a long breath, and looked around at the other children, who watched him somberly. "I will ride back to the shieling." He stood. "And I will be back— with Catriona."

"You will have to go to Kilernan to get her, then," Mairead said easily, and fed the cheese to Tomas.

She was gone when he arrived. The hut was empty but for the cow, and the hearth was cold. He frowned over that; Catriona had been careful never to let the fire go out, fearing bad luck.

The cow lowed, a mournful, lonely sound, and stepped across the disheveled room, knocking over a stool as she went, bending her head to nibble some oats left in a sack. The other garron was gone. Even Cù was gone.

Kenneth patted the cow's shoulder and fetched a bucket of water for her, frowning as he worked. He looked at the neatly made bed, then glanced away. Haunting memories of the love they had made there hurt him keenly.

Catriona had clearly gone back to Kilernan. Had she decided to marry Parlan after all, finding a MacDonald more to her liking than a Fraser? He sucked in an angry, wounded breath and stomped out of the house, shutting the door firmly behind him.

Hoofprints marred the snow all around him as he trudged toward his garron. Several horses had been in the yard since he had left earlier. The MacDonalds had come for her, then; Parlan and his cousins, or even

Hugh MacDonald, who had sent word through Parlan that he would fetch his niece for Twelfth Night.

Kenneth scowled as he swung up into the saddle. Had she gone willingly, or had she gone with regrets? Had she decided to wed Parlan to gain a MacDonald home for her eight cousins? He squeezed his eyes shut in grief at the thought.

He spun the garron and began to ride out of the yard, but something in the snow caught his gaze. Reining in, he looked down at an image of a flower in the snow, made by the repeated impressions of a slender, graceful foot.

A snow rose, he realized with a sense of shock. Nearby, glinting on the crusted snow, he noticed the discarded silver brooch, its rose quartz stone pale and perfect. Dismounting, he picked up the jewelry piece and stared at the design in the snow.

The brooch, he was sure, had been flung down in haste. The flower design had been made earlier, for its edges were blurred. He wondered if his anger and sense of rejection were misplaced. Perhaps Catriona had not left here voluntarily.

Perhaps she had dropped the brooch as a message, as a plea for help. He could not ignore the possibility.

He would ride to Kilernan and face Hugh and Parlan—and Catriona as well. Only then would he know for certain how she felt about him. Only then could he prove to her that the MacDonalds were no threat to him.

An idea occurred to him then, wild in its newness, bringing with it fresh hope. Perhaps, if he acted on it, he could honor all the pledges: Lachlann's, the legal bond, and, most important, his own to Catriona. He thrust the cross pin of the brooch into his plaid, and rode out.

"And so, Catriona needs our assistance," Kenneth finished. He looked at the steady, caring gazes that watched him somberly. "It is a risk, I know, but we must ride to Kilernan and free her if she needs it. I cannot do it alone. I need your help."

Patrick nodded first, and looked at his brothers and sister. Each one in turn nodded, including Tomas and Edan. "We would do anything to help Triona," Patrick said. "But what can we do against Hugh MacDonald?" He inclined his head toward the younger ones. "They are children, and you are a Fraser. The MacDonalds will not even let you into Kilernan Castle."

"They will not let a Fraser inside, true," Kenneth said. "But they will let you in, I think. Listen, now. We have much work to do before the feast tomorrow evening."

Chapter Ten

∽◆∾

A raucous mixture of laughter, rough voices, and the strong thrum of a wire harp filled the vaulted hall of Kilernan Castle. High stone walls soared into shadow deepened by the rising smoke of wall torches. Benches creaked under the weight of fifty MacDonalds seated at tables, eating a variety of roasted meats, savory vegetable dishes, and sweet cakes, and drinking wines and *uisge beatha* from flasks and cups handed back and forth.

Catriona sat beside her uncle at a table near the blazing hearth, and flicked at a small, dry pea, spinning it idly on the table; she had found it in her cake earlier, and had been named the Twelfth Night Queen. Parlan had put it there she was certain, forcing this night of revelry upon her, just as he and her uncle had taken her away from the shieling the day before. But she had acquiesced and gone with them. She knew that she must leave before Kenneth returned for her, or she would have to surrender to the strength of her love for him.

Sighing, she glanced at Parlan and her uncle, who sat to either side of her. They ate with lusty appetites and swallowed drink strong enough to take most men to their knees. She had eaten little, and had sipped less.

"The queen is not merry tonight," Hugh MacDonald remarked. "Eat up, girl, and drink. And smile. Soon you will be wed, and Kilernan will be yours. I will announce your marriage tonight."

She looked at him, noting the florid stain in his cheeks and his constant grin, which meant that he was quite drunk. She was familiar with that flushed, hearty look, having seen it on her uncle's face frequently throughout her life.

"I wish to go to bed," she said, beginning to stand.

Hugh MacDonald grabbed her arm. "Stay," he barked. "You are the Queen of the Revels tonight. You cannot go until the celebration is over. We are waiting for you to choose your king." He grinned and waved his hand toward Parlan.

Parlan leaned toward her, grinning, his breath soured by wine and meat, and held a bit of cake near her mouth. The spicy, sweet fragrance nearly made her ill. Catriona shook her head in refusal. "Eat it," Parlan said. "The cook made it for this feast, from English flour, and sugar and raisins and ginger. You will not taste a finer Twelfth Night cake in all the Highlands."

She shook her head again, and Parlan crammed the piece into his own mouth. "You must do as I say when we marry."

"I have not agreed to wed you," she said, between her teeth.

Hugh leaned over. "You came back to Kilernan, girl, and that means you agree to many things," he said, and belched.

"You both must promise to bring the MacGhille

children to live here," she said. "Then I will consider wedding Parlan."

"Hah! You have a will like an ox," her uncle said. "My nephew will do well to wed such a strong woman." He grinned. "Parlan! Did you find that Fraser who was about last week?"

Parlan shook his head. "He went back home, I'm sure."

"The rascal," Hugh said. He lifted a brow at Catriona. "Where is that silver brooch you always wear?"

"I—I lost it," she said.

He scowled. "You did not send it to a Fraser and ask them to honor that foolish promise, did you? They would take the silver, and leave you, girl. You know that. I've told you their pledges are worthless. Mac-Donalds keep pledges, not Frasers."

"I believe that the Frasers are men of their word, Uncle," she said quietly.

He growled in disagreement and swallowed more drink. "Ah!" he called suddenly. "Good! Now the revelry begins at last! The guisers are here from the *clachan*!" He gestured toward the door.

Catriona barely looked up as the troupe of guisers entered the hall. The men cheered and laughed as the lads danced and sang, wending their way through the large chamber. One of them beat a skin-covered drum, and another played notes on a wooden pipe; all but one wore loose, hooded robes of pale wool, their faces painted in frightening or comical masks. The oldest lad, taller and larger than the rest, wore an animal hide.

The old bard played a tune on his wire-strung harp to keep time with the spirited rhythms of the drum and pipe. Clapping and singing began among the

MacDonalds who watched, howling with glee as the guisers pranced and chanted, tumbled and cavorted.

Catriona watched, her attention captured by the music and antics. The group of guisers included children, but that was not unusual. The smallest child, robed like the rest, was lifted and passed among the older lads; guisers traditionally celebrated the youngest among them as a symbol of luck.

Any household on New Year's Eve and on Twelfth Night would welcome a group of guisers, both as lighthearted entertainment and as a means of clearing away lingering evil spirits. Catriona sighed, watching the performers, and thought of Kenneth, who had come to her house on New Year's Eve, and had vowed to bring her good luck. But she would not let him attempt it, fearing what her uncle and Parlan might do to a Fraser in their midst.

Now the guisers began a mock battle, initiated by one of the smaller lads, who kept tripping on the hem of his voluminous robe, raising hearty laughs from the men watching. He fought a "bull" in the form of the tallest lad, who wore an animal hide that covered his head and torso, with deer antlers fixed to his head. Beneath the hide, Catriona saw a red-and-green MacDonald plaid, and long, muscled legs cased in deerskin boots.

The comical battle continued between the roaring "bull" and the robed little hunter, who bravely climbed on his quarry's back and rode him around the hall. Then Catriona sat up abruptly.

She had seen those deer-skin boots before; just yesterday she had watched a pair of strong, agile hands lace them, hands that later had loved her into ecstasy.

Chills cascaded down her spine. She narrowed her eyes and watched more carefully.

Her uncle chuckled beside her, enjoying the simple, amusing battle. "Look at that brave little one! Punching the bull with his tiny fist—and the bull goes down! And again! Ha-ha!"

Catriona did not laugh. Parlan guffawed beside her, and choked on his drink, coughing until he was red-faced. Catriona stared at the bull, and at each guiser in turn. She now recognized every one of them, from Kenneth down to little Tomas, carried by his older brothers. And the hunter, quite clearly, was Mairead.

She frowned, wondering why Kenneth had come to Kilernan Castle, and why he had brought the MacGhille children. She twisted her hands in her lap anxiously and watched the antics.

The little hunter won the battle, but the fallen bull sprang to life again. He chased the guisers from the hall—and perhaps to safety if trouble began, Catriona thought—but for one older lad; Patrick, she guessed. The bull ran, roaring, around the hall, with this guiser in pursuit, banging on the drum.

They came to the table where Catriona sat with her uncle and Parlan. The white-robed guiser, Patrick, his face painted green and black, bowed low. "Queen of Twelfth Night," he said, "your wish is ours to fulfill. Whatever you want shall be yours. Who shall be your king? Who shall rule your hall?"

Catriona glanced at him and at her kinsmen, and at the bull, whose face and torso were covered in the shapeless animal hide. She straightened.

"What better king for a Twelfth Night Queen than a bull who cannot be defeated, even in death?" she said. "Surely he is an enchanted king from some magical land." She held out her hand to the bull. Beside her, Parlan sputtered a protest, and Hugh chortled with laughter, guzzling his drink.

Kenneth bowed low in acceptance, snorting and pawing the ground. He came closer and shifted until he stood between her and Hugh MacDonald. She could smell the stale animal hide, and saw his hand, long-fingered and strong, at his belt. He wore a red plaid, borrowed, she guessed, from the children; his own blue-and-green tartan would be recognized here as a Fraser weave.

"And who shall rule your hall?" Patrick asked.

She paused, and saw Kenneth's hand tighten in the shadows beneath the hide. She saw Parlan scowl, and saw her uncle slit his eyes toward her, waiting.

"I rule this hall," she announced. "And I shall send the bull out to graze." She gestured imperiously, earnestly. "Go now. Please. Go!"

Laughter rose around the hall. Parlan chuckled heartily, and her uncle slapped his knee and pointed, imitating her.

The bull moved like lightning then, tearing off his disguise. Shoving Hugh facedown on the table, Kenneth twisted the man's arm and pressed a knee hard into his back. Then he touched the point of his dirk to Hugh's neck. Patrick dove at the same time, wrenching Parlan's arm behind him, and holding a dirk to his neck as well.

Catriona gasped and jumped to her feet, backing away. Throughout the hall, men rose to their feet, shouting as they came toward the main table.

"Hold!" Kenneth roared. "Hold! If any man comes near, your laird will die at the point of a Fraser blade!

And his nephew will follow, cut by one of your own pups! Hold now!"

Breathing hard beneath Kenneth's restraining hand and knee, glancing wild-eyed at the dirk near his head, Hugh managed to nod. "Listen to him!" he bellowed. He swiveled his eyes. "I know you! You are a Glenran Fraser! By God! Catriona, you sent that damned brooch to them! And look what treachery!"

"Catriona did not invite me here," Kenneth said. "I am Kenneth Fraser of Glenran, come of my own will, with something to say to you, Hugh MacDonald, and to all the MacDonalds of Kilernan. First, though, I ask your pardon for the blade at your throat, for we do not trust one another well just now. And I thank you for your hospitality." He smiled easily.

"Hospitality?" Hugh choked out. "What do you want here?"

"Peace," Kenneth said clearly. "And promises. I wish to remind you of a paper pledge you signed long ago, when you agreed to end the feud between our clans. Let it be newly agreed in words between you and I, and witnessed by all men here."

"Ach," Hugh grunted. "You know I must agree to that, on pain of death from the crown. I have no choice, whether or not you hold a blade to my throat."

"I will not draw your blood," Kenneth said, sliding a meaningful glance toward Catriona, "if you will listen well, and give your solemn promise before all men here."

"Promise what?" Hugh growled.

Watching, Catriona fisted her hands at her sides, wondering what Kenneth meant to do. She glanced from Kenneth to Hugh, then from Patrick to Parlan, who looked ill. Kenneth looked at her once, his dark eyes full of storm and determination. His presence, his intensity, swept through her like the pull of a lodestone.

"Tell me, Hugh," he said. "Who owns Kilernan? Who holds it by right of the Regent of Scotland?"

Hugh was silent, his face florid, his breath coming in gasps. "Catriona," he growled at last. "It is hers by right."

"And you have kept the property well for her, for which she surely thanks you. But now, I think, she is ready to manage it with her own hand and her own judgment. Tell her."

"A bargain," Hugh gasped out. "If Catriona promises to wed the man I choose for her, I will make this pledge. Kilernan must remain a stronghold for Clan Donald."

Catriona sucked in a breath and stared at Kenneth. His mouth tightened. "Catriona?" he asked, without looking at her.

She had no choice. For the sake of Kenneth's life after this moment, for the children, for Kilernan, she had no choice. "I—I promise," she murmured.

"Then I bestow Kilernan back into your keeping, now that you are old enough," Hugh said. "Before all men here, I pledge this," he added when Kenneth pressed the dirk point to his neck.

Kenneth looked at the silent, frowning Highlanders gathered nearby. "Catriona MacDonald is the owner of this castle. Your loyalty is owed to her now. She is her father's daughter, brave and strong and fair-minded. Follow her always, and show her your support."

Catriona watched him, tears glinting in her eyes. Kenneth Fraser had fulfilled the promise of the snow rose, but the price was high: she would gain Kilernan, but she must lose the man she loved.

He barely glanced at her as he looked down at Hugh. "Now, MacDonald," Kenneth continued. "The Twelfth Night after Christmas is the Epiphany, when three wise kings offered gifts and homage to a child in a manger. Will you honor that by offering gifts and protection to a few children in need?"

"The MacGhille children," Hugh muttered. "Catriona holds Kilernan, and she has the right to bring the waifs inside its walls if she wants." He groaned, a low, sober sound. "Let me up, Fraser. I will not come after you, nor send my men."

"Then I will trust you." Kenneth let go and stepped back, though he held the blade steady. Beside him, Patrick slowly released Parlan. Hugh muttered to him, and laid a restraining hand on his arm. Catriona sensed no threat there, though; Parlan looked as if he might faint or be sick, either from strong drink or the shock of being bested so easily.

Kenneth glanced at Catriona. "You wanted Kilernan taken without bloodshed," he said softly. "It is done. You wanted a home for your young cousins. That, too, is done. Hugh MacDonald will not go back on his word to you. Every man here will hold him to his promise." He gestured toward the men who stood watching them.

"Uncle?" Catriona asked. "Will you forget this pledge later, when it suits you?"

Hugh wiped sweat from his brow. "I gave you my word before a host of men, on a holy day," he muttered. "I will not break that. I have pride and a heart, girl, though you do not think so. Kilernan is yours, as it always was. I only kept it until you found a strong husband. Parlan will do well by you."

Catriona hesitated, dreading what she must do next. "Thank you, Kenneth Fraser. Thank you—" Her voice trembled uncertainly. "Go now," she urged him. "Please. You must leave."

Hugh watched them. "You know this Fraser!"

"I know him well," she said softly. "Let him return to his home in peace, Uncle." Hugh scratched his head, grumbling indistinctly.

"If I must go," Kenneth said, looking at her evenly, "let me first ask a favor of the Twelfth Night Queen. She may grant requests on the last night of the Yuletide season."

Catriona inclined her head, determined to answer whatever he asked her with calm and pride, though her breathing grew quick. She knew that Kenneth must leave here, yet she longed for him to stay, however foolish the thought.

"What is your request?" she asked.

"All I want," he said, "is to know the queen's dearest wish." He stepped toward her. "Then I will leave."

Her heart surged. She watched him, and sensed the hush all around her. She drew a quivering breath. "All I truly want," she murmured, "is for you to be my luck, and my own. Forever." She looked up at him through a glaze of tears, then glanced away. "But that is just a foolish wish."

"Wishes are often blessings." He moved closer. "Catriona MacDonald, listen to me well." He tipped her chin up with a finger. "I am your luck, and I am yours."

"Holy saints," Hugh mumbled. "Look at that."

"And if I leave here," Kenneth continued in a whisper so low only she could hear it, "I will never give up. I will be back for you."

A hot tear slid down her cheek. She took his hand

and turned to her uncle, who watched her with a stunned expression.

"I choose my king for this night," she said.

"You would choose him for your husband," Hugh murmured.

"I would," she said softly. "But I made you a promise."

Hugh sighed. "I am no fool, girl. I know a brave, good man, a man to respect, when I meet one—though he be a Fraser." He rubbed his whiskery jaw. Then he looked at Kenneth. "Would you hold Kilernan for MacDonalds, or Frasers?"

"Kilernan can be a fortress of truce between our clans," Kenneth answered. "The pledge of peace will always hold here."

Hugh nodded brusquely and scratched his head. "Catriona, wed this man." He grinned sheepishly. "Do what I say, girl. It is a wise choice for all of us."

She smiled. "I will, Uncle."

Parlan sputtered. "Hugh—"

"Hush up," Hugh snapped. "I have other nieces."

Catriona looked at Kenneth through joyful tears. He drew her into his arms and kissed her, his lips gentle, his breath full of life. "I told you I would bring you luck," he said.

"Ah, and you did," she answered, and laughed softly. "You surely did."

"The star!" A murmur rose among the men gathered in the hall. "The Epiphany star!" The crowd parted to admit one of the small guisers, who walked toward the main table, carrying a candle.

Kenneth put his arm around Catriona as they watched the final ceremony of Twelfth Night. Catriona rested her head on his shoulder and let the tears glide freely down her cheeks.

Mairead came toward them, her white robe trailing, her small hands clasped around a thick, blazing candle. The light pierced the shadows in the dimly lit hall as she held the flame high. She lifted her face to the golden light, and her eyes, blind and seeing, glittered like pale jewels.

"Twelfth Night is the last night of the Yuletide season," Catriona murmured. "It is the day of hope, the day when we truly realize all the blessings of the year to come."

"There will be many years full of blessings for us, love."

"Is it so?" she asked, her tone light.

"I pledge that it will be so," Kenneth whispered. "Here. This belongs to you." He lifted his hand and pinned the snow rose brooch to the shoulder of her plaid. Then he kissed her, while the child circled the light of promise and hope around them.

SUSAN KING was raised in upstate New York and moved to the Washington, D.C. area as a teenager. She earned a B.A. in studio art and an M.A. in art history from the University of Maryland. She has lectured in art history, art theory, and historical research, and is a Ph.D. candidate in medieval art history at the University of Maryland. Susan is a member of Romance Writers of America, of Novelists, Inc., is on the board of directors of Washington Romance Writers, and is a Fellow of the Society of Antiquaries of Scotland.

Following the birth of her third child, Susan took a leave of absence from graduate school. Gaining inspiration from a multitude of research notes, she began to write historical fiction to counterbalance life with three sons. Her first novel, *The Black Thorne's Rose,* set in thirteenth-century England, was published by Topaz in September 1994.

Since then, Susan has explored her fascination for Scottish history with award-nominated books such as *The Raven's Wish,* set in the sixteenth-century Scottish Highlands, and *The Angel Knight,* set in medieval Scotland. *The Raven's Moon* was a lead title for Topaz in February 1997, and *Lady Miracle,* a sequel to *The Angel Knight,* was released in September 1997.

Susan lives with her husband and three sons in Gaithersburg, Maryland.

The Best Husband Money Can Buy

∽◌∾

BY MARY JO PUTNEY

Chapter One

❦

London, 1818

It was Emma Stone's annual day for sadness.

She returned to her room after an exhausting session of trying to drum manners and mathematics into her charges, and found a letter waiting for her. The heavy, expensive paper and Vaughn seal were instantly recognizable, as was the exquisite script that said, "Miss Emma Vaughn Stone."

She picked the letter up with a sigh, not yet ready to open it. There was no need to, really. Inside, in the handwriting of the Duchess of Warrington's secretary, would be an invitation to the annual Vaughn Christmas gathering at Harley, the family seat. Two weeks of talk and laughter and celebration among dozens of Vaughns of varying degree, with the duke and duchess presiding over the festivities.

Nostalgically she thought back to happier days when she'd attended every year. Troops of young cousins galloping through the house and grounds. Older Vaughns fondly remembering their shared past. Feasts that made the tables groan. The candlelit Christmas

Eve service in the castle chapel. She could almost
smell the roasting chestnuts . . .

Face set, she broke the seal and looked inside. The
invitation was exactly like all the others, even though it
had been over ten years since she had attended one of
the gatherings. Ten long years since her parents had
died and left Emma impoverished.

Her mother had been a second cousin of the duke,
and every year she had brought her husband and
daughter to Harley for Christmas. Emma wondered
how much longer it would be until she was dropped
from the list. Even if she could take a fortnight off
from her governess position, she would not go to
Harley. She was too poor, too insignificant, to belong
in that gilded world anymore.

It hurt to receive the invitation every year and know
that she could not attend. It would hurt even more
when the Warringtons finally stopped inviting her. The
annual invitation was her last fragile connection to her
happy childhood.

Unbearably restless, Emma caught up her cloak so
that she could walk through the London streets. For
the next few hours, she'd think of the past, a self-
indulgence she allowed herself only once a year. By
the time she returned to the Garfields' house, she
would be tired enough to sleep, if she was lucky.

Giving silent thanks for the fact that it was her half
day off, she went out into the raw December afternoon.
As her long strides carried her east along the Strand,
she thought of those distant golden holidays, and wondered what had happened to her grand relations. There
was quiet young Lord Brandon, known as Brand, who
was son and heir to the duke. He had two younger sis-
ters within a few years' age of Emma. And Cecilia,

who like Emma was a distant cousin. Unlike Emma, she was wealthy and beautiful.

And, of course, there was Anthony Vaughn, Brand's best friend, another distant cousin who would someday be Viscount Verlaine. Five years older than Emma, Anthony had been the leader of the younger generation, outrageously handsome, and sometimes merely outrageous, but so charming that everyone always forgave him. At Emma's last Christmas at Harley, it had been obvious that he and Cecilia were heading for a match. They'd made a stunningly attractive couple. Emma had come across them kissing in a corner once. She'd made an embarrassed retreat, unnoticed by the young lovers.

Actually she had usually gone unnoticed, being plain and shy. She'd never minded that. What mattered was that she had belonged.

Emma detoured to the Covent Garden market to buy herself a nosegay of flowers. It was an expensive luxury at this season, but one that she permitted herself now and then. To always watch every penny was bad for the soul. She loved flowers, and this small bunch of chrysanthemums would brighten her drab room for days.

She continued eastward into the old City of London, the financial and merchant district, until a glance at the gray sky showed that it was time to turn back. Though Emma did not worry overmuch about her safety during her walks, she knew better than to risk getting caught on the streets after dark.

On impulse she decided to visit the church on the corner. Like most of the parish churches in the City, it was suffering as residents moved farther from London's center. Still, the church was handsome, and it would be a welcome respite from the cold wind.

Inside, she sat for a few minutes and gave a prayer for her parents. They had died of a fever when Emma was at school in Bath. That terrible shock had been followed by another when she returned home to find that after the debts were paid, there would be no money left. Her amiable father had inherited a modest independence, and spent every penny of it, along with his wife's marriage portion. There would be no income or dowry for his daughter.

The day after Emma's parents had been buried, a letter came from the Dowager Duchess of Warrington. In crisp, formal words, she offered the orphan a home at Harley. Even at fifteen, Emma had known what that meant—a lifetime as a poor relation, entitled to room and board in return for performing menial services for the duchess and other members of the household.

If she'd been pretty, she might have accepted. Many people came to Harley, and there might have been a man willing to marry an attractive girl with no dowry.

But Emma was tall and robust and unremarkable, with dark hair and freckles and eyes of shifting color that never stayed the same long enough to be called gray or green or hazel. If she'd gone to Harley, she would have spent the rest of her life—decades, probably—as an unpaid servant. Inevitably she would be known as Poor Emma. That is, if she were noticed at all.

Luckily there had been another choice. The headmistress of Emma's school offered to let her stay and complete her education in return for helping with the younger students. Within two years, Emma had been a full-fledged teacher.

She quite enjoyed teaching, so when the head-mistress retired and sold the school, Emma had become a governess. Usually governesses were older, but it was one profession where plainness was an asset. She'd spent several years with the family of a pros-perous doctor. When the daughters no longer needed her, she'd taken her current position with the Garfields.

The Garfields. Emma sighed at the thought as she got to her feet and began to stroll around the church. There was much carved wood, and several fine funeral brasses.

She was almost ready to leave when she discovered a coffin lying in a side chapel. The pine box looked very stark, with no mourners or flowers or even any candles lit. Tucked in the corner where the rail met the wall was a book open to show blank pages. Curiously she looked closer, and saw a note asking those who prayed for the deceased to leave their name and address.

A harried curate emerged from the vestry and walked down the aisle past her. Hesitantly, Emma said, "Excuse me, sir. Who was this man?"

The clergyman paused. "Though Harold Greaves was a resident of this parish, he never came to services, so I know very little about him. He was sixty-six years old. Died of an apoplexy, I believe. He'll be buried tomorrow."

"He had no family?"

"Apparently not." With a nod the curate continued on his way.

Emma stared at the empty condolence book. It seemed unbearably sad that a man should have lived sixty-six years and left no one to grieve.

For a moment she wondered who would mourn her

death. Then, ashamed of the self-pity she'd been indulging in since receiving the invitation to Harley, she knelt beside the coffin and prayed for the soul of Harold Greaves. As she did, she imagined him as a small child. Since no infant survived without being fed and washed and tended, there must have been someone who cherished him then. In his sixty-six years, surely he had made some friends. She prayed that he had known his share of happiness and satisfaction, and that his death had been a swift and easy one.

Gradually, a sense of peace came over her. She hoped that meant Mr. Greaves was resting easy. A little stiff from the cold stone floor, she got to her feet. After a moment of struggle with her own selfish impulses, she laid her nosegay on the coffin. For her, there would be other flowers, but not for Harold Greaves. May his soul rest in peace.

Not wanting to leave the pages of the condolence book so desolately blank, she used the pencil lying in the middle to write her name and the address of the Garfields' house. After a moment's thought, she also printed out the words of the Twenty-third Psalm. *Yea, though I walk through the valley of the shadow of death, I will fear no evil, for Thou art with me. . . .*

After she finished the psalm, she left the church, walking hastily, for it was almost dark. But the sense of peace stayed with her. It was true that she did not have the comfortable life with husband and family that she had grown up expecting, but she was alive and healthy and she'd never gone hungry.

Counting her blessings, she hurried home.

Five days after Emma received the invitation to Harley, a footman interrupted her French lesson with the two Garfield daughters. "The mistress wants you to come downstairs," he said slyly. "You have a caller."

"For me? How odd." Wondering who could possibly want to see her, Emma got to her feet. "Letty, Isabelle, work on your translations until I return."

Letty rolled her eyes elaborately while her younger sister giggled. The two girls were unrewarding students, interested only in clothing and endless speculations about the men they would someday marry. They were also idle and spoiled by their mother. Emma hoped that in time she would be able to inspire them with some respect for learning, but she wasn't optimistic.

"Maybe Miss Stone has a gentleman caller," Isabelle whispered.

Letty sniffed. "An old thing like her? Hardly."

Emma didn't know if she was supposed to hear the interchange or not, so she decided to ignore it. Still, her color was high when she went downstairs.

Mrs. Garfield was seated in the drawing room with a silver-haired gentleman on the chair opposite. As he got to his feet, she said with obvious disapproval, "Mr. Evans insists that he must speak with you privately about a most important matter." Her eyes narrowed to slits. "I'll have no goings on in my house, miss."

Mr. Evans said in a formidably well-bred voice, "I assure you, Mrs. Garfield, my business with Miss Stone is entirely professional." His tone was enough to rouse Mrs. Garfield and send her from the room. Then he turned to Emma.

"Sir, are we acquainted?" she asked, her brow furrowed. "If so, I'm afraid that I have forgotten the circumstances."

He smiled and looked much more approachable. "We are not acquainted, Miss Stone. I am a solicitor with news I think you will welcome. Please, do sit down. This will take some time."

Welcome news? As Emma settled on the sofa, she tried to think of any aged relations who might have left her a legacy, but without success. The rich Vaughns all had closer kin to leave their money to.

The solicitor resumed his seat. "First, are you the Emma Stone who five days ago left your name in the condolence book of Mr. Harold Greaves at the church of St. Pancras of the Field, in the City?"

Startled, she said, "Yes. I'm sorry, I meant no harm. Is there some family member who was offended by a stranger praying for Mr. Greaves?"

"Quite the contrary. Mr. Greaves was a widower. He and his wife had no children, and there are no other close kin." Mr. Evans paused, his eyes distant. "He and his wife were very close. After she died several years ago, Harold became something of a recluse. They were both good friends of mine as well as clients."

"I'm sorry for your loss," Emma said politely. She managed, barely, not to ask what this had to do with her.

"My friend left a most unusual last will and testament. He said that because he had no surviving family, anyone who freely prayed for his soul would receive 'the sum total of his worldly goods.' " The solicitor smiled. "You were the only one to sign the condolence book. Therefore, Miss Stone, you are the sole heir of Harold Greaves, merchant of London."

"Simply for spending a quarter of an hour in prayer?" Emma said incredulously.

"It was a quarter hour that no one else spent," Mr. Evans pointed out. "Harold always had a great appreciation for disinterested goodness. He would be happy to know that you prayed for no other reason than the simple caring of a good heart."

Emma held very still, trying to absorb the solicitor's announcement. Merely because she had chanced to wander into that small church, then spent a few minutes praying, she was now an heiress. She wondered how much Mr. Greaves had left. It would be a great blessing to have several hundred pounds as a cushion against unemployment or illness. Even fifty pounds would be very welcome.

Mr. Evans said jovially, "Aren't you going to ask how much you will inherit?"

Emma colored. "I'm curious, of course, but it seems rather vulgar to ask. Still, I assume that you would not be here unless there was some amount left after paying Mr. Greaves' funeral expenses."

"There is indeed." Mr. Evans paused portentously. "It's too soon to give an exact figure, but it is safe to say that your inheritance will be slightly in excess of one hundred thousand pounds."

Emma's jaw dropped. Sure she had not heard correctly, she repeated, "You said in excess of . . . of one hundred pounds?"

The solicitor chuckled. "You didn't mishear. The estate is a little more than one hundred thousand pounds. You are now a very wealthy young woman, Miss Stone."

There was a roaring in Emma's ears, and for a moment she thought she would faint. A hundred thousand pounds! The daughter of the richest banker in Britain had gone to her husband with a dowry of one hundred thousand pounds. It was a fortune worthy of a duke's daughter.

Could this be some kind of dreadful joke at her

expense? Her gaze went to the solicitor's face. Sober, respectable, patently honest. Exactly the kind of solicitor that a rich merchant would have. She tried to clear her throat, but her voice still came out as a squeak. "Excuse me, sir. I . . . I'm having trouble taking this in."

"Naturally. Strokes of fortune such as this are life-changing." He cocked his head to one side. "Do you have any idea what you will do with your inheritance?"

The question focused Emma's churning thoughts. "I wish to tithe a tenth of the amount to charity. For the widows and children of our gallant soldiers who died fighting Napoleon, I think."

"Very proper," Mr. Evans said approvingly. "What else?"

Emma could travel to Italy and Greece and all those wonderful, exotic places that were no more than names on the map. Buy a house, or even an estate. Do a thousand things.

Did she want to do them alone? She realized with shock that she had just been given the chance to obtain the most powerful desire of her heart—a home and family of her own. She could once more have a place where she belonged.

Struggling to control her excitement, Emma said, "I'm going to get myself a husband, Mr. Evans. The best husband money can buy."

Chapter Two

❦

The solicitor blinked at Emma's bald announcement. Then he gave an unprofessional grin. "You're a very direct young lady, Miss Stone. What sort of husband would that be?"

"I'm not that young, Mr. Evans, but I am practical and not at all romantic." At least, not in the last ten years. Once Emma had been as romantic as any young girl. A man's face appeared in her mind. Ruthlessly she suppressed the image. "I want someone of good character who will treat me with kindness and respect. Well-bred. Pleasing to look at, but he needn't be handsome. In fact, it would be much better if he is not."

If a handsome man married a plain woman, everyone would think it was only for money. Emma did not want that to be said of her, even if it was true.

The solicitor gave an approving nod. "In other words, what any wise woman would want in a husband. But you mentioned 'well-bred.' Did you mean a titled aristocrat?" He hesitated, then said with some awkwardness, "Forgive me, but men of that class can be . . . difficult. There are those who would happily take your money while despising you for being of lower birth."

She raised her chin. "My mother was a Vaughn. No man would dare look down on my birth."

"You are one of the Vaughns of Harley?" Mr. Evans' raised brows were a surprised comment on her status as a little more than an upper servant.

"The relationship is close enough that I am invited to the castle on great occasions," she said dryly, "but not close enough for me to have any money."

As she spoke, Emma suddenly realized that she could accept the Christmas invitation to Harley. That prospect was far more vivid and compelling than the abstract knowledge that she had just inherited a fortune. She could return to the scene of her happiest days, a Vaughn once more. She wanted to laugh aloud with joy.

The solicitor's tone changed from avuncular interest to crisp professionalism. "No matter whom you marry, I suggest that you allow me, or another competent solicitor, to set up a special trust so that, say, half of your capital is reserved to you and your children. Normally a woman's property automatically becomes her husband's when she marries, but a woman of great wealth, such as you are now, often prefers to keep some control in her own hands."

She was now a woman of great wealth. Emma wanted to laugh again, this time in disbelief. "An excellent idea. I've seen women ruined by profligate husbands." She bit her lip. "I have no idea how to manage so much money. Will you act for me, as you did for Mr. Greaves?"

"It would be my honor, and my pleasure," the solicitor said promptly.

"I shall need rather a lot of help, and not only financial." She smiled with wry self-mockery. "Would you be able to use your connections to compile a list of possible husbands? Men who fit the requirements I mentioned earlier, and whose circumstances compel them to seek a rich wife. In other words, the better grade of fortune hunter."

Mr. Evans regarded her with fascination and a certain shock. "As I said, you are . . . admirably direct. I shall make inquiries among my legal colleagues about suitable candidates. Character will be of the utmost importance in these circumstances."

His eyes narrowed thoughtfully. "Actually I can think of several men who might suit myself. There's the Honorable George Martin, a widower with four fine children. A very worthy gentleman. Or Sir Edward Wyckham, a rising young politician. He has great ability, but he'll need a wife of means to make the most of his opportunities." The solicitor smiled dismissively. "We wouldn't want you to pledge yourself to a charming wastrel such as young Lord Verlaine."

"Verlaine?" She caught her breath. "If the current viscount is a young man, I presume that means the second viscount had died and his son Anthony has inherited."

"Yes. Sorry, I forgot that Verlaine is a Vaughn," Mr. Evans said, expression stricken. "He is related to you?"

"A distant cousin," Emma said, her heart pounding. "I . . . I remember him from Christmases at Harley. I'm fearfully out of touch with the family—I had presumed that he'd married another of my cousins. Or is he a widower?"

"As far as I know, Verlaine has never been married. Certainly he is single now." The solicitor frowned. "If you know him, you'll also know how unsuitable he would be. Too handsome, too charming, and thoroughly unreliable. His name is a byword for every kind of wild escapade. They say he gambles heavily. I know for a fact that his estate is on the brink of foreclosure."

Anthony. Single and in need of a rich wife. "I agree that he is probably inappropriate. Still, Verlaine has the advantage of being known to me." She rubbed her damp palms on her skirt. "Please look into his circumstances. If it appears that he would be interested in the kind of . . . arrangement I propose, he might be worth considering."

"As you wish," the solicitor said without enthusiasm. "But I will be able to present much better prospects."

"I'm sure you can," Emma said, pleased with her calm tone.

Yet after she and the solicitor concluded their business and he took his leave, she leaned back in her chair, her cold hands locked together. A fortune, Christmas at Harley—and Anthony. Granted, he'd always been a bit wild, but there had been no real vice in him. In his casual way, he'd been kind to her. If he really needed money enough to be willing to marry for it . . .

She tried to control her turbulent thoughts, but without success. She wanted to buy herself a husband. If so, why not Anthony Vaughn if he was willing?

Anthony, the only man she had ever loved.

Events moved quickly after Mr. Evans left. Full of curiosity and bad temper, Mrs. Garfield had immediately confronted Emma about the purpose of the solicitor's visit. Since Emma no longer had to tolerate her employer's rudeness, she promptly quit her position, effective in one week.

Another governess was found. Emma silently wished her well with the Garfield daughters. Then, because she needed a maid to be considered respectable, she hired away one of Mrs. Garfield's housemaids. Becky was a pleasant, quiet young woman who was bullied unmercifully by the housekeeper because she could read and write and wanted to better herself. She accepted Emma's offer to be a lady's maid with relief and enthusiasm.

The day after Emma and her new maid took up residence in the very expensive and fashionable Grillon's Hotel, a sheaf of papers arrived from the solicitor. Each page listed a prospective husband. With amusement, Emma noticed how Mr. Evans had done his best to make each sound appealing. One man had "a bright, engaging manner," while another was "owner of a splendid Yorkshire estate, only moderately mortgaged."

She paged through the pile impatiently. The very last was "Anthony Vaughn, third Viscount Verlaine." No enticing descriptions for him, only comments like, "His estate, Canfield, is on the brink of foreclosure." "Gambles heavily" came with the grudging note, "Usually wins, though he has never been publicly accused of cheating."

Emma smiled at that. Unless Anthony had changed beyond recognition, he would never cheat.

Then she lowered the paper, her expression sobering. She was a fool, of course. She had never really known Anthony well. The last time she'd seen him, he had been a man grown while she was still in the schoolroom. She'd spun dreams around him, cherished his occasional friendly words, and loved him with the innocent fervor of a very young girl. In another year or so, she would surely have outgrown her infatuation, if she had continued in her old life.

But everything had changed irrevocably when she was fifteen, and she had never had a real chance for romance. The closest she had come was when a drunken guest at her former employer's had cornered her for a kiss. It had not been an enjoyable experience. No wonder her old dreams about Anthony had stayed alive in her heart.

She glanced back at the dossier, and realized that Anthony had rooms on Bruton Street, literally around the corner from Grillon's Hotel. It wouldn't hurt to walk by. In fact, it might be a good idea to call on him. As his cousin, it wouldn't be too improper for her to do so. A single short visit should be enough for her to strike him from the list of prospects. Then she would be free of her childish dreams, and able to put him from her mind forever.

Quickly, before she could become frightened by her own audacity, she donned her cloak and went off to call on her cousin.

Her resolve faltered when she reached the building where Anthony lived. It contained several sets of rooms for gentlemen, with Anthony's flat on an upper floor. She stared at the plain facade, wondering if she dared enter. It wasn't too late to turn back, and doing so would probably save her great humiliation.

But she had to know. Jaw set, she went up the steps and into the common hallway. There was a desk for a porter, but he was away from his post. Not sorry to be unobserved, she continued upstairs.

Anthony's flat was easily identified by a card in a

small brass holder on the door frame. To her surprise, the door itself was slightly ajar. She knocked lightly.

When no one answered, she pushed the door farther open. Then she gasped, horrified by the sight of bodies lying on the floor of the drawing room that lay just beyond the tiny vestibule. The flat looked like a massacre had taken place.

Then she heard heavy snoring and smelled the sour scent of spilled wine and sickness. Her nostrils flared as she moved forward into the drawing room and examined the scene more carefully. Apparently she had arrived the morning after an orgy. Empty wine bottles were everywhere, along with at least a dozen disheveled young men and almost as many women. Not, clearly, the respectable sort of female.

But none of the drunken men were the one she sought. Emma paused uncertainly, knowing that a sensible woman would leave instantly and have strong hysterics outside in the street. But she had already come this far, and she did not want to leave without seeing Anthony. She might not have the courage to return.

An open door at the far end of the drawing room led to a shadowed bedroom. Inside, she could dimly see a bed with a man who might be Anthony sprawled on his back on top of the rumpled counterpane. She preferred not to consider what condition he would be in, or what might be sharing his bed.

She began picking her way among the tangled bodies, doing her best not to touch any. Halfway across the room, one of the sleepers groaned, then rolled over and caught her right leg. "Nice ankles," he said hazily. "C'mere, darlin'."

He tugged with one hand while his other fumbled

with his unbuttoned breeches. She jerked free, stamped smartly on his fingers, and continued toward the bedroom.

A manservant emerged from another door, which led to a small kitchen. When he saw her, a look of horror came over his face. "I beg your pardon, miss, b . . . but his lordship is not receiving."

Emma paused. "Is he in the bedroom?"

"Yes, but this is no place for you," the valet said desperately. "Leave your card, and I'll see that he receives it."

Emma arched her brows and used the manner she had learned from the Dowager Duchess of Warrington. "You needn't be concerned about my reputation. Lord Verlaine is my cousin, so there can be no impropriety in my visit." Ignoring the valet's sputtered protests, she resumed her progress.

Luckily the sleeping man was more or less decent, though his coat and cravat were off and his shirt gaped at the throat, revealing a distracting triangle of bare flesh. Anthony, as handsome as ever, with the powerful build and waving dark hair that looked so much better on Vaughn men than on unfortunate females like her.

She studied the strong-boned, never-forgotten face. It had been so many years. Even in his present condition, rumpled and unshaven, he was magnificent.

Suddenly his eyelids flicked open. She caught her breath, wondering how she could have forgotten the impact of those piercing, light blue eyes. The force of his gaze made her feel like a butterfly pinned in a specimen box.

She was on the verge of flight when he said in a rumbling voice, "You're obviously a Vaughn, but damned if I know which one."

She took a deep breath. "I'm your cousin, Emma Vaughn Stone. You probably don't remember me, but my family always spent Christmas at Harley."

For an endless moment he regarded her unblinkingly. "Ah, yes. Little Emma Stone. A third cousin or some such."

"Second cousin once removed, I believe." She gave him a hesitant smile. "Though I wouldn't swear that's the precise relationship."

He regarded her dourly. "I once fished you out of the lake when you broke through the ice when skating."

"I remember. Not one of my better moments." She had clung to him like a monkey, shivering violently, after he pulled her from the water. He'd immediately carried her up to the house, talking soothingly the whole time. Looking back, that was probably the day she had fallen in love with him.

He sat up and swung his legs over the bed, moving with an effort that said a great deal about his previous night's activities. "Did you come here to play memory lane? If so, your timing is very poor."

She agreed, but now that she had begun, she wanted to get this interview over with quickly. "My purpose is quite different. Would it be possible to have a serious conversation with you?"

He groaned and buried his head in his hands. "Miss Stone, the last thing on earth I want is a serious conversation with anyone."

Perhaps, but he was coherent, and it spoke well for his basic good nature that he could be polite to an unexpected visitor when he probably felt like Vulcan's hammer was pounding on his skull. She turned to the valet, who had been hovering by the door. "Please make a pot of strong coffee for Lord Verlaine."

Years of teaching had given her some skill at persuading the recalcitrant. Very soon she and Anthony were sitting in the tiny kitchen with a pot of coffee on the table between them. Not the best setting for evaluating a potential husband, but at least the kitchen was private.

Anthony had taken the chair by the wall and promptly slumped against the whitewashed plaster, three-quarters asleep. She put a steaming mug of coffee in his hand. Eyes closed, he took a deep swallow, his Adam's apple moving. After a second draft, he sighed and opened his eyes. "Miss Stone."

"Emma," she said shyly. "After all, we are cousins, and you have known me since I was in the nursery."

"Very well, Emma." He drank more coffee. "To what do I owe the honor of this visit?"

She hesitated, then decided on bluntness. It was her chief talent. "I had heard you were in dire financial straits. On the verge of losing Canfield, in fact."

His expression turned to granite. "Our relationship is nowhere near close enough for you to speak of such matters. I'll thank you to leave now."

She swallowed hard. Angry, he was formidable. "I'm sorry. I know that was impertinent. I only ask because . . . perhaps I can help."

"No one can help," he snapped. "In three days, the mortgages will come due and the property will be taken from me. For two years, ever since my father died, I've been trying to pay off his damned debts, and now it's too late."

Her eyes widened. Anthony's father had been a charming, amiable fellow, but she remembered whispers that he was a gamester. "So your gambling has been an attempt to earn enough to pay off the mortgages."

Anthony's eyes narrowed. "How the devil did you know that? Even my best friends have assumed that I was playing only for sport."

She shrugged, unable to explain. "An educated guess."

He poured more coffee and added milk, his expression haggard. Desolate, even. "I needed forty thousand pounds. I'd managed to accumulate half that. There was no chance of borrowing more—believe me, I'd tried. My father's history of gambling made the banks consider me a poor risk. With only a few days until foreclosure, I had to throw caution to the winds." His eyes closed with pain. "Yesterday I bet the whole amount on a single game, double or nothing. If I'd won, Canfield would have been saved."

There was a hushed silence before she said the obvious. "But you didn't win."

His mouth twisted. "The cards were against me. The Deity, if there is one, apparently didn't want to see me remain a landowner."

"So you are not a gamester by temperament," she said thoughtfully.

"Believe me, if Canfield was secure, I'd never touch another deck of cards in my life," he said bitterly. "My father did enough gambling for both of us."

She did believe him. Her hands locked around her mug until the knuckles whitened. The worst charge against Anthony was that he was a hopeless gambler, but if that wasn't true, it changed everything. "Perhaps . . . perhaps we could help each other. I have just come into an unexpected legacy. I would like to marry and have a family, but as a governess I've had no opportunity to meet eligible men."

She stopped to gather her courage before continuing:

"Purely by chance, my solicitor mentioned that your property was on the verge of foreclosure. Since I am in need of a husband and you are in need of a fortune, I . . . I thought perhaps you might be willing to consider a . . . a marriage of convenience."

"What?" His mug, which was halfway to his mouth, slammed down on the table, and scalding coffee slopped across his hand. "You want me to *marry you*?"

His appalled expression was worse than a slap in the face. How could she have been so brazen, so *stupid,* as to suggest that a handsome, fashionable man like him might consider marrying a woman like her?

Face burning, she jumped up and grabbed her cloak from the back of her chair. "It was just a thought, and obviously a bad one. I'm sorry for disturbing you, Anthony. Lord Verlaine." She turned and bolted toward the kitchen door.

His chair scraped the floor, and in one bound he crossed the kitchen and caught her arm. "Wait! I'm sorry, Emma. I intended no insult." He turned her to face him. "This is just so . . . so unexpected."

Though she was a tall woman, he loomed over her, intimidatingly large. The reality of him was very different from her hazy childhood memories. He was a man now, not a youth. A man who was strong, virile, and forceful. For a woman who'd lived the last decade in a world of women and children, the effect was rather overpowering.

Her gaze went to his unshaved chin. The dark stubble was surprisingly intriguing. She wanted to touch it, discover the texture of those very masculine whiskers.

She wrenched her gaze away. "I'm sorry. It was presumptuous of me to march in like this."

"Unusual, perhaps, but not presumptuous." He studied her, his gaze piercing. "I keep wondering if I'm dreaming this whole scene out of a desperate desire to save Canfield."

"This is no dream," she said with conviction. He was too vivid, his hand on her arm too warm and strong, for this encounter to be anything but real.

He released her arm and made a courtly gesture toward the table. "Come sit down again, Cousin. You were quite right to say that we must have a serious conversation."

Chapter Three

∽◦◦∾

Anthony Vaughn poured more coffee for himself and his guest. Even after two cups, he still felt as if he were standing next door to death. He shouldn't have drunk himself into a stupor last night, and he definitely shouldn't have invited so many of his rackety friends to join in a perverse celebration of his disastrous gaming loss. He wondered vaguely when the whores had come. There had been none present when he had passed out.

He put that aside to concentrate on more important matters, namely, his amazing cousin, who sat across from him looking every inch the meek, dowdy governess. Yet it must have taken courage for her to come here and make her startling proposition.

Thinking back, he remembered her as a quiet child who tagged around after him with huge, speaking eyes. But there had been many children at Harley during the holidays. Except for the incident on the ice, he recalled very little about Emma.

First things first. He said, "You have forty thousand pounds?"

After a moment's hesitation, she said, "If we were to

marry, you would immediately have fifty thousand pounds at your disposal."

It was enough to save Canfield, and make necessary improvements as well. Enough to live like a gentleman again. But still—marriage? It was a state he had not contemplated since dear damned Cecilia.

He studied his long-lost cousin intently. When he'd first seen her picking her way through the tangled bodies of his dissolute friends with catlike care, he'd thought he was hallucinating. But he could not have imagined such a startling mixture of shyness and candor. She had the Vaughn height, square jaw, and dark hair. Though no beauty, she was presentable, or would be when decently dressed.

That was all very well for a cousin, but a wife? Yet what were his choices? Marry this disconcertingly direct but not unpleasant woman, or lose Canfield.

Put in those terms, there was really no choice at all. As a boy, he'd taken for granted that Canfield would be his one day. It wasn't until his father's death, when he realized that he was on the verge of losing the estate, that he had recognized how much he loved the place. More than loved—in a very real way, being Verlaine of Canfield defined him. Without it, he was merely an idle, careless fellow of good birth and small accomplishment, as useless as a dandelion.

He said carefully, "If you want children, it would have to be more than a marriage of convenience."

Emma turned beet red and looked away. "I understand that, of course. What I meant was that it would not be a love match."

An understatement. He asked, "What would you expect of me in the way of husbandly duties?" When she blushed again, he added, "I mean that in the broadest possible sense."

She thought before replying. "If we were to marry, I would ask that you treat me with courtesy and consideration, especially in front of others. I do not want to become a laughingstock—the desperate woman who bought herself a husband who cannot care for her." Her voice was rich and smooth as fine brandy, surprisingly provocative for a woman of her very proper appearance.

"That is hardly a problem. I would be no kind of gentleman if I treated you any other way. What else?"

Her gaze dropped. "Though I want children very much, I would prefer for that part of the marriage to be delayed until we are . . . are better acquainted."

A little relieved, he said, "A quite understandable desire. Do you have any other requirements?"

She shook her head mutely.

"If that is all you want, you would be a very easily pleased wife," he said dryly. "If we do agree to this, we would need to marry immediately, within the next two days, for me to save Canfield. Would you mind that?"

After a brief hesitation, she said, "Not under these circumstances."

He sighed and bent his head, running his fingers through his tangled hair. Marriage was for life. It was not a commitment he had ever thought to make to a virtual stranger. That was one reason why he hadn't looked around for an heiress when he discovered his financial problems. And, of course, he'd thought he would be able to save Canfield through his own efforts.

But how much did one person ever really know another? He'd thought he'd known Cecilia, and had been pitifully wrong. Emma Stone would probably make an easy, sensible wife, and she was not quite a stranger. Growing up in the same extended family surely counted for something.

He raised his gaze and studied his cousin again. Her face was so pale that a ghostly scattering of freckles showed across her high cheekbones. She was as nervous as he, and with good reason. When a woman married, she gave her body, her name, and her worldly goods to her husband. Perhaps that was why Emma had made her proposal to a man with whom she had at least some acquaintance.

Honor compelled him to say, "Are you absolutely sure you want this, Emma? My situation is urgent, but yours is not. You're young. You can afford to take more time searching for the mate who will best please you." His mouth curved without humor. "Remember the old saying, 'Marry in haste, repent at leisure.' "

Her gaze slid away from his. "I could spend years looking, but it wouldn't guarantee a better decision in the end. A man eager to marry a fortune is bound to make himself agreeable during the courtship. How would I know his true nature? With you, at least, I already know that you are pleasant to servants and patient with small brats who follow you around."

Bemused, he said, "Did I call you a brat?"

"Yes, though not unkindly." She smiled a little. "Younger children are more aware of older ones than vice versa. It's not surprising that you scarcely remember me, while I recall you quite vividly."

Though Emma had courage and honesty, her opinion of her own worth was not high, he realized. His shock when she'd suggested marriage had hurt her badly. Obviously she didn't think a man would marry her for any reason except money.

His thoughtful gaze went over her full, womanly

figure. While his preference was for ethereal blondes, it would be no hardship to lie with Emma. No hardship at all. If he satisfied her in bed and treated her with courtesy everywhere else, she would be content with this marriage. As for him—he would have Canfield.

He hesitated a moment longer, knowing that his life was about to change forever in ways that he couldn't even imagine. Then he took Emma's cold hand between both of his and said very formally, "My dearest cousin, would you do me the honor of becoming my wife?"

Face pale, she said, "The honor would be mine, Anthony."

The deal was done.

Heavy silence fell between them. Having agreed to marry, what came next? Anthony said, "I must call on your solicitor and discuss the financial settlements. I'll also go to Doctors' Commons for a special license, and arrange for the ceremony to take place day after tomorrow. Do you have any preference as to place or time?"

She shook her head. "Whatever is convenient. I'm staying at Grillon's Hotel. You may notify me of your arrangements there." She pulled paper and pencil from her reticule and printed out a name and address. "My solicitor."

After handing him the paper, she got to her feet. "I'll leave you now. You have much to do."

She was right, and he was going to have to do it while suffering from the prince of hangovers. He stood, thinking there should be something more to commemorate such a significant occasion. He took her hand. "Until our wedding day, Emma."

She flinched when he dropped a light kiss on her

hand. He wondered if she was one of those women with a constitutional dislike of physical intimacy. Well, it was too late to worry about that now. He would have to hope that his proven expertise with the fair sex would not fail him.

Taking her arm, he escorted her to his front door. Several of his friends were beginning to wake up, usually accompanied by low moans. His valet, Hawkins, had wisely set basins near the afflicted. Emma did a fine job of ignoring the whole decadent scene. Really a most sensible woman.

He squeezed her hand meaningfully at the front door, and she left him with a shy smile. Halfway back to his bedroom, one of his awakening friends, Matthews, muttered, "That must be the ugliest whore in London. Very proper of you to throw her out."

A surge of unexpected anger burned through Anthony. He bent over and grabbed Matthews' shirtfront in both hands, lifting him half off the floor. "You are speaking of my affianced wife," he said in his most menacing tone. "Do I make myself clear?"

Matthews' eyes widened until they resembled bloodshot gooseberries. "S . . . sorry, Verlaine! No insult intended, upon my word, no indeed!"

He was still babbling apologies when Anthony dropped him back to the floor and returned to his bedroom. Mercifully Hawkins had left a pitcher of hot water on the washstand. As Anthony splashed water on his face, his spirits began to rise. Canfield was saved. The Lord moved in mysterious ways His wonders to perform, and the Deity had outdone himself today.

Two days later, Emma donned her Sunday best dress for her wedding. Becky suggested a more elaborate hairstyle, but Emma rejected it on the grounds that she would look silly. She did spare a regretful thought for her childhood dreams of a romantic courtship, an adoring bridegroom, and a ceremony in the Harley chapel, where she would be surrounded by fond relatives. But those things were trivial. What mattered was that she was marrying Anthony, a fact so wonderful that she had never dreamed about it, at least not seriously.

At eleven o'clock punctually, Mr. Evans came for Emma and Becky. He had agreed to be a witness to the ceremony, while Becky would be maid of honor. On the short ride to the local parish church, Emma asked, "What did you think of Anthony?"

The solicitor said cautiously, "While I cannot approve of such haste, I was not unfavorably impressed by the young gentleman. He has a good head on him, and he was very reasonable about the settlements. Very reasonable indeed."

High praise from a lawyer. The carriage halted in front of the church, and she descended into drizzly rain. It would have been nice if the sun had come out, she thought wistfully. Everything about this wedding was drab and hurried.

Telling herself again that the details didn't matter, she entered the church, and saw that Anthony had already arrived with a friend to be groomsman. Elegantly dressed in a dark blue coat and immaculately starched cravat, he was so handsome that she almost bolted from the church. How could a barnyard hen mate with a lordly peacock?

Then Anthony saw her and came down the aisle with a smile. He was carrying a small nosegay in one hand.

Presenting it to her, he said, "I thought you might like these."

The flowers were tiny winter roses, white mixed with palest pink and bound together with a silver ribbon. Heaven only knew where he'd found them in December. The exquisite blossoms made the rest of the ceremony's shortcomings fade into irrelevance. "Oh, Anthony," she breathed. "They're perfect."

All doubts gone, she took his arm and they walked together to the vicar. This marriage was right. She knew it.

Chapter Four

✦✦✦

The newlyweds had their first quarrel shortly after the wedding breakfast. Mr. Evans and Anthony's groomsman had left after they'd all shared an excellent meal in a private room at Grillon's Hotel. Since Anthony's bachelor rooms were hardly suitable for a new wife, he had engaged a suite at the hotel. One with two bedrooms. As he'd thought dryly when booking the rooms, the least he could do with Emma's money was use it to ensure that she was comfortable. His valet and her maid had moved the necessary personal belongings into the suite, then been given the rest of the day off.

As Anthony escorted Emma up to the suite, he considered carrying her across the threshold. He decided against it, since this would not be their home, and the gesture seemed entirely too intimate at their present stage of acquaintance. Ironic to feel that way about his wife on their wedding night.

He had another fleeting thought, this time about Cecilia. The only time he'd ever thought about wedding nights had been when he'd thought they would marry. She had been beautiful—small and graceful and blond, the complete antithesis of Emma. He immediately suppressed the thought as disloyal.

As they stepped into their handsome sitting room, he said lightly, "Welcome to our temporary home, Emma Vaughn Stone Vaughn." He smiled. "Lady Verlaine."

Smiling, she removed her bonnet. "That's rather too many Vaughns, isn't it?"

"Exactly the right number." He pulled a set of papers from inside his coat. "Here, Emma, a wedding present of sorts. The paid-off mortgages on Canfield."

After a brief glance, she handed the documents back. "I'm glad."

He set the papers aside. "With the mortgages cleared, the property will soon be producing a comfortable income. I'm letting go the rooms on Bruton Street, but within a year or two, we should be able to afford a house here in town if you'd like that."

"That would be nice, but for now I'm looking forward to living at Canfield."

He nodded. "It will be good to be back. I thought we could go early next week."

Her dark brows drew together. "Wouldn't it be easier to go directly from London to Harley Castle? Canfield is the opposite direction."

Startled, he said, "Harley? We aren't going there."

"We aren't?" She stared at him in dismay. "Whyever not? It's been ten years since I've been able to attend one of the Christmas gatherings. I ... I've been looking forward to returning."

His face tightened. "I haven't been for nine years myself, and I have no intention of going now."

She slowly sank onto the sofa. "All this time I've imagined you at the castle with the rest of the family every Christmas. Why did you stop attending?"

"I doubted that I'd be welcome," he said brusquely.

She gazed at him with her large, changeable eyes, which were a smoky gray at the moment. "How could that be?"

Could she really not know? Remembering that her parents had died suddenly and she had disappeared from the family circle, he supposed it was possible. "You never heard that Cousin Cecilia married Brand?"

"Brand!" Emma exclaimed. "But I always thought that you and she would make a match of it. I . . . I did wonder what had happened when I learned you were unwed, but I had no idea that she'd married Lord Brandon instead."

Edward Alexander Vaughn, Marquess of Brandon, their mutual cousin. Heir to the Duke of Warrington, and once, long ago, Anthony's closest friend. "Why shouldn't she marry Brand?" he said with acid humor. "He will have far more wealth and a much better title, and he always doted on her."

Emma gazed at him, her eyes darkening. "I see."

She probably *did* see; the damned woman seemed able to read his mind. It gave her an unfair advantage.

Her gaze dropped, and she slowly peeled off her gloves. "I shall write the dowager duchess again and say that we cannot come after all."

The dowager duchess was Brand's grandmother, and the benevolent silver-haired despot of Harley and the whole sprawling Vaughn family. Anthony felt a pang as he thought of her elegant presence and dry humor. Since she no longer came to London, he hadn't seen her in nine years. He missed her. "You'd already written an acceptance?"

"Yesterday. I told her of our planned marriage and said we would arrive next week." Emma sighed. "I'm sorry. It never occurred to me that we would not be going."

Despite her calm words, Emma's disappointment was palpable. He prowled around the drawing room, feeling like a complete villain. Though he no longer went to Harley, he hadn't suffered during the intervening years. He'd finished his education at Oxford, gone on the Grand Tour after Waterloo made the Continent safe for Englishmen again, and generally enjoyed the life of a privileged young gentleman right up until financial disaster had struck.

During those same years, Emma had been living a miserable existence as a teacher and governess, probably sleeping in icy garret rooms and stoically enduring employers who weren't worthy to tie her shoes. It was all too easy to imagine her secretly dreaming of happier days at Harley. And they *had* been happy days—the best of Anthony's life. He felt another pang. God, why had everything gone so wrong?

Even as the question formed in his mind, he reminded himself that the fault was his. Nor did he have the right to deny his wife what she so much desired merely because he'd acted like an idiot many years earlier.

For a cowardly moment he considered telling Emma to go alone, but that would be contemptible and unfair to her. He stopped pacing and turned to her. "If you are set on the visit, I suppose we must go. I am too much in your debt to refuse."

Instead of looking grateful, she said, "Don't say that. Indebtedness is a poor foundation for a marriage. You will soon hate feeling obligated, and then you will hate me." Her lips curved in a wry smile. "I don't want that."

He felt as if he'd just been struck a solid blow to the midriff. Who would have thought that this woman, whom a week earlier he would have passed on the street without a second glance, would be able to get into his mind so effortlessly? After drawing a deep breath, he said, "You are very wise, and very generous."

"Not really. The bargain we struck is a fair one. My money paid the debts incurred by your father, and in return I have secured a fine home and a distinguished rank in society." A hint of irony sounded in her husky voice. "Not to mention a husband that all women will envy me."

"I shall do my best to forget my sense of obligation," he said, thinking she overrated his desirability. When he was trying to raise money to save Canfield, parents had kept their eligible daughters far away. "I'll be a properly arrogant husband in no time."

Her face lit up as she laughed. He realized that he hadn't seen her laugh before. Amusement transformed her from sober governess to a vividly alive woman.

That realization was followed by another; he *wanted* to take her to Harley. Not because he was in her debt, but because he wanted to please her, since she asked so little for herself. "Since you've already written to the dowager duchess, we really ought to go to Harley. I promise I won't be a martyr over it."

She caught her breath, hope in her eyes. "Are you sure? I really don't want to go if a visit would be painful for you."

Ruefully he recognized that his accommodating wife was making it easy for him to be a coward. He must take care that she didn't undermine what character he possessed. "I expect that the visit will be awkward, at least at the beginning. But actually, having just married makes this the perfect time to return. If I don't now, I may be condemning myself to a lifetime of exile. I've just realized that I don't want that. Harley and the family gatherings were too important a part of my life to throw away without at least attempting to mend those burned bridges." His tone turned dry. "Of course, Brand may throw me out, but at least I will have tried."

Surprised, Emma said, "Surely he would not behave so rudely. I remember him as being very even-tempered."

Anthony hesitated, reluctant to lose his bride's good opinion, but knowing it would be unfair to take her to Harley without telling her the whole story. "Even a steady man reacts badly to being told his adored fiancée is marrying him for his money and title. That every night he and Cecilia lay together, she'd be thinking of me."

Emma winced. "Anthony, you didn't."

He sighed. "I'm afraid I did, along with some other equally insulting comments. We got into a ferocious fight. I'm bigger, but Brand was murderously angry. If our fathers hadn't intervened, it might have ended in pistols at dawn."

"Thank heaven it didn't come to that," she said vehemently.

"I wouldn't want Brand's blood on my head," he agreed.

Amused, she said, "You're that sure you would have won?"

"I'm a far better shot." He had a brief, horrifying image of him and Brand facing each other with guns in their hands. Thank God that hadn't happened.

"But if there had been a duel, wouldn't the choice of weapons have been Brand's? As I recall, he was a superb swordsman."

She was right, he realized. "I never thought of that, probably because the quarrel didn't go so far. I left Harley the same day, and have never been back. Once or twice Brand and I have met in public. He always gives me the cut direct."

"So much has happened that I never knew about," she said pensively.

He resumed his prowling as he thought about the return to Harley. Brand's parents and grandmother would not allow any scenes, but the situation would still be strained. Sadly he thought of all the boyhood escapades he and his cousin had shared. They'd gone to school together at Winchester. Countless nights had been spent commiserating about the horrors of school, or sneaking out to buy the extra food necessary to growing boys.

That closeness was no longer possible, not with the shadows of Cecilia and Anthony's own insulting behavior between them. But if he apologized profusely, perhaps they could at least be civil to each other in the future.

Lord, what would it be like to see Cecilia again? He wasn't sure if he loved her or despised her. Both, perhaps. She was the only girl he'd ever loved, and she'd made a fool of him. Her betrayal had left permanent scars. If financial necessity hadn't driven him to marry Emma, it was quite possible that he would have spent his life as a bachelor.

He ceased his prowling and studied his wife, who still sat peaceably on the sofa, giving no hint of her thoughts. He felt a curious duality. He liked her, and his respect for her intelligence and honesty was growing hourly.

At the same time he saw her as the drab governess

whose appearance had been designed to avoid notice. She had been right to say that people would wonder why the fashionable Lord Verlaine had married such an unprepossessing woman.

After a moment spent deciding how to present his case in a way so it would not sound too insulting, he said, "You asked to be treated with courtesy and respect for the sake of your pride. I, too, have pride. I don't want to go to Harley and have the family judge me a fortune hunter who has taken advantage of your honesty and innocence."

Her expression closed. "Does that you mean you've again changed your mind about going there?"

"It means that we'll both benefit by appearing fond rather than barely acquainted. And that we must get you to a modiste and order you a new wardrobe immediately."

Taken aback, she said, "I wouldn't object to some new gowns. But you can't make a silk purse from a sow's ear."

Uncomfortably aware that she had sensed what he wasn't saying, he said, "How fortunate that we don't have to. Come. I'll take you to Madame Chloe. There's no time to waste if we're to have you turned out properly by next week."

"Very well." She got to her feet and retrieved her bonnet, saying darkly, "Just remember what I said about sow's ears."

"Actually your ears are quite well shaped and attractive. After your gowns are ordered, we must stop at the jewelers for some earrings that will do them justice."

As she blushed and pulled on her gloves, he realized that he was looking forward to playing Pygmalion to her Galatea.

* * *

Emma's mother had spoken enthusiastically of the joys of visiting a London modiste, but that was one of many experiences that poverty had stolen from Emma. She tried not to gawk when Anthony swept her into Madame Chloe's shop. The luxuriously decorated salon reminded her of the dowager duchess's boudoir. In such a temple of feminine fashion and frivolity, Anthony's powerful, broad-shouldered figure looked almost indecently masculine.

Madame Chloe herself, a handsome woman of mature years, came forward to greet them, her expression brightening at the sight of Anthony. With a trace of French accent, she said, "Milord Verlaine. What a pleasure to see you again."

As Emma tried not to think what other women her husband had brought to the salon, he said breezily, "The pleasure is mutual, madame. Our visit is something of an emergency. My wife's trunks were destroyed in a fire at a coaching inn." He shook his head sadly. "She was forced to borrow clothing from the vicar's wife, a worthy woman, but not fashionable. Everything must be replaced, from the skin out."

Chloe may or may not have believed his lie, but she laughed good-naturedly. "You have come to the right place." Her eyes narrowed critically as she studied Emma. "You have a really lovely complexion, Lady Verlaine. And your figure—*magnifique*."

Emma blinked. It was true that her skin was nice, but her figure was altogether too . . . too much. Definitely not the figure of a fashionable sylph. Meekly she said, "I put myself in your hands, madame."

Without further ado she was whisked off to a private alcove. Luckily Anthony did not accompany them.

Chloe gave whispered instructions to an assistant, who darted off. By the time Emma had been stripped down to her shift and measured, the assistant had returned from a nearby shop with a mound of exquisitely sewn undergarments.

Emma donned a lovely new lawn shift, then allowed herself to be laced into a set of surprisingly comfortable quilted dimity stays. Chloe explained that it would take several days to make proper shifts and other garments, and that she hoped milady was not too offended at having to make do with ready-made items. Emma was hard-pressed not to laugh. The unmentionables that the modiste was apologizing for were the finest she'd worn in many years.

Madame Chloe held up a shimmering green garment. "This gown is being made for another client who is of similar size and figure. Lady Wolverton will not mind if you try it on for just a moment to get the effect."

Emma raised her arms, and whispering green silk dropped over her. After the fastenings were secured, she turned to look at herself in the mirror. Her jaw dropped. The image she saw was not of the familiar dowdy governess, but a striking, fashionable woman. Even her eyes were unfamiliar as the green gown made them glow like jade. Voice hushed, she asked, "Is this really me?"

"Indeed, my lady. It is the real you," Chloe said with satisfaction. "Lord Verlaine will be most pleased."

Then the modiste swept Emma into the main salon so her husband could survey the results. Emma was tempted to cover the large expanse of bare flesh visible above her décolletage, but managed to restrain herself. The problem was not with the gown, but her unfashionable self.

Anthony was gazing out the window at the afternoon traffic outside, his expression pensive. When she entered the main salon, he turned and became very still. After a long moment, he said softly, "Well, well, *well.*"

"It's the stays," Emma blurted out. "I'm not really shaped like this."

He grinned as he circled around her. "My dear, no woman is shaped precisely like that, which is why stays were invented. And believe me, you shape up very well."

She blushed to the roots of her hair. But she was not displeased. She studied herself in the salon mirrors. She was not a delicate fashionable beauty, and she never would be. But she had a kind of forceful splendor that made her a woman who would not be easily overlooked. It was a heady thought.

Emma clung to that satisfaction through a long, tiring afternoon while endless fabrics and patterns were chosen. By the time they left, she was exhausted. In the carriage, she sank back into the velvet squabs of the seat. "What a very unusual wedding day."

Anthony chuckled. "It was time well spent. Tomorrow we'll visit jewelers and find you shoes and stockings and such like. The other important thing is your hair."

He leaned forward and removed her bonnet, then pulled out the pins that secured the knot on her nape. Her hair tumbled over her shoulders. Gently he brushed the dark waves back, the skim of his fingertips on her ear and throat sending sparks through her. She caught her breath, shocked that such a casual touch could stir her so.

Apparently unaffected, he said, "Tomorrow, a hairdresser. Your maid—Becky, I think?—must learn how to do new styles."

It all sounded wonderful, but Emma could not dismiss a flash of concern. "Anthony, can we afford all this?"

He frowned, and for a moment she feared that her question had angered him. But his voice was even when he said, "Your wardrobe will cost a pretty penny, but it's a necessary expenditure, one that I allowed for when estimating our expenses. You must trust me when I say that I have no desire to live in debt again, Emma."

She gazed at him, enchanted by his serious expression, the way his attention was concentrated on her. This glorious male creature was now her husband. *Hers.* "I trust you, Anthony," she said softly. "Never doubt it."

She had never been happier in her life.

The Dowager Duchess of Warrington chose her moment carefully. The Vaughns were just finishing dinner, but it was not yet time to rise. Her gaze went over her beloved family. Her son James, the duke, with his quiet dignity and dry humor. Her daughter-in-law Amelia, a woman of wit and laughing charm. Sarah, her youngest granddaughter, who would be presented to society in the spring.

The dowager's eyes clouded when she looked at her grandson, Brand, who would be the next duke, and his wife, Cecilia. Oh, they'd produced two fine boys dutifully enough, but something was wrong between them, and both were too pigheaded to ask advice from those who were older and wiser.

Concealing her thoughts, the dowager said, "I've

received most of the replies for the Christmas gathering. Besides the usual guests, there will be a few who are less expected."

She took a sip of wine as every gaze turned to her. Setting down the crystal goblet, she said, "Verlaine will be coming with his new wife."

Her statement produced absolute silence. The duke and his wife exchanged a swift, startled glance. Brand's face became as expressionless as marble while Cecilia's gaze dropped to the meringue swan on her plate. Only Lady Sarah, too young to remember what had happened, said brightly, "Cousin Anthony? Marvelous! He hasn't come for Christmas in donkeys' years. Whom did he marry?"

"A Vaughn connection, actually." The dowager glanced toward her son. "Emma Stone. The daughter of your second cousin. She used to come with her parents, Jane Vaughn and Sir George Stone. They both died of a fever ten years back. Luckily the girl was at school, or she might have died, too. She has not been here since then."

Amelia pursed her lips. "Jane Stone's daughter. I remember her. A nice child. Quiet, but with very speaking eyes and excellent manners."

James said with a barely discernible hint of irony, "How pleasant it will be to see them both again." He studied his son, who had said nothing. "I didn't realize that you still sent invitations to such distant relatives, *Maman*."

"That is why family gatherings should be left in the hands of the old," she said serenely. "We have the time and memory to maintain the family connections. It wasn't easy keeping track of Emma, but I made sure that she received an invitation every year. She would always return a pretty note, regretting that she could not attend."

"I shall be glad to see Emma," Cecilia said with a touch of defiance. "I've wondered what had become of her. She was nice, and so clever. How lovely that she and Anthony have discovered each other after so many years." She cast a wistful glance at her husband, but he would not look at her. A muscle jerked in his jaw as he stared at the tapestry on the opposite wall.

Slowly the dowager drank the last of her wine. Though fireworks were not traditional at Christmas, they would certainly take place at Harley this year. God willing, they'd shed some light on corners too long filled with shadow.

Chapter Five

❧

Emma eyed a piece of toast doubtfully. "I don't think I can eat. I'm too excited at the thought that today we're actually going to Harley."

Her husband picked up the toast and put it in her hand. "Eat," he ordered. "You'll make yourself ill if you set off on a long coach trip with an empty stomach."

Pleased by his concern, she obediently spread honey on the toast and took a bite. It did taste good. Her gaze went around the attractive room. In the week of their hotel honeymoon, she'd grown fond of the place. Every morning their breakfast was served on a small table in a corner of the drawing room. Several newspapers arrived at the same time, and she and Anthony had fallen into the habit of sharing a leisurely meal, reading and discussing the news of the day.

Her husband had been surprised the first time she'd offered an opinion, but he'd adjusted very quickly. Now he seemed to enjoy their discussions as much as she did. Later in the day, after they had done the shopping and fittings necessary to her transformation, he would take her to see sights that she'd had no chance to visit when she was working.

Her gaze went to the doors that led to the two bedrooms. In that area their honeymoon was sadly deficient. Anthony was always charming and considerate, but he'd made no attempts to bed his bride. Was he taking her desire to wait too seriously, or was he simply not very interested?

Granted, before their hasty wedding Emma had felt skittish about giving herself to a near stranger, but time was rapidly curing her of that. The yearning she'd felt for Anthony when she was a girl had returned tenfold. She loved every casual touch, even if he was only helping her from the carriage. She loved looking at him, studying the strong planes of his face, his easy, athletic movements. She delighted in small discoveries like the faint scar on his chin, and enjoyed the irrepressible tuft of hair that lived its own life, wild and free, no matter what Anthony did to try to tame it.

Her husband divided the last of the coffee—another taste they shared—between their cups. "Do you know, my worst fear when we married was that we wouldn't have anything to say to each other," he said thoughtfully. "But I've noticed no shortage of conversation."

She gave him a smile of suspicious innocence. "That's because you're so extremely interesting that there is always something to discuss."

"Flatterer," he laughed, his gaze warm. "You have a wicked sense of humor."

She wondered if he was going to lean forward and kiss her. Apart from the briefest of pecks at their wedding ceremony, they hadn't kissed at all.

After a suspended moment he drained his coffee and got to his feet. "I'll go order the carriage and summon porters for the baggage. We must be off soon if we wish to make Harley in one day."

She nodded, suppressing her disappointment. Having asked for time to ease into the intimacy of marriage, she supposed she had no right to complain at receiving more than she'd bargained for.

They made good time, and arrived at Harley just as full dark was settling over the rolling hills. As they rattled up the long driveway, Emma peered out the carriage window. "Look! The Christmas candles are lit. I'd forgotten all about them."

Anthony looked past her and saw a lattice of lights, one candle in every window of the massive building. There was enough moonlight to recognize the pale stone and graceful proportions of one of Britain's grandest homes. It was a palace, really, almost as large as Blenheim or Castle Howard. "I'd half forgotten the candles, too. Yet now that I see them, they remind me of everything I've ever loved about Harley."

"I'd given up believing that I'd ever return," Emma said softly. "Now that I'm here, I'm frightened. I've lived in a different world for the last ten years. I don't belong at Harley anymore. I keep thinking that the dowager only invited me from courtesy, believing I would never accept."

The darkness made it easy for him to reach out and take her gloved hand. It was large and capable and well formed, like the rest of Emma. "Even if that were true, which it isn't, you would still be welcome here as my wife." He stopped, struck by the irony of his words. "That was a silly statement, wasn't it? I'm the one wondering if I'll be thrown out bodily."

Her hand tightened on his. "Of course not. It's been

nine years. You say that Brand and Cecilia have two children now. He probably barely remembers your fight."

Anthony wished he believed that. But he didn't.

Their carriage pulled up in front of wide, torch-lit steps. Instantly footmen emerged to take their baggage. With a steady stream of Vaughns arriving, the servants had their routine down to a fine art. While two footmen went for the baggage, another opened the carriage door and flipped down the folding step. Anthony climbed out first, then turned to assist Emma. She gave him a tremulous smile as she stepped down.

She looked so vulnerable that he wanted to take her in his arms and murmur comforting words in one elegant ear. In fact, he would like to take her in his arms anyhow. She had blossomed under the ministrations of Madame Chloe, the best hairdresser in London, and sundry jewelers, shoemakers, and others. Under his breath, he whispered, "You look every inch a Vaughn."

Her smile widened and became more confident. Arm in arm, they climbed the steps. A footman opened the massive front door and bowed them in. No sooner had they entered the huge, three-story entry hall when a gaggle of children, aged between about six and twelve, ran shrieking through the far end of the space. By the time Anthony blinked, they'd come and gone.

Emma laughed as her gaze went to the fragrant greenery and bright ribbons that decorated the hall. "Lord, that brings back memories. Remember how exciting it was to arrive here and see all the cousins for the first time in a year?"

"Vividly." On his last visit, the cousin Anthony had longed for most had been Cecilia. Tonight he would see her again. The thought knotted his stomach.

Before Anthony could say more, a relaxed woman of middle years came forward to greet them. It was the Duchess of Warrington herself, Brand's mother. "Anthony, how wonderful to see you again," she said warmly. "And, Emma, how splendid you look. It's hard to believe you're so grown up."

She kissed Emma's cheek, then turned and offered her hand to Anthony. As he bowed over it, she said with a twinkle, "The dowager and Cecilia and I have been taking turns receiving people since yesterday morning. I'm so glad that you two arrived on my shift. Having you both here again is quite the most exciting event this Christmas."

Emma said quietly, "I can't tell you how much it means to be at Harley again."

Anthony added, "How is everyone? The duke, the dowager . . . " After the faintest of pauses, he added, "Brand. Cecilia. Your daughters."

The duchess's mouth twisted ruefully. "Brand is . . . stubborn. Cecilia and her boys are very well. Anne and her husband arrived earlier today, and you won't even recognize my Sarah. She's all grown and chafing to be presented."

Three chattering females entered the hall. The oldest called out, "Verlaine, you rascal, what's this about a wife?"

"Aunt Fanny!" Anthony exclaimed, giving her a big hug. Turning to the younger women, he said, "And these dazzling creatures must be my cousins Rebecca and Louisa."

Both girls giggled, and Louisa hugged Anthony. When he emerged from her embrace, he said, "You already know my wife. She was Emma Stone, you know."

His Aunt Fanny, actually a first cousin once removed, said in a booming voice, "Of course I remember little Emma. Not that you're so little now." Her gaze went over the subject of the discussion. "Pure Vaughn," she pronounced. "Has Verlaine got you with child yet, girl?"

As Emma turned scarlet, Anthony recalled that Fanny had always been an earthy sort. Putting one arm around his wife's shoulders, he said firmly, "Behave yourself, Aunt Fanny. We haven't been married even a fortnight yet."

Fanny shook her head with regret. "You should have waited and had the wedding here. Always good to have another reason to celebrate."

The duchess intervened, saying, "We've never lacked for celebration, Fanny. Now, let me take these young people to their room so they can freshen up." She whisked Anthony and Emma up the sweeping stairs.

As they climbed, she said with a mischievous smile, "You're the last to arrive. The house is packed to the rafters. As newlyweds, I'm sure you won't mind sharing a bedroom. I've put you in one of the towers."

Anthony darted a look at Emma. She looked startled, and rather alarmed. That was something they'd both overlooked—with the house full, married couples were required to share quarters. Since many of them were used to having separate rooms, there were always good-natured complaints about the crowding.

They had to climb three flights of steps to reach their room. There were no less than four stops to greet other Vaughns who were coming and going along the halls and stairs. Anthony was better remembered, not only because he'd already reached adulthood on his last visits, but because he'd always been outgoing. But

Emma was greeted warmly, too. The exuberant welcomes created the holiday spirit she remembered so well. Though not every member of the family loved every other member, for the next fortnight, there was goodwill enough for all.

When they reached their assigned chamber, the duchess said, "Because so many guests have just arrived today, dinner will not be formal." She smiled. "Not much changes here, you know. Tomorrow will be a formal dinner, the night after is Christmas Eve and the service in the chapel. And so it will go until the Twelfth Night ball."

"The events might not change, but the people do," Emma observed. "This will be my first time dining with the adults rather than at the children's table."

"Why, so it is. You were still in the schoolroom the last time you came for Christmas." The duchess's expression became grave. "Such a terrible thing, your parents' deaths. *Maman* and I were sorry that you would not come to us afterward. But you obviously decided wisely, for you are blooming now." She turned to leave. "I mustn't keep you talking. It isn't much more than half an hour until we dine. You remember the bell, I'm sure."

"Who could forget it?" Anthony said feelingly. He took the duchess's hands. "Thank you for having us here, Aunt Amelia."

"The pleasure is mine. Family is the touchstone of life. We're fortunate that Harley is large enough to hold so many Vaughns. I think of us as traveling through time together. There are constant changes— births, marriages, deaths—yet as a family, we are whole and healthy." With a last smile the duchess left.

When they were alone, Emma removed her bonnet,

saying, "As a child I wished that the towers were round, not square, but this is still one of the nicest rooms in Harley."

"We must have received it because of our status as newlyweds," Anthony replied. With typical Harley efficiency, their baggage had already been delivered. While he and Emma had socialized, her maid and his man had done the unpacking and vanished again. The mechanics of life always flowed smoothly here.

As Anthony removed his cloak, he added, "I'm sorry you don't have a private room. Shall I have a dressing screen brought up?"

Emma made a face. "Everyone in the household would know, and since we're just wed, speculation would be rampant. We'll manage well enough."

She went to the window, where a Christmas candle burned inside a special fixture designed to protect against fire. Every afternoon during the holiday season, a servant came around to clean the fixture and put in another candle that was designed to burn until dawn in a custom that was at least two hundred years old. Musingly Emma said, "I like being so high. When I was little, I would climb out on the roof and scamper around."

"In December?" His brows arched with surprise. "You were an intrepid little thing. Roof walking can be dangerous, especially when it's icy."

"I only went out during mild weather, and I stopped entirely when my mother found out and made me promise not to do it again." Gazing out at the dark landscape, she said dreamily, "I used to imagine flying off the roof and soaring over the hills."

Anthony had an unsettling image of her lying broken and lifeless in the wintry courtyard far below, her dark

hair fanned about her and a glaze of ice crystals on her
face. "I'm heartily glad that you never actually tried to
fly."

"I've always had a firm grasp on the difference
between dreams and reality. At least I did as a child." She
turned back toward the room. "I'd forgotten how women
always flutter around you. Do you ever tire of it?"

He almost passed the comment off with a light reply.
But the subject was one that should not be dismissed.
"I suppose women like me because I like them. I'm not
particularly flirtatious, you know."

She sighed. "I know. Just as flowers cannot help
attracting honeybees, you can't help attracting
females."

He'd always been grateful for that quality, but he
understood that Emma might be less than enthused by
the effects. "I can't stop them from buzzing, but you
are my wife, Emma," he said seriously. "My one and
only."

She nodded and spoke no more on the subject, but he
sensed a certain sadness in her. He hoped that she wasn't
beginning to regret her hasty marriage. He would have
to try harder to make sure that she didn't.

A raucous bell clamored through the building. Even
with a closed door between them and the source of the
sound, it made a shocking amount of noise. Emma
jumped and Anthony winced. "The fifteen-minute bell.
Since it will take us easily five minutes to walk to the
salon, that gives us only ten minutes to get ready."

Emma frowned and went to the wardrobe. "Even
though the duchess said this wouldn't be formal, I'll
feel better if I put on something fresh." She took out a
green gown. "Heaven only knows where Becky is.
Could you help me with this, please?"

"Of course." Anthony came up behind her and began unfastening the complicated tapes and buttons of her traveling dress. When he was finished, he slid the garment down her arms. He swallowed hard when he saw the creamy slope of her shoulders. She had the most deliciously touchable skin he'd ever seen. It cried out for caresses.

Emma stepped out of the travel dress. Her shift and stays and petticoats covered as much of her as most gowns would, but there was a wicked sense of intimacy in seeing her in her unmentionables. He remembered what Madame Chloe had said about Emma's figure: *magnifique*. The modiste had been right. Emma was no fashionable sylph, but a woman of lush, sensual curves. He wondered how the weight of her full breasts would feel in his hands. A stab of swift heat ran through him.

Struggling to suppress that response, he went to the dressing table, where Hawkins had laid out his brushes and other personal items. If there were more time, he would have shaved. Luckily his chin was still presentable, though only just.

"I need more help." Emma had pulled on the gown, but could not manage the fastening herself.

Silently Anthony moved behind her again. His imagination was rioting. He wanted to lock the door and miss dinner and seduce his wife. But that really was not possible tonight, when they were both making a kind of homecoming.

Fingers uncharacteristically clumsy, he began tying the tapes. She'd put on a perfume with a complex, provocative scent. Not for her the girlish, floral fragrances.

His fingers brushed Emma's back as he tied a hidden bow. A little shiver went through her. Hoping it was a shiver of pleasure, he leaned forward and kissed the juncture of her shoulder and throat. Her skin was silky warm under his lips. He wanted to lick her from head to toe. He settled for tracing the elegant curve of her ear with his tongue. Emma stiffened.

Though he'd had his fair share of female companionship, he wasn't such a coxcomb as to believe that he could infallibly sense what a woman wanted. And understanding this particular woman was more important than any of his casual affairs. "Whenever I touch you, you seem to pull away," he said softly. "Would you rather I stopped?"

"No," she replied, her voice constricted. "I don't dislike your touch at all." She swallowed, her throat going taut. "Quite . . . quite the contrary."

Thank heavens for that. With the lightest of touches, he put his arms around her and cupped her breasts. She gasped, and he felt the hammering of her heart under his hands. Then, very gently, she leaned back against him in a silent gesture of trust and surrender. Her warm curves fitted against him as perfectly as matched puzzle pieces.

His own heart hammering, he said with deep feeling, "I really, really wish we didn't have to go down to dinner."

She turned her head and glanced up at him with an expression in her eyes as old as Eve. "We'll be back here later, and all the more eager for having waited."

He chuckled. "You've the makings of a wicked wench."

"Good," she said with great satisfaction.

Moving away from him with obvious reluctance, she went to finish her toilette. Anthony combed his hair rather blindly, since most of his attention was on the vivid memory of Emma in his arms. There was a gentle sensuality about her that made him simultaneously want to protect her and ravish her. Was this what marriage was about? Please God, he'd learn soon enough.

"I'm ready," Emma said with a touch of nervousness. "Do I look all right?"

He turned and surveyed her from head to foot. The shade of green she wore did wonderful things for her creamy skin and made her changeable eyes into a striking light green. Her softly waved chestnut hair was also far more flattering than the severe style she'd worn when they met. "You look perfect. Not too formal for tonight, but every inch a lady." He walked toward her. "There's only one problem."

Her expression, which had brightened, became anxious again. "What's wrong?"

"This." Women often wore a gauzy scarf called a fichu around the neck as a way of making low-cut gowns more modest, and adding a bit of warmth as well. Emma had donned such a scarf. He swept the fichu away, exposing the dramatic swell of her upper breasts. "You won't need this. With so many people present tonight, the rooms will be warm."

She blushed scarlet and instinctively brought her hands up to cover her bare flesh. Dropping them again, she said apologetically, "I feel very bare."

"I've a cure for that." He went to his dressing case and pulled out a worn velvet box. Inside was a triple rope of pearls and a pair of matching earrings. "Not too many heirlooms survived my father's debts, but these did. They were my mother's, and now they are yours. Merry Christmas, Emma."

Emma caught her breath. "My mother had a necklace much like this, but hers had to be sold." A glint of tears in her eyes, she lifted the necklace and pressed it to her cheek. "Pearls have such a wonderful feel. Silky. Almost alive."

"They must be worn to be at their best." He took the necklace from her and clasped it around her neck. It was a lovely neck, long and graceful. He kissed the nape under her upswept hair. She made a small, breathy sound, and this time he knew that it was not distress.

Fingers not quite steady, Emma put on the earrings, then turned for his inspection. He said with absolute conviction, "You look lovely, Emma. Any man would be proud to have you by his side."

She gave him a smile so radiant that for a moment she took his breath way. "I'm very glad you think so."

He offered her his arm with a courtly bow, and together they went to rejoin their family.

Chapter Six

∽≈∾

Bubbling with anticipation, Emma held Anthony's arm as they went down the icy halls and staircases. He wanted her! Even an innocent could recognize the desire in his voice and his touch. He hadn't been uninterested before, merely giving her the period of adjustment that she'd requested.

Well, she was ready to be a wife now. In fact, she was eager for this long-awaited evening to be over so they could return to their room, and the waiting bed.

The thought made her glance up shyly. He met her gaze, and gave her an intimate smile. *His one and only.* The knowledge made her want to turn somersaults the way she had when in the nursery.

Almost floating, she let him guide her toward the main salon, where the adults were meeting for predinner sherry. The great house looked exactly as she remembered, with the scent of pine boughs and the bright colors of holly berries and scarlet ribbons everywhere. Christmas at Harley was magical.

The salon was already teeming with people and noisy with talk when they entered. Emma looked around, trying to put names to faces. Most were cousins of some sort, though older family members had generally been made honorary aunts and uncles. Heavens, Aunt Agatha had put on weight. Lord only knew who that tall youth was, except that he was obviously a Vaughn. And was that young woman in blue her cousin Margaret, or could it be Margaret's sister, Mary?

Someone called out, "Verlaine has arrived!"

Emma smiled a little wryly, knowing it would be like this for the rest of their lives. It was Anthony whom people would remember, Anthony who would bring that smile to their faces. He had the same effect on her. As long as he was hers, she didn't mind sharing his attention at gatherings such as these.

People crowded forward to offer hugs and best wishes on their marriage. Emma knew she must be glowing like a Christmas candle. She'd dreamed of this warm welcome for ten years, and never believed she would feel it again. Once more she was a Vaughn among Vaughns. And to judge by the admiration in men's eyes, Anthony had not been lying when he said that she looked well.

The dowager duchess entered the room through another door, and many of the group around Emma and Anthony went to greet her. The dowager had been a great beauty as a girl. She still was.

As the crowd thinned, Emma saw a young woman standing by the great fireplace, her gaze turned in their direction. Emma caught her breath with surprise. It was Cecilia, and she hadn't changed at all. She must be near thirty, but even after two children, she was slim and graceful. As beautiful as she had always been.

Taking leave of the ancient aunt with whom she had been speaking, Cecilia came to greet the newcomers, her golden hair shining in the light of dozens of candles. Coming to a stop, she said, "It's wonderful to see you again, Emma. I'm so glad you're here."

The warmth in her voice seemed sincere; Cecilia had always been very pleasant to Emma. It wasn't her fault that her petite blond beauty made Emma feel like a giant graceless ox by comparison. Barely managing a smile, Emma said, "Thank you, Cecilia. You look marvelous. Do your children favor you or Brand?"

"They are unmistakably Vaughns." Cecilia's face tightened, and she turned to offer Anthony her hand. "Verlaine. It's been a long time since you've come to Harley."

"Cecilia." Anthony bowed over her hand, then straightened, still holding it. "It's ... it's good to be here again." The tension between him and Cecilia was palpable.

Emma felt as if she'd been struck a physical blow. Of course there would be some reaction when two people who had once been sweethearts met again, but she had not expected Anthony to turn to marble. Blast it, she thought he'd put his feelings for Cecilia behind him! Instead he was gaping like a mooncalf.

The two were still gazing at each other as if they were alone in the room. Feeling invisible, Emma released Anthony's left arm. He didn't even notice.

The moment stretched for a painful eternity. Then a tall, dark-haired man who looked like a slightly smaller version of Anthony materialized by Cecilia's side. It was Brand, looking as if he wanted to do murder. Taking his wife's arm, he said in a low, bitter voice, "Since this is my father's house, I cannot ask you to leave, or even cut you, Verlaine. But do not expect civility."

Anthony tore his gaze away from Cecilia and looked

at his former friend. Visibly struggling to collect himself, he said, "I had hoped we would be able to make peace, Brand. I behaved badly the last time I was here, and you have my most sincere apology." He extended his hand tentatively.

His cousin looked as if he wanted to cut it off. "I'd rather invite the Great Plague to dinner than take your hand, Verlaine." He pivoted and stalked off, taking Cecilia with him. She cast a last miserable look over her shoulder, then went obediently.

Unable to face Anthony, Emma also spun away. She walked rather blindly through the room until she almost ran into an elderly man, Lord Edward Vaughn, the present duke's uncle.

"Emma, my dear child, how lovely to see you," he said jovially. Taking her hand, he drew her under a beribboned kissing bough that hung in the arch which divided the salon into two parts. Every open arch in Harley had a similar kissing bough. After a swift peck on the cheek, he said with twinkling eyes, "One of the advantages of being an old man is that I can now kiss all the pretty girls, and my wife won't have my head for it."

Laughing, she said, "You're not that old, Uncle Edward. Not even seventy, and looking ten years younger." All of the Vaughns aged well; in another forty years, Anthony would look very much like Lord Edward. Thinking of Anthony sent a pang through her. With a determined smile, she said, "Where is Lady Edward? I haven't seen her yet."

"Charlotte sent me to get you." Taking Emma's arm, he escorted her to a corner where his round, cheerful-looking wife was relaxing on a sofa. "Doesn't get around as well as she did, but she can still ask questions!"

Gratefully Emma sank down beside Lady Edward and prepared for a good-natured interrogation. At least it would keep her from thinking about Anthony, and his reunion with the divinely beautiful Cecilia.

After Brand towed Cecilia away, Anthony took a deep, slow breath, startled at the turmoil of his own feelings. He thought he'd gotten over Cecilia years before. After all, she'd dropped him like a hot coal once she received a better offer. Yet seeing her had knocked him heels over head. He'd forgotten the impact of her beauty.

Yearning for Emma's good sense, he looked around and couldn't find her. Damnation, what must she be thinking? He had a fair idea, and the thought was disturbing. He was about to start searching in earnest when the dinner bell rang. The dowager duchess appeared beside him with feline suddenness. She even had the sleekness and composure of a small, silver-haired cat. "You shall take me into dinner, Verlaine, and then sit beside me," she announced.

One did not refuse an order from the Dowager Duchess of Warrington. He offered his arm. "It will be my honor, Grandmère. I haven't seen you in far too long."

Not that she was his grandmother, but every Vaughn under the age of fifty called her that. As he led the dowager into the dining room, his heart gave a painful twinge. If he could not make peace with Brand this Christmas, he would be unable to return. A gentleman did not make another man uncomfortable in the man's own home. Aloud, he said, "Where do you wish to sit, Grandmère?"

She gestured. "Here, at the foot of the table."

Anthony pulled out her chair, then took the right-hand seat. The long table was set for at least fifty people, he guessed.

The dowager explained, "The rest of the year, Amelia takes her place at this end as a proper duchess should, but tonight, since we dine informally, she can actually sit by her husband."

Sure enough, the duke was taking his seat at the far end of the table, and his wife was next to him. They both had mischievous expressions from flouting convention. Breaking the rules was part of the holiday fun.

"I'm glad to see that you're finally settling down, Verlaine," the dowager said in a low voice meant only for his ears. "I had begun to despair of you."

"I see you haven't lost your taste for assault, Grand-mère," he said pleasantly.

"At my age, there isn't enough time to waste it on social inanities." She regarded him unblinkingly, her pale blue eyes like aquamarine. "I was particularly pleased to hear that you'd married Emma Stone. You need a wife like her, with a brain in her head and a steady disposition."

"Happy though I am to be here, I'm beginning to remember the drawbacks of attending gatherings with people who have known one since the nursery," he said dryly.

She laughed. "Everyone knows your business, and has opinions on how you should run your life. It's part of belonging to a family, Verlaine." Her expression sobered. "I've been worried that you might go the same way as your father. You're very like him, you know. Charming, handsome, everything comes to you easily. Too easily. He never grew up, and the same could happen to you."

"I can't say that I appreciate the comparison," he said coolly. "My father was an irresponsible care-for-nobody who very nearly lost the family patrimony."

"It's a man's duty to care for his inheritance and pass it on to his children, and he failed badly in that," she agreed. "But from the tales I've heard of your gambling and wenching, your behavior has not been any better. I trust that you now intend to start acting like an adult."

Having delivered that blow with the expertise of a prizefighter, she turned to the man on her left. Anthony clamped down on his irritation. As soon as his father had died and the state of the Verlaine finances was revealed, Anthony had retrenched and done everything he could to save the estate. But it was also true that until that appalling day, he'd lived extravagantly, as if his income was drawn from a bottomless well.

For the life of him, he still couldn't think of any method other than gambling that he might have used to earn the money to redeem the mortgages. One certainly could not borrow such a sum from a friend, the banks had refused him, and he had not wished to turn fortune hunter. So he'd gambled, saving his winnings, never allowing wagering fever to overcome good sense, never spending money needlessly.

Yet in the end, gambling hadn't been enough. He would have lost Canfield if not for Emma. Most of the damage had been done by his father, but Anthony would have born the blame in the eyes of the world, just as he would have had to live with the consequences of his father's selfishness and waste. For two years, that bitter knowledge had eaten at him like acid. When he had a son, he'd do better by the boy.

It was the first time he'd seriously thought about

having children, and he was surprised at the complicated emotions that accompanied the idea. Children,
and Emma would be their mother. Her blood would
flow in their veins, as would his.

It was one of the most obvious facts in the world, yet
he had never really thought about it with respect to
himself. Lord, what could a man do for his children
that was more important than choosing a good mother
for them? And Emma would be good—he knew that
without question. Kind, patient, and intelligent, not to
mention healthy and with a wry sense of humor that he
was appreciating more and more.

Automatically he looked for her. She was sitting
near the far end of the table, smiling at some comment
made by her dinner partner. Anthony's mouth tightened. Perhaps he shouldn't have removed her fichu—
the fellow was leering down her bodice as if she was
the next dinner course.

Jealousy was also a new experience, one he didn't
like. He'd never felt jealous of his mistresses. If they
fancied another man, he'd always let them go cheer-
fully. But Emma was his wife. He found, rather
uncomfortably, how much difference that made.

Luckily the woman on his right was exchanging a
year's worth of news with her other neighbor, which
relieved Anthony of the obligation to talk. He toyed
with his leek soup and thought about what the dowager
had said. *Charming, handsome, everything comes to
you easily.* Emma and her fortune had certainly come
easily.

As he sipped his wine, he wondered about that
stroke of luck. Would she have found him and suggested marriage if he'd been ugly? What a sobering
thought. He'd always known that beauty gave a woman

power, while taking for granted the advantages that his own face and athletic form gave him.

Yet he could no more take credit for his looks than for his title and station in life. His appearance was pure Vaughn, and the Verlaine title and fortune had been granted to the naval grandfather who'd been a famous admiral until his heroic death in battle.

By comparison Anthony was forced to admit that he was basically a worthless fellow. He had spent his life pursuing pleasure. His father's death had sobered him, and his desire to save Canfield had given him a worthy goal, but he had still essentially been living the life of a heedless young man about town.

I've been worried that you might go the same way as your father. You're very like him, you know . . . He never grew up, and the same could happen to you . . . I trust that you mean to start acting like an adult.

His gaze went to Emma again. Perhaps being an adult was a matter of letting go of the youthful belief that the world was a place of infinite possibilities. Not everything was possible. Every choice eliminated a myriad of other paths.

By marrying Emma, he had forfeited the right to marry any of London's dazzling beauties, just as she had given up the chance of a husband who might be more clever or worthy than Anthony. Since they had chosen each other, it was up to them to make their marriage closer to heaven than to hell.

With a wry smile, he realized that that was probably a very adult thought.

Determined to enjoy the evening, Emma managed to shut away the memory of that horrible moment between Anthony and Cecilia. She laughed her way through dinner with a cousin by marriage she'd never met. Afterward, as the men sat over their port, she made the rounds of her female relatives, exchanging hugs and news.

After the gentlemen joined the ladies, an impromptu concert began. Three young female cousins began singing carols while another played the pianoforte. Soon the instrument was surrounded by Vaughns who joined in. Emma did her share of singing, her heart aching a little as she watched some of the older couples. Lord Edward and his wife sat on a sofa, his arm around her waist. The duke and duchess were discreetly holding hands as they joined in the carols.

Would Emma and Anthony have that fondness for each other when twenty or thirty years had passed? Or would they be like Brand and Cecilia, who stood side by side with frozen faces, neither touching nor looking at the other?

Depressed by the thought that the odds were against her and her husband developing a long-term affection, Emma slipped away while the party was still going strong. No one would miss her, least of all Anthony, who was spreading his charm lavishly about the gathering.

She made the long climb to the tower room through silent passages. It was a welcome surprise to find a small fire burning when she arrived. The Harley coal bill for this fortnight would be astronomical.

After changing to her heaviest nightgown and a matching robe that went over it, she sat down at the dressing table and pulled the pins from her hair. As she was lifting her brush, the door opened and Anthony entered.

Their gazes met in the mirror. Voice carefully neutral, she said, "I thought you would be downstairs longer."

He closed the door and leaned back against it. "I made my excuses when I saw you leave. It took me a few minutes to break away, or I would have escorted you up."

She wondered if he'd come because of the sensual promise that had been between them when they dressed for dinner. Unfortunately she was no longer in the mood to consummate her marriage even though Anthony looked almost irresistible. Tall and broad-shouldered, with his waving dark hair and piercing eyes, he was a man too splendid to be the husband of Emma Stone. He was any young girl's dream. He'd been her dream.

She began brushing out her hair. Deciding that it was time for an inane comment, she said, "It was lovely to see everyone again."

"You're wondering about Cecilia," he said quietly.

She had not expected him to broach such a delicate subject. "As a matter of fact, I am." Looking in the mirror rather than at his face made it easier for her to ask, "Are you still in love with her?"

He hesitated. "No. At least I don't think so. But seeing her again was a shock. It brought back what it felt like to be twenty." His mouth twisted. "I'd forgotten how wretched a time that was."

She turned to look at him directly. He was doing his best to be honest with her, and for that she was grateful. But she was not very reassured by the fact that he "didn't think" he was in love with Cecilia. "Brand looked as if he wanted to do murder."

"I really don't know why, since he got what he wanted—Cecilia. He hardly has cause to be jealous when I haven't laid eyes on her in nine years." Anthony sighed. "I always thought of him as having an easy disposition. Perhaps I didn't know him as well as I thought. There is a lot I didn't know."

Emma suspected that when a woman came between two men, the emotional equation could change dramatically. Certainly Brand appeared to have changed from the young man she remembered. But what did she know? She was just an aging spinster who had bought herself a husband. She began to braid her hair. "Perhaps when Brand gets over the shock of having you here, his mood will moderate."

"Perhaps," Anthony said, clearly unconvinced.

Emma tied the end of her braid, then rose and went to the bed. Outside scattered flakes of snow were falling. She hoped they would continue. She'd always loved the beauty and silence of new snow. After taking off her robe and laying it over a chair, she slid under the covers.

His voice as neutral as hers, Anthony said, "Can you spare a blanket? I'll make up a bed on the floor."

It would be much easier if he wasn't near her, but she couldn't be so selfish. "You'll freeze on the floor," she said in her most practical governess voice. "The bed is quite large enough for two." Then she rolled onto her side away from him, pulling the blankets protectively around her in an unmistakable sign that she would not welcome any amorous overtures.

She heard the rustling sounds of undressing. Before dinner, she would have peeked so she could admire him. Not now.

He put out all the candles except the one in the window, which had a tin reflector that sent most of the light outdoors. Then the mattress sagged as he lay down.

Though he didn't touch her, she was acutely aware of his nearness. Her husband. It was entirely within her rights to roll over and cuddle up against him. Perhaps he would draw her close and tell her how lovely she was, and how he was much happier to be with her rather than Cecilia . . .

She shouldn't have thought of Cecilia. Now the image of her husband and the woman he had loved was burning in her brain. He had never looked at Emma like that. With brutal honesty, she recognized that he probably never would.

It had been a mistake to try to build a new marriage at Harley. They were surrounded by too many ghosts, not all of whom were dead.

Swallowing hard against the painful lump in her throat, Emma closed her eyes and ordered herself to sleep.

Chapter Seven

❧

Hours passed, and Anthony's breathing had long since become slow and regular, but Emma still couldn't sleep. Never having shared a bed with a man in her life, she was painfully conscious that Anthony's warm, very male body was mere inches away. With one half her mind on him and the other spinning ever more depressing visions of what her marriage might be like, sleep was impossible.

Finally, with an exasperated sigh, she slipped from the bed. The room was chilly, so she quietly put another scoop of coal on the fire. Then she went to the window. The light snow had intensified into huge soft flakes floating thickly through the windless air, covering the world with a pristine white mantle.

Unable to resist, she detached the Christmas candle fixture from the sill and set it aside. Then she opened the casement window and leaned out. The air was fresh and pure and stimulating, cold but not unpleasantly so. She inhaled deeply, feeling refreshed.

An outrageous idea struck her. She'd always loved both snow and the roofs of Harley. Why not go out? The roof wasn't really dangerous in this area because a low decorative balustrade ran along the edge. Between the angled roof and the balustrade was a two-foot wide walkway. She could easily step down onto it and go exploring.

She glanced back at Anthony. Her husband was sleeping as if he'd been drugged. He'd never know that she was gone.

The idea of going outside seemed somehow right. Being a little outrageous would make her feel less like plain Emma Stone, and more like the dashing Lady Verlaine that she wanted to be.

She felt her way to the wardrobe and located her cloak and half boots. After sliding her feet into the latter, she tossed the cloak over her nightgown. Then she clambered out the window. The snow was three or four inches deep.

Loosely closing the swinging casements behind her, she set off along the narrow walkway, her cloak swirling around her ankles. The slanting roof was to her right, and the vast open spaces of the night on her left. It was wonderfully quiet. The snowflakes caught and magnified the subtle light, turning it into a pearly, otherworldly glow. Her worries began to dissolve, leaving her with a sense of serenity.

After walking across the long straight central block she came to an awkward corner where the east wing met the main building. Rather than risk scrambling across it, she folded down into the corner. The sheltered position gave her a splendid view of the snow-covered planes and angles of Harley. Seen from this perspective, the great house was strange and lovely. Haunting, in fact.

Alone in the night, she was able to relax in a way that had been impossible in the bedchamber. She thought about Harold Greaves, lying in a new grave beside his wife. Was the snow also falling over their resting place in London? Mr. Evans had said they were close as only a childless couple could be.

She closed her eyes and offered a prayer that Mr. Greaves had been reunited with his wife in some better place. Every day she made at least one such prayer. It seemed the least she could do. Strange how her life had been changed utterly by a man she would never meet.

She wrapped her cloak closer. The cold was slowly seeping into her, but she wasn't ready to go inside again. Later. For now she would simply let her mind drift. . . .

Anthony awoke when something banged hard nearby. The wind had blown open the casement windows and snow was swirling into the room. It took a moment longer to remember where he was. Harley. Emma. The tower room.

Where was Emma? Not beside him in the bed.

He sat up and scanned the room, but the faint light of the fire did not reveal her. He rose from the bed and lit several candles. No Emma, yet the door was still latched from the inside. How could she have left?

His gaze went to the open window, and he stiffened. The Christmas candle had been removed from the sill. Oh, God, no. Earlier she had talked about her childhood fantasy of flying from the roof and soaring over the hills. She couldn't possibly have been so upset about his encounter with Cecilia that she would have jumped. Could she?

Cold with fear, he threw open the casements and looked down into the courtyard, terrified that he would see a broken body far below. He could see nothing unusual . . . but if she had jumped, the snow might have covered her by now.

His hands locked on the sill until his fingers whitened. If she had done something terrible because of him . . . may God have mercy on both their souls.

Then he noticed faint marks on the narrow walkway below the window. Footsteps, perhaps, though so full of snow as to be almost invisible. But why the devil would she be out on the roof in the middle of the night?

Rather than struggle with boots, he slipped his feet into a light pair of evening shoes. Then he threw his cloak over his nightshirt and climbed out onto the roof. The snow was about six inches deep, and the same rising wind that had blown the window open swirled clouds of icy crystals around him.

Grimly he started walking. Under other circumstances, he might have enjoyed the unearthly beauty of the scene. Instead he moved along the slippery walkway as quickly as possible, his attention divided between his footing and the ground far below.

He was nearing panic when he finally found her huddled in a corner. In fact, he almost fell over her. An inch or more of feathery snow covered her cloak, making her almost invisible in the white night. She was so still, he feared that she was dead.

Heart hammering, he dropped to his knees beside her. Lacy flakes coated her face and dusted her dark lashes. Taking her hands, he said urgently, "Emma! Emma, are you all right!"

Her hands were like ice. He began chafing one of them between his. "Emma, damn it, wake up!"

Her lashes fluttered open, and she stared blankly at him. Praise God, at least she was still alive. He said sharply, "Can you walk?"

She blinked at him, dazed. "Anthony?"

"Yes, it's me. What the devil are you doing out here in the middle of a snowstorm?" He stood, then took both her hands and pulled her up. She didn't fall, quite, but she swayed badly. He caught her around the waist.

Her tall body sagged against him. "I . . . I think I fell asleep."

"Idiot," he said brusquely. Half carrying her, he started the long trek back. The walkway that was adequate for one was hazardous for two, especially covered with soft, sliding snow. He took the outside edge himself, keeping one hand on the top of the balustrade and the other arm locked around his wife.

The trip back seemed three times as long as the one out. Emma moved stiffly, sometimes slipping on the soft snow. Once her feet went out from under her, and they both almost went over the edge. She seemed unaware of how close they had come to death, but Anthony was sweating with strain by the time they reached the tower room.

Knowing this last bit was the most dangerous, he braced one foot against the balustrade, then scooped Emma up and maneuvered her through the window. After setting her on her feet inside, he climbed through himself and latched the window tight.

He dropped his cloak and kicked off his ruined shoes, then turned to his wife. Emma was shivering uncontrollably. He tossed aside her cloak and seated her in a chair by the fire. After throwing coal on lavishly, he brought a branch of candles close and examined her. Though she seemed barely aware of her surroundings, he couldn't find signs of frostbite on her face or hands or feet.

He hesitated, considering what to do. Putting her in a

hot bath would probably warm her quickly, but finding servants to heat the water would take time. Too much time. Even locating brandy would take longer than he wanted. She needed to be warmed up immediately.

The best way to warm her was probably with his own body. He found a heavy pair of his socks and put them on her icy feet. Then he drew her upright. "It's back to bed, my girl."

He tugged her nightgown up over her head. She didn't resist, except for a faint squeak of protest.

Under other circumstances he would have paused to admire the lush femininity of her body, but not this time. He tucked her into bed and pulled the blankets over her, adding the spare from the wardrobe. Then he snuffed all but one candle, stripped off his own garments, and slid under the covers.

Lying on his side, he drew her into his arms so that her spine was pressed into his stomach and her bottom was against his groin. Damnation, but she was cold. He breathed warm air on the back of her ear and began rubbing the chilled length of her arm.

"What . . . what are you doing?" she said, sounding more aware.

"Trying to keep you from the death by freezing you so richly deserve." He slid his knee between her icy thighs.

She stiffened and tried to wriggle free, which only pressed her icy but shapely rump into him harder. He tightened his arm around her and began massaging the cold curves of her hip and thigh. "Hold still. The sooner you warm up, the less likely you are to come down with lung fever."

"Why . . . why didn't you just leave me out there?" she asked a little breathlessly.

"Because losing my wife after less than a fortnight of marriage would look like damned carelessness on my part," he retorted.

"It would have been worth a little gossip," she said hazily. "I have another forty thousand pounds in trust for me and my children. If I died now, you'd inherit the lot."

His hand stilled. Christ, did she realize what she was saying? "If I understand you correctly," he said acidly, "you didn't trust me enough to reveal the truth about your fortune, and you're now suggesting I should have murdered you for your money. Why the devil would you marry a man you find so contemptible?"

"Better the devil you know . . . " she muttered as she tried to writhe away again.

As he caught at her, his hand came down on her breast. The soft weight fit his hand perfectly. She inhaled sharply, and they both became very still.

He released her breast with reluctance. She may or may not be getting warmer, but he certainly was. "So I'm the devil you know. How flattering. Remind me to thrash you someday when the circumstances are more appropriate."

"You wouldn't dare!" she said indignantly, sounding more herself.

"I restrain myself only because my mother taught me never to strike a female, no matter how richly she deserves it." Though his voice was dryly humorous, he was uncomfortably aware that she would not have made her bizarre suggestion about leaving her to freeze if she didn't secretly fear that he didn't want to be married to her.

If she had died through no fault of his own, would he be relieved to be rich and free again? The answer in his head was an instant, vehement *no*. It was time to be an adult. To take on responsibility, to build a family. And if Emma was not the wife he would have chosen, she was the wife he had, and he was not displeased by that. Not displeased at all.

He began rubbing her again. She was noticeably warmer. As his concern receded, sexual awareness became impossible to suppress. He had a beautiful, naked female in his arms, and she was his wife. Or almost.

He wanted, rather desperately, to make love to her. Yet on a level beyond arousal he sensed that this was a critical moment. What he did now would influence the rest of his life. He moved his hand from her side to the front of her body, stroking from magnificent breasts over curving torso down to her soft belly. Her skin was satin smooth and blessedly warm.

"Your view of my character is rather unflattering, and I can't say that I blame you for that," he said quietly. "I've been an irresponsible, frivolous fellow most of my life, and you and I married for mutual convenience, not love. But I assure you, Emma, I do take our marriage seriously."

He propped himself up on one elbow and gazed down at her as he tried to shape what he wanted to say. "I will do my best to fulfill the vows I made on our wedding day, as I trust you to honor the ones you made to me. If we do that, perhaps in time love will come. If not love, surely we can manage caring and respect."

She rolled onto her back and looked at him. In the dim light of the single candle, her eyes were a smoky gray, and fully aware. Their gazes held for a long, long moment.

Then she raised her left hand and touched the side of

his face with gentle fingers. "Caring and respect are easy, Anthony," she whispered. "You already have mine."

He did not deserve so much from her. Turning his head, he tenderly kissed the shiny new wedding band he'd slid onto her finger the week before. That, at least, he had bought with his own money. Softly he said, "With this ring I thee wed."

He laid her hand on the mattress. "With my body I thee worship." Then he leaned forward and kissed her. Her mouth was warm and soft and welcoming.

"As long as we both shall live," he said huskily as he moved his lips to her throat.

Her arms came around him hard, and once again they were flesh to flesh. But this embrace was not for warmth or consolation. It was wholly carnal as the desire in him sang to the sleeping desire in her.

Her response was hesitant at first, but as honest and true as Emma herself. He caressed her lavish, womanly body, searching for what pleased her, and discovered that everything did. Every touch, every kiss. Every gentle exploration, every discovery of a new, secret place.

Despite the urgency of his own craving, he took his time. It was very much in his best interest for her to be a joyous, ardent partner. The longer he denied himself now, the more unselfishly he wooed her, the greater the reward for them both.

He pleasured her until she gasped with wonder, her body convulsing and her arms locking desperately around him. Then, when her ragged breathing slowed, he claimed the final intimacy that made her his wife. At first she stiffened from the pain. Panting with the effort of restraint, he held still and soothed her with soft words and gentle kisses until she relaxed and began to pulse against him.

Together they found a rhythm that went from mutual exploration to fierce possession to the final madness. And in the end, she cried out his name in a voice that pierced him to the heart.

They both collapsed, spent and shaking. He buried his face in her thick silky hair as he struggled for breath. How strange that he, who considered himself a master of the amatory arts, should have learned so much from her. His sweet, wise, brave wife.

As his breathing slowed, he rolled onto his side and drew her once again into his arms. Soon she was asleep, her head trustingly on his shoulder.

He stayed awake a little longer, drowsy but struck by the wonder of what had taken place between them. Letting his hand rest in her tangled hair, he murmured, "My one and only." Then he, too, slid into sleep.

Chapter Eight

❦

Emma awoke the next morning to blue skies and pale wintry sunshine. The events of the previous night might have seemed a dream, except that Anthony slept beside her. He was gloriously naked, with one powerful arm wrapped around her waist to hold her close. She should be embarrassed at being equally naked, but her sense of well-being was too great. The sheer animal warmth of her position made her want to purr.

She was in love. What she had felt for Anthony when she was a girl had not been mere infatuation, but the first distant notes of what was now a grand symphony of emotions. Whatever the future held, that love would always be an integral part of her.

She lay in mindless contentment until she succumbed to the need to stretch. When she moved, Anthony's eyes opened. His dark lashes were really ridiculously long, a devastating frame for his light eyes.

His mouth curved into a smile. "Remember—any more night walks on the roof in snowstorms, and you get thrashed."

"Yes, my lord and master," she said, her meek words belied by her saucy smile.

His hand moved lazily, possessively, to her breasts. "I'm going to like being married to you. I'm glad you were foolish enough to propose to me."

The desire to say that she loved him was almost overwhelming. Firmly she clamped down on it. This was not the right time for such a declaration; it might never be the right time. At least they had become friends. Not only had Anthony risked his life to rescue her from her own foolishness, but they had shared profound intimacy.

Some of her pleasure dimmed as she realized that for him, sexual relations must be a matter of course. Needing to know how he felt about what they had done, she said shyly, "Last night—is it always as nice as that?" She felt herself blushing. "The . . . the being married part, I mean."

His brows arched, and she could feel her heart sinking. Why had she assumed that he had taken any special pleasure in what she had found so rapturous?

"Nice?" he repeated in a deep, ominous voice. "We discover a rare degree of passion together, and all you can say is 'nice'?"

Even as she recognized that he was teasing, she blushed some more. "Well, I have nothing to compare it to. I would appear foolish rhapsodizing over something that was utterly routine." She paused pensively. "Though if that was routine, no married person would ever get out of bed."

He laughed and caught her in his arms, rolling her over so that she was lying on top of him. "No, my sweet Emma. Last night was not routine by any standard. It was special." He kissed the tip of her nose. "As special as you are."

She didn't think it was possible for her to be any happier. Stretching out along his warm, muscular frame, she said softly, "I'm glad you think so."

He skimmed his hands slowly down her back and hips, stirring delicious sensations in places that she hadn't even known existed before the previous night. "Are you sore this morning?"

"Only a little. I'm not the least bit refined or delicate, you know. My mother once said that with all the riding and tree climbing I did, I'd have an easy wedding night. She seems to have been right." Emma rocked her hips against his provocatively. "I'm certainly not sore enough to forgo what I think is about to happen."

"Delicacy is overrated," he said huskily. "Let's *not* get out of bed all day."

And he pulled her head down for a kiss.

They did rise in time for a very late breakfast. In the cheerful confusion of the house party, they hadn't been missed. Emma was glad when Anthony suggested a walk after they'd eaten. Much as she loved socializing with her long-lost family, she wanted to savor the enthralling new intimacy between her and her husband.

The previous night's storm had transformed the landscape into white sculptured shapes of unearthly beauty. As the wind blew icy plumes from the drifts, they set off along an untouched lane.

The snow was about six inches deep, which made walking awkward, but Anthony helped Emma through the drifts and kissed her at every stile. When they reached the shelter of a beech wood, she gave into temptation and flopped on her back in a drift. "I'm going to make an angel," she said as she energetically waved her arms up and down through the soft snow. "I haven't done this since I was a child."

Anthony laughed and dropped beside her. "Neither have I. Why do we stop doing things like this when we grow up?"

She propped herself on one elbow and studied her husband's snow angel critically. Since he was unhampered by skirts and his cloak was less voluminous, his angel was better than hers. "I don't know, but perhaps that's one reason for having children. One can pretend to do childish things for their sakes rather than for oneself."

She hesitated, then said awkwardly, "I should have told you about the other forty thousand pounds. It wasn't that I didn't trust you, but . . . " Her voice trailed off. She *hadn't* trusted him. But she did now. "I'll tell Mr. Evans that I've changed my mind about putting the money in a trust."

Anthony said gravely, "The gesture is much appreciated, but it's not necessary. You had every right to protect your future from a man who might be irresponsible. In fact, based on my history, probably was." He reached out and took her gloved hand in his. "We don't need the money. Now that the mortgages are cleared, Canfield will give us a very comfortable living. Keep the trust for our children."

She squeezed his hand, loving the way he said "our children" so naturally. It was tacit acknowledgment of the fact that they were going to build a life together.

His expression became less serious. "We've done snow angels. Now it's time I taught you about snow devils."

Her brows drew together. "I've never heard of them."

A wicked light in his eyes, he stripped off his gloves and tossed them aside. "I should hope you haven't."

Then he pounced, trapping her with his body as his cloak fell around them both. As she gave a squeak of surprise, he captured her mouth in a mesmerizing kiss.

It was a wonder they didn't melt the snow.

Anthony and his wife finished a thoroughly decadent day by napping after their walk. When they rose and prepared for dinner, he wondered if his intrepid bride would have been as eager for another passionate session as she had been for the earlier ones. He'd been too drained to find out, but was sure that by the end of the evening, when they went to bed again, he would have recovered sufficiently to offer another example of husbandly devotion.

Smiling for no particular reason, he glanced at Emma, who was putting on a pair of gold earrings he'd bought for her. Even though he'd always fancied petite blondes, he must admit that his wife, who was exactly the opposite, was quite irresistible. Even now, when desire was temporarily sated, he wanted her. It was impossible to imagine *not* wanting her, no matter how many years they were married.

The dinner bell clamored through the long halls. Emma rose from the dressing table and turned. "Do I look all right?"

He found her lack of confidence rather endearing. "You look magnificent," he said with complete sincerity. "That shade of russet silk is perfect for your coloring." And this time she was not covering her bountiful curves with a gauze scarf.

She smiled and took his offered arm. "The only

drawback to a formal dinner is that I can't sit next to you."

He said meaningfully, "That doesn't matter, since you'll sleep next to me."

Her blush was so enchanting that he paused to nibble from her ear to her shoulder. She tasted delicious. Both of them were breathing more quickly when he escorted her from the room. If it weren't for Brand's enmity, this would be a perfect holiday.

After a long and lavish dinner, the duchess rose in the signal for the ladies to withdraw. As the crowd of chattering women made their way to the drawing room, the dowager duchess appeared beside Emma. "Come, child. I want to talk to you. We've scarcely had a chance so far."

"So many Vaughns, so little time," Emma said with a laugh. "You're in such demand, Grandmère, that I didn't wish to monopolize you."

"Then I shall monopolize you instead," the dowager said tranquilly. In pale, ice-blue silk and ostrich plumes, she was as lovely now as in the portrait Gainsborough had painted when she was twenty and a newlywed duchess.

When they reached the drawing room, the dowager steered Emma to a pair of wing chairs set in a quiet corner. As they seated themselves, she said, "Is Verlaine treating you well?"

Emma blushed. "Very well, Grandmère. We have much still to learn about each other, but we . . . we seem to suit."

"I guessed as much," the dowager said, her faded blue eyes twinkling, "when I saw you coming in from your walk this afternoon. Such a quantity of snow on you both."

Another blush. Really, Emma thought with resignation, she'd blushed more in the last few days than the previous ten years.

"I'm so glad you married Verlaine," the dowager said seriously. "He has a good heart, but he needed an anchor, a sense of direction. You'll give him that, I think."

Startled, Emma said, "I thought the benefits of this marriage went mostly to me."

"Not at all. A good marriage is a benefit to both partners," the dowager said briskly. "You will give Verlaine stability, and he will teach you to laugh and enjoy life."

Emma looked down at her wedding ring, absently turning it on her finger. "I haven't had many opportunities for laughter in the last ten years."

The dowager sighed. "I wish you had come here. Even if you wouldn't stay at Harley, surely we could have found better employment for you than what you had."

Emma glanced up. "You were the one responsible for the fact that every year I received a Christmas invitation, weren't you? That's how you know about my various employers."

The dowager nodded. "I was afraid you might be lost to us, so I did my best to ensure that wouldn't happen. You should have come long ago."

Emma had not known that anyone was so interested in the welfare of an orphan who was a mere connection, scarcely a member of the family at all. A little defensively, she said, "I wanted to be here, Grandmère, but I could not have left my work for so long. Nor could I have come as a beggar."

"You have your share of Vaughn pride," the dowager said dryly. "I know it well." Laying a gentle hand on Emma's, she continued in a softer voice, "But, my dear girl, I want you to know that you would have always been welcome."

Emma swallowed hard, torn between tears and a strong desire to kick herself. The dowager was right— it was foolish pride that had kept her away, far more than her circumstances. Still, she was here now. She gave the dowager a heartfelt hug. It healed a loneliness deep inside to know that she never really stopped being a Vaughn.

When the Duke of Warrington gave the signal that it was time to leave the port decanter, Anthony held back as the rest of the men—including Brand—got to their feet and ambled off to rejoin the ladies. In a group so large, it was proving fairly easy to avoid his glowering cousin.

It was a Harley custom to have casual dancing the evening before Christmas Eve. Anthony had always enjoyed the event more than the grand Twelfth Night ball that would end the house party. For some of the younger guests, this would be the first public dancing of their lives. That had been true for Anthony a dozen years earlier. He smiled at the thought of how grown up he had felt then, when in fact he'd been the merest boy.

He joined the stream of Vaughns heading toward the ballroom, where a pianoforte was playing seductively. Emma would have been too young to dance at Harley during her last visit. He looked forward to introducing his wife to the polished dance floor.

A small hand touched his arm. He turned and found Cecilia regarding him with great tragic eyes. "Anthony, I must talk to you," she said urgently. "In private."

He hesitated. "It would not look good for us to go off together."

"No one will notice." She touched his arm again, seeming on the verge of tears. "Please, Anthony."

He glanced around, but didn't see Brand. With so many people milling about, a brief absence would not be noted. "Very well, Cecilia," he said without enthusiasm. "Where shall we meet?"

She thought. "The gallery."

"You go ahead. I'll follow in a moment."

She nodded and headed down the passage that ran to the main hall. Anthony waited until she was out of sight, then followed at an unhurried pace. The gallery was a long chamber on the floor above. It served several purposes, from providing an exercise area in inclement weather to displaying paintings and fencing foils.

When Anthony arrived, Cecilia was lighting more candles with a Christmas candle from one of the windows. She glanced up nervously at his entrance, then replaced her candle in its window fixture. In the soft light, she looked fragile and almost unbearably lovely, as petite and exquisite as a gilded marzipan holiday angel.

Wryly recognizing that he was not the kind of man who could stay angry with an attractive woman, Anthony said, "What did you wish to discuss with me, Cecilia? Is something wrong?"

She nodded, her eyes brimming with tears. "Will

you talk to Brand? He has the absurd notion that you and I have been having an affair."

"What!" Anthony stared at her, shocked. "Where did he get such a ridiculous notion?"

"I have no idea." Tears began spilling from Cecilia's blue eyes. "Oh, Anthony, everything has gone wrong, and I don't know what to do."

According to Anthony's mother, it was a gentleman's duty to allow a lady to cry all over his best waistcoat if she was in distress. Recalling that Cecilia had always had a tendency toward melodrama, he put an arm around her soothingly. "Surely things aren't that bad, Cecy."

She clutched at him, weeping harder than ever.

Brand chose this inauspicious moment to enter the gallery. He stopped dead in the doorway, his face going dead-white. Then he strode forward, eyes blazing. "Damn you, Verlaine! I knew I'd find you with Cecilia in your arms."

"If so, you're cleverer than I," Anthony said with exasperation. "She's your wife, Brand. Let her cry over on your shoulder." He disentangled himself from Cecilia, hoping that would defuse a potentially volatile situation.

No such luck. Brand stalked over to the rack of fencing foils and grabbed two of the weapons. "Tonight I'm going to do what I should have done nine years ago." Grimly he flicked the protective buttons off the points of the foils, then tossed one of the weapons hilt first to Anthony. "I challenge you to a duel. Right now, right here."

"For God's sake, Brand!" Anthony exclaimed as he reflexively caught the hilt of the foil. "It's bad form for you to challenge a guest, or for me to accept. For that matter, if you're the challenger, I get to choose the weapons, and I don't choose swords."

"We'll do it *now*!" Brand barked at he stripped off his close-fitting coat. *"En garde!"*

Beginning to feel seriously concerned, Anthony removed his own coat, keeping a wary eye on his angry cousin. "This is ridiculous. I'm damned if I know what I've ever done to make you so eager to kill me."

"Oh, you most assuredly will be damned," Brand said in a voice like a whip. "Prepare yourself, Verlaine, because tonight justice will be mine."

Then, as Anthony stared in stunned disbelief, the man who had once been his best friend lunged at him with glittering blade and murderous eyes.

Chapter Nine

∽∾∾

After her audience with the dowager duchess, Emma left the nearly empty drawing room to go to the ballroom. She was looking forward to her first waltz with Anthony. He was undoubtedly a superb dancer. She was badly in need of practice, but she didn't think that would matter.

As she entered the hall that led to the ballroom, she saw Cecilia slip away from the crowd ahead and go down the cross passage that went to the foyer and the main staircase. Emma thought nothing of it, until she saw Anthony leave as well—going the same way as Cecilia.

Emma stopped in her tracks, her stomach turning. Surely Anthony could not be having an assignation with Cecilia, not after what had transpired between him and Emma last night and today.

She swallowed hard and told herself not to be a ninny. The fact that Anthony and Cecilia had gone off in the same direction was hardly proof of amorous intentions. Fiercely she told herself that she must learn to trust her husband or she would go mad, for there would always be women hovering around him. Nonetheless, not ready to face the laughing people in the ballroom, she sank into a chair tucked beside a massive carved console table.

Until now she had not let herself wonder if Anthony would be a faithful husband, because the answer was probably not one she would like. Many men of his class had mistresses, and a man who loved women as Anthony did was a prime candidate for infidelity. Her heart bled a little at the thought.

Would she still love her husband even if he was unfaithful? Probably—but if that ever happened, part of her would retreat from him. Never again would there be the openness and trust they had shared today.

She sat very still and concentrated on her breathing until it was regular again. There. She had faced the worst. If Anthony was unfaithful, at least she would be a little prepared. *But—please, God, don't let it happen.*

She was about to continue to the ballroom when she saw Brand stalk out and head in the direction that Anthony and Cecilia had gone. His face was like granite. Merciful heaven, had he seen them leave? If he caught the two of them together, there would be hell to pay, even if the meeting was perfectly innocent.

Swiftly Emma considered what to do. Go for the duke? He would certainly put a quick end to any conflict. But by the time she found him, it might be too late. Better to follow Brand, and hope that she could head off any trouble.

She got to her feet and walked after Brand, her long legs covering the ground quickly. By the time she reached the great hall, he was disappearing from sight on the upper floor, heading toward the gallery. Emma followed, praying that she was being an absolute idiot and nothing untoward was going to happen.

Halfway up the stairs, she was halted in her tracks by

a woman's scream. Merciful heavens, Cecilia! Lifting her skirts indecorously, Emma raced upward, knowing with icy certainty that years of festering anger had reached the explosion point.

Anthony's mind was stunned by Brand's attack, but years of fencing practice saved him. As Cecilia screamed, Anthony knocked aside his cousin's blade. Retreating, he exclaimed, "Christ, Brand! Have you gone mad?"

"It's you who are mad, to meet my wife in my own house." Brand attacked again, this time controlled and far more dangerous than in his initial lunge.

With a shriek of clashing steel, Anthony countered well enough to save himself from injury, but this couldn't last long. Brand had always been a better swordsman, and now he was in a blind rage.

Hearing the door open, Anthony spared a swift glance, hoping to see the duke or one of the duchesses. They were the only people Brand might heed. Instead Emma entered. Christ, she was the last person he wanted to see. If he was going to be spitted like a lamb for roasting, he did not want his wife to witness it.

In the instant that his attention was divided, Brand drove in again, slashing at his opponent's sword arm. Anthony managed to block his cousin's blade, but only just. The sleeve of his shirt was ripped from elbow to wrist. Knowing he could not retreat forever, Anthony stood his ground, fighting back furiously. He managed to battle Brand to a standstill as their blades shrilled together with metallic fury.

Then heavy folds of fabric whipped violently between them, trapping the foils and knocking them downward. With amazement, Anthony saw that Emma had wrenched one of the great tapestries from the wall and slammed it over the dueling weapons. She looked like a furious Valkyrie.

"Bloody hell!" Brand sneezed from the dust released by the tapestry. "For God's sake, Emma, stay out of this, or you'll get hurt."

Not moving, Emma snapped, "What the devil is this all about?"

"It's none of your affair." Recovering from the shock, Brand wrenched his weapon free from the heavy fabric and prepared to resume fighting.

"Not my affair when you're trying to kill my husband?" she exclaimed. "*Men!* Of course this is my affair."

Deciding it was time to take a hand, Anthony hurled his foil away. The sword flew across the gallery and stabbed into the wall about a yard above the floor, then hung there, quivering. "Enough, Brand! I won't fight you any more, not when I haven't the faintest idea why you're so outraged."

For a terrifying moment, it appeared as if Brand might renounce a lifetime of gentlemanly training and attack an unarmed man. Then Emma grabbed the cowering Cecilia's hand. "Come on, Cecy, make yourself useful."

She hauled her smaller cousin between the men so that the two women formed a barrier. Then, with a practiced schoolteacher voice, she ordered, "Brand, explain yourself."

He looked mulish, which at least was an improvement over homicidal. Since he seemed unwilling to speak, Anthony said helpfully, "From what Cecilia told me, Brand suspects me of having an affair with her."

Emma's face tightened, but her voice was calm when she asked, "Are you?"

"Don't be absurd!" he retorted. "Until yesterday, I hadn't laid eyes on Cecilia in nine years."

Emma turned to Brand. "You heard what Anthony said. Do you honestly think they're having an affair?"

Brand wiped his brow with one forearm. Though he still looked dangerous, the wildness had faded from his eyes. "There might not be a physical affair," he admitted gruffly. "But Anthony has stood between Cecy and me every day and night of our marriage. When he fought me after she accepted my proposal, he said . . . " Brand stopped and swallowed hard. "He said that whenever I bedded my wife, she would be thinking of him. And he was right, damn him!"

Cecilia gasped. "Brand, how can you say that? I could have married Anthony if I wanted to, but I chose *you*. What made you think I secretly preferred Anthony?"

"Everyone always did!" Brand stared at his wife, his expression anguished. "He was always the leader. Smarter, more charming, more handsome, everyone's darling—including yours. You only married me because I have a greater fortune and title."

Anthony cringed as he remembered how he'd flung both those taunts in Brand's face when they'd fought over Cecilia. Who would have believed that his angry words would have taken such poisonous root?

Exasperated, Emma said, "Don't you two ever *talk* to each other?" She unobtrusively removed Brand's foil from his relaxed grip. "Cecilia, why did you marry Brand instead of Anthony? I'm sure you had your reasons."

"I married him because I loved him, of course." She hesitated, then said painfully, "I loved them both, really, even though they're so different. But I'd always thought that Brand's feelings for me were more those of a brother. Anthony was the one who treated me like a sweetheart. He and I both drifted into thinking that we would marry, even though he hadn't formally offered."

By this time tears were running down Cecilia's cheeks. Emma wordlessly produced a handkerchief from somewhere and handed it over. After Cecilia had blotted her eyes and blown her adorable little nose, she continued, "Then Brand asked me to be his wife, and I realized that he was the husband I wanted, not Anthony." She stared at Brand beseechingly. "Do you remember what happened after I accepted?"

Her husband turned an interesting shade of red. "Of course I remember," he said stiffly. "But that is hardly something to be discussed before others."

Blushing herself, Cecilia gave a nod of agreement. "I didn't accept because of your fortune or your title, though of course I didn't object to becoming a duchess. But what I loved was your . . . your steadiness. The way you made me feel cherished. Special." She gave Anthony an apologetic glance. "Marrying Anthony would have been very jolly, but he would always have mistresses, and we might have ended up in debtors' prison. I didn't want that. I wanted *you*."

Anthony felt a sharp pang at her words. She hadn't trusted him. It was not flattering knowledge. Yet he could not blame her for her mistrust. Emma hadn't entirely trusted him, either.

Brand swallowed hard, a muscle jumping in his throat as he stared at his wife. "I . . . I wasn't second best?"

"Never." Cecilia's tears began flowing again. "But after we married, I began to wonder if you'd ever really loved me. As time went on, and you became colder and colder, I . . . I decided that you had only wanted me because Anthony did. You two were always competing, and I was merely one more prize. Once you had me, you lost interest."

Anthony winced. He couldn't speak for Brand, but he had to admit that there had been an element of competition in his courtship of Cecilia. She'd been the prettiest girl around, so he had assumed that he, dashing Anthony, everyone's darling, deserved her.

Sometimes he didn't like himself very much.

Speaking as if he and his wife were alone, Brand said hoarsely, "How could you think that, Cecy? You're the only woman I've ever loved. But you never said that you loved me, not once."

"You never said that you loved me, either," she said starkly.

"At first it seemed unnecessary," he said. "Later, I couldn't because I started thinking that you had married me for the wrong reasons. It was like . . . like acid in my belly."

Cecilia went into his arms, sobbing, "Oh, Brand, Brand. Why didn't we talk like this years ago? I've always loved you, even when I was sure that you didn't love me."

Brand embraced his wife with feverish intensity, his own eyes glittering with tears. They clung together for a long moment. Then he looked up and said haltingly, "Anthony, I'm sorry. I've behaved abominably. I wanted to blame you for wrecking my marriage, because that was easier than blaming myself. Can you forgive me?"

Anthony realized that he was being given a golden opportunity to act like an adult. "Much of the fault was mine, Brand. I didn't want to believe that Cecilia preferred you, so I said things no man should ever say to another. I'm sorry." He offered his hand.

Brand reached out and grasped it fervently. With surprising pleasure, Anthony realized that once again they could be friends. If the truth be known, he'd missed Brand far more than he'd missed Cecilia.

Emma, who had been watching approvingly, made a small movement of her head toward the door. Understanding, Anthony ended the handshake. "Can you forgive me, too, Cecilia? I never meant to injure your marriage."

She gave him a teary smile. "Brand and I did most of the damage ourselves. From now on we'll do better, won't we, dearest?"

"We will, darling. I swear it." Brand bent his head and kissed his wife passionately, one hand slipping down her back to pull her against him. The air crackled with sexual tension.

Knowing they would not be missed, Anthony collected his coat. Then he and Emma quietly left the gallery. "I'd forgotten what a watering pot Cecilia is," he murmured when he'd closed the door behind them. "Thank heaven you're not like that."

After donning his coat and straightening his cravat, he draped his left arm around his wife's shoulders and they made their way down the stairs. "That was a very timely intervention, my dear," he said sternly. "But don't you *ever* put yourself between two armed men again, or I'll have to thrash you. You could have been killed."

She said demurely, "If every day you forbid me from another thing on pain of being thrashed, very soon I'll be restricted to sitting by the fire with a book."

He smiled, but it quickly faded. "Who would have thought that the angry words I yelled at Brand nine years ago could have such terrible, lasting effects? I almost ruined his marriage. I swear before God, Emma, I never meant for that to happen."

"Words have power, Anthony," she said quietly. "Especially angry words thrown by someone like you, who affects people so strongly."

Everything comes to you easily. Too easily. "If I have power, I've used it badly," he said with self-disgust. "I've lived my life on the surface, sliding from one thing to another with never a serious thought in my head."

"That's probably true," Emma said with a depressing amount of objectivity. "But as Cecilia said, they did most of the damage to themselves. If either of them had had the courage to admit their love, they could have saved themselves years of misery."

"Perhaps in the long run their marriage will be better for having been tested like that. I hope so."

"You have also used your power of words for good, you know," Emma said quietly. "I think I remember every friendly word you ever said to me when I was a child. And there were many, even though you couldn't have been particularly interested in a plain, shy girl years your junior."

"Was I kind, Emma? I hope so." He smiled ruefully. "I have to admit that I don't remember that much about our encounters. You were merely one of many smaller Vaughns."

They'd come to an archway that divided two halls. A kissing bough hung there, so he stopped and turned Emma to face him. As he studied the strong, well-shaped planes of her face, the intelligence and warmth in her eyes, he wondered how he ever could have thought her plain. "I don't want us to become like Brand and Cecilia—hurting each other by not saying what we mean." He grinned. "Luckily, as alarmingly honest as you are, I don't think that will be a problem."

Her gaze dropped. "If I must be honest, then I shall have to admit that I've always loved you, Anthony, even when I was a child. When Mr. Evans mentioned that you were in desperate financial straits, I dismissed every other possibility and ran straight to you, hoping you were desperate enough to marry me," she said haltingly. "Luckily you were."

She looked up again. Her great eyes, more gray than green tonight, were regarding him without hope or illusion. She did not expect love, but she did deserve honesty.

What did he feel for this woman who was his wife? Respect, certainly. Desire absolutely. Liking and protectiveness and a hundred other things. In fact, he recognized with lightning bolt suddenness and power, he was in love with her. It was so obvious. So right. The passion and intimacy and laughter between them were the truest thing he'd ever found his life, entirely different from his boyish yearning for Cecilia.

It took a moment for him to collect his scattered thoughts. Then, his gaze holding hers, he said slowly, "I can't claim to have loved you most of my life, Emma, but rather to my own surprise, I seem to have fallen quite madly in love with you."

Holding her face between his hands as if she were made of rare, fragile porcelain, he kissed her, the first kiss of true love he'd ever given in his life. In it was tenderness and desire and a growing sense of awe. Emma kissed him back with a sweet intensity that brought her spirit closer to his than he would have dreamed possible.

After a long, long embrace, he lifted his lips a few inches and said huskily, "Yesterday the dowager said that things come easily to me, and she's right. Through no effort or virtue of my own, I've acquired the best of all possible wives."

He ran his admiring gaze over Emma's richly curved body. "It's something of a bonus that you're the most alluring woman I've ever known. What more could a man ask of the only woman he'll ever lie with again?"

She caught her breath. "Do you mean that, Anthony?"

Fidelity struck him as a very adult, very desirable trait. "I swear and vow, Emma, that you will be my one and only as long as we both shall live."

She gave him such a shining smile that he almost kissed her again. He was halted by the dowager duchess's amused voice. "I'm glad you two found a kissing bough to misbehave under. We wouldn't want the children corrupted."

Anthony and Emma jumped as if they'd been caught picking pockets. Then they both turned to the dowager, who was gliding over the polished floor toward them.

Calmly she asked, "Did you get Brand and Cecilia sorted out?"

"Yes, Grandmère," Emma replied as if it was perfectly natural for the dowager to know everything. Perhaps it was.

Anthony added, "I suggest that you avoid the gallery. I think they may be reconciling in a manner that would embarrass anyone who accidentally interrupted them."

Amusement gleamed in her blue eyes. "Well done, both of you. Christmas should be a time of reconciliation. By that measure this may be the best Christmas we've ever had at Harley."

Almost simultaneous, Anthony and Emma said, "It's the best I've ever had." Then they looked at each other, laughing with the sheer pleasure of being in love.

The dowager studied them both thoughtfully. "I've talked to Amelia and James, and they agree that it would be a very good thing for the two of you to exchange your vows again tomorrow night before the Christmas Eve service. That way, the whole family can celebrate with you. Emma, James would like to give you away, if you agree."

Emma inhaled with delight. "I would like that above all things. Anthony?"

"An excellent idea." He put his arm around her waist. "I wonder if Brand would stand up with me? When I was younger, I'd always assumed that someday he would be my best man. This would be a way to put the past behind us."

"I suspect that he would be very honored by such a request." Smiling with satisfaction, the dowager turned and floated away.

Emma glanced shyly at Anthony. "I used to dream of being married at Harley. In my wildest dreams, I even imagined marrying you."

"I think a second ceremony will be most appropriate." Anthony drew her into his arms again. "After all, when we married in London, it was a marriage of convenience. This time, my dearest, it will be a pledge of love."

Tears filled Emma's eyes. Wiping at them with one hand, she said tremulously, "Now you're going to think that I'm a watering pot, too."

"As long as you're *my* watering pot," he said tenderly.

Emma laughed and slid her arms around his neck. "If I'm your watering pot, then you're the cleverest bargain I ever made." Her smile turned wicked. "The very best husband money could buy."

Author's Note

∽∾∽

Though it may have read like a product of my fevered imagination, the incident that inspired this story is quite real. The October 3, 1996, edition of the *Baltimore Sun* ran a short filler story about a Spanish businessman who happened to stop into a church while visiting Stockholm, Sweden. The church was empty except for a coffin. The Spaniard, a devout Catholic, knelt and prayed for twenty minutes or so, then signed a condolence book that asked for the names of anyone who prayed for the deceased. No one else had signed.

After returning home, he received a call from Stockholm announcing that he would inherit the entire fortune of the man who had died, a successful real estate dealer who had left no close relatives. The Spanish gentleman's generous act of faith had made him a millionaire, and provided me with an irresistible hook for a story.

All of which goes to prove, once again, that truth is stranger than fiction!

An acclaimed and award-winning author from her very first book, MARY JO PUTNEY is known for her sensual, intelligent, and emotionally powerful stories. Called by *Romantic Times* "one of today's great romance writers," her books appear on numerous bestseller lists. She has won many awards, including two Ritas from the Romance Writers of America, for *Dancing on the Wind* and *The Rake and the Reformer*, and a Career Achievement award from *Romantic Times* magazine. A native of upstate New York, Mary Jo now lives in Maryland with her nearest and dearest, both two and four footed.

A Light in the Window

❦

BY JUSTINE DARE

❦

Wyoming Territory, 1878

It was night, it was a stable, and he'd followed a light, but that was definitely where the similarities to another Christmas season ended.

Stupid thought, Morgan Blaine told himself as he shivered slightly, and pulled his bedroll blanket tighter around him. The movement made his rifle slide down the bed of hay, and he risked the chill to pull it within reach. Not that he was expecting any trouble, not in this quiet out-of-the-way place, but he was trespassing, and if the owner of this small homestead took it in mind to protest, he might have need of the weapon. It was a tidy, well-built place; he'd noticed metal hinges on the doors instead of the easier rawhide, and the barn at least was in decent repair. And that oddly bright light in the window had seemed warm and welcoming, even to a homeless stranger. It was the kind of place a man protected.

He closed his eyes in determination. He'd thought he would be asleep as soon as he found a place to lay his head, but somehow the rest he so badly needed eluded him. His mind was restless, although he wasn't sure why. It wasn't like he cared, and anyway, he'd known it was December. It was hard not to when the briskness of the air here in the Wyoming Territory had long since given way to the crisp cold of winter. Storms had already whitened the mountains, and each week saw the snow line creep lower toward the high plains. Tonight even the lower elevations were getting a taste of what was to come. Soon the thick blanket of white would be here to stay.

But until he had walked into that saloon a couple of miles back and been met with a drunken and off-key rendition of a song about one-horse sleighs, and had seen the small, crooked tree in one corner, decorated rather ludicrously with empty shot glasses and a length of yellowed lace he didn't want to speculate about, he hadn't realized just how close—two more days, the bartender told him—Christmas was.

He'd lasted long enough for one shot of whiskey that was a little too reminiscent of stuff he'd tasted in the back hills of Tennessee, but was warming nonetheless. Then he'd looked around again, at the tawdry tree, the faces of the men who had no place else to go—or nowhere they wanted to go—on this cold night, and worse, the faces of the three women, who had had no place else to go for far longer, and he'd known he couldn't stay. He never stayed around people this time of year. He'd ridden out of the small town of Granite with a sense of relief, stopping only when he'd been drawn to this place by that light casting its glow out into the snowy night. No matter that he'd ridden into town thinking he would welcome human company for a change.

Human company, yes, he thought now as he listened

warily to the small noises coming from a stall at the other end of the small barn, but not human misery. Not that he was any better off. He had nowhere to go, either, and nothing to do when he got there. He didn't even have anywhere to be, and hadn't for what seemed like a very long time.

In the distance a coyote yipped. An answer came; even the wild ones had company tonight, Morgan thought. Save one, he amended wryly, thinking of his imperious aunt's declaration that he was such a one, wild, uncivilized . . . and unfit to bear his father's name. As a child, he'd been hurt by her words, although he'd hidden it well behind a mask of insolence. As an adult, he'd wondered at her perception; how had she known even then?

The small sounds came again, then a quiet footstep.

Human company.

He had it after all, it seemed. He sat up and quietly hefted his Winchester. More footsteps, furtive, closer, and his nerves hummed to attention, sleep forgotten. No, they weren't furtive, just . . . light, he thought.

A shadow moved at the corner of his vision. He rolled to his knees and brought the rifle to the ready. In the next instant he realized two things: he indeed had human company, and he was aiming a good foot too high.

He let out a breath, shivering with the force of old, ugly images, relieved he hadn't shot before he'd looked. He lowered the Winchester slowly, feeling nearly as wide-eyed as the barely three-foot-tall child who stared back at him from beneath long, silver-blond bangs and the brim of a too big hat. Yet there did not seem to be any fear in those huge dark eyes, only curiosity.

"Are you Jesus?"

For the first time in longer than he could remember, Morgan was taken utterly aback. He stared at the child, who answered his own question before Morgan could even begin to think of anything to say.

"Nah, guess you're too big. Jesus was a baby. And it's not Christmas yet anyway."

The child's gaze flicked from the straw that clung to Morgan's jacket to the blanket crumpled beside him to the saddlebags he'd been using as a pillow, then down to his own bundle, a rolled-up collection of clothes and some other oddly lumpy things, from what Morgan could see.

"Did you run away, too?" the child asked.

Now, that, Morgan thought, was a good question. And he wasn't sure he wanted to face the answer to it. The child just looked at him, waiting, with a patience uncanny in one so young. A boy, he thought, although the soft, thickly lashed brown eyes could have been a girl's. Or a fawn's.

"I had to run away," the child said confidingly when he still didn't speak. "My aunt, she doesn't really want me here. She only took me because they said she had to."

Morgan winced. It was an accident, the child couldn't have known. And it only hit a raw spot because he'd just been thinking about his haughty Aunt Abigail, not because it still bothered him. He was long past being bothered by such things. Hers had been only the first harsh lesson; he'd since become used to not belonging, and it meant little to him. As did most things. His heart was as impervious as the granite of the Rockies, and he liked it that way.

"Doesn't anybody want you, either?"

Morgan didn't know if it was the poignant words themselves, or the fact that the child uttered them without emotion, evincing nothing more than curiosity, that made him speak at last.

"No," he said. "And I don't want anybody."

The child sighed. A boy, Morgan thought with certainty now; even at this age there was something masculine about the way the child stood, hands jammed into the pockets of his wool pants.

"Me, neither," he said. "But I'm just a kid, so I have to have somebody."

It was spoken in the weary tone of one much older, and Morgan couldn't help wondering what had brought the child—what was he, five? Six? Seven at the outside—to this pass. Nor could he help remembering just what it had felt like, to not belong anywhere, and how hard it had been to cover up the fear.

"Your aunt?" he asked, remembering what the boy had said. "This is . . . her place?"

The boy nodded, and Morgan's lips quirked, but something in that wide-eyed gaze kept him from smiling at the fact that the runaway child had only made it as far as the barn.

"It is now. They gave it to her," the child said, "but she had to take me along with it."

"They?"

"The sheriff, and some fella in town who does . . . law things."

"A lawyer?" The child nodded, and Morgan wondered if the "law thing" had been a will left by the original owner.

"But she hates me. She's old, and she cries all the time since she came here. But it's hers now, and she doesn't want me here, so I have to go."

Morgan didn't know why he was carrying on this

conversation, but he couldn't seem to help himself. "Go where?"

The boy gave a shrug that was as ancient as his early words had been. "Don't know. Just . . . away. I hate it when she cries."

At least she does cry, Morgan thought, remembering his own aunt, who, if she'd ever had any tender feelings, they had toughened to saddle leather long before he'd ever been dumped on her doorstep. He'd been a little younger than this boy, just as scared, and as determined not to show it.

"What about your uncle?"

"Don't got one. My Aunt Faith, she never got married."

A spinster, then, like Aunt Abigail. Faith, he thought. Even the name sounded like she was as starched, stiff, and stern as the old lady who had raised him—at least she had until he hadn't been able to stand it anymore and had lit out after his twelfth birthday. After Abigail had told him his gift was to have been his father's watch, but he obviously didn't deserve it, now or ever. He'd known then there was nothing he could do that would ever change her opinion of him. He hadn't known why she hated him, but it was as real a part of his life as the fact that his eyes were the same odd blue-gray as they said his father's had been.

"Where're you goin'?" the boy asked.

"Tonight?" Morgan asked, his voice sharpened by the stirring of memories he'd thought deeply and forever buried. "Nowhere, if I don't have to. It's cold out there." He eyed the boy warily. "Is your aunt likely to come chase me out of her barn?"

"Nah. She'd probably let you stay, being as how it's snowin' and all. It's only me she doesn't like."

"You think she'd want you out in that snow?"

The shrug came again, and Morgan felt something tighten in his chest; the boy was trying so hard to pretend he didn't care, never realizing all his fear and uncertainty was showing clearly in his eyes.

"She'd say she wouldn't, pretend that she cares, but I know she don't mean it."

"How do you know?"

"Because at night she prays for me to go away."

Morgan blinked. This aunt must be truly heartless; even Aunt Abigail hadn't gone that far. She'd been too busy reminding everyone that she'd taken in her sister's only child out of the Christian charity of her heart; he'd often thought she'd actually miss him when he left, simply because with him would go her opportunity to parade her goodness before the world. Of course, she'd probably made as much out of his wretched ungratefulness, leaving the perfectly good home she'd provided for him, because it was her duty.

"Is she . . . really your aunt?"

The boy's blond brows furrowed. "My ma is her sister. That means she's my aunt, doesn't it?"

He nodded. "Where is your mother?"

For the first time the boy looked away. He stared at the pile of hay Morgan had been lying on. He stared at the barrel of the lowered rifle. He stared at his own small feet. Morgan wished he hadn't asked. And then wondered why he cared at all; he knew nothing about kids, or talking to them, so he never did. He didn't even like being around them; they brought back too many memories. He avoided them whenever possible, so why was he sitting here talking to this one?

"I . . . don't know," the boy said, misery in his tone. "She went away. That's why they gave our house to my aunt. But Mama's coming back, I know she is."

Morgan frowned. "What about your father?"

"He died a couple of years ago, when I was little. I don't remember him much."

Morgan would have chuckled at the three-foot-tall boy's reference to when he was little, but again something in those wide brown eyes stopped him. He knew how it felt; both of his parents had died when he was even younger, and his life had never been the same. *It'll only get worse, kid,* he thought, but didn't see the point in saying it; the boy would find out soon enough.

With a little shock, Morgan realized that within three minutes he'd learned more about this child than he knew about anybody he'd met in the past twenty years. And the kid was making him think about his past more than he had in all that time. And that made him plumb edgy.

"Look, kid—"

"My name is Zach."

"Okay, Zach, I'm tired, it's cold, and I want to go to sleep. So why don't you go on back to bed?"

The blond bangs moved slightly as the boy gave a shake of his head. "She's cryin' again tonight. I gotta go. I'll come back when Mama comes home."

Morgan looked at the boy's lightweight wool coat, and at his patched trousers, and knew the kid would be frozen inside an hour out in that snow at night. He tried to tell himself he didn't care, but for some reason his mind wasn't buying the notion. And this Zach looked like he had a stubborn stripe, and having one a mile wide himself, he knew what result prodding it would get.

"You do what you have to," he said, shrugging. "But if it was me, I'd spend the night here in this warm barn, and worry about lighting out in the morning."

Zach considered this thoughtfully. "You would?"

"No sense a man freezing his . . . toes off if he doesn't have to," Morgan said with another shrug.

"I s'pose not," Zach agreed with a solemnity that seemed again beyond his years.

Morgan straightened his blanket and stretched out once more on the bed of hay. He situated his rifle within easy reach, gave Zach a sharp nod, as if what the boy did was of no consequence to him, then closed his eyes.

He closed his eyes, but he was fully aware of the boy's slight movements as he considered things, apparently dragging a toe over the ground as he thought. Then came the rustling of hay as he settled down a few feet away. Still telling himself what the boy did was no concern of his, Morgan nevertheless remained awake until he heard the boy's breathing even out into the regular rhythm of sleep. Only then did he let himself drift into the light, never too deep sleep he allowed himself on the road.

Which meant, he thought as the peaceful tendrils began to numb his mind, most of his life.

Faith Brown lay in the small bedroom, staring at the open beamed roof of the cabin through eyes that were again reddened from tears. Although the snow that had begun a little past midnight had abated, the layer on the roof was thick, and left the little house very quiet. And isolated.

She'd never felt so lost, so utterly alone, so overwhelmed. She missed Hope terribly, she hadn't even gotten to say good-bye, Zachary hated her, she couldn't keep this place—small as it was—going on her own like Hope had. She was going to fail, fail herself and her little nephew, and have to retreat ignominiously in defeat.

Sleep seemed farther away than ever, and at last, as dawn began to brighten the winter night sky, she got up. She shivered as she pulled on her cotton wrapper— it had been plenty for the warm rooms above the dress-maker's shop in St. Louis, but it was decidedly lacking here in the Wyoming Territory in December. But it would do long enough to stir up the fire on the hearth, and she could stay there until she was warm enough to face dressing. In fact, she thought, she would take her dress with her, warm it by the fire, then it wouldn't be quite so awful.

She gathered up the simple gray wool dress along with her undergarments and the single petticoat she'd quickly been reduced to since coming to the wilds of the Wyoming Territory. Anything more was beyond a nuisance, she'd learned it was dangerous the day her favorite blue dress had caught fire. If it hadn't been for Zachary's curiosity about why her dress was smoking, she could have been badly hurt.

And that, she thought sadly, was probably the most the boy had spoken to her since she'd arrived here a month ago.

Carrying her clothing out to the main room of the small but sturdily built three-room house, she bent over the hearth and poked at the embers until they glowed, then added a log. Then, defiantly, she added another. The supply of wood was low, but she was determined that today she would master the knack that had eluded her so far; that of handling the big ax that had given her only blisters and very little firewood, and had twice nearly added her foot to the small kindling pile.

She would learn, she thought determinedly as the

edges of the logs flickered, then caught. She would learn how to split wood, to care for the small ranch, and she would learn to make Zachary, if not love her, at least not hate her. She would not go back to St. Louis and surrender to a lifetime of drudgery, not when she had a chance at something she could love, a chance for a place to belong.

She warmed her dress before the fire, then hastened back to her room to put it on; it would hardly be proper for Zachary to pop out of the small, curtained-off alcove beside the fireplace, where he slept, to find her in her chemise and underdrawers.

Someday, she thought in exasperation as fingers rapidly growing cold again wrestled with the interminable shoe buttons, someone would make a sturdy shoe you could just slip on, like a man's boots, and women would rejoice.

Quickly she pulled her hair back, and twisted it into a severe coil at the back of her head. No longer did she wrestle with the fashionable cascade of ringlets from the back of her head. It had done her little good even in St. Louis, where no one noticed she was alive once they'd gotten a look at Hope's vivacious blond beauty; here the elaborate style was just another nuisance she'd discarded like the extra petticoat.

When she went back into the main room and saw the curtains around Zachary's alcove still closed, she walked over and pulled the coarsely woven cloth aside just enough to peek at the small, narrow bed Zachary slept in. It was empty. A frown puckered her forehead. While the boy was usually up and outside early, it wasn't usually this early, before the sun had even fully risen.

She sighed. It was if he couldn't bear to be in the house with her. She tried to understand, the boy's entire world had changed, and she'd not seen him since he'd been a baby, so it was only natural he be somewhat untrusting. But, still, it stung. She could charm the wildest creature, even injured ones trusted her, but she couldn't get one small boy to even look her in the eye.

It was only then that she noticed the hooks that held his clothes were empty, and that the carved wooden top that was his most precious possession because it had been made by his father was gone as well. And this was no weather for spinning a top.

She grabbed her heavy cloak from a peg beside the door, tugged it on, and stepped out onto the porch. She stopped, her breath caught in her throat, as much from the vista before her as from the cold. As far as she could see, the land was coated in crystalline white, the first rays of sunlight bouncing off the new fallen snow until it hurt the eyes. In all directions the pristine blanket lay unbroken, undisturbed.

Undisturbed.

Her brows lowered. If the snow was undisturbed, if there was no sign of life except for the faint, barely discernible tracks of some small creature skittering along the surface, then where on earth was Zachary?

It struck her with the fierceness of a blow, the absence of child-size footprints in the snow that had begun at midnight, long after she had thought the boy sound asleep, and the absence of his clothes and most precious toy.

"Zachary!" she cried out. Or tried to; her voice was so hoarse with fear she doubted it carried past the edge of the small front porch.

Frightened now, she plunged into the snow and headed for the barn. The snow came up halfway to her knees, making the going difficult, but she slogged on, her gaze fastened on the barn, praying that when she got there she would find the boy safe. Surely he wouldn't run away, not now, not when she'd told him a storm was coming.

She didn't even try to open the big, heavy barn door but rather slipped through the smaller, person-size door just to the side of it, mentally breathing a thank-you to the two-years-dead Allen Phillips for having thought of it.

Her mare and the pony nickered a soft welcome; she'd moved them inside last night when she'd been certain she could smell snow coming. Hope had always believed her foretelling, even when their parents had laughed, but even they finally had to admit she was right more often than not in predicting St. Louis's occasional snows in the winter.

She saw the small shape huddled under a blanket she didn't recognize, and breathed a sigh of relief. It was Zachary; that silver-blond head was unmistakable. So he'd only come as far as this, last night. Perhaps it was just that simple, he couldn't bear to be in his mother's house with her. Faith felt the pain of rejection clutching at her; she wanted so much to help the boy, to reassure him, but she didn't know how. She'd never been around children much, and she supposed she was missing some crucial part of her that made such nurturing second nature to most females; she quite simply didn't know what to do.

He'd had a restless night, it seemed; there was hay tossed all around. And she really didn't know where he'd found that blanket; it wasn't one of the ones from the house. Maybe he—

She stopped in her tracks when she heard a snort and an unfamiliar black equine head came over the stall railing to her left. She should have been worried, should have immediately thought of what trespasser had come in with this animal, but instead all she could do was stare at the finely drawn head, the flared nostrils, and the liquid dark eyes of what was the only horse she'd seen since she'd left St. Louis that could truly match her own little mare, Espe.

"Oh, you're a beauty," she breathed, stepping closer cautiously. But it was a caution born of respect, not fear; if there was one thing in life she was certain of, it was her knack with animals.

Even with his rather shaggy winter coat, the horse gleamed in the faint light. He stretched out an inquiring nose, and Faith held out her hand for a sniff. He was clearly not fearful of a stranger, at least not here and now, and showed every sign of being well and gently treated. And the moment she realized that, her innate fear of whoever had come with the animal faded.

"Good way to lose a finger or two."

The deep, rumbling voice came from so close by, she nearly screamed; only the fear of startling the horse kept her silent. The animal's ears flicked in the direction of the voice, but he kept looking at her.

"He doesn't cotton much to strangers."

The warning came out of the darkness beneath the hayloft, behind where Zachary was sleeping, and it irritated her that he wouldn't show himself.

"And I don't cotton to trespassers," she retorted.

There was a silent moment, then, unexpectedly, a low chuckle. She peered into the shadows, only barely able to make out the shape of a man. A very large, very powerful-looking man.

"Just trying to save your hand."

"He seems perfectly friendly." To prove her point, she took a slow step closer to the horse. "Aren't you, boy? You're not about to bite me, now, are you?" She was crooning in the low, coaxing voice she used with unknown or wounded creatures. It had worked for as long as she could remember, and it worked again. The animal nudged her hand and, certain now, she gently patted the velvety muzzle. Then she slid her hand up under his jaw and rubbed at the spot between the wide bones. The horse let out a whicker of pleasure. "No, of course not, you've the look of a gentleman. And you're not hiding in the shadows, afraid to show your face, now, are you?"

"And you're not one to hide what you're thinking," the rumbling voice came again, making an observation rather than asking a question.

On the words he stepped out of the shadows. Faith's eyes widened; Lord, he was big. Not just tall, although she'd bet he topped six feet easily, but broad and strong, even more powerful-looking in the light than the shadows. His hair was coal dark, and long enough to brush his shoulders, and a jagged scar marked his left temple from hairline to just in front of his ear. His eyes, to her surprise, were light, although she couldn't tell if they were blue or gray in the rather dim light inside the barn.

Not that it mattered; more than anything else his eyes were cold and hard. Flint hard, like some of the men she'd seen come home from the war, looking as if all gentle feeling had been burned out of them. And she suddenly reassessed her dismissal of her fear; it was possible, she supposed, for someone to be kind to his horse while he slaughtered people by the dozen.

"You have a knack," he said, gesturing at the horse. There was nothing of admiration in his voice; he spoke as unemotionally as if he were observing that the snow had stopped.

"Yes," she said, uncertain of what else to say. "I always have had."

He studied her silently, for so long that she felt a nearly overwhelming urge to look away. But in the same way she sensed that the horse wouldn't hurt her, she knew that to betray fear to this man would be foolish. He was the kind who would not miss such a revealing slip. What he would do with the knowledge was something she couldn't guess at. But she didn't wish to find out in an unpleasant way.

"I'll pay for the night I spent here," he said abruptly.

Under his steady gaze it took her a moment to realize he was referring to her calling him a trespasser.

"That's . . . not necessary. I'd not begrudge anyone shelter on a night like last night."

He lifted a dark brow, but it didn't seem a questioning gesture rather than one of affirmation, as if he'd had something he'd already thought confirmed.

"Thank you . . . Faith."

She stared at him. The simple sound of her name in that rumbling voice seemed to paralyze her. It was a moment before she was able to think enough to wonder how he had—

"Zachary," she said suddenly, realizing he must have talked to the boy, and learned her name.

He nodded. "I didn't know what went with the 'Miss,' or I'd have been more . . . polite."

"Brown. I'm Faith Brown."

"Miss Brown," he amended, and inside her a tiny voice bemoaned the loss of the way he'd said "Faith" in that deep, rough voice.

"No sense in going backward," she said, not quite believing she was saying it. "Faith will do."

He looked at her again for a long silent moment, as if he were puzzled about something. Then he glanced over his shoulder, to where Zachary was stirring, perhaps roused at last by the mention of his name. The boy sat up, rubbed at his eyes, looked around in some bewilderment, as if he couldn't recall how he had come to be here Then his gaze fell upon Faith and the stranger, and his eyes rounded to half-dollar size. He scrambled to his feet, bits of hay clinging to him, and to the blanket he let slip away from his small shoulders.

"Zachary," she began, but before she could get out another word, he backed away. He picked up a bundle that she saw was made up of all the things missing from his little space.

"I was leavin'," he said. "I'da been gone, 'cept he"— he nodded toward the big man—"told me not to go while it was still snowin'."

This confirmation of what she'd guessed gave her another heart-deep pang. She had no idea what to say to the boy, so instead she looked at the man.

"In that case, I suppose I must thank you."

"Common sense," the man said with a shrug that could have meant anything from "you're welcome" to a disavowal of any concern over the boy's welfare.

"Which children sometimes lack," she insisted. "So thank you, Mr. . . . ?"

"Just . . . call me Morgan."

Had he hesitated, or was it her imagination? A dozen reasons, none of them very pleasant, as to why he might be undecided about giving her his name came to her, but she wasn't certain enough to press the issue. Nor

was she sure she would even if she was certain; he had
the look of a man it was wiser not to question.

She glanced at Zachary, who was staring up at the
big man with more than a touch of awe in his face. She
could see why; not only was it his size, but in the black
pants, shirt, and coat, with a Winchester rifle balanced
easily in his right hand, he was an intimidating figure.

"I'm . . . glad you didn't leave," she said to the boy,
haltingly.

"Sure," Zachary muttered, clearly not believing her.

Faith sighed. She wished she knew what she'd done
to make the boy dislike her so. He was already looking
at the stranger with more feeling than he'd ever given
her. Was it simply because he was a man? Or was it
that anyone, even a stranger, was better than her?

She shivered. Whether it was because of her nephew's
continued coldness, the chilly temperature even here in
the barn, or some stab of foreboding brought on by the
man before her, she didn't know. She suppressed the
urge to run. *Where will you run to?* she chided herself.
*All the way back to St. Louis? There's nothing for you
there.*

And before she realized the words had formed in her
mind, she was saying them. "I was about to put coffee
on. Could I . . . offer you a cup?"

The man called Morgan looked startled, then thoughtful.

"Yes, stay," Zachary said excitedly. His gaze flicked
to Faith, and for the first time had a tinge of warmth in
them. She knew it wasn't for her, but it was nice to see
anyway.

"I thought you were lighting out," Morgan said to
the boy, again without emotion, as if it meant nothing.

"I was," the boy said. "But I'll stay if you do. For
now," he added with another quick glance at Faith.

"Don't worry," she said wryly, "I won't assume you've changed your mind about me."

To his credit the boy colored slightly. But he looked at Morgan eagerly. "Will you stay?"

Morgan turned that cool, assessing gaze back on her. "I'd be obliged for a cup of fresh coffee . . . Faith.

She nearly shivered again, but it had nothing to do with cold this time, and everything to do with the sound of her name in that low, rough, rumbling voice.

"All right," she said, striving to keep her own voice from shaking. "Come on to the house."

She darted out of the barn without waiting for an answer.

Well, now, Morgan thought as he watched her scamper away. *So that was old, weepy, spinster Aunt Faith.*

The spinster was fact, he guessed; she had the look and the nervousness of a woman not used to being around a man. And true, she was perhaps not a girl any longer, but if she was old, he wasn't at all sure what that made him; he had to have a few years on her. And he believed the crying part; her eyes were swollen, her nose reddened.

But it was a cute nose. Little and tilted slightly upward. And even the puffiness of eyes that had probably spent the night weeping couldn't disguise the warm, cinnamon color of them. He wondered if her hair, when—if, he amended silently—she took it down, had the same cinnamon tones.

His mind shied away from that image, just as curiosity about just how long her hair might be struck him. He purposely thought instead that she'd covered her nervousness well, with quick retorts that had made him grin inwardly, and even chuckle out loud a couple of times. Maybe it was that sassy mouth that had resulted in spinsterhood; it would take a brave man to take on a woman with a wit that lively. Although the female shape beneath the plain dress might make one think it worth the price, if one were of a mind to settle down. Fortunately he'd never been of that mind in his life, and wasn't going to begin now.

"Are you comin'?"

The boy's question was urgent, as if he were afraid Morgan would change his mind. "I'll be along," he said. "Why don't you go on ahead and help."

The boy looked taken aback. "Help? I can't make coffee."

"I reckon you could stoke the cooking fire or some such."

Zach grimaced. "With what? We're 'most out of firewood, and she can't chop worth a row of beans. About cut off her own foot the other day."

The scorn in the boy's voice was plain, and Morgan felt an unwanted pang of sympathy for the apparently beleaguered Faith Brown. "So you're better at chopping, I suppose."

The boy shook his head, and Morgan guessed the point had been beyond the child. "Mama wouldn't let me handle an ax. She said I had to be tall as her rocker 'fore I could do it."

"So she chopped the wood, then, after your father died?"

Zach looked startled. "Mama? 'Course not. She had a man in to do it, Mr. Talley from town, usually, he'd do it if she fed him. Lots of the menfolk from town would help with chores and fixin' things for that. She was a real good cook. Not like my aunt," he finished with that same note of scorn.

"So it was okay that your mama couldn't chop wood, or do other hard work, but not your aunt," Morgan said musingly, wondering why he was bothering to try to point out the unfairness of his view to a child who probably couldn't comprehend it anyway. But to his surprise, Zach looked a bit chagrined. He pressed the advantage, still not sure why.

"What *can* she do?" he asked.

The pale blond brows furrowed. "I dunno. She sews some, I guess. Mama said that's what she did back in St. Louis."

He said the town's name as if it were as foreign as France or China, and Morgan bit back a smile. But then what the boy had said registered. She'd had on a plain, simply cut gray dress, the only other color on it a touch of some white frilly stuff at the neck, but it had fit her like a glove, and set him to wondering if he really could span her waist with his hands.

If she'd made that dress, she did more than "sew some"; that dress had had none of the potato-sack–like fit he associated with most clothing sewn by the wearer. When she'd reached up to pat his horse's nose, he'd been able to picture exactly what she would look like beneath the gray wool, and he'd been a little startled when he'd realized just how modest the dress actually was, revealing nothing compared to the fashions he'd seen in Denver and San Francisco.

"And," he said thoughtfully, remembering, "she charms horses."

"I guess," the boy said. "Mama always said she had a way with them, when they used to ride together back in St. Louis, when they were little. That's why she gave her that mare."

The boy pointed toward the far end of the barn,

where a horse and a pony he assumed was the child's occupied the end box stalls. He'd purposely kept his own animal here at this end in a straight stall, away from the other two; the stallion was very well mannered, but no sense in taking chances, although the little sorrel mare had clearly not been in season. He'd liked the trim lines and intelligent look of the flaxen-maned mare, and she looked fit and strong.

"She wants to raise horses, like my pa did. She cares more about that mare than anything else," the boy added morosely.

"Including you?" Morgan guessed.

The boy shrugged, but his answer was eloquent in the slump of his skinny shoulders.

"Let's go," Morgan said suddenly. He'd had enough of chin-wagging with this boy. And he felt suddenly in genuine need of that promised cup of coffee. No matter how bad a cook she was, it couldn't be any worse than what he'd brewed on the trail, using grounds that had been leeched of all their taste a hundred or so miles back.

He gave his horse, the animal who had nearly made a meal of more than one set of unwary fingers in the past three years, a curious, sideways glance as he passed.

He had a feeling there was much more to old, weepy, spinster Aunt Faith than there appeared.

"What's your horse's name?"

Faith knew it was a silly question, but she felt like she had to say something. Just listening to Zachary's excited chatter was painful; he hadn't said more than a sentence or two in a row to her in the entire month she'd been here, but he talked to Morgan as if they were old friends. It wasn't that Morgan hadn't led a fascinating life—he'd been to so many places she'd

only heard of, seen so many amazing things—but the
boy's garrulousness made her all the more aware of
how miserably she was failing at carrying out her last
promise to her sister.

"He doesn't have a name," Morgan said.

"Why?" she asked as she watched him finish the last
of the biscuits and gravy she'd fixed for breakfast; she
hadn't been hungry herself, and Zachary usually just
picked anyway, but it seemed only polite to offer a plate
to Morgan, and he'd accepted it graciously enough,
thanking her. And he'd eaten most of it, with no comments of the kind she'd come to expect from Zachary;
the boy made it clear that no food that wasn't prepared
by his mother could possibly be edible.

"Horse doesn't need a name."

"But what do you call him?"

He shrugged. "Horse."

Zachary snorted. "Better'n some silly name like
Espe."

Faith blushed. "Among many other things, Zachary
doesn't care for my mare's name."

"Espe?"

"Yes." She went on hesitantly. "It's . . . Latin."

Morgan lifted a dark brow at her. "You speak Latin?"

"Oh, no," she said hastily. "but Dr. Ward, in Granite,
does. He helped me pick the name."

"Dumb name for a horse," Zachary put in again.

Morgan ignored the boy and asked her, "What does
it mean?"

"Hope. I named her for my sister."

Zachary's head came up sharply. Morgan shifted his
gaze to the boy. "Still think it's a silly name?"

The boy flushed. "I . . . "

"A man should always be sure he knows the whole

story before he goes passing judgment on folks," Morgan said mildly.

Zachary ducked his head, his excitement at their guest quenched for the moment by his embarrassment.

"I saw your mare in the barn," Morgan said, lifting his cup to his lips for another sip. "She's a good one."

Faith's enthusiasm bubbled up, making her forget her troubles for the moment. "She's smart and strong and quick. I've been training her, and even though it's only been a few weeks, she's learning quickly. She's a wonderful horse. She's the last of Parson's get." At his look she added, "My sister's husband bought him from a reverend. They raised horses to sell, until . . . "

"Parson was the horse that killed my pa," Zachary said.

Faith turned on the boy. "That's not true, Zachary Phillips."

"Is, too."

"It is not. You were barely four, you can't remember."

"Mama told me—"

"That innocent animal did not kill your father. It was an accident, and if anything Parson died trying to save him, crossing that river. I know your mother never told you such a tale, and I will not have you saying such things now that she's gone."

Zachary stared at her, his eyes wide. He scrambled to his feet. "You don't know anything about my mother! You say she's dead, but I know she isn't, she comes to see me, in the night. You're lying, and I hate you!" he yelled, then turned and darted out of the house.

Her heart sinking, Faith rose to her feet.

"I'd let him be," Morgan suggested, in that same unemotional tone.

"But if he runs away again—"

"Won't." Morgan nudged the bundle that sat on the floor by the boy's now empty chair, the bundle of all his belongings.

"Oh." She sat down again, letting out a long breath.

"Interesting," Morgan observed.

"What is?" she asked, still staring at the door Zachary had slammed behind him.

"You'll let him say blame near anything about you, but you get all in a pucker when he talks bad about a horse."

"That's different," she said, a little lamely.

"Mmm."

Whatever *that* meant, Faith thought. She dragged her gaze from the closed door; obviously the boy would be gone for a while. She hoped not long; it was sunny, and the snow was already beginning to melt, but winter was here and the weather could turn crazy at any time, with little warning. It was the nature of life here on the high plains at the foot of the towering Rockies.

"He told me he didn't know where his mother was."

Faith flinched, and felt the sudden sting of moisture behind her eyelids. "She died five weeks ago. Some kind of fever. I came as soon as she sent for me, but . . . it was too late. She went so quickly . . . " She wiped at her eyes. "Zachary hasn't accepted it yet. Keeps waiting for her to come back."

"His father didn't."

Morgan's voice was cool, detached, and Faith couldn't help thinking his words rather cruel. But for some reason it helped Faith regain control and blink back the tears that were threatening yet again. As she did, she wondered if he ever let down his guard.

"He saw his father," she was able to explain after a moment. "They brought his body home when they found it. When Hope took ill, Zachary went to stay with the schoolteacher, so he wouldn't catch the fever. He never saw her again." She hesitated, then gestured toward the small window at the front of the house. "I didn't realize what he was thinking until he got upset when I tried to move that lamp there in the window. Said his mother would never find her way home without the light. It was what she used to do when his father was gone, put the lamp there, to guide him home." She gave a helpless shrug. "I think he doesn't believe it was really her in the box they buried."

"Especially if he sees her at night."

"I dream about her, too," Faith said quietly. "A lot. Hope was . . . beautiful, and sweet, and kind, and good. Our parents hated it when Allen took her out here, into this wilderness they called it. They kept begging her to come home, up until they were killed in a steamboat explosion five years ago." She sighed. "I'm almost glad they . . . weren't here to know she died so young. She was the most precious thing in the world to them."

"But they still had you."

Faith grimaced. "You don't understand. Hope was the special one, the beautiful one, everyone loved her."

"I see."

She glanced at him, and her breath caught at the suddenly piercing steadiness of his gaze. He was looking at her as if he did indeed see, including what she'd not told him, that sometimes, despite her tremendous love for her sister, she'd ached inside for wishing she could be more like her, for wishing she wasn't her plain, ordinary self. She went on hastily, before she betrayed any more.

"I asked her again to come home after Allen was killed, but she insisted on staying, on keeping this place so that Zachary could have his inheritance from his father."

"And instead you ended up here."

"I know it sounds . . . crazy, but she loved it here so much, the way she wrote about it made it sound so beautiful and open and free . . . I wanted to come. It seemed a place to belong, and that's all I've ever wanted." Heavens, she sounded like some whining, self-pitying old maid for sure, Faith thought, and quickly changed the subject. "I hope Zachary doesn't go too far. It could be dangerous."

He nodded. "This is a mite different than St. Louis."

She blinked and drew back. St. Louis? How had he known St. Louis was home? For an instant she wondered just how much those eyes—they were a rich blue-gray, she'd noticed when he'd come into the house—really saw. Then she realized where he must have gotten the information; the same place he'd learned her name.

"You and Zachary seem to have talked of a lot of things."

"He mentioned you used to sew there."

Her chin went up; she was used to the disparaging opinions of those who made it clear what they thought of females who had to earn a living because no man had found their other meager skills enough to overlook their plain appearance.

"I was a seamstress there," she said rather defiantly. "A good one."

"I know."

She blinked again. "What?"

He nodded his head toward her. "Your dress."

She knew she was gaping at him, but the thought of a man who rode in out of nowhere looking dark and

deadly dangerous, noticing the details of a woman's
dress astonished her.

She thought she saw his lips twitch, as if he were suppressing a smile, although she found it hard to believe.
Any lightness of spirit seemed foreign to him, and if she
hadn't known that it had to be him she'd heard chuckling
in the barn, she wouldn't have believed it.

"I knew a woman once who spent more time and
money on dresses than she did anything else," he said.
"And her fanciest Paris gown didn't fit like that."

Faith felt herself blush, although she wasn't sure
exactly what it was she was blushing about. He hadn't
said anything untoward, not really. And then the heat
faded from her cheeks as she found herself wondering
just who that woman was.

"Your . . . wife?" She hazarded the guess tentatively,
wondering why her heart was starting to pound as she
awaited the answer.

Morgan snorted. "I'm not fool enough to marry a
woman like that. She was my . . . aunt."

That pause before he spoke that last word made her
wonder what he was thinking, whether it had been
meant for her, Zachary's aunt, in particular in a way she
didn't understand. She looked at his impassive face,
thinking it doubtful that anyone, man or woman, ever
truly knew what this man was thinking. He changed the
subject rather abruptly, so abruptly she got the feeling
he would rather have just walked out, and probably
would have had she not just fed him.

"The boy said you wanted to raise horses, too."

"I wanted to. I love them, and I'm good with them."
Faith sighed. "But it was just a . . . silly dream." Her
mouth twisted. "I don't know whatever made me think
I could run this place. I can't even get one small boy to

speak to me. Everything I do is wrong, the way I dress, the way I talk, even the food I fix, because it's not like his mother's. He hates me because I'm not her."

Morgan looked thoughtful for a moment, then said, "He thinks you hate him."

Faith gasped. "What?"

"Says you pray at night for him to go away."

"I never," she exclaimed. "I only . . . " Her voice trailed off, and she put a hand to her mouth. When she went on, it was in a barely audible whisper. "I only said . . . I prayed, asking for help, telling God I . . . couldn't do this. I never meant . . . how could he think I meant that?"

"Zach's just . . . confused right now. It's tough, getting used to being an orphan so young."

Something about the way he said it, some faint bit of emotion that marred the utter detachment she'd almost grown used to, made her ask softly, "How old were you?"

"Younger than Zach. I don't remember them at all," he said, then his eyes narrowed, as if he hadn't meant to answer at all.

"Both your parents? Together?"

"Yes." He stood up abruptly. The conversation was clearly at an end. His part of it, anyway. "Thanks for the coffee. And breakfast. It was good."

"You're welcome."

Before she could say another word, he was gone.

His horse looked at him curiously. And Morgan couldn't blame the animal; he'd put the saddle blanket on and taken it back off again twice now. The dark head had come around, the alert ears swiveled toward him, as if awaiting some kind of explanation of this odd behavior.

"I wish the hell I knew," he muttered.

He should be riding out of here right now. Hell, he should be already gone. Long gone. The snow had stopped for now. But there was more coming, he could feel it, and if he didn't get out of here now, he could well end up stuck here for longer than he wanted to think about.

Of course, another ten minutes was longer than he wanted to think about. Determinedly he reached for the blanket again.

Hope was . . . beautiful, and sweet, and kind, and good. Hope was the special one, everyone loved her.

Faith's words echoed in his head again. And again he tried to quash them. What did he care about the hurt feelings of a girl he'd never known, a girl who had clearly lived in the shadow of a prettier, doted-upon sister? He didn't give a damn about anybody's hurt feelings, and had more than once observed that it was better to do as he did, and make sure you had no feelings to be hurt. It was a lesson he'd learned early and well.

"She's not dead. She's not."

Morgan's hand was halfway to his rifle before he recognized the small, insistent voice that came from above him. Damn, he hadn't even heard or sensed the boy in the loft practically over his head. "Keep this up, and you'll be bucking out real soon, and they'll bury you under a board that says you got snuck up on," he muttered to himself.

"I've seen her, 'most every night."

Morgan slowly picked up the blanket he'd dropped

when the boy had startled him into going for his Winchester before he said, "But not in the daylight."

Silence met his words. He put the blanket back once more, settling it carefully over the stallion's withers and sliding it back so there was no twisting of winter coat that might irritate the already spirited animal.

He kept his voice toneless. "Most folks would call that a dream."

"No, it's real, I see her!"

Morgan heard a scraping sound as the boy scooted toward the makeshift ladder of cross pieces nailed to one of the support beams of the loft. Zach came down rapidly, skipping the last three rungs in a sort of scrambling jump. The boy froze when the stallion snorted and danced sideways. Morgan calmed him with a quiet word and a pat; the animal was well mannered, as stallions go, but he wasn't used to children. The horse eyed Zach warily as he let Morgan nudge him back in position. The saddle blanket slid from his back, landing with a faint plop. The horse stretched out to nose the blanket as if suspecting it of having taken on a life of its own. Morgan stared at it, wondering if there was some kind of message for him here.

"I didn't mean to scare him," Zach said, eyeing the horse, "but it's true. I see her."

Morgan stifled a sigh. He'd been right to stay away from kids. Dealing with them was too complicated. And too painful.

"And I suppose she explains where she is," he said dryly.

"No," the boy said. "She doesn't 'xactly talk to me. She's just . . . there. She smiles at me, like she always does when she comes to check on me, to make sure I'm all right."

A sudden memory of a slender, sweet-smelling woman with dark hair and laughing eyes, bent over him and kissing him good night, flashed through Morgan's mind. He nearly flinched; he hadn't thought of her in so long he'd thought the images permanently vanished from his mind. How could he blame this child for hanging on to a much fresher memory, when this one from his earliest days was still with him after nearly thirty years?

"Aunt Faith says I see her because I'm wishing so hard that she'll come back. But she's there, I know she is. I can even smell that sweet stuff she used in her hair when she washed it. I'm not lying, really."

Morgan dragged in a breath. "You're sure it's not your aunt, checking on you? Her hair . . . smells like flowers."

Lilacs, he thought, amazed that he could even recognize the scent. But he did. And the fact that his mother had rinsed her hair with the same scent was a fact he'd forgotten until now. This was why the fragrance had seemed familiar when Faith had been close enough to him for him to catch a faint whiff of it.

"Nah, it ain't her. She's not pretty, and nice, like Mama."

"She was nice enough to come here to take care of you." Morgan wasn't sure why he was defending her; maybe because, unlike his own stiff-necked, self-centered aunt, Faith at least cared about the boy. Whether he believed it or not.

"Only because she had to," Zach insisted. "But she can't take Mama's place," he ended fiercely.

"I didn't notice she was trying to," Morgan said. "But she cares about you, boy. If she didn't, she wouldn't have come."

"But Mama asked her to."

Clearly the idea of anyone saying no to his beloved mother was more than the boy could believe.

Hope was the special one, everyone loved her.

Suddenly weary of it all, Morgan reached for the saddle blanket one last time.

"Are you leavin'?"

"I am."

"Oh." The boy gave him a sideways look. "You could stay. Have supper with us."

Morgan's mouth quirked. "I thought your aunt couldn't cook."

The boy lowered his gaze. "Well . . . maybe she's not so bad."

"She just doesn't cook like your mother."

"She doesn't even try."

"Well, now," Morgan said, "you'd think if she was really trying to take your mother's place, she'd at least try."

Zach looked startled. Morgan said nothing, just letting the boy think about it. He brushed some straw off the saddle blanket before putting it back on the stallion's back.

"She calls me Zachary all the time."

A hanging offense for sure, Morgan thought, stifling a grin. "I thought that was your name."

"I like Zach better."

"And when you told her this, she said she liked Zachary better?"

The boy had the grace to look a bit chagrined. "I . . . never told her."

"Mmm. Doesn't seem quite fair to feel mad at somebody for something they don't know you don't like."

"Maybe," Zach admitted grudgingly. He walked over

to Morgan's saddle, inspecting it with the curiosity of a child. "How come you only carry a rifle?"

"It's enough. Don't need a belt gun."

"But most folks wear one."

"I don't. They only make you a target."

The boy seemed to accept it, a good thing since he wasn't about to explain any further. Then, as he once more put the blanket on the by now disgruntled horse's back the boy said hopefully, "It might snow some more tonight. You should stay."

"Smells like it's a day or so off."

Zach looked even more startled. "That's what Aunt Faith said. I thought smelling snow was silly."

Did she, now? Morgan thought. Maybe she wasn't quite as unfit for this life as she seemed to think. If she was in harmony with the land enough to sense the weather, and she could charm all horses the way she'd charmed this one . . . well, others had started with less and made it.

But more had died in high plains winters.

It had been an easy season, so far. If it hadn't been, he never would have left the Washington Territory. He still wasn't sure why he had, except that he never stayed too long in one place, and the time he'd been wandering around out there was more than he usually gave any one place. Even the five years he'd spent working cattle drives had been years spent in motion, along the Sedalia Trail, the Chisholm Trail. At forty dollars a month, he hadn't had much to show for it but a distaste for working twenty hours a day and a desire never to eat hot trail dust behind a moving herd again. So here he was, in the Wyoming Territory, looking to head out before more snow flew.

He wondered if Faith Brown had any idea what she was in for when winter truly set in.

Faith heard the sound for several seconds before she realized what it was. Of course, she might have recognized it sooner had she not been so lost in silly daydreams. And had she heard it anytime recently, the rhythmic, efficient sound of an ax in the hands of someone who knew how to use it.

She caught herself running toward the window and made herself slow. She was twenty-seven years old, after all, and should be far beyond such silliness as daydreaming of things that could never be, beyond running to a window in hopes of seeing a dark, dangerous man who was only passing through anyway.

But she did go to the window, and she did peer out toward the woodpile. And he was there, amid the snow, his long, lean body moving with a grace she couldn't help but admire as he so easily wielded the ax she found so difficult to handle. He'd shed his heavy coat, so she could see the muscles in his back and shoulders and arms flex and stretch as he swung the heavy splitting ax again and again. It seemed to take him only moments to reduce the already cut wood into stove wood, and pieces that would fit the fireplace.

She moved slightly, so that she couldn't be seen should he happen to glance up. She watched as he turned to the biggest log, some kind of pine, she thought, vaguely remembering Hope writing something about Allen spending days on end dragging deadfalls down from the higher country. Morgan studied the small gash, which was all she'd managed to inflict on the downed beast. She could imagine what he was thinking, what a fool she was to even think she could survive in a place like this, a woman alone, and a woman without the skills necessary for life here. Maybe she should just give up, take Zachary, and go back to St. Louis. She had little money left, especially if she had to hire things done that she was too stupid or weak to do herself. There was enough to perhaps get them through one more winter, but after that she would have to be making some, and that seemed unlikely. She could get her old job back with Mrs. Lane, she knew that, and even though it would be cramped in her old rooms with another person there, Zachary could have the small sitting area for a room of his own, which was more than he had now, and she—

Morgan swung the ax, and she stopped her own thoughts, determined not to think about really giving up. Hope had wanted more than anything for Zachary to have this small legacy from his father, and this place was the only home the boy had ever known.

The solid thunk as the ax blade bit deep reverberated in the still air. Again and again it came, and Faith watched with fascination. She told herself it was because she was curious about how different this motion was than when he had been cutting the smaller pieces, how he was now putting the full power of his strong body into each stroke. She told herself it was not because she simply wanted to look at him, wanted to be able to stare without him knowing, without him thinking she was a foolish old spinster, hungry for the sight of a man. And apparently she was just that, she thought sadly. Although it was odd, she'd never felt compelled to stare at any of the men she saw in St. Louis.

She didn't know how long she'd been standing there, engrossed in the easy movements, in the subtle power of him, she only knew that he was nearly through the big log in what seemed like a very short time. Then she stifled a tiny scream as he suddenly stopped, turned his head, and stared at the house as if he were perfectly aware that she'd been watching all this time.

She jerked away from the window. She was trembling. She stared at her hands, seeing the quivering. It was because she'd been caught, she told herself. Not that he really could have seen her, she'd been careful, but he'd seemed to know anyway, the knowledge had seemed clear in his eyes, even from here.

She fought the urge to draw back into some shadowy corner of the house and hide until he was gone. Gone from the woodpile, gone from the ranch, gone from her world. Her small, narrow world. But on the day she had resigned herself to her life, to never having the husband and family she'd once longed for, she'd sworn she would get something from life in return; she would no longer be afraid to do or say whatever she wanted.

Of course, she'd managed a lot more saying than doing, she admitted reluctantly. She'd had grand plans. She was going to keep her promise to her sister, she was going to make sure Zachary kept what Hope had wanted him to have, and she was going to make a home for herself and her nephew together. A family, as much a one as she would ever have. She'd come here with every intention of accomplishing all those things. And she was no closer to doing so than if she'd just stayed in St. Louis. Farther from it, probably; if she'd sent for Zachary, at least she would have been in familiar territory, not in a place where she couldn't do something as simple as chop wood.

As she thought it, the steady blows of the ax began anew. She couldn't stop herself from looking once more, at the striking tableau of dark man and white snow. It struck her then, what the simple act of chopping wood meant here. It meant survival, through a kind of winter she knew she'd never seen before. Morgan was giving them a gift it would have taken her weeks to match. And here she was, hiding, watching him secretly, with a kind of interest that would have embarrassed him had he known, and most likely should be embarrassing her. But she couldn't find it within herself to feel that way. It wasn't as if she were . . . expecting anything, she was too old and settled in her spinster ways for that, but she could look couldn't she? Look at and appreciate a fine figure of a man?

And she could thank him. Should thank him.

Quickly, before she could cravenly change her mind, she grabbed her cloak and stepped outside. She arrived at the woodpile just as a final blow separated a large piece from the rest of the long trunk. She saw Zachary sitting atop the far end of the log. The boy watched her, with an intentness she found rather disconcerting; it was as if he'd never seen her before.

Morgan upended the shorter piece he'd just cut, then straightened to look at her silently.

"I . . . we thank you," she said. "You didn't have to do this."

"You gave me shelter in a storm, and you fed me this morning," he said with a shrug.

She refrained from pointing out that she hadn't offered him shelter, he'd simply taken it. "I don't think biscuits and gravy count as a meal worth this kind of labor."

"I didn't have to fix it myself, and that's worth a lot. And it was good." Then, with a sideways glance at Zachary, he added, "Wasn't it, boy?"

Zachary's dark brown eyes darted from Morgan to

Faith. Then he lowered his gaze to pick at the bark of the log. "Yeah. I guess so."

"Guess your Mama didn't get around to teaching you manners, and to be thankful," Morgan said mildly.

"She did so!" Zachary's head came up sharply as he spoke, as quickly as a protest rose to Faith's lips. But Morgan gave her a quick, hard glance that quieted her, and after a moment, to her surprise, Zachary said, albeit rather sullenly, "Okay, it was good. I liked the gravy."

Faith stared at the boy. It was the first positive thing he'd said since she'd come here. She looked at Morgan. His expression was unreadable. Her gaze returned to the boy's bent head, his blond hair so much like Hope's, silky and shiny. Tenderness flooded her at the sight of this last tiny bit of her sister that still lived, and she hated herself for having grown into looking upon him as an adversary.

"Thank you very much, Zachary," she said softly.

The boy's head came up again. His eyes once more flicked to Morgan, then back to her. "I don't like bein' called that. I like Zach."

"Oh. I'm sorry, I didn't know."

"That's what he told me," the boy said, nodding toward Morgan. "Said I shouldn't get mad if'n you didn't know I didn't like it."

Startled, Faith stared at Morgan. His face was still impassive, that unreadable expression never wavering. She turned back to her nephew.

"I'll try to remember . . . Zach. But you may have to remind me a few times, until I get the knack."

"Okay."

It was a small truce, brought about by a source

she never would have expected, but it made hope soar within her.

"Maybe you could show your thanks by toting some of that wood inside," Morgan said. As usual, it was spoken in the tone of suggestion, not command, as if it mattered little to him if the boy did as he said. As perhaps it did, Faith thought, fearful she was reading too much into Morgan's continued presence, and his obvious effort to snap Zachary—Zach, she reminded herself—out of his sullenness.

The boy hesitated, clearly not certain he wanted to go quite that far with his acquiescence.

"More snow coming," Morgan observed, lifting his head as if to sniff the air. "A warm fire'd be a welcome thing."

Zach's eyes widened. "Then, you're stayin'?"

For a split second, Morgan looked startled, and that in itself so surprised Faith that she spoke before the man could give the boy the negative answer she'd read in that brief, unguarded moment.

"You're more than welcome," she said, drawing his steady gaze to her. "For supper at least. We owe you another meal, a real one, for all this work."

She saw him start to shake his head. Zach apparently saw it, too, for he chimed in swiftly. "Please? Then you could show me that kind of snare you were talkin' about, to catch rabbits."

Morgan never looked at the boy, he simply stared at her, those blue-gray eyes searching her face, her eyes, as if he could see clear to her soul.

"A woman alone should be careful about who she invites to supper," he said at last.

"Yes," she agreed, holding his gaze levelly. And for an instant saw that surprise flicker in his eyes once more. And then, to her shock, he lowered his eyes as if he could no longer meet her gaze. But he nodded in acceptance of the invitation, and Faith's heart gave an odd little leap in her chest.

"I'll finish this up." His voice sounded oddly husky.

"And I'll take the wood in," Zach said, as if a moment ago it hadn't been a chore he'd been none too happy about.

A few hours later, Faith set a big pot of savory stew on the table. She'd used up far too many of the precious stores she'd purchased in Granite two weeks ago, but it somehow seemed important. And proper; Morgan had worked hard all afternoon, rarely stopping even for a breather, there was nothing left of the big log and even the smaller pieces were trimmed and cut. Even Zach had been helpful, stacking the wood against the house until the pile got too high for him to reach. Then Faith herself had stepped in, stacking as the boy ran back and forth with as much of the wood as he could manage, trying to keep up with Morgan's killing pace.

"If you're careful," he'd said, "it'll hold you until spring."

"We can't begin to thank you," she said now as she served up the stew with thick slices of the bread she'd baked yesterday.

He indicated the steaming bowl she set before him. "This is thanks enough."

He took a bite of bread, and a spoonful of stew. Faith held her breath; she'd never thought much about cooking, thinking herself average at it, until Zachary— Zach—had kept telling her she wasn't as good as his mother.

"And good," he added, and she breathed again.

"You must be starved, after all that work. Eat up."

He nodded, and for a while the only sound was of good food being consumed.

"Where'd you come from?" Zach asked Morgan when he'd slowed down his gobbling. Faith supposed she should hush him, it was not a question that was asked here in the West, she'd soon learned. Hope had written her that people didn't much care where you were from or if your family was important; they only cared about who you were now. It had been, she supposed, another reason she'd wanted to come here instead of sending for Zach to come to her.

Besides, she was immensely curious to hear the answer herself.

"Came here from Washington Territory," Morgan said, and Faith didn't miss the slight evasion.

"I don't know where that is," Zach said frankly.

"Northwest of here."

"Oh. How'd you get there?"

"Rode."

"Your black horse?"

"No. A cow pony I picked up down in Texas, when I was working the cattle drives."

"Oh. Was he a good horse?"

Morgan nodded. "Not quite as good as the black, though. He's the best horseflesh I've straddled since the Pony Express."

"You rode with the Pony Express?" Faith asked.

"For a few months, part of the Nevada run."

"But that was . . . so long ago," Faith said. "The telegraph's been up for over fifteen years. You couldn't have been more than a boy."

"Sixteen," he admitted.

"And they let you ride? Wasn't it dangerous?"

"That's why they preferred orphans."

"Why'd you stop?" Zach asked, clearly intrigued.

Morgan's mouth twisted. "I grew."

Zach blinked. "Huh?"

"Nearly six inches over the winter of sixty-one. I just got too darned big."

Faith stared at him as Zach chattered on, asking question after question about where the fascinating visitor had been. And it seemed he'd been everywhere, from Denver to California and most points in between. But Faith wasn't really listening, she was trying to picture him as a boy, as anything other than the man he was now.

Not too darned big she thought, *but just right. Just about perfect, in fact.*

She felt her cheeks heat at her wayward thoughts, and bent her head over her cup of coffee to hide it. She'd nearly recovered her poise when Zach innocently shattered it again.

"You're not gonna sleep in the barn again, are you?" he asked Morgan. "It's a lot warmer here in the house. You should stay in here."

Faith's breath stopped in her throat. Morgan paused in his chewing of another slice of bread. After a moment he resumed, then swallowed.

"Hadn't heard I was staying at all," he said.

Zach looked crestfallen. "But I thought . . . " The boy's voice trailed away.

"Now, Zach, I'm sure he has more important things to do than . . . " Her own words trailed away as Morgan looked at her, an oddly intent expression on his usually unreadable face.

"Some things," he said, "need an invitation."

Faith blushed. "Oh! But ... of course you're welcome to stay. It's the least we can do."

"Lot of protection in that word," he said in that detached, observing tone she was coming to know all too well.

"What word?" she asked, feeling a touch of irritation.

"We," he said, glancing at Zach for a moment before turning back to her. "You don't need it. Not from me."

Faith drew back slightly, stung, but struggling not to show it. While she knew there were men who preyed on women in vicious and filthy ways, she doubted very much that Morgan was one of them, so she knew he was mocking her. He had to be; no one could think she needed the kind of protection he was referring to, the kind that made it hazardous for a woman to be alone with a man. She was hardly the type to incite a man to uncontrollable urges.

"I get your meaning," she said tightly, "there's no need to ridicule me."

His brows lowered. "You may have gotten my meaning, but I think you misread my intent. I only meant you're safe, Faith."

"Of course I am," she said, her voice still sharp.

He looked at her closely then, studying her with that intentness she found so unsettling. "It's never good to assume too much," he said quietly.

It was beyond bearing. She gathered up her scattered pride and lifted her chin as she said coolly, "I know what I am, and what I am not. I know most pity women like me, but I want none of that. Not from anyone, and especially not from you."

"Whatever I feel for you, Faith Brown," Morgan said, "it's surely not pity."

* * *

His own words haunted him that night as he lay down on the pallet she'd fixed for him on the floor near the fire. What in Hades *did* he feel for Faith Brown?

Concern, he supposed. It was natural that a man worry about a respectable woman alone in still wild country. True, she was fairly close to town, such as it was, but she was still alone out here on this place, and some no-account could stumble upon her at any time and she'd be trapped and helpless, her and the boy.

And maybe he felt a little empathy. He knew what it was like to have a dream, but not the means or knowledge to carry it out, or to have life take that dream away, through no fault of your own. And he supposed, in her way, Faith felt as much an outcast as he always had. He'd never considered what happened to women who never married; if he thought of it at all, it was to picture them as bitter old maiden aunts like his own, or schoolmarms who were happy enough with their lot in life. But just as he once had, Faith wanted a place in life, a place to belong. He'd given up on it long ago, he'd learned that the only thing you really owned was yourself, and counting on anything else was for fools.

And if he were honest, he supposed he could admit to a bit of admiration for her. She'd left an apparently comfortable, if not enjoyable life behind to come out here and try to carry out her sister's last wishes, to keep this place as the boy's heritage, and to raise him herself. Not in the way Aunt Abigail had, to tout her own nobility to her friends, but out of love for her dead sister, in a place and among people strange to her. And she was determined to succeed, to make a home, to make a boy lost in his own grief love her, and to see that he got what his parents had worked so hard for. And even the fact that she seemed doomed to failure didn't keep her from trying. Yes, if he were honest, admiration would be in there as well.

But none of that, not concern, not empathy, not admiration explained why he was lying here listening for any sound from the small bedroom at the back of the house, when he should be exhaustedly sleeping after the work he'd done today. Why he'd found himself taking deep breaths, drawing in that sweet lilac scent whenever she was close enough. Why he'd found himself listening to the soft rustle of her skirts with a strange kind of pleasure. Why he suddenly found brown eyes the color of cinnamon so warm and lovely. Why he'd spent so much time wondering all over again just how long her hair was.

And what it would feel like sliding over his skin.

He shuddered suddenly as his body cramped with violent longing. He rode it out, nearly groaning aloud. He'd been a long time without a woman, but he hadn't even been aware of wanting one until now.

You've waited too damn long, if you're getting yourself in a state over old, weepy, spinster Aunt Faith, he told himself harshly.

He should have stayed in that saloon in Granite, tossed a silver dollar at one of the hard-faced whores, and taken her every way he could think of, until he was drained and dry. That he hadn't been the slightest bit interested then wasn't any consolation now. He should have done it. The blonde had looked like she hadn't been at it quite so long, and there had been a flicker of interest in her eyes when he'd walked in; that always helped, made him feel a bit less like he was a chore a woman had no choice about. He didn't mind paying for his pleasure, much preferred women he could walk away from without a backward look, and if there was something missing from the encounters, it was surely something he could live without. As he did so many other things. It was worth it, never having to say good-bye.

"Damn it," he muttered, shifting again on the blankets. It was too damned warm in here; he should have stayed in the barn. At least there, sleeping in his clothes would be a necessity, not a concession to sharing a roof with a woman who would probably faint dead away at the sight of a less than fully dressed man. And who could sleep with that damned lamp burning? He should just turn the damned thing out. The boy was long asleep by now, after his day of doing chores apparently never asked of him.

But he left the small china lamp burning. Something about the way Zach had put it in the window, something about the look on the boy's face as he made sure it glowed out into the night, kept him from putting it out. He could think of a dozen reasons it was foolish, from drawing unwanted attention to the waste of kerosene, but he still didn't douse the wick.

Gettin' soft, he muttered inwardly.

"Soft in the head," he answered his own thought aloud, and then shook his head at his own craziness.

He had finally dozed off when a scraping sound brought him to his knees, Winchester in hand, ready to fire. He froze when he saw a small figure in a white nightshirt that reached almost to the floor.

"Morgan!" At Zach's excited rather than frightened voice, he removed his finger from the trigger. "Come look, she's here! Mama's here!"

"Zach," he began, but the boy scurried back to his little alcove. It was to the side of the fireplace, to take advantage of the warmth of the fireplace; a wise placement for a child, he thought. And then he followed the boy, thinking he would at least get him back to bed. He caught a glimpse of white near the bed, but when he stepped past the curtain, the boy was off to the other side. Morgan frowned, wondering what he'd seen.

"She's gone," the boy said, his voice laced with disappointment. "But she was here, honest. She was here, and she smiled at me, and touched my face, and—"

"Easy, Zach," Morgan said, lifting the boy and putting him back in the narrow bed. "There's nothing here."

"But she was," the boy said doggedly.

"Okay, okay, easy now." He was talking much as he did to a nervous horse, soothing, almost crooning. The boy seemed to react to the tone if not the words, and looked at him pleadingly.

"You believe me, don't you?"

Morgan chose his words with a care he found painful; this was why he didn't talk much to women or kids, he thought. "I know you believe you saw her."

"I did."

Stubborn, Morgan thought wryly, apparently runs in the family. "If it was your mother, then you know she meant you no harm. So you can go back to sleep now. It's nearly midnight."

The boy was reluctant, but he lay down. Morgan pulled the covers over him, and a moment later was staring in amazement as the boy went swiftly back to sleep.

Wish it was that easy for me, he thought.

He turned to go back to his restless bed, then stopped. He sniffed the air, catching an unmistakable whiff of lilac. That explained it, he thought. Faith had been checking on the boy.

Except that there was no way on earth she could

have done it without waking him. Not when his senses were trained by a lifetime of wariness to function even when he was sleeping. Not when he'd been half awake anyway.

Not when he was so damned attuned to every little move she made that she could hardly breathe without alerting him.

No, she hadn't left her room. He would have known. Hadn't he been lying here for hours, wondering what she'd do if he went to her? What she'd do if he betrayed the promise he'd given her, that she was safe from him?

There's no need to ridicule me.

Her words, and the tightness in her voice when she'd said them, dug at him now like claws. He'd only meant to assure her he wasn't the kind of man to make advances on a respectable woman, a woman who would rightfully expect something in return from him, something he would never be able to give. He'd never meant to imply that it was because she really was . . . old and weepy.

Because she wasn't, not really. She was no girl, it was true, but she was hardly old. Younger than he was, anyway. And as for weepy, he was beginning to doubt Zach's perception of that; if she wept, she did it alone and silently. He'd only seen her even close to tears once, when she'd told him about her sister's death, and that hardly counted as weepy.

And, in fact, she wasn't that ill-favored. Perhaps she'd just gotten into the habit of thinking of herself that way, compared to the sister everyone seemed to think had been so beautiful. But in her own way, she was pleasant enough to look at. Those warm, cinnamon eyes, that slight tilt to her nose, the determined chin . . . and those curves that proved she was more woman than girl, curves that made his hands itch to touch, to trace, to cup . . .

He groaned. He rolled over, welcoming the painful pressure when the part of him that had responded so eagerly to his own thoughts met the not-too-soft pallet of blankets. He willed himself not to move, to give his body only one way to ease the pressure; to give up on foolish notions like finding old, weepy, spinster Aunt Faith attractive.

The small shelf clock, an oddity for Morgan, who was more used to judging the time instinctively, chimed the midnight hour he'd mentioned to Zach. And in the next moment, he heard faint sounds of movement from the bedroom. Had she been awakened by their voices, their movements?

He lay still, listening. This proved, at least, that she hadn't gone to check on Zach without him knowing. That sweet fragrance must have just lingered in the air after she'd gone, like the way the echo of a meadowlark's morning call lingered in your ears in the spring. Or else he was completely crazy now, and hearing and scenting her like an old dog running on only distant memories of the hunt.

He heard the bedroom door open. Then quiet, light footsteps across the floor. Headed his way.

He held his breath, not daring to look at her, for an instant his imagination leaping out of control, picturing her coming to him, her hair down and loose, her cinnamon eyes warm with wanting. His body surged in response, and he nearly called out her name.

She walked past him. And out the front door.

He expelled a long, compressed breath, cursing himself for a fool. Faith Brown was every bit the virginal spinster, and picturing her coming to any man that way was foolish; picturing her coming to *him* that way was worse than foolish, it was looking for the long end of a square quilt. He was a drifting man, never staying in one place, and with nothing in particular to recommend him except a good horse and an ability to stay alive under chancy conditions. Not much to offer a woman like Faith. Not that he was an offering man, either.

"You've gone crazy as a loon," he muttered to himself as he sat up. "You should be wondering where the hell she's going at this hour, not about . . . things that can never be."

He waited, thinking perhaps she'd gone to the privy out back, but when she didn't return after a few minutes, a frown creased his brow. He sat there indecisively for another few minutes, an act uncharacteristic enough to make him uneasy. Finally he yanked on his boots and rolled to his feet. The Winchester, as always, was at his side, and he picked it up without thought and headed for the door.

He stepped outside in time to catch a glimpse of something moving behind the barn. He moved to one side, far enough to see, yet remaining in the shadow of the house while the moonlight reflected off what remained of the night before's snow.

He wasn't surprised to see Faith; he'd expected as much. What he was surprised to see was that she was leading the sorrel mare. The horse was bridled, but not saddled. Curious, Morgan moved swiftly but with care through the snow, ready to dodge out of sight at any moment.

Faith pulled her heavy cloak to one side. And Morgan stopped dead in his tracks, staring.

Beneath the cloak she wore trousers, and even from here he could see the outline of her legs against the moonlit snow. He'd seen women in divided riding skirts before, and in the wilder parts of the country even in pants. He could even see the need for it, here in the wilder reaches. But somehow those he'd seen before had never affected him as anything other than an oddity.

And then she startled him anew, leaping to the back of the little mare with the grace and agility of a rider long used to such action. And the mare came alive, dancing in the shallow snow, her tail up, her head alert; she, too, was obviously long used to this. Faith settled on the mare's back, balancing easily. Morgan caught the sound of her voice in the still night, faintly, not enough to make out words, but enough to hear the same crooning, loving tone she'd used to charm his stallion. The mare's ears swiveled, one forward, betraying eagerness to be off, one back, listening to what was clearly a beloved voice.

Morgan watched as she leaned forward to pat the mare's neck. The sorrel snorted with pleasure, prancing as Faith guided her to the edge of a clear, flat spot just west of the barn. Then he heard a short, sharp cry that sounded like "Now!"

The mare exploded into motion, hooves digging, sending up a spout of snow as she leapt away. In no more than three long strides she was stretched out and running, tail straight out, eagerness in every stride. And Faith was with her, not clinging, but moving with her, as if she anticipated every motion, as if there were some uncanny link between them. With no saddle, and seeming to barely move, she crouched over the mare's neck until they indeed seemed one being, with one heart and one mind and both set on running free.

Morgan watched with a touch of awe as they raced

across the clearing, Faith's cloak whipping behind her, woman and horse in an amazing picture against the moonlit winter landscape. A moment later the hood flew back, and Morgan's breath caught as her hair streamed out, long and free and flying.

His gut knotted, his body clenched. His lips parted as he struggled to breath, knowing the air was there, but seemingly having forgotten how to take it in. He wondered if some part of him had known, had sensed that beneath the prim, tidy surface had lain this wildness, if this was what he'd been responding to unknowingly, this hidden fire.

He stood there staring long after the pair had disappeared over a rise.

He was looking at her so oddly, Faith thought as she sipped at the steaming coffee. And he looked tired, although he'd been asleep when she'd slipped out last night, and had barely moved when she'd come back two hours later. She knew, because she'd stood there far too long, risking him waking up and finding her staring at him simply because she hadn't been able to stop. She'd never been so close to a sleeping man before.

And though she would have thought that asleep he would be less . . . well, just less, he was not. She'd watched the firelight play over him, gleaming on the raven hair, turning his skin to gold and his lashes to dark thick semicircles on his cheeks, and making that firm, usually stern mouth seem softer. And he'd seemed more intimidating to her asleep than awake. At least her heart had pounded more, and her breath came more quickly.

It could have been simply that she was still excited, of

course. She smiled inwardly, remembering the exhilaration of that midnight ride. Espe had been ready, eager to run, and when she'd reached the clearing, she'd let her loose, savoring the fi eedom as much as the horse did.

"You're looking . . . pleased this morning."

They were the first words he'd spoken, and the husky timbre of his voice sent a shiver down her spine. She'd come out a bit late this morning, after her ride, and it wasn't until she'd seen the pot on the stove that she realized the smell of coffee had awakened her. It was a new and unexpected experience, having a man do something even as simple as fix coffee in the morning, and she was grateful he hadn't seemed to require anything other than her brief "Yes, thank you" when he gestured with the pot.

She couldn't think of a thing to say in answer to his comment, so she said nothing. But he kept looking at her, until she finally resorted to staring into her cup as if it held the answer to his odd mood. When the silence spun out, she began to feel a strange tension, unlike anything she'd ever experienced before. Finally, almost desperately, she turned to the age-old topic.

"I believe it will snow again tonight."

"Smells like it."

She looked up at him, surprised by his words. "Yes. Yes, it does." He seemed to find nothing odd in the exchange, and Faith felt a warm little glow inside. "Seems right, on Christmas Eve."

"Mmm."

There was no determining what that meant, so Faith didn't try. "Do you miss Christmas at home?"

"No."

"I mean, before your parents . . ." She trailed off, hating the chill that came into his eyes anytime she asked him anything even vaguely personal. And realizing that he'd never asked her a question at all, except for that moment when he'd been surprised by Espe's name being Latin. She thought about it for moment, wondering why. When the answer came to her, it was painfully simple; asking questions of others implied they had the right to do the same, and he'd made it quite clear he didn't like being asked questions. He'd answer generally, about where he'd been, what he'd seen, and he showed a patience with Zach that surprised her, but then, the boy didn't ask anything . . . dangerous.

Her own choice of words surprised her, and she found herself looking at him thoughtfully.

Zach joined them sleepily, rubbing at his eyes as he came out of the alcove. Faith noticed Morgan looking at the boy carefully, but when Zach simply climbed into his chair and mumbled a greeting, he seemed to relax. When she suggested flapjacks for breakfast, Zach merely nodded, but Faith thought it a great improvement over the sullen responses she'd been getting up until today.

"I think," she said brightly after they finished, and Morgan—and Zach, at Morgan's prompting—had thanked her for the meal, "we should go find a nice little tree to bring in and fancy up for Christmas Eve."

She saw a flicker of interest in Zach's face, but it faded quickly. "I don't care about Christmas," the boy muttered.

"Then perhaps I shouldn't make that apple pie I was planning," Faith said, knowing from Hope's letters that the boy adored it. She'd found a cache of dried apples on a shelf in the small pantry, and had put them to soak last night.

Again Zach's expression lightened for a moment,
but again the gloom descended. "Won't be as good as
Mama's."

*You'll let him say blame near anything about you,
but you get all in a pucker when he talks bad about a
horse.*

Morgan's words echoed in her mind, and when she
glanced at him he seemed to be waiting. For something.

"I wouldn't be so sure, young man. Who do you
think taught your Mama?" Faith asked.

Zach's eyes widened. "You?"

"I most certainly did. If there's one thing I can do in
the kitchen, it's bake pies. Now, back to that tree. We
could pop some corn, and I'll string it," she said as if
the boy hadn't spoken, "and I've got some ribbons we
can tie on the branches. What else do you suppose we
could do?"

"Mama used to put some little candles on it," Zach
said, almost unwillingly.

"Do you know where she kept them?"

He nodded, hesitated, then scrambled out of his chair
and disappeared into the small pantry. He came back
clutching a small bundle wrapped in paper. He unrolled
it carefully, exposing a dozen small candle stubs.

"Perfect, Zach. Will you pick out a tree for us?"

"Well . . . okay." He still sounded grudging, but now
it sounded a bit forced. At least Faith wanted to think
so. Then he brightened. "Maybe we *should* have a tree.
Maybe Mama will come home, then."

Faith winced, but recovered quickly. "Go get dressed,
then," she said, and the boy went quickly enough.

Only then did she look at Morgan, who had been
pointedly silent throughout the exchange.

"I . . . he's changed since you came. Thank you."

Morgan shrugged.

"I hope you like dumplings," she said. "I thought I'd—"

"I'm leaving, Faith."

She fell silent, heat flooding her face. She lowered her eyes to the table. "I . . . I'm sorry. I thought you'd at least stay through Christmas."

"Why?" He said it as if the day were like any other, as if it truly meant nothing to him. She raised her head, and saw nothing in his expression to deny her thought.

"Because you shouldn't be alone on Christmas, if you have people to be with," she said.

"I don't."

"You have . . . us," she said, hating the way she sounded.

He set down his cup. He leaned forward. And when he spoke, it was very slow and quiet.

"Listen to me, Faith Brown. I have no one. That's the way I want it. I don't want to have anyone, be close to anyone. You can't count on anyone but yourself. People leave. They always leave. And if they don't, I do, and I'll be damned if I'll be made to feel guilty about it when I go. So don't be including me in your plans, and don't be giving me those looks meant to set a man afire, because I don't want it. Or you."

Faith stared at him, a riot of emotions stirring. So many emotions she couldn't even begin to sort them out. All she could think of, sillily, was that he'd just given her the answer to something she'd once asked him.

"That's why your horse has no name, isn't it? That would make him more than just a thing, it would make him a creature that matters, that you care about. And you don't want that."

He gaped at her, as if stunned that after what he'd said, this was all she had to say. She nearly laughed.

"You must think me a fool, Morgan. But it's you that's a fool. Do you think I don't understand about people leaving, and how it hurts? My sister left me, my parents left me . . ."

She swallowed, her throat suddenly tight. Had he really thought she would believe he could ever care for her? Her, plain, quiet Faith Brown? She knew, to her humiliation, that she had more than once looked upon him with the kind of longing a woman had for a man. But she was far from foolish enough to believe he might return her feelings.

She stood up, gathering what she could of pride and composure. And she was proud that her voice was fairly steady.

"I suppose I have . . . looked at you," she admitted. "I've never been so . . . close to a man before. But I know quite well I'm not a woman to . . . start a fire in a man like you. Or any other man. That's for women like my sister: beautiful, gentle, sweet, all the things men want. I spent most of my life learning that lesson, and I don't need you to teach it to me again."

She turned then, and didn't stop when he called her name. She stepped outside into the brisk morning air and closed the door carefully behind her, not allowing herself the satisfaction of slamming it to give vent to the turmoil inside her.

When he joined her outside, Zach's mood, which was willing if not enthusiastic, lightened her own. He approached the job solemnly, trying to pick the best of the small fir trees that grew close enough to the house to be carried back. She supposed Allen had brought a bigger tree down from the higher country, but this was the best she could do. At least Zach wasn't pointing out to her that she couldn't do this as well, either.

"Mama didn't really want a tree, after Papa died," Zach said, as if he'd read her mind. "She only did it for me."

"It's hard to find any joy when you lose someone you love," Faith said softly. "But you have to believe they would want you to go on."

The boy trekked on, still in search of that perfect tree. They walked for several minutes before he spoke again.

"Did you really love my Mama?"

"I did, Zach. So very much. It was a . . . different kind of love than yours, but it was very, very strong. It still is." She stopped, making him look at her. "I know you don't believe it, but I love you, too. So much it makes me cry, sometimes. But I'm afraid I won't do right by you, because I don't know much about little boys. Sometimes . . ." She took a deep breath. "Sometimes I even pray for help, to know what to do so you'll be happy."

Zach stared at her. "That's what you pray for? Not for me to . . . go away?"

If nothing else, bless Morgan for telling her this, Faith thought. "Of course I don't want you to go away. I loved your mama, Zach. And you're part of her, the only part I have left."

His eyes were wide. "If you love her, then why don't you see her like I do?"

"I don't know Zach," she said honestly. He was talking to her, really talking to her, and she couldn't bear to see him turn cold and sullen again because she denied what he thought he'd seen. "Maybe . . . you

need to see her more, because . . . you had her for a
shorter time."

He seemed to consider this for a moment, but he said
nothing. They walked on for a while, and then he
pointed out a nicely shaped tree.

"We could carry that one, couldn't we?" he asked.

She looked at it doubtfully. "I don't know. Maybe
we should find a smaller one."

"I'll carry it."

Even as she gave a start of surprise, Faith noticed
she was the only one; Zach had apparently realized
Morgan had followed them. She very pointedly didn't
look at the tall man, but kept her gaze fastened on the
tree Zach had chosen.

"You better chop it, too," Zach said. "She'll hurt
herself."

Faith turned to look at the boy; the words were very
like the cutting remarks she'd grown used to hearing,
but there was something missing from his tone. The
nastiness was gone, leaving behind a sort of wryness
that was strangely adult and very male.

"I'll chop it," Morgan said, and proceeded to do so
in a half dozen solid blows. It would have taken her the
better part of an hour and probably cost her some blisters and possibly blood, and he'd done it without even
taking an extra breath.

"Thank you," she said stiffly as he reached between
the branches, grasped the tree by the trunk, and hoisted
it to his shoulder.

"You're welcome," he said, and if there was an
apology in his tone, she chose to ignore it. "Zach, run
ahead and find a bucket to put this in. We'll fill it with
wet dirt to prop the tree up."

"Yes, sir!" Zach yelped and raced ahead with the

first display of genuine six-year-old energy Faith had seen from him.

Morgan slowed his steps, waited until the boy was out of earshot, then looked at Faith. "I'm sorry," he began.

"Don't be. You were kindly warning me about being a foolish woman," she said formally. "I can only assure you it wasn't necessary."

"Lord, you can talk like a schoolmarm when you're mad." She stopped, startled by his exasperated tone. "Faith, I know I hurt your feelings, and I didn't mean—"

"You don't know anything about my feelings."

"I . . . maybe I do." He looked at her, and she saw in his eyes something she'd never expected to see, a softness that stopped her breath in her throat. "My aunt . . . the one I told you about . . ."

He stopped, and Faith felt a clutching in her stomach; now that he'd at last begun to talk to her, would he stop before he'd really started? She prompted, "The . . . clothes aunt?"

His mouth twisted ruefully. "Yeah, that one. Back in Connecticut. She was my only relative, so she . . . took me in, after my folks were killed. Even though she . . . hated me."

"Surely not," Faith exclaimed.

"She did," he said flatly, and Faith knew that whether it was true or not, Morgan believed it was true, which made it the same thing in the end. "It took me a long time to figure out why. It was . . . confusing, because one day she'd be talking about my father, saying how wonderful and noble he was, and how I wasn't fit to carry his name, and the next she'd be screaming and hitting me because I looked like him."

Faith's brow furrowed. "I don't understand."

"Neither did I, until a got older and put a few pieces together. A letter I found, and a couple of servants who didn't worry much about talking in front of a kid."

So he'd come from a wealthy family, she thought, remembering rather inanely her mother complaining about finding good help. She filed this tiny bit of knowledge away in a place within her she hadn't been aware of until now, a place where she'd been hoarding what little she knew of this man.

"Anyway, I finally realized that my aunt . . . had been in love with my father. But he loved my mother, her sister. The one everybody said was . . . prettier, and sweeter. He married her, and my aunt . . . never married anyone. And Aunt Abigail never forgave her sister for that. Or me."

Faith stared at him. What was he saying? That he thought she'd loved Allen? That she would hold a grudge against an innocent child? She'd wished he would share something of himself with her, and now that he had, it hurt more than she could have imagined. And it took every bit of nerve she had to speak.

"I never loved my sister's husband. I always loved my sister. And I would never blame an innocent child!"

His brows lowered. "I didn't say that. I only meant . . . your sister, you said everyone thought she was the beautiful one—

"So you think I was jealous of her?"

Faith had fought that assumption most of her life; no one seemed able to believe that she had loved Hope for the same reasons everyone else had, they seemed determined to assume that because Hope had been so beautiful, her plain older sister must have been envious. She'd grown used to it. Or thought she had; but hearing it from Morgan brought on all the old pain as if it were new. The problem was, she wasn't certain if it was being accused of a jealousy she'd never felt, or Morgan's agreement that she had reason to be jealous that hurt.

"I didn't say that, either," Morgan snapped.

They heard a call as Zach came out of the house, clearly wondering what was keeping them. The boy began to trot toward them. Faith looked back at Morgan.

"I am only human," she said carefully. "And I often wished I could be more like my sister instead of what I am. But I was never, ever jealous. I loved her. I love her still."

"What're you doing?" Zach asked. "I thought you were bringin' the tree."

"He is," Faith said, her voice sounding much cooler than she felt. "That is, if he's through being hateful."

She turned on her heel, then nearly slipped in the slushy, melting snow, ruining her dignified retreat. Her cheeks flamed, and she was grateful her back was to him.

"Hateful?" she heard Zach ask.

"Boy don't ever try and talk about feelings to a woman," Morgan said, sounding genuinely exasperated now. "You try and help, and they just twist around what you say until you don't even recognize it."

Faith kept going. But the color in her face rose even higher.

Again he didn't know why he was still here. He'd intended to go. He'd even started to saddle the stallion again. But the look the horse had given the saddle blanket, as if he expected to be playing the silly game Morgan had invented last time he tried to saddle up, had been too much. He'd snapped at the animal in a tone he rarely used, and the horse had looked askance at him.

"Just never mind, horse," he'd muttered. And Faith's words had come back to him as clearly as if she'd been standing there speaking them again.

That's why your horse has no name, isn't it? That would make him more than just a thing, it would make him a creature that matters, that you care about. And you don't want that.

He'd always thought of his life as pretty much the way he wanted it. But now it seemed like a hollow, empty thing. Or he did; he wasn't sure there was much difference. What he was sure of was that he'd had enough of being here, enough of wearying himself being patient with that kid, of feeling like the boor his aunt had called him every time he refused to answer one of Faith's questions, of having her probe at his past, and then act like he'd slapped her when he finally gave her a piece of it, of being eaten alive by needs he'd never felt before.

But here he was now, his stomach pleasantly full, his mind unpleasantly so. He told himself it was because Zach had practically begged him to stay, but he'd never let anybody's requests sway him before, not if his mind was set on hitting the breeze. It certainly wasn't because of Faith. She hadn't asked, hadn't given the slightest indication she still wanted him here; she'd seemed more surprised than he was that he had stayed.

So he was already feeling proddy, and his mood wasn't improved any by the realization that, instead of welcoming Faith's polite but utterly impersonal manner, he missed her straightforward speech, her openness, even her damned questions.

"The pie was good," he said into the silence.

"Yes," she agreed shortly.

"It was," Zach agreed. "Maybe you did teach Mama."

"Thank you, Zach." The difference in her demeanor was obvious. And it grated.

"So who taught you?" Morgan asked.

"I taught myself," she said, not looking at him.

"Can't be any tougher to run this place than to learn to bake a pie like this." Morgan wasn't sure what kept him trying, beyond sheer stubbornness.

She said nothing, just gathered up the dishes.

"Let me help," he said, rising to his feet.

"No." Then, as if it were an afterthought, she added a very formal, "Thank you."

Morgan's lips tightened. He barely resisted the urge to turn on his heel and walk out, get his horse and leave, no matter that it was nearing nightfall. He wasn't sure why he didn't. He stalked across the small room and stood in front of the tree they'd brought in.

"It's pretty, ain't it?" Zach asked as he came to stand beside him.

"Yeah." It was kind of cheerful, Morgan had to admit, with the strands of white popcorn, the bright ribbons, the candles burning.

"Have you ever made a better one?" the boy asked.

"I've never made one at all."

Zach's eyes rounded. "Never? Why?"

He opened his mouth to give the boy some meaningless reason that was nevertheless the truth, such as he was usually on the road, or in some saloon that didn't run even to the amount of Christmas spirit he'd seen in the place in town. But what came out instead startled him.

"I . . . lost the meaning of this day a long time ago."

"How can you lose Christmas? It's always there, every year."

"I think . . . it's myself I lost," Morgan whispered.

He heard a slight sound, and looked up to see Faith standing there staring at him, her eyes wide, and every bit of emotion and gentleness he'd so missed was glowing there.

He wanted to run. Some gut-deep part of him knew what that look meant, knew what it offered, and he wanted to run.

"Christmas is presents and songs and food and . . . and . . ."

"And family and love," Faith said softly, putting her hands on the boy's shoulders when he ran out of words.

Morgan shuddered, fought it by clenching his jaw, and sucked in a strangled breath as she spoke of the very reason he'd made sure to be alone on this of all days, as she spoke of the things he'd seen in her eyes.

"I have to put the lamp in the window. Mama will come back for Christmas," Zach declared. "I know she will."

"Zach," Faith reproved him gently.

"She won't miss Christmas, she loves it, she'll come back," Zach insisted, reaching for the pretty little lamp. "But she needs the light in the window."

"Zach, please, you know she can't come back," Faith began, reaching for the lamp. Zach pulled it away.

"She will. I know she will." Zach looked at Morgan pleadingly. "Tell her. You almost saw Mama, tell her. She'll come back, won't she?"

Morgan didn't look at the boy, he looked at Faith. And it was all there in her face, in her eyes, in the way she gently held the boy, all the things he'd never allowed himself to want, never dared think of, because he knew too well what would happen, knew too well the pain that was inevitable once you let anyone become too important to you.

"Tell her," Zach pleaded again, clutching the lamp to his thin chest. "Then she'll let me put Mama's lamp in the window, so she can find her way home."

Learn it now, boy, Morgan thought, while you're young enough to get over it quickly. He grabbed the lamp away from the boy. The glass chimney wobbled, then fell, hitting a branch of the tree and then rolling to the floor. The sound as it cracked was no harsher than his voice.

"She won't. You're fooling yourself. She wasn't there. She's gone. Forever. She's in that box they buried. Dead is dead, boy. They don't ever come back. Not ever."

Zach stared at him, his eyes first wide with shock, then brimming with tears.

"You lie! She's *not* dead, she's not!"

The boy turned and ran out the door into the night. For once, Faith didn't go chasing after him; she must have decided the boy needed time to deal with this alone. Instead she stood still, staring at Morgan. Once more her face was unreadable, but he knew what she had to be thinking.

"Go ahead, say it," he told her bitterly. "I'm a cold-hearted bastard who just ripped the heart out of a little boy."

"As someone once ripped it out of the little boy you were?" she asked softly.

She didn't wait for him to answer but simply knelt to pick up the glass chimney of Hope's lamp. It was cracked nearly from bottom to top, and she set it aside carefully. Then she walked to the rocker that had been her sister's and took up the shirt of Zach's she'd been mending, sat down without another word, and began to work.

It was just as well; he had nothing to say. He'd already said far too much; that look of betrayal in Zach's eyes was seared into his soul. He had some ugly memories he carried, never able to rid himself of them, and he knew he'd just added another.

He sank down onto the folded blankets by the fire; the fact that Faith had left them there instead of putting them away told him she expected he would stay the night again. Yet again he thought of leaving right now, but he couldn't seem to find the energy to even move. He stared into the hearth wondering, if hell was truly leaping flames and eternal torment, how it differed much from life.

He listened to Faith's slight movements as she stitched, saw out of the corner of his eyes her sure, easy, efficient movements as she worked at the familiar task. He looked away, unable to reconcile this quiet, comfortable scene with the image burned indelibly in his mind of a jubilant woman riding free under a winter moon. The idea that both natures could be combined in the same woman astonished him, and excited him in a way he didn't understand or know how to deal with.

He didn't know how long he'd been there when he heard Faith move. She put down her sewing and stood. He didn't look at her until she had walked across the room and taken her cloak from beside the door. She would be going to talk to the boy, he thought; a glance at the small shelf clock told him Zach had been gone for nearly two hours.

She said nothing, just went out and closed the door quietly behind her. Faith Brown was not given to slamming doors to vent her feelings, it was clear. Nor did she yell, or pout; instead of giving in to anger, she merely put on that mask of cool politeness that would make a man welcome a fit of temper. Morgan wondered how she did let it out; it had to come out somehow.

And then he realized he knew; she ran wild with her mare under the night sky.

The fire had the room comfortably warm, but he shivered, and knew that it had nothing to do with cold and everything to do with the crazy emotions careening around inside him. He'd worked so hard all his life at never feeling anything soft or gentle, knowing that those things only opened the door for pain, the kind of pain Zach was feeling right now. If you didn't care, you couldn't be hurt when those you cared about left you. It was a simple, logical way to live.

Only now did he realize it was a damn cold way as well.

The flames burned on the hearth; his gut burned inside him. Resin snapped as it heated, and a log broke and fell. He got up and put another one on the fire; they'd be cold when they came back in. Unless, he thought wryly, they both decided to spend Christmas Eve in the barn, to stay away from him, the despoiler of celebrations.

He heard hurried footsteps on the small porch, and a moment later Faith came in. Alone. She pulled off her cloak but did not hang it up; she tossed it on the table as she passed. She hastened past him into the bedroom without a word, but her worried expression spoke for her. He followed her, catching the door she'd pushed before it closed. He shoved it back. And stopped dead when he realized she was tearing off her clothes in a furious hurry.

She already had her shoes off, and for a moment he just stared as she tugged at the buttons of her bodice until enough were undone that she could pull it off over her head. A long strand of hair came loose from the severe coil at the back of her head, and the image of it streaming out behind her came back to him with stunning force.

Clad only in her chemise from the waist up, she bent to slip off her skirt. Morgan's pulse began to hammer in hot, heavy beats, and when he glimpsed the soft, swaying curves of her breasts and the shadowy valley between them as she moved, his body responded with a swiftness that took his breath away.

She straightened with the skirt in her hands. He had a moment to see womanly curves and long legs beneath white cloth that seemed both modest and incredibly suggestive, before she realized he was there and gasped, holding the skirt up in front of her. She stared at him, eyes huge in her suddenly pale face.

With an effort that told him just how close to the edge he was, he made himself look only at her face.

"What's wrong?" he asked, unable to control the urgent note of need in his voice, but hoping that in her innocence, she wouldn't understand it for what it was.

"I . . . Zach is gone. I have to go find him." She raised the skirt slightly. It covered her breasts, but left him with a view of her bare feet and delicately slender ankles. "Will you let me dress, please?"

He didn't move. It took a moment for him to beat down the rising heat and concentrate on what she'd said. "Gone?" Of course he was gone, they'd both seen him run out of the house.

"Yes. Will you go, please?" He still didn't move. "Fine, then," she said, her voice tight, her cheeks flaming. And dropped the skirt to the floor.

Morgan had a momentary view of what he'd imagined to be beneath that dress, now hidden only by the thin linen of her shift and drawers. And then she was pulling on the trousers he'd seen her wearing on that night ride he couldn't put out of his mind. As she reached for a heavy shirt of some homespun-looking material and began to wrestle it on, things finally began to register. Unlike her tidy self, she had tossed her dress on the floor. She was redressing in front of him. She was putting on her riding clothes. And the urgency of her movements finally snapped him out of his haze.

"What do you mean, Zach's gone?"

She glared at him, her embarrassment vanished now. "What I said. He's gone. He took his pony. I found the tracks heading into the trees up the hill."

He frowned. "Up? Toward the mountains?"

She nodded. "And snow's coming. Fast."

He shook his head, able to see through the tiny window behind her what she had not yet noticed. "It's already here."

She whirled to look, a small sound of distress escaped her, and she raced to the small cupboard and took out a pair of high, lace-up boots. She sat down on the edge of the bed and began to pull them on.

"Stay here," he said. "I'll go find him."

Her head came up sharply. "No."

"Faith—"

"I'm going." She turned back to fastening the boots.

"There's no need. That's a big storm coming in. I'll go."

"Zachary is my responsibility."

He winced, although he knew she hadn't meant anything other than the literal meaning of her words. But he couldn't deny the sense of guilt that was prodding him. "And him taking off like that is mine," he said grimly.

She looked at him for a moment, and he had the uncomfortable feeling that she was seeing much more than this moment. Her next words proved him right.

"You're absolved," she said. "You can stay safely . . . alone."

"I'll go," he repeated, reduced to repetition in the face of a perceptiveness he found hard to face.

"You do as you wish." She stood up. "As I suspicion you always do."

His mouth twisted; she sounded exactly like he did, when he was making sure it seemed as if something meant less than nothing to him. He'd never thought about how it really sounded. Or he'd never cared.

"But you're going anyway."

She didn't even look at him. "I am."

He'd always known that he generally got done what he wanted to do. When others gave up, he kept on. Aunt Abigail had called it stubbornness; he'd thought of it as determination. Whatever it was, for the first time in his life he knew he'd met its match in the woman before him. She would be going with him.

She'd never been so cold. Nor had she ever seen snow like this, a wall of white coming down so thick it seemed solid rather than flakes. But she couldn't stop, not when Zach was out here somewhere, as cold as she was, and scared. The trail the boy and his pony had left had been buried under fresh snow an hour ago, but she refused to quit.

The big black beside her slowed, then halted, and she reined in Espe to look back at Morgan.

"We've got to stop," he said.

"No."

"Faith, you can't see a foot in front of you. Neither can the horses. We've probably been riding in circles. There's a bit of shelter on the lee side of those rocks over there—"

"I'm going on." It was hard to say, her lips were so cold.

"Damn it, it won't do Zach any good if you freeze to death out here."

Freeze to death. The words rang in her ears, and the ugly vision she'd been fighting for the last hour came viciously back to life, a vision of a small boy, frozen and lifeless in this swirling white world.

"N-no." she stammered. She bit back a sob.

"For God's sake, don't cry," Morgan said. "Your face will freeze."

"It's already frozen," she snapped.

"Get down," Morgan said fiercely, in a voice that brooked no argument. "We're stopping. At least until this lets up a little."

"No," she repeated doggedly.

In answer he dismounted and pulled her from the little mare's back. She tried to fight him, but instead found herself sagging against him, marveling that he still seemed so strong, when she was about to cave in, body and spirit.

"We're not quitting, Faith. Just resting for a while. We need it. The horses need it."

His voice was soft, gentle, as she'd never heard from

him before. And the quiet reassurance was the one thing that could have convinced her; she let him lead her to the rocks.

The biggest boulder was better than horse-high, and provided a windbreak. The lower portion had been hollowed out slightly by wind or water or weather, and gave them a tiny bit of shelter from the snow. He untied his bedroll and put it down for her sit on. As she watched rather numbly, Morgan worked swiftly, using their slickers to give the horses what shelter he could, then managing to start a small fire at the edge of the slight overhang with some mesquite he found that was dry enough to burn. Then he sat down beside her.

When she shivered, he moved closer. He cradled her gently against him, moving only to open up his overcoat and invite her inside. She went, letting him tuck it around her, nearly shuddering at the welcome warmth. Oddly she felt him shudder as well, but supposed it was because she'd brought cold air with her. She could feel the steady thud of his heart beneath her cheek, and snuggled closer. The beat faltered, then raced as if to catch up, and she leaned her head back to look at him curiously. The fire was too small for much light, and he was little more than a shadow in the darkness, but in her mind she saw him as clearly as if the sun were pouring over them instead of this blizzard of snow.

For an instant his arms tightened around her, until it almost hurt. And then, before she realized what was happening, his mouth came down on hers.

She'd been kissed once or twice, by supposed suitors who had changed their minds about her attractions the moment they laid eyes on her sister. Or perhaps that had been the attraction in the first place, she'd finally realized. But nothing had ever prepared her for this.

For an instant she wondered how it could happen, how such heat could happen when the world was freezing around them. But then the blaze raced along her every nerve, and she could think of nothing but the feel of his lips and the strength of his arms as he pulled her ever closer.

He brushed his tongue over her lips, creating more, sudden heat, like a shower of sparks. She gasped at the fire that shot through her, and then settled somewhere within her like a hot liquid pool. He took the chance she unwittingly offered him and probed further, and the feel of his tongue gently tasting her turned that hot liquid into a boiling mass of sensations she'd never known.

"Faith."

He whispered it against her mouth, and it made her quiver. His hands moved, slipping down her body to her waist, and pulling her tight to him. She felt him move his hips slightly, felt the digging pressure of something hard against her belly. She gasped when she realized what it must be, but the heat that rippled through her was not from embarrassment, but of some new, strange feeling she'd never experienced.

He moved then, pulling her down on the opened bedroll, coming down over her, his weight oddly pleasant atop her. His hands moved again, to her breasts, cupping, lifting, and before the shock of such an intimate touch could grip her it was shoved aside by the greater shock when his fingers rubbed over the tips. For a split second she realized in wonder that her nipples were hard, almost aching, and then it went through her like a wildfire, hot, pouring sensation that blazed a path from his fingers to some low, deep, hollow place inside her.

He groaned, something that sounded like her name. Then she heard something very odd and realized it was herself, moaning, almost whimpering. It was a begging little sound, and she didn't even know what she was begging for, only that she wanted it more than she wanted anything except to find Zach . . .

Zach.

She wrenched her mouth away. She stared up at Morgan, who was breathing as quickly as she, as if he'd felt the same sudden shortness of air. He was looking at her, and in that instant she saw all the emotions that he never let show. She saw heat, need, and oddly, a gentleness that was almost tender. And it made her want even more to sink back into his arms, to let this rising heat carry her with it to whatever end was in store.

"Zach," she said, almost desperately.

Before the echo of her voice died away, Morgan's face was back to its usual expressionless state. He released her and drew back instantly, and she felt bereft in a way she didn't understand.

"I can't . . . we have to . . . he's out there all alone, and probably scared, Morgan."

He leaned back against the rock. "I know."

"I'm so worried. The snow's not letting up, we really can't see, and when we find him, I don't know how we'll find our way back, and—"

He lifted his arm, hesitated, then put it around her again. "We'll find him. That's all that matters."

"I should have just let him put the silly lamp in the window, it wouldn't have hurt anything—"

"It's not your fault," he said, sounding grim. "It's mine. I shouldn't have turned on him like that."

Faith nearly shivered again at the pure emotion in his voice, this man who never let down his guard but had now done so twice: once when he held her in his arms, and now, when he was castigating himself over Zach.

"He . . . needed to hear it," she said.

"But not like that."

"Perhaps. But it needed saying, and I don't know if I could have said it at all."

"You would have," he said, with what she could have sworn was a sigh. "And you would have done it . . . with kindness. Not anger."

He spoke as if it were a memory. "Is that how it was done to you?" she asked softly.

He laughed, a harsh, bitter sound. "Exactly. And then I do it to that boy. Makes me no better than her, doesn't it?"

She didn't have to ask who the "her" was. But, anxious not to talk about what had just passed between them, she asked instead, "Was she so very awful?"

"She was—is still, for all I know—a very . . . righteous woman. I suppose it was all she had."

She took a deep breath before saying something that had been preying on her mind for some time now. "I . . . think I understand now what you were trying to tell me, before."

He hesitated, and she wondered if he was deciding whether to answer at all, or just go on in the safe silence he preferred. When he finally spoke, she felt as if each word were a small treasure handed to her.

"I never meant to hurt you," he said. "I just . . . Aunt Abigail had a beautiful sister everyone loved, just like you did. But she . . . she became bitter, grew to hate my mother. And when she was gone, she switched that hate to me. And did her best to make sure everybody in

Hartford felt the same way, and she was a powerful voice around there."

"That's awful, Morgan," she said, not sure what to say in the face of such hatred where there should have been love.

"I reckon it wasn't really her fault. She wasn't as strong—or as loving—as you are. I know you loved your sister. That's the difference between you. And Zach will see it, too, when he gets his grieving done."

The simple but clearly heartfelt words nearly stopped her breath in her chest and gave her hope where she'd nearly given up. Perhaps she *could* still reach Zach. When they found him, and got him home, she'd try again. And again, and again, however long it took.

"Thank you," she whispered. He shrugged. "Don't," she said. "It *does* mean something, it is important, that you . . . cared enough to say that." She felt him go still as she said the forbidden word, and hastily went on. "We'll find him, and tell him that people you love may never come back, but if you love and remember them, they're never lost forever."

Morgan made a disparaging sound that told her what he thought of that idealistic statement.

"Your aunt, is she . . . still alive?"

It was all she could think of to say. After a long moment when she thought he wouldn't, he answered.

"I don't know. I left the day I turned twelve, and I've never been back."

"Twelve? So young?"

"No point in staying. I knew by then she'd never change her mind about me."

"But . . . where did you go?"

"West. Made it to Denver just after they changed the

name. It got too big too fast, so I headed south." His tone turned wry. "Then they hit gold at Pike's Peak, and it got crowded there, too." His voice turned oddly wistful. "Thought about going back to the states, when the war started. But I hated the place, and everybody who looked at me the way my aunt did, so I didn't see any point in fighting and maybe dying for it. Idaho Territory was new then, so I hit out for there for a while."

"You've been . . . everywhere, it seems."

"Been around," he agreed.

"And you never stayed anywhere?"

Again that hesitation, and she sensed it was almost a physical effort for him to go on. But he did.

"Never found anyplace that made me want to stay. Or come back."

Or anyone.

Faith's mind provided the answer her heart didn't want to hear. No one would ever hold him, no one would ever bring him back to someplace he'd already been.

She lapsed into silence; there was, it seemed, nothing more to say. Morgan remained silent as well, and the only sound was the occasional snap of the wood, and then the loud crack of a branch, apparently breaking under a too heavy load of snow.

She looked toward the sound, even knowing she would see nothing but the night. But there was a strange glow in the distant trees, much as she would imagine their little fire would look from there. It vanished, and she would have thought she'd imagined it had not Morgan gone still beside her, his head turned in the same direction.

"Did you see it?"

He nodded, but put a finger to her lips to hush her.

She felt a little jump of her pulse at the touch, and he pulled his hand away so swiftly she wondered if he'd felt the same little jolt she had. But he said nothing, just stared.

So did Faith, and after a moment she saw it again, a faint light, gold like reflected fire in the snow.

The snow. "How can we see that, when the snow is coming down so thick?" she asked, looking in another direction and realizing she still couldn't see beyond a few feet.

"I don't know," Morgan said, but he was already on his feet before the last word left his lips. "Stay here."

"No," she said quickly, "it might be Zach, maybe he managed to build a fire."

"Maybe." But it could be somebody else as well. Stay here."

"No," she repeated determinedly, scrambling to her feet. She ran to Espe, and untied the slicker Morgan had put over the mare.

"Faith," Morgan said warningly. She turned on him.

"Zach is mine now. I love him, and I will not leave him to anyone else, especially if he's in danger. Not even you."

His eyes widened at her last words, but she didn't explain. She couldn't; she wasn't even sure what she'd meant herself. Instead she tugged her cloak tighter around her and started toward the light. She heard Morgan mutter something she guessed she was glad not to hear. In a moment he'd mounted and caught up with her.

"At least stay close," he said. "I don't want to be hunting for you, too."

A sharp retort rose to her lips but she bit it back,

thinking she'd best save her energy for riding rather than waste it arguing.

She didn't realize for several minutes that the light didn't seem to be getting any closer. She looked back over her shoulder, and their own fire had vanished behind the thick veil of snow.

"I don't understand," she said after they'd gone farther and the light still hadn't changed.

"Neither do I," Morgan said, sounding grim.

They kept on. The snow got thicker. It began to swirl around them as the wind picked up. And the light never seemed to get any closer. It was as if they were following some phantom, forever ahead of them, leading them on some foolish chase . . . or to their doom. Faith shook her head, trying to rid herself of the ghastly images.

The stallion snorted as Morgan reined in suddenly. Morgan's hand shot out to Faith's shoulder, and she pulled Espe to a halt beside him.

"What?"

"I thought I saw something . . . there!"

He pointed to a thick stand of trees. Faith leaned forward, peering through the snow. And she saw the little shape of Zach's pony, head down, rump to the wind. And beside him, a smaller shape huddled on the ground.

"Zach!"

They got to him in a matter of seconds. Fear clawed at Faith, but eased when the boy opened his eyes.

"You came," he whispered.

Faith gathered him up in her arms, heedless of the snow and chill. "Of course I did," she said, hugging him tightly. "I love you, Zach. And we're all we've got now, baby. We have to take care of each other."

Any other time she was sure Zach would protest that

"baby," and the fact that he didn't—and that he was hugging her back—now told her how scared he'd been.

Morgan took the boy up on the black, leaving Faith to lead the pony. She watched as he wrapped his coat almost tenderly around the child, who was so pale it frightened her. He seemed groggy, and she feared it was from more than sleepiness. She needed to get him home, into a warm bed with some warm liquid in his belly.

But she didn't know where home was. She didn't even know where their fire and meager shelter was.

"The light," she began, looking in the direction where the golden glow seemed to paint a path through the falling snow. "What *is* it?"

"I don't know, but it's in the right direction," Morgan said. "Let's go."

They slogged on through the night and the cold and the snow. Faith's hands grew numb, until the only way she could be sure she still held the pony's reins was to turn and look. Espe plodded on steadily, her staunch courage never faltering, step after step after step down the strange path of light.

It seemed endless, and as Faith grew colder so did her hope. The light was some cruel kind of torture, taunting them, always retreating, never to be reached. Or perhaps they had already died, she thought a little wildly, and this was their hell, not the fires of the eternal pit, but an endless chase through the snowy night.

As if in answer, a gust of wind sent a wet mass of snow into her face. She ducked her head, amazed that anything could feel any colder than she already was. She kept her head down, her weary body moving instinctively with the mare's slow but steady walk. It was no more than she deserved, she supposed. She was a fool, and had been acting the part ever since Morgan had arrived. Dreaming silly dreams, thinking wicked thoughts. She'd been tempted by the fire, so it was fitting that she die in the ice. Without ever knowing what it was she'd hungered for when he'd kissed her, without ever knowing—

"Faith."

Morgan's voice came out of the night toward her. She was too tired to even lift her head.

"Faith, look."

Some strange note in his voice energized her. She looked up. He was staring ahead of them, and she turned her head.

It was the house.

And in the window, casting a golden glow across the snow in a razor-straight path, was Hope's lamp.

"He's sound asleep," Faith said as she pulled the curtains closed. "And he doesn't seem to be feverish."

From where he stood by the window, Morgan glanced at her, nodded, then turned his gaze back to what he'd been staring at.

A lot of impossible things had happened here, he thought. He'd stayed when he'd wanted to go. He'd found himself talking to a child, and pouring his guts out to a woman. He'd lost his customary detachment and couldn't seem to find it again. He'd been listening, and talking, and worst of all feeling.

And he'd found what he never expected to find, a woman with both a gentleness of soul and a wildness of spirit, and with more quiet courage than he'd ever seen before.

But even more impossible was the thing sitting right

in front of him; a small, china lamp sitting where it could not be, the glass chimney whole as it could not be whole . . . and casting a light far beyond its reach, far enough to guide them home through the snow.

And that was the most impossible thing of all, that when he thought of this place, when he thought of Faith, home was the word that came to his mind.

She came up behind him, quietly. He felt her warmth, and was seized by the memory of her mouth beneath his, soft and warm and sweeter than anything he'd ever tasted. He didn't look at her, didn't dare. In that moment she seemed more impossible than the lamp before him, and her light seemed as bright. He felt as if he were teetering on the edge of a precipice, and he could either retreat, with the knowledge that he had run like a coward, or leap off and hope he could fly.

"Maybe Zach was right," she said softly. "Maybe Hope really was here."

"If you believe that, you're as big a fool as the boy." But he felt a shiver as he spoke, for he had no other explanation for glass that had been broken and was now whole, for a tiny lamp that had impossibly cast a lighted path through a storm.

Her voice was calm. "Perhaps I am."

He turned on his heel then, and walked over to where his Winchester lay on the table. He picked it up, then turned to look at her. "I'm leaving," he announced baldly.

"I know." She eyed the weapon. "You don't need that to convince me."

Taken aback by her tone and the odd light in her cinnamon eyes, he stared at her, brows furrowed.

"I know you'll leave, Morgan. I never expected anything else, not really. But you don't have to leave . . . now."

His fingers tightened on the stock of the Winchester, until he knew without looking his knuckles were white. And then she took a step closer, looking up at him, and what he saw in her face made his gut knot as tightly as his hand.

"Stay tonight," she whispered. "With me."

He groaned, his body suddenly as hard as the knot in his belly. "Faith." It came out low and husky, and he couldn't go on.

"Out there it seemed like you weren't . . . repelled," she said hesitantly. "I know it wouldn't be . . . real, not from love, but it doesn't have to be for a man, does it? You kissed me, so . . ."

He made a sound that was half laugh, half groan. When he spoke, his words were purposely rough. "Lady, I was so damn hard, and you were so hot in my hands, you're lucky I didn't take you right there in the snow."

"Then . . . even though I'm plain—"

"God, Faith, don't." All the things she was to him rushed to his lips, and biting them back was one of the hardest things he'd ever done. "Why are you doing this?" he asked, barely able to get out the words past the aching tightness in his throat.

"Because we could have died tonight. We nearly did. And I don't want to die never knowing . . ."

Her nerve, that steel-strong courage failed her then, and she lowered her eyes. But not before he'd read the hunger in them. A hunger, a stark longing that was his undoing; his body rose to it with a speed that took his breath away.

He couldn't fly off this precipice. He knew he couldn't. He would crash on the rocks below, and probably take her with him. But he couldn't run, either. He couldn't run from the precious treasure she was offering him. If she made one more move toward him, he would take it if it damned him to hell.

So he had to make her move away.

"You never asked what my last name was."

She looked startled at the sudden shift, and lifted a delicately arched brow at him. "It's not Morgan?"

"That's my first name." He took a breath, then said it. "My name is Blaine. Morgan Blaine."

She studied him for a moment. "Whatever that is supposed to mean to me, I'm afraid it doesn't."

Of course, he thought ruefully. She'd been in civilized St. Louis, and while the story had been widespread in the West, back in the states they had bigger things to talk about than one man who'd shot down two boys not even ten years older than Zach when they'd taken a notion to steal the stage-line payroll from the coach he'd been riding shotgun on. He'd shot first and only seen their unmasked faces later, and the images had haunted him for fifteen years, and would haunt him until he died.

"You'd better know who you're asking to . . . share your bed, Faith Brown," he said harshly, and told her in cold, brutal words what had happened fifteen years ago, told her just what kind of man he was.

"I quit wearing a gun that day," he finished coldly. "What shooting needs doing I do with the Winchester. But nothing will bring those boys back. I killed them, and they were children."

She had paled slightly, but her voice was level as she asked, "Were they armed?"

"Yes, but—"

"Were they man-size?"

"Almost. But I still should have—"

"Was it your job to protect that coach?"

"Yes, but—"

"Did you know they were just boys?"

"Not until . . . after. But that doesn't—"

"Change the ugliness of what happened? No. But it does mean it wasn't your fault. You weren't responsible for what they did, Morgan. They took that out of your hands when they put on guns and came after that stage."

He couldn't speak, he just stared at her, stunned.

"And you couldn't have been much more than a boy yourself. You've carried the guilt all this time. Punishment enough for something that wasn't your fault."

He felt something let go inside him, some easing of pressure like a long festering wound cleaned and beginning to heal.

"And it doesn't change my mind," Faith said softly. "I know I'm not beautiful—"

He broke then. "Hush," he said, his voice hoarse. He reached for her, and she came to him easily. "I'll move on," he warned her again, "I don't know how not to."

"I know." She slipped her arms around him. "But stay tonight. I've never asked for any gift at Christmas, Morgan. But I'm asking for this one now. And when Christmas is over, you'll ride out, and I'll not try to hold you."

He didn't know exactly what caused the unbearable ache in his chest, the simple honesty and courage it had taken for her to do this or the idea that anyone could look upon him as a gift. He'd spent his life half convinced his aunt had been right, that he was a mistake, worthless, somebody nobody would want, had they a choice.

But Faith Brown was looking at him with longing, with

need, and something else he didn't dare name, offering herself with no demands, no expectations. She deserved more, he knew she did, but God help him, he couldn't walk away. Maybe it meant it was true, that he was as bad as he'd feared, but he couldn't walk away.

He carried her to the small bedroom. His hands shook as he fumbled with her buttons, noting in some corner of his mind that wasn't already beyond thought that her men's clothes didn't seem odd to him at all now, they were simply part of her. In fact, he found himself even more aroused, because they brought back so vividly the memory of her racing across a snowy meadow in the moonlight.

She shivered, and he saw the shy uncertainty in her eyes when she at last stood naked before him, but he reached out to cup her face in his hands.

"Don't ever say you're not beautiful," he whispered, meaning it; she was the loveliest thing he'd ever seen, her body curved and warm and female, and a heat as old as time warming her eyes. "You're perfect in all the ways that matter, inside and out."

She reached for him then, her fingers going to the buttons of his shirt. His patience broke at the first touch of her fingers on his skin, and he pulled away to shed his clothes himself. He saw her eyes widen as she looked at him, took in the fierceness of his arousal.

"If you're going to change your mind, do it now," he said thickly. "Because once I touch you . . ."

His words trailed away as she shook her head. Then she held her arms out to him, and they went down to the bed together.

It took every bit of endurance he had to go slowly, but he held back until she was whimpering, consumed with pleasure but moaning for more. With a quick but heartfelt apology for having to hurt her, he thrust past the slight barrier and at last slipped into her, shuddering at the welcoming slick heat of her flesh. For an instant she tensed at the pain, but then he felt her hands tighten on his back, and she shifted beneath him, reaching. He moved, slowly at first, but then faster as she began to move with him.

And he found in those moments that the woman he'd seen racing under the winter moon was as real, as wild, as passionate as he could ever have imagined. And when she cried out his name as her flesh clenched around him, his body arched into her hard and deep as he shuddered, a guttural cry breaking from him, and in the instant he felt the scalding heat as he poured himself into her, the word in his mind was forever.

He kept his eyes on the stallion's bobbing head as they walked. The horse's hooves crunched the snow rhythmically. And his thoughts settled into the same steady rhythm, and the word repeated in his head with every step was *coward*.

And he knew it was true, it had been cowardly of him to slip out before dawn, with no good-byes. But although she'd promised not to try to hold him, that had been before, before a night spent in pure wonder at what could happen between a man and a woman. After a night like that he knew no woman could help but expect more. It was what women had used for centuries to bind their men to them, to give them such heaven in the night that they would never want to leave come the dawn.

And he hadn't wanted to. He wanted night after night of that hot, sweet pleasure, countless, endless nights. And he wanted mornings as beautiful as Faith had looked curled up in his arms, her hair lying across his chest, her soft, warm breath brushing over his skin.

Hot, clawing need shot through him, nearly doubling him over in the saddle. Proof enough, he thought as he fought it down, that he was right. He'd had to ride out of there. He'd had to.

He was only vaguely aware that it had begun to snow again. He welcomed it, knowing the house would be out of sight now, and that he no longer had to fight the urge to look back; now there would be nothing to see through the darkness.

The stallion moved on steadily, despite his earlier protest at leaving the relative warmth of the barn. Thinking of his stealthy departure made Morgan grimace; he'd known he was in a bad way when his throat had tightened when he'd peeked in at Zach, sleeping peacefully like some golden angel come to earth, but when he'd found himself stopping in the stable to pat Espe in farewell, feeling an odd sense of loss, he knew it was worse than he'd realized.

And he knew he was thinking of these things to keep from thinking of how utterly, wrenchingly hard it had been to lose Faith.

Lose Faith.

His mouth quirked at the irony of the words. As if he'd ever had any faith to lose. As if he'd ever had anything to lose.

The stallion snorted and tossed his head. Morgan knew it was to shake off the snow, which was coming down heavily now, but it seemed to his weary mind that it was a declaration of disgust with his rider's self-pity.

He rode on, heedless of his direction. He'd thought that the farther he got the easier it would be, but with every step the stallion took, the pain grew rather than lessened. It tore at him, like white-hot talons ripping away at every vital part. He clenched his jaw, then bit his lip until it bled, fighting pain with pain, but it wouldn't stop, just kept rising within him until he felt something he hadn't felt since he was a child, the sting of tears in his eyes.

Finally he pulled the horse to a stop. Snow swirled around him, as it had last night. There had been moments when he had thought they would die out here, when the cold was too cold, when the way was hidden. But the light had come, and against all reason they had followed, and it had shown them the way. And in the quiet, soft night, he'd found more than just the way to shelter, he'd found the way home.

Home.

For the first time he thought of it as not a place he'd never known, but a person he'd finally found. And he'd run away from her, as he'd run away from so much in his life. There had been some excuse for it when he was twelve, he supposed, but now?

He realized that Faith, in her quiet way, had shown more courage than he ever had. She might be afraid, she might be uncertain of her abilities, she might despair that she could not do the task she'd set herself, but she had never given up, had never, ever run away.

Zach is mine now. I love him, and I will not leave him.

Her words came back to him, and he knew that any-one that Faith loved would be able to count on that love forever.

Anyone that Faith loved.

The stallion snorted, shook his head again, and shifted sideways to turn his back to the wind, seeking some relief. Morgan barely noticed. Snow swirled around him, and the darkness closed in, but it was no

colder or darker than his soul, and he felt a deep
despair at the thought of going on like this, forever
cold, forever dark, and he wished there were a light
like the one that had led them last night, to show him
the way, because he had never felt so completely, desolately lost. But it would take a miracle to see that tiny
light from here, and he didn't know anyone less de-
serving of one than he.

The stallion's head came up sharply, and the animal
danced as if it had scented danger. Morgan was jolted
out of his dazed state and raised his eyes.

Before him a pure, golden light arrowed its way
through the storm and the darkness.

Faith refused to give vent to the ache in her chest.
She'd known he would go, and should have known
better than to think he would say good-bye. She would
not hate him for leaving, nor would she regret what
she'd done; he'd left her, but he'd given her a miracle
before he'd gone, shown her a beauty and taught her a
glory she'd never even dreamed possible. How could
she hate him for that? She could only pray that he was
all right on his journey, in this wicked weather. And try
not to wonder where he would go.

She checked on Zach again. After his ordeal he was
still asleep, and once she was assured he was suffering
no ill effects or fever, she left him to it. She would
make him breakfast when he awoke, and give him the
small gifts that were all she had to give. Not much of a
Christmas morning, she thought, But she hugged the
memory of the night to her, ignoring the pain of
waking to find Morgan packed and gone, and told herself she'd been given more than she had ever expected.

She walked over to the tree, and carefully lit the

candles again. She stood there looking at it, remembering Morgan's words when they'd finished it.

I think it's myself I lost.

"Please," she whispered, "someday, give him the gift of love. Even if it's not from me."

A sound from the door made her whirl around, her heart leaping to her throat. She stood there as the door swung open.

"Morgan," she breathed, staring at the solitary figure in black.

"I . . . was lost," he said, his voice low and wondering. "I didn't think I'd ever find my way."

She sensed that he was talking about much more than simply losing his way in the snow. She went to him, quickly, seeing in his face the bemused wonder she heard in his voice.

"But the light . . . it came. Like last night."

Instinctively Faith glanced at the window where Hope's lamp sat, although she knew it was not lit. She'd not refilled it, being almost wary of touching it after what had happened, and it had been burned out when she'd awakened at dawn to find herself alone.

Morgan looked toward the lamp, too, and shook his head in denial. "I saw it," he said. "It led me back."

He shivered then, and Faith took his arm. "Come over by the fire. You must be freezing."

"Not anymore," he whispered. He looked at her then, and what Faith saw in his eyes made her hold her breath, waiting, not daring to think, not daring to hope, simply waiting for his next words. "I don't ever want to be that cold again, Faith."

Still she waited, afraid to speak.

"You said you were asking for a gift," he said, reaching out to touch her face with hands that were still cold.

Faith didn't care; she lifted her own hand to press his to her cheek. "But you were giving the greatest one of all, weren't you? And I almost didn't recognize it in time."

"You've never really seen it before," she said, knowing what she was admitting, but suddenly feeling as reckless as if she were racing Espe under the moon.

"Love." His voice seemed to catch on the word.

"Yes."

"But you didn't . . . tell me."

"What difference would it have made? You're not the kind of man to be held by ties not of your own choosing."

"And if I did choose? Would you trust me to be bound by the choice?"

She gathered all her courage and faced him straight on. "If you loved me back, I would."

He smiled then, and it was a smile the like of which she'd never thought to see on his face. "Then, trust me, Faith. Because I do love you."

With a joyous little cry she was in his arms. And they lost track of anything except each other until Zach stumbled sleepily out of the alcove, came to a halt, and stared at Morgan.

"Thought you were leavin'," he said. "An' why are you kissing Aunt Faith?"

"Sit down, Zach," Morgan said with a grin. "We've got some talking to do. I need you to help me name my stallion. And how do you feel about raising horses?"

It was much later, cuddled on Morgan's lap as they sat before the Christmas tree, that Faith sleepily asked, "Do you think Zachary will ever be happy again?"

"He will. It will just take time. But he's got you— us—to love him. He'll be all right."

"Someday," she said, snuggling closer, "we'll tell him."

"Yes," he said. "Someday we'll tell him."

In unison they turned to look. Hope's lamp sat in the window, its light only a small, circular glow now. Yes, Faith thought, someday they would tell him about the light. When he was ready to believe in Christmas miracles again.

For now, it was enough that they believed.

JUSTINE DARE (who also writes as Justine Davis) is the author of over thirty books, and has been called by *Romantic Times* magazine "a dreamspinner of unparalleled magic . . . an extraordinary storyteller." Her books appear regularly on national best seller lists, including the *USA Today* list. She is a three-time winner of the coveted Romance Writers of America Rita Award, and has received a Career Achievement Award and several Reviewer's Choice awards from *Romantic Times*. Justine has been a guest lecturer at UCLA, many regional and international conferences, and has been featured on CNN. She has accomplished all of this while, up until recently, working at a full-time career in law enforcement. Justine lives in San Clemente, California, where her passions outside of writing are her husband, music, and driving her restored 1967 Corvette roadster—top down, of course.

Boxing Day

꙰

BY JILL BARNETT

For those readers who
wanted an older heroine.
Thanks for the idea and
Happy Holidays.

Chapter One

❦

Conn Donoughue had a right hook as strong as a pint of Irish porter. For ten years he'd lived by his fists, fighting opponents who—when they would wake up—claimed his shoulders looked as wide as two grand pianos. And his fists? They swore they never saw them coming.

When he'd first stepped into the ring, no one knew who Connaicht Tobias Donoughue was. Until he fought. Then no one forgot the man they called the Irish Giant.

By age twelve, Conn had already grown over six feet and could rest an elbow on his grandmother's head while she looked up at him, as if he weren't almost twice her size. She would shake one gnarled finger somewhere below his square chin and lecture him about the three *H*'s: Heaven, Hell, and Hard Work. He grew even taller over the next few years, thriving on stories of his grandparents' flight from Ireland to America, where there was opportunity for a new life.

His grandmother died in '83, and Conn had no family left. He had worked at a carriage factory for fourteen hours a day since he was ten years old. At first he had been a water boy, carrying buckets of water to cool the hot iron of the wheel rims.

Eight years later, he was earning five dollars a week running the huge grinding machine that turned out carriage rods. He wasn't afraid of hard work. He never was late or missed a day's work.

Two months after he had buried his grandmother, the factory changed owners. The new owner fired every Irishman employed there and refused to pay their week's wages. The next day the workers gathered at the factory to demand payment.

And it was that day that changed his life—for Conn's first fight was with a hired hoodlum who blocked the entrance to Tanniman's Carriage Company. He won the match and payment of the back wages.

His second fight was two nights later in Brooklyn, where he fought a local boxer in a roped-off gravel lot behind O'Malley's Tavern. He won ten dollars. His third bout was in a cow pasture outside Hoboken. Word had spread from tavern to tavern about this new fighter. There was a crowd of three hundred. And Conn had a new line of work.

Over the next ten years, the Irish Giant grew to be a legend in the boxing ring. He had lost count of the number of fights he'd fought. The number didn't matter. But there was one thing he didn't lose.

Connaicht Tobias Donoughue never lost a fight.

Giant Gymnasium sat in the belly of New York. Housed inside a three-story brick building with black iron fire escapes that zigzagged like fencing scars down the east wall, the gym was wedged between Pasterini's Custom Bootery and the Havana Cigar Company. Pasterini's had a singular boot-shaped canvas awning dyed the colors of the Italian flag. A porcelain flange sign in the shape of a cigar band was bolted above the heavy doors of the cigar shop, where a slogan painted in gold on the glass windows claimed Havana's sold the finest stogies in the States.

The narrow street had a mishmash of merchants and shops, most with living quarters and multiple flats abovestairs. No building was the same height or style. Each had personality, unique and diversified, like those who lived and worked there.

In deference to the Christmas season, Pasterini's front window had a crèche made of real alligator displayed inside a brown patent leather manger. The cigar shop was more traditionally festive. Boxes of imported hand-wrapped cigars and exotic tobaccos with names like Oasis Flame and Spanish Spice were displayed in shiny red tin boxes painted with women's profiles and tucked inside carved ebony humidors that had sterling silver lids.

The German-owned butcher shop displayed a Christmas tree of goose feathers dyed in patriotic red and blue and natural white with ornaments of stars and stripes. Instead of an angel, a pasteboard likeness of Uncle Sam topped the tree. A wide strip of ribbon that looked like the sateen banner worn by the winner of the Miss Brooklyn Bridge contest angled across the tree and boasted beer-fed beef, plump fresh chickens, and the best of traditional Christmas geese.

Those newfangled electric light and telephone lines strung around the neighborhood twined together like Barnum's trapeze nets over the old cast iron street poles. Someone had made an effort to celebrate the season and had tied red and green shimmery ribbons on the street poles the day after Thanksgiving. Now, a few days later and after last night's sloppy hail and rain, the soaked ribbons pooled at the bottom of the street lamps waiting for the street sweeper's broom.

There was no Christmas garland on the entrance to the gymnasium. No holly branch or evergreen wreath. Just a big old pine plank door with three cracks—one from when Murray Ryan took a swing at Otto Rhinehold and missed. The other two were from the whiskey bottles Duncan Fogarty's old lady heaved at him when he forgot to come home for a week.

The stoop was dark and dank, with cement steps and a rusty iron railing that was bent from where an ice wagon spilled its load. Inside was better. A wide lobby with a built-in desk met the sportsmen who entered. Behind the leather-topped counter was a wall of numbered mail cubbies lined with worn green felt and stuffed with white notes and envelopes for the gymnasium members.

Just to the left stood a set of swinging doors painted a washed-out green. The doors had brass hand plates screwed into the wood and oval frosted windows the size of a boxing glove. The constant dull, but rapid thud of fists punching a sparring bag came from behind the doors. There was a round of male laughter, the heavy bounce of a medicine ball, and a distant tooth-ringing sound of fencers parrying their foils.

Behind those doors it was a man's paradise.

The gymnasium air was heavy and warm; the room smelled of camphor wax and cigar smoke . . . of men, sweat, and the primitive need to beat the hell of out of something.

Another round of bawdy laughter came from a smoky corner where three men stood around a desk as big as a wagon. Propped atop the battered desktop was a pair of size eighteen feet, crossed casually and shod in a pair of Tony Pasterini's calfskin boxing boots.

Conn Donoughue stretched back in his oversize leather chair with wooden rollers on the bottom that looked like clenched fists. He rested his arm behind his head and blew ten consecutive smoke rings from one puff of a five-cent cigar. After a moment he straightened, planted those huge feet on the wooden floor, and clamped his white teeth down on the stogie.

He stared at the three men opposite him for a long moment. His face broke into a cocky grin, the smoldering cigar still clamped in his back teeth and sticking out of the side of his mouth. "I win."

A slew of curses filled the air: Italian, Spanish, and fractured English mixed with one voice of German dialect. Within seconds one twenty-dollar gold piece, an ornate silver belt buckle, and a large mahogany box of imported cigars plunked down on Conn's massive desk.

Cuba Santana, owner of the cigar shop, stared up at the dissipating smoke rings that floated toward the high ceiling. He shook his head along with one raised fist. "Santa Maria! I thought no one could blow ten rings!"

"They said no one could knock out the Bronx Bruiser, but Conn, here, did it in two rounds." Tony Pasterini picked up the expensive belt buckle he'd lost, swiped it down his wool vest to polish it, and with a look of regret tossed it back on the desk.

Pete Hassloff turned toward Cuba and shrugged. "Das ist Conn's dammit Irish luck, by golly."

Originally from Hamburg, Pete was the neighborhood butcher. His dream had been to come to America, and now that he was here, he butchered the meat and the language.

All were friends, but Conn had known Tony the

longest. Ever since that fight behind O'Malley's Tavern. And even after all those years, Tony was still his closest friend.

Conn tucked the gold piece and buckle into a black safe with gilded curlicues on the door, then rolled his chair back to the desk and snapped open the polished cigar box. He took out a cigar with an impressive black band embossed with gold. He drew the stogie across his upper lip, took a deep breath, and closed his eyes. "Ah . . . These are some fine cigars, Santana."

"They oughta be. They cost a fortune."

Conn opened his eyes and looked at Cuba. "But not to you, my friend. What's your markup on these babies?"

"Three hundred percent," Tony said in a wry tone.

Santana rubbed his chin, then absently tugged on the corner of his handlebar mustache. "I don't charge three hundred percent."

Tony gave a snort of disbelief.

"At Christmas I always hike 'em up five hundred percent." Santana's dark face broke into a sly grin. That grin turned into a laugh, and the curly tips of his mustache shimmied despite the thick coats of wax that made the hair look like curled tar.

Pete clucked his tongue and gave Santana a disapproving look. "Das ist hard for you to see your head when ist daytime."

Conn looked at Tony, whose frowning face looked as confused as he was.

"Face myself in the morning," Santana explained. For some reason Cuba could understand Pete no matter how convoluted his phrases were.

"Ya." Pete nodded, waving a hand. "Das ist vhat I said."

The swinging doors blasted open and slammed against

the gym walls. Lenny the towel boy came rushing inside. He raced over to the desk and gave Conn a panicked look. "We've got trouble, boss."

"What kind of trouble?"

Lenny glanced at the doors. "She's here again."

The gym grew suddenly quiet. Fencing partners stilled, their foils held in midair and their meshed masks suddenly cocked back. Punching bags quieted, and the medicine balls no longer bounced on the wooden floor. Iron weights and wooden dumbbells rattled onto the storage racks, and an Indian club smacked a trainer in the head. The boxers had frozen in the rings and stared at the door with horror. It was almost as if they expected to see a Republican walk in.

Conn looked away and groaned. He stared at the desk for a second, then snatched up the cigar box. He stood. "Here you go, boys! Light 'em up! Quick!"

Within seconds the men were tossing around matchboxes and expensive stogies instead of Indian clubs and exercise balls. The air swelled with a chalky shroud of sulfur and cigar smoke. Moments later the room looked as if a volcano had erupted in it.

The green doors swung open with a sharp rattle. Small heels moved across the wooden floor—click, click, click—like Kaiser Wilhelm's soldiers.

And there she was. Conn's landlady.

Chapter Two

⌒∾⌒

Eleanor Rose Austen stopped when she was inside the center of the gymnasium and waved away the clouds of stinking cigar smoke. It proved to be a futile exercise. Rather like trying to put out a fire with an eye dropper. She fiddled with the button on one kidskin glove and scanned the room.

The men looked like smoky shadows—ghosts on a misty moorland. She blinked back the teary sting of smoke, then slowly scanned the room again, her hands now planted on her hips in a determined manner.

She didn't care about the ghost shadows. She was looking for a giant.

One huge shadow stood in silhouette near the far north corner of the room. A cloud of smoke puffed upward in a mad rush from a bright glowing red dot. It was one of those vile cigars that—she looked around her—all the men in the room smoked.

She cocked her chin at a brave angle, raised her index finger high in the air, and marched through the fog toward that huge shadow. "Yoo-hoo . . . Mr. Donoughue!"

The huge shadow ducked.

"I see you!"

The shadow ducked even lower.

As if a man the size of the Manhattan Life Building could hide from her. *Really.*

The smoke had grown thicker the closer she got to him. She kept walking.

A moment later she poked her index finger into Conn Donoughue's mountain of a chest. A big mistake; it was a bare and hairy chest.

She froze. In all this smoke, the man could easily be naked. Good grief . . . All the men could be naked.

Eleanor stood still as a stone, masking her reaction and trying not to do something emotional and silly, like turn and run . . . or even more foolish—take a closer look. The air began to clear a bit. Her line of vision was level with her finger, which was buried in a thick patch of curly red chest hair.

Now what?

Don't look down. A little voice inside her head kept chanting away. Don't look down, Eleanor. Don't you do it!

But she had always had a small problem with doing what she was told. Her gaze just dropped all on its own.

A few seconds later she looked up. "You're wearing athletic shorts."

"Abercombie and Fitch."

"Mr. Donoughue—"

"You sound disappointed. I can take them off if you want, sweetheart."

She choked on a breath of air or smoke, or on his words. It took her a second to stop coughing. She could hear some of the men behind her laughing quietly. She inhaled slowly and looked up—way up into Conn Donoughue's grinning face.

"What did you just call me?"

"Sweetheart?"

"That is not my name."

"Okay, how 'bout Nellibelle?"

She flinched. *Nellibelle? It made her sound like a cow.*

He held his arms straight out from his side. He reminded her of the Brooklyn Bridge. "Just pull this little string here at my waist, Nellibelle, and everything I have is all yours."

"No, thank you. If I needed a jackass, I can buy one at the local stable." She smiled sweetly.

He laughed. The sound was deep and loud like a tuba, and seemed to go right through her no matter how stiffly she stood there.

"My name is Eleanor, not Nellibelle."

He hitched his hip down on the corner of his desk, but he was still taller than she was. "I had a cat named Nellibelle. She used to crawl into bed with me, curl up and purr."

Make laughter filled the room. She closed her eyes and felt foolish for egging him on. This was humiliating and belittling. When those men laughed at her, it choked more from her than any cigar smoke ever could.

But she would never let him or the other men know it. She didn't respond again. It wouldn't do any good to spar with him.

She just turned and walked away, her spine rigid and her head held even higher than when she had come inside. She slapped her palm flat against the swinging door and paused halfway through the opening.

She looked back at the men. Some still grinned but Donoughue's cocky look seemed to fade before her eyes. That wasn't at all what she expected to see. She had thought he'd be looking immensely pleased with himself.

Instead they both stood there watching each other for the longest time. The laughter in the room died. The silence seemed to stretch out like a long road, the kind that beckons you toward a wondrous thing so far out of reach you had forgotten it even existed.

Something passed between them. Something chilling and intense. Something deep that she had never before felt. Almost spellbound, she could not tear her gaze away from him, even though she wanted to. This one man had a hold over her that she could not control. With sudden clarity she knew how weak and frightened and powerless a small animal must feel when it was caught in a trap.

After a moment Eleanor noticed that the men were staring back and forth between the two of them with expressions of surprise or curiosity.

She straightened her shoulders. "Gentlemen." She let the word hang there, so it was clear that was the last thing these men had behaved as. She fixed her most honest look on Donoughue. "I didn't come here for this."

He started to walk toward her, his expression filled with another emotion she didn't care to see. It was pity.

Her hand shot up. "Stay there." Her voice sounded raspy and sharp, almost as if she was going to cry. "Please. Don't." And for a brief instant she didn't know if she was talking to him or to herself.

He did stop. Just stood there looking at her.

"I'm moving into the flat upstairs." Her words came out in a rush.

The moment seemed to hang in the air like the cigar

smoke. It was awkward and she could feel her nervousness. Her face felt hot, and her hands were clenched at her sides.

She knew the moment her words had registered. His face showed it. Now she had his attention for something other than his juvenile entertainment.

"What the hell do you mean you're moving upstairs? I live there."

"I own the building."

"I have a lease from your grandfather. Legally you have to uphold that agreement. And you know damn will I've offered repeatedly to buy this building."

"Yes, you have. Almost as often as you've cursed at me."

"You won't sell."

"You're right. I won't."

"Why the hell not? I've offered you a fair price."

"I just told you why. Because I'm going to live here."

His expression hardened. "Not in this lifetime, lady."

She sighed. It truly was like talking to a brick wall.

He took two huge steps closer. "You are not moving onto the third floor."

She stood a little straighter, the door pressed against her back.

He moved even closer, trying to intimidate her.

She still only stood level with his shoulder. She raised her chin. "You're absolutely right. I'm not moving onto the third floor." Her tone was casual.

"Damn straight." He gave his head a sharp nod as if to say his word was law.

"I'm moving in above you."

His eyes narrowed. He was not a happy man.

"The fourth floor," she explained simply.

"I store my extra supplies and equipment on the fourth floor."

"I know. That's the reason I came here today."

"Well, Nellibelle." He crossed his hammy arms over his chest. "I don't think there will be room for you *and* those weights *and* my sporting equipment *and* the gym supplies."

"There will be plenty of room once you move everything out."

"Like hell I will! I pay rent!"

"Not for the fourth floor, you don't. I suggest you read your lease. You have two days to vacate the fourth-floor loft. Happy holidays, Mr. Donoughue." Eleanor turned and marched right out the door.

She stood with her back pressed against the cold damp brick building. Her chest was heaving from a horrid case of nerves.

What a foolish thing she was. She was no giddy girl, the kind that would get flustered at the mere sight of a man. She was a woman. And not even a young woman.

But one who was forty years old.

Irritated with herself for reacting like she was, she exhaled sharply. Her throat was dry to the point of soreness, and her breath had that brittle taste of cigar smoke.

The air outside was cold now, much colder than it had been before she went inside. Yet here she was sweating as if it were July. She fanned her face a little, and the pheasant feathers on her Sunday hat fluttered.

Just like her silly old heart.

She had met Conn Donoughue on a half a dozen occasions since she took over ownership of the building, and still she reacted to him in the same insane way each time. It was as if he were a huge dipper of peppermint ice cream.

Eleanor loved peppermint ice cream.

And Eleanor loved Conn Donoughue. She had taken one look at him, and suddenly she wasn't the old Eleanor anymore. She was one big heartache. From that moment on, she had known that nothing would ever be the same again. She had fallen for him so deeply and quickly that it was like being slapped right in the face.

He was a boxer who was too young and too handsome, especially for a forty-year-old woman who had long ago accepted the fact that love and passion and desire were not to be a part of her life.

He had smiled at her the first time they met. She remembered being so amazed that someone who was so tall and so big could smile like that. So she had just stood there and stared at him.

He had reddish blond hair, deep blue eyes, and an angled face that was unforgettable; it haunted her at the most awkward times. There was a bump on his nose. But she liked it because it gave character to what would have been a too handsome face.

At that first meeting, she had come to her senses a little late and realized he was watching her stare at him. She'd felt herself blush, so hot that she had been certain her face was as pink as a cabbage rose. She had felt so very silly. Forty-year-old women should be past the age of blushes and sheep's eyes and other flirtations.

Years ago she had thought she was through with those white-hot dreams of desire and love, the ones that grow up with you. The same ones where she would awake in a deep sweat because her own body didn't know that what she was experiencing was just a dream.

Since that first meeting, at the strangest times during the day, she would feel dizzy and light-headed. She would stare off at nothing almost as if she were searching for a reason why this was happening to her.

But the only explanation she could come up with was Conn Donoughue. He had brought all that youthful craziness and hope back. Feelings that should have died long ago. Sometimes it seemed to her as if the world just didn't work right.

He had invited her to dinner soon after that first meeting. She had forgotten herself and had gone out that evening feeling like a young girl again. All through dinner he had been charming and attentive. She just fell all that much harder for him.

He danced with her and pulled her closer than a man should. He would lean down to say something to her, and she could feel his breath in her ear and goose-pimples covered her from head to toe. He took her back to Mrs. Waverly's and kissed her under the lamplight on the stoop.

And while she was trying to calm her heart, he went and ruined everything.

He leaned against the building with his arms crossed in that male way he had, and suggested they "get down to business." He wanted to buy the building.

She was so humiliated that she had refused his offer with a stubbornness that he didn't appear to understand. And perhaps neither did she.

From then on they'd been adversaries.

He hounded her to sell. She stubbornly refused. She had even resorted to dropping by unannounced and pointing out infractions in the lease agreement.

It was her right. Besides, it irritated him, which was the reason she did it.

Eleanor straightened and pushed away from the building. She adjusted the velvet collar on her wool coat, pulling it up around her neck as if it could block out everything she was feeling. A minute later it was snowing those small and white wet flakes that seemed to melt just the instant before they touched you.

She squared her shoulders and walked down the sidewalk without glancing back. Snowflakes sprinkled her face and floated in her mouth. She went as far as the corner where the cable car stopped every half hour, and stood there for a minute. But she wasn't looking for the car or listening for the ringing of the trolley bell.

She was staring at the windows of the gym.

It wasn't even five o'clock, but lamplight shone in shapes of dim yellow boxes from a window on the third floor. She had forgotten how very dark it could get at this time of year.

She wondered if he was reading the lease. It was there on that paper in black and white. The top floor and the roof had been excluded from the lease agreement by her grandfather.

She knew why. Half the roof was paneled with long panes of glass that framed the night sky and made it look as if it were lifted right from a Van Gogh painting.

Gramps had always fancied himself somewhat of an astronomer. She'd heard him say that someday he would move his telescopes and charts to the old building. If the stock market did well, Gramps had been determined to renovate someday, perhaps even turn that building into a small neighborhood observatory.

But then her family had always been filled with hopeless dreamers. She never knew if for Gramps it was only a far-off dream or if he would have actually done it. Although it hadn't mattered because he never had the chance.

The market crashed in 1893. And so did their world. After two years of struggling and unexpected poverty, Gramps died. The only thing he still owned was the building, which was leased for five years to the gymnasium.

At that moment the cable car clanged its way up the street, and the people who stood on the corner began to crowd together. Heat from the anxious huddle of commuters blocked out the cool air for a brief moment. Blessedly the snow had stopped falling.

Eleanor shifted to hold her place at the edge of the curb. The cable car clacked to a stop, and the crowd swarmed forward. She jumped up the steps, dropped two pennies into the coin box with a clink, and turned to look for a seat.

Rows of couples stared back at her: men and women, fathers and mothers, husbands and wives, friends and lovers. She gripped the handrail above her as the car filled, then the trolley jerked forward. For the hundredth time she wondered how she could feel so alone in a city that was so very crowded.

A husband and wife sat next to where she stood, her hand in the leather strap that hung from the handrail above. The couple was talking about what to buy the children for Christmas.

She turned away only to see a handsome young pair across the aisle share a long look of first love. They shifted closer like turtledoves when the cable car turned another corner. She saw the young man discreetly take a hold of the girl's hand. The girl looked up shyly, and they exchanged a smile so full of feeling it hurt for her to watch.

She stood there tall and stiff and feeling achingly empty inside. At that moment she was more lonely than she could ever remember feeling. It was as if she were on the outside of a huge window where she could only look on as the world merrily went by on the other side. Over the years she had thought she'd gotten used to this lonely life, accepted it the same lost way someone learns to accept going through life on a wooden leg.

But all around her people chattered and laughed. She stood there, her body rocking to the cable car motion, her mind rocking with an odd mixture of loneliness and desire.

The car moved down the blocks while she stood there not seeing anything. People got on. People got off. But even when there were empty seats, she did not sit because she didn't notice.

At a crowded intersection, the brakeman clanged out "Jingle Bells" on the trolley bell. That did make her smile.

Ten minutes later she was off the trolley and moving down the street toward her rented rooms. It was raining now, and she began to run past the pushcarts filled with vegetables and fruits that refrigerated trains brought up from Florida, past the couples shopping for supper.

She only had a half block to go when the winter skies just opened up. Rain was coming down so hard it could blind you if you looked up into the sky.

She made a dash for cover under the red canvas awning at the Paris Café. She huddled there watching the rain splatter down as if the sky were a river. With the downpour came a gloomy darkness, and the lamps outside the café fluttered on.

Startled, she turned around. There, through the windows, she could see the waiters setting tables with candles and roses and wineglasses for two.

Twos. All around her was a world of twos.

She turned and bolted from beneath the awning. Rain pelted her face as she ran down the street and the cold water on the sidewalk splashed over the tops of her calfskin boots. By the time she made it to the stoop, she had pheasant feathers straggling in her face, and her coat felt like she was wearing a sandbag.

She was wet and freezing. Her shoes squished into the drafty linoleum in the foyer, and she closed the front door. Turning, she slapped the feathers out of her eyes and shook out her coat.

Mrs. Waverly was leaning against the wainscoted wall of the dining room and shouting into the shiny black horn on the wooden telephone box. "I heard you, Sally! The train is coming in at four o'clock on Thursday. I'll be there. Don't fret so."

She nodded at Eleanor and pointed to the table near the stairs, where she would put any mail that had come. Eleanor walked over and picked up the envelopes. She thumbed through the ones that were most important.

Every week she sent out a new batch of applications. And every week the responses said the same thing. No positions available at this time.

Mrs. Waverly hung up the telephone. "I swear that girl gets worse every day. If it isn't one thing, it's another. She's called me six times already today."

"I'm sure she's just excited to be coming home."

"I suppose you're right. A girl's wedding is the most important day of her life."

Eleanor stood stoically silent.

Mrs. Waverly retied her ruffled chintz apron with

the print of cabbage roses and looked up. She nodded at the envelopes in Eleanor's hand. "Any luck?"

She shook her head and tucked the letters into her coat pocket. "I'm certain there will be something available soon."

"You know how very sorry I am, my dear."

"I know. You don't have to keep apologizing about the move." Eleanor gave her landlady a smile.

"If Sally wasn't coming, you could stay indefinitely and not have to pay one single penny."

"I know that. But Sally needs you. And it will be special to have her and your new son-in-law living here. Besides, which, I have a perfectly good place to go. Really."

"That horrid gymnasium?" Mrs. Waverly snorted.

"It's actually better inside than it looks. I'm certain I can find a position after the holidays. Then I'll be able to fix it up just the way Gramps would have liked."

"It's a hectic time of year for you to be looking for work. Nothing gets done during the holidays. People don't seem to pay attention. Why that daughter of mine wanted a Christmas wedding I'll never know."

"I think a Christmas wedding would be lovely."

"I suppose." Mrs. Waverly planted her hands on her rounded hips and asked, "Do you know why Sally called this time?"

Eleanor shook her head.

"That silly girl wanted me to make certain the florist had Christmas lilies. I told her it was Christmas. Of course they'd have Christmas lilies." The older woman sighed. "There's already enough to do at this time of year without having all this brouhaha. Oh, which reminds me. One of those Stadler boys came by this afternoon, and said they'd have the wagon here at seven Wednesday morning. They'll have your things moved out and into the new place by noon."

Before Eleanor could thank her, the telephone rang with a loud shrill ring.

"I wonder who this could be," Mrs. Waverly said in a wry tone. She grabbed the ear piece, tapped on the speaking horn, and listened for a second. "Yes, Sally. It's me." She glanced at Eleanor and rolled her eyes. "Yes, Sally. I'll check it. No, the florist is closed. I'll have to call tomorrow."

She was feeling her aloneness so acutely today. Why? Because she had chosen to face Conn Donoughue? Maybe it was because of the holidays. Maybe she was turning into a lonely old woman who did nothing but dream of what could never be.

Eleanor just felt all used up. After a moment she turned and trudged up the staircase to her rooms. She had her things to pack.

Chapter Three

❦

Early Wednesday morning Conn awoke to the sound of someone singing Christmas carols. He groaned and rolled over, flinging his arm over his eyes to block out the shock of daylight.

To hell with King Wenceslas.

The ceiling thundered as if all the king's horses and all the king's men were having a melee right above him. He crammed a pillow over his head and tried to go back to sleep.

It worked until something thumped down the stairs. Something heavy. Something big. Something loud.

Conn rolled his legs over the side of the bed and sat up. There was another loud thud. He buried his pounding head in his hands.

He glanced up, wincing. The banging around on the fourth floor was so loud the old gaslight in the center of the room shook. It sounded as if the whole building rattled.

Conn stood up, scowling at the ceiling. Who the hell was moving in? One stubborn pain-in-the-butt woman or New York City's mounted police?

He stepped into his pants and shrugged on a wool

shirt. Grumbling under his breath, he tied his shoes and crossed to the room. He threw open the door.

There in the hallway near the stairs was a cumbersome oak cabinet rocking back and forth in midair. Two men, one under it and one behind it, were trying to move the cabinet around the turn in the third-floor landing and up the next flight of stairs.

One of the men swore. "Stop telling me how to do it, Jimmy, and just back up so we can get this blasted thing up the stairs."

"Yoo-hoo!" Nellibelle leaned over the banister and shook her finger at the movers.

One of the men groaned, "Not again."

Conn knew just how he felt.

"Don't scratch the wood please!"

The tallest mover shifted to get a better grip on the cabinet and leaned his head over to the side. "We got it, Miss Austen."

She started to say something else but her gaze flashed to Conn. For just an instant her face froze in a sick look; it was the same look he'd seen on people who had just swallowed a rotten oyster.

A second later she popped up quicker than his best punching bag. She stared at him the way she had when they'd first met and her face began to turn pink. Her chin shot up, and she spun around and disappeared into the doorway of the fourth-floor apartments.

Conn looked at the other men and shrugged, then pushed away from the doorway. "You want some help?"

The mover took in his size with a quick and rapt once-over. He had seen that look a million times.

"Yeah. We'd appreciate it. Jimmy, set down your end and take this other corner." He turned to Conn. "Thanks. It's been a long morning."

"I'll bet it has." Conn hunkered down and picked up the bottom of the cabinet.

Ten minutes later the cabinet was against the west wall of the fourth-floor flat. Nellibelle was hovering around it, trying to decide if they needed to move it a little to the right.

Again.

He watched her purposely ignore him. But he could see her nervousness—the wringing of her hands, the way she darted back and forth like a confused bee, and her stubborn determination not to look at him.

His immediate reaction was to think of things he could do to force her to look at him. Stand in front of her. Walk toward her until he had her backed against a wall. Grab her and kiss her like he had the night he walked her home.

He paused and made a big to-do of eyeing the cabinet, moving to stand in front of her and tapping one finger against his chin. "I think it's too far to the left. You should move it to the right, Nellibelle."

She stiffened and looked at him, her expression all pruny. He could almost hear her teeth grind.

He gave her an innocent look and casually pointed at the cabinet with his thumb. "It's too far to the left."

She turned back around and without looking at the cabinet nodded to the movers. "Move the cabinet more to the left, please."

He laughed to himself. Dealing with her was no different than maneuvering one of his opponents into taking a frustrated swing at him.

The movers picked up the cabinet again and began to lift it. The rope securing the doors closed slipped down, and the mirrored doors swung open.

Conn grabbed her under one arm, swung her off her

feet and out of the way. She gave a shriek of protest and squirmed. A second later an iron bed frame unfolded from the cabinet and slammed to the floor.

He set her down while she was still muttering something about an oaf and walked over to the iron frame. He turned back to her. She was swiping back a hank of black hair from her red face.

He pointed to the bed. "What the hell kind of bed is this supposed to be?"

She raised her chin. "It's a folding bed."

"Why?"

"Why what?"

"Why would anyone want a folding bed?"

"For convenience of course."

"What's convenient about a folding bed? Looks damn inconvenient to me."

"It saves space."

He eyed the bed. "Who cares about space if it's too short to sleep in."

"It's not too short for me."

He let his eyes roam slowly from the top of her stuck-up head to her feet pressed together at the ankles in that annoying prim way she had. "Doesn't look to me as if you'd fit. Unless you sleep with your knees all drawn up."

"How I sleep is none of your concern, Mr. Donoughue."

"You'd never catch me in that bed."

"There is a God."

The movers laughed out loud. He wanted to laugh, too, but he didn't. Instead he stared at her long enough to annoy her. She gave him a smile that held no humor and spun around.

He waited until she was halfway across the room. "We could always use my bed."

She stopped as if she had run smack dab into a wall. She turned slowly, her jaw set and her words gritty. "Mr. Donoughue—"

Ignoring her, he strolled around some of the trunks and crates that separated them, peering inside. "So what other kind of contraptions do you have around here?"

"I don't recall inviting you in here."

"You didn't." He scanned the room. It was a huge cavernous place. It wasn't dark like his flat. Half the roof was glass. It let sunlight in, but it also leaked whenever it rained. He knew because it had leaked on some wooden boxes, damaging a shipment of leather elbow pads and knee guards.

"I think the movers will be able to handle the rest of my things. *Alone*." She walked toward him. "I don't want to keep you from whatever it is you do."

"You're not." He turned his back on her and strolled over to an overstuffed chair, sat down, and made himself comfortable, then crossed his hands behind his head and propped his feet on a crate of dishes packed in excelsior.

She watched him from a face that was half offended and half frustrated.

He would have stayed there all morning if Lenny hadn't come running upstairs all in a panic. Beckman's Laundry Wagon had forgotten to deliver last week's load of towels.

A few minutes later Conn was walking down the street toward Beckman's. He stood on the corner, where a uniformed copper on horseback controlled the traffic.

Conn glanced back at the gym. He could see those old glass transoms on the roof. He watched them for a few lost minutes. He heard the police whistle and turned around just in time to catch the man next to him staring up in awe. Conn was used to it.

He glanced down at the man who tried to cover his embarrassment by quickly looking away. After a minute he turned back and caught Conn's eye. "Looks like rain," the man said.

"You think so?" Conn glanced up. The sky was turning a dull gray color that could mean rain.

"Yeah, with those clouds it'll be pouring by tonight."

The policeman's whistle blew again, and everyone began to cross the street. Conn was in the crowd but a head above everyone else. The wind picked up and ruffled his hair. He turned around, walking backward across the street. He looked back at those leaky glass windows on the slope of the roof.

Grinning, Conn turned back and stepped up on the opposite curb. He shoved his hands in the deep pockets of his pants and strolled down the street—whistling.

The first raindrop fell on Eleanor's forehead around midnight. Her eyes shot open. The second drop plopped on her nose and dripped down her cheek. After the third drop, she sat up.

Her roof was leaking.

She threw back the covers and got up. The rain outside was coming down harder, pattering a constant beat on the glass and the roof tiles. Drops of water splattered all over the floor and on what little furniture she still owned. She rushed toward the kitchen nook and took out her cast iron pot and a frying pan, then rushed back and placed them under the worst leaks.

Her china cups caught smaller leaks, and along with her few soup bowls, they were scattered haphazardly over the plank floor like croquet wickets. She rum-maged through trunks and wooden boxes searching for vases and goblets, anything that could hold water.

By the time she found one new container, the smaller dishes were overflowing and rainwater was spreading over the floor and under the boxes of things she hadn't yet unpacked. She moved back and forth, trying not to panic. She would tuck a vase under one arm, and race across the floor to catch a cup or bowl or pan before it overflowed. She'd shoved the vase under the leak, and run back to the old porcelain sink drain or the narrow water closet and dump out the bowl of water, only to rush back and find five containers overflowing.

The rain came down so hard it hit the roof like buck-shot. The leaks began to pour instead of drip. Still she raced back and forth. Water pooled all over the floor, and she tried to mop it up with towels and extra blan-kets, linens, anything that could soak it up.

Panicking, she spun around and started running. Too fast. She slipped. Lost her balance. Her ankle gave out, she went down, sliding across the wet floor like a duck on ice.

She hit a patch of dry wood and skidded to a stop. She gripped her ankle and groaned, her body curled like a comma. For a pain-filled moment, all she could do was lie there while the rain fell all over her.

I'm okay . . . I'm okay . . . I'm okay.

But she wasn't. Her ankle throbbed, and an aching pain shot up her leg and felt as if someone had tried to twist her foot off. She just lay there, waiting for the pain to subside. Part of her wanted to cry, but she wouldn't let herself. She shifted into a sitting position, then rolled onto her knees and pushed herself up. Very carefully she put weight on her injured foot.

It wasn't too bad. She began to walk slowly across the wet floor. She was okay. It was sore, but she could walk almost normally.

Rain dribbled onto her hair and down her back from the roof. Not that it mattered since her nightgown was soaked on one side and damp on the other. She stared up at the glass. She could see the cracks. She stared at them for a few minutes, then began to gather pieces of clothing from her trunks, anything she could use to stuff the leaks.

She gathered up an armful of undergarments, since they were the thinnest fabrics, then she hobbled over and picked up the broom. Within moments she was atop the bureau, using the broom handle to stuff stockings, hankies, a thin corset cover, even bloomers, anything that would plug up the cracks between the glass panels.

Eleanor moved from piece to piece of high furniture—her grandmother's armoire, the old cherry wood buffet, and the round oak table—until she had stuffed the biggest leaks. The cracks on the arch of the roof were too high, but luckily they were over areas where there was no furniture. She put her largest pots and other containers under those.

An hour later she had all the leaks plugged.

Then a new one started right over her bed.

She limped over to the bed, crawled up, and stood on the mattress. She tossed the last two stockings and her broom on top of the oak cabinet, then pulled herself up, scrabbling until she was kneeling on it.

Slowly she stood, then stuck a stocking on the end of

the broom handle and stretched up as high as she could. She was just an inch or two short. With her weight mostly on her good foot, she rose on her tiptoes, teetering just a little. She straightened her back for balance. Every time she thought she had the crack plugged, the stocking would slip and fall.

By the fifth time she had learned to catch it with the broom handle so she wouldn't have to keep crawling down to pick it up. This was one of those times when you wished you had too many stockings. It took thirteen tries before she had stuffed the stocking in the narrow leak.

One more leak.

She put her last stocking on the broom handle, stood on tiptoe again and stuffed it into the leak on the first try.

Slowly she put back the broom. *Please stay . . . please stay . . .*

She turned slightly and braced her back flush against the wall and waited. The stocking stopped the leak and stayed there.

She took a deep breath. She'd done it.

A second later the other soaked stocking slipped from its crack and slapped her smack across the face.

The broom slipped from her hand.

She fell. Face forward.

She screamed. Her body hit the mattress so hard the bedsprings screamed with her. The bed frame bounced upward and slammed her into the back of the cabinet.

She saw stars.

It took a moment to realize what had happened. She tried to move and couldn't. The mattress was pressed against her. She could wiggle her hips a small bit. She needed a little more room to be able to force the bed frame back down. She took a deep breath—of mattress—and butted the back of the cabinet with her backside.

The cabinet rocked back.

There was a loud bang. A small click of metal catch.

The cabinet doors! Oh my God . . . They closed!

She opened her eyes.

Eleanor was stuck inside the bed cabinet.

Chapter Four

❦

Conn woke up when small pieces of ceiling plaster fell on him.

"What the hell?" He sat up, shaking the plaster off his head. Still sleep-startled and half wondering where he was, he scanned the dark room.

It was still night. A storm had broken; he could hear the rain against the windows. He was in his bedroom. Awake.

He thought he heard a familiar shriek. He scowled up at the ceiling. What was she doing now?

He looked down at the dusty bedding.

Cracking the plaster, that's what she was doing.

He threw back the covers and chalky bits of the ceiling bounced like craps dice on the wooden floor. He stood and took a step. Chips of plaster jabbed his bare feet and crumbled like sand when he walked on them. Muttering, he dusted off his feet and staggered over to the next room.

He looked at the clock. It was three in the morning.

Frustrated, he leaned one shoulder against the wall and stared at the floor. He needed some sleep. Not much. Just a few consecutive hours. She was going to make his life miserable, living above him like this. He could see it coming.

There was a loud banging against the wall upstairs. Even the dead couldn't sleep through that. Behind him he could hear the patter of plaster on his bedroom floor. His hands itched with the need to wring her damn neck. Conn took a deep breath, then stood there for a moment, rubbing a hand over his eyes.

The noise continued. Muffled, but it continued. The gaslight shimmied and rattled. That was it!

He grabbed a pair of trousers and pulled them on, buttoning them as he moved toward the door. Once in the hall, he ran up the stairs, glared at her door, and then pounded it with his fist.

He waited, rocking on his feet in anticipation.

But there was nothing. He hammered the door again and waited. All he got for his effort was some more noise. He pounded on the door so hard, they could've heard it in the Bronx. "Open this damn door!"

Nothing.

He knew she was in there. An eternal minute passed. Maybe he was scaring her, which was not a smart move. He leaned toward the door. "Nellibelle?"

Nothing.

He drummed his fingers against the doorjamb. He took a deep breath for patience. "Miss Austen?" He paused, then called out. "Eleanor?" He pressed his ear against the door and listened.

For just a second he thought he heard her. It sounded like she was shouting from miles away. Something cold and wet pooled under his bare feet. He looked down, instinctively stepping back.

Water seeped out from under the door. He tried the doorknob but it was locked. He rattled the handle, then, without another thought, he stepped back and rammed his shoulder against the door.

It flew open with a loud crack.

A good inch of water flooded the hall. The floor inside the flat was soaked. He walked in and looked up. From all over the roof panes hung soggy women's clothing.

Not clothing, exactly, but underwear. Water dripped onto the floor from drenched black cotton stockings. More water poured from a couple of those thin corset cover things women wore that always took forever for his big hands to unbutton.

Staring up, he moved to the center of the room. A pair of white lacy bloomers dropped on the floor in front of him like a sodden flag of surrender.

"Nellibelle?"

A muffled call for help came from deeper inside the apartment. He looked around, then crossed room. "Where the hell are you?" He peered around the corner, but then heard something behind him and turned around.

That oak cabinet with the stupid and useless bed shuddered like it was alive. A voice came from deep inside it. "Help! Help!"

Swearing, he crossed the room and jerked open the doors. The bed fell forward so fast he had to jump backward so it didn't hit him.

It banged against the watery floor with a loud crashing splat. Nellibelle bounced up off the mattress with a shriek. Her tangled mass of wet hair flew outward; it looked like floating black spaghetti.

Momentum made the front legs of the bed frame collapse.

Before he could move, she hit the slumping bed again and rolled down the mattress. She landed on the wooden floor with a hard wet thud that made him wince.

He moved to her side and hunkered down. "Are you all right?" He reached out tentatively and touched her shoulder.

She shifted slightly.

He heard a choking sound. "Nell? Uh . . . Eleanor? Are you crying?"

"Yeeeeeesssssssss!" she wailed all curled up in a pitiful wet ball.

He scooped her into his arms, and water dripped down to his hands and onto the soaked floor. He held her tightly against his chest, and she turned into him as if she were trying to hide, sobbing the whole time.

He patted her back a little tentatively. "Don't cry. Okay?"

She cried harder, then slid her damp arms around his neck. She buried her head against him.

He could feel her, every soft feminine inch of her. He had to remind himself just who he was holding in his arms. He looked down at her and saw nothing but a small woman with a mass of hair that hung past her butt. Her bare feet poked out of the hem of her night-gown. They were pink and narrow and looked as soft as she felt. He studied the back of her head, then spoke to it because he couldn't see her face. "Tell me where it hurts."

"All over." Her words were muffled against his shoulder and neck.

He rubbed her back with one hand, making soothing circles to stop her pitiful crying. "If I'm going to help you, then I need you to be more specific."

"Okay." It was barely a whisper. She said nothing more, just hiccuped against him as she tried to catch her breath.

"Please. Tell me, sweetheart. What hurts the most?"

The silence dragged on. Finally he felt her take a deep quivering breath, then she muttered, "My pride." She tightened her arms around him and began to cry all over again.

Eleanor's pride was still smarting a few hours later. She was wearing a huge flannel nightshirt with sleeves that came to her knees and sitting on the most dangerous place she could think of—Conn Donoughue's bed.

Bed. The word was enough to make her want to crawl in a hole and never come out. That whole cabinet fiasco was so embarrassing. She felt foolish. What a goose! All that silly crying. She'd never done that before. Whenever she was around him, she was not herself. That was the trouble with love. It made you act in the most irrational ways.

The more she thought about it, the more she realized that love was a lot like the winter weather. It came at the worst time and made your life as difficult as possible.

Emotions were so hard to understand. Like the way snow and ice always fell, then melted. There was no reason why, it just did. Love was the same; it just smacked you right in the face for no logical reason at all. You could ask yourself why forever, but that didn't change the fact that you loved the person you were destined to love. And it seemed, she was destined to love Conn Donoughue.

To make the whole thing even worse, he had been really kind to her. A perfect gentleman.

She drew his brush through her hair with hard quick strokes that hurt, a handy way of punishing herself. Her scalp was tingling and felt abused, but she kept brushing through her long straight hair, more out of nervousness than need or self-anger.

Heat swelled from a corner woodstove that crackled with burning splits of live oak. The brush stilled in her hand. She watched the sparks from the fire and realized that for the first time she'd awakened that night, she was actually nice and warm.

He strode back in the room balancing a tray and set it down on a table. He picked up some ice wrapped in a towel. "Let me see that ankle again."

Reluctantly she stuck her foot out from beneath the flannel shirt. Her ankle was so swollen and purplish gray that it looked like it belonged on a circus elephant.

Conn stood next to the bed, looking every inch the giant they called him. But he leaned over and placed the wrapped ice on her foot with such gentleness, she couldn't believe it. He made a point of tucking it around her ankle in the exact place it ached. She was so stunned, she ended up just sitting there staring at his wonderful hands.

"That should bring down the swelling," he told her.

"Thank you." She couldn't look him in the eye. She was half afraid he would be able to read her thoughts.

"Here."

She looked up.

He was holding out a blue earthenware mug. "It's soup, not poison." She could hear the smile in his voice.

She took the mug with two hands and looked in it.

"Go on. Taste it."

She slowly raised the mug to her mouth and took a tiny sip. Frowning, she looked down at the mug, then glanced up and took another bigger sip.

He was smiling at her. No cynicism. No double meaning. Just a sincere amused smile.

"It's good."

He crossed his arms and leaned a shoulder against a nearby wall. "My grandmother always gave me a mug of soup in the winter. After I came home from work."

"You worked?" The minute she said the words, she wanted them back.

He laughed.

"I didn't mean that the way it sounded. I had assumed boxing was your only profession."

"I didn't start fighting until I was eighteen. Before that I worked in a carriage factory."

"Really?" She took a drink. "For how long?"

"Eight years."

She choked on the soup. "You worked in a factory when you were just a little boy?"

"I was never a *little* boy."

She subtracted the years. "Ten is too young to be working."

"We were poor. By then it was just my grandmother and me. If I didn't work, she would have had to. She was all Irish, still had a brogue. The only job she could have possibly gotten would have been as a scrubwoman. She was seventy years old."

She could hear the tenderness in his voice as he spoke about his grandmother and told her how she had raised him after his parents died when he was a baby.

"She wasn't afraid of hard work, and neither was I. She didn't like it at first, but I had fought so hard to get the job, and I'd already been working there a week before I told her. She gave in, mostly I think because it was an honest job. No one took advantage of me.

Within a couple of years I was bigger than most of the men, so I never had any trouble."

He straightened. "I guess I'd better let you get some sleep. Tomorrow I'll have some of my friends help me, and we'll see if we can fix the roof."

She searched for the right words, but could only say, "Thank you." She paused, then added, "For everything you did. The cabinet, the soup, the ice, and the bed. The shoulder to cry on. I'm not normally like that. I . . . well, I haven't been very—You and I are usually not—"

"I know. You don't have to say it, Nellibelle."

She wanted to tell him how very much she hated that name, but she just couldn't bring herself to destroy this moment.

"When we're around each other, it's almost like we're in the ring together. You come out punching."

She was quiet for a second, then had to admit, "I do, don't I?"

"Yeah, you do."

"But you don't make it easy on me." She sat up straighter and saw him break into a smile.

"No. I don't."

She laughed then, too. "I think that's the first thing you and I have agreed on since—" She cut off her words. It would be a mistake to mention that horrible dinner together and what happened afterward.

He knew exactly what she meant. She could see it on his face. She felt her own flood with color.

He didn't speak, thank God. Didn't tease or give her a knowing smile. He just nodded.

She stared at her hands, folded in her lap. Then she gave him a direct look. "Thank you, again. For all you did for me tonight."

"Sure. It was nothing." He turned and left the room.

She flopped back on the bed with a huge sigh. She stared up at the dark ceiling. He was a nice man. Under all that bluster and cockiness, he was a good person. Kind. He loved his grandmother. He had honor and scruples, even when he was ten. Who would have thought it?

The lamp went out, and she could hear him settle in on the sofa. She reached over and turned down the gas lamp. Then she lay there.

It was almost too quiet. She could hear nothing but her own heartbeat, which sped up. He was there, just around the corner. And she was here, sleeping in his bed. She turned on her side, then sat up and adjusted the ice and drew the covers over her.

Her head sank into his feather pillow. She turned her face into it and breathed in. Conn. It smelled masculine. She turned and grabbed the other pillow, hugging it to her chest, and she curled onto her side, then closed her eyes.

"Nellibelle?"

She resisted the urge to moo. She flopped over on her back. "Yes?"

"Don't think I'm some kind of hero or anything."

What was this all about? "Why not?"

He was quiet.

Of course he was somewhat of a hero in her eyes. He'd rescued her—a damsel in distress. She smiled.

"You still awake?" he called out.

"Yes."

"I have a confession to make."

"What?"

"I knew the roof leaked."

A moment later she heaved the pillows across the room.

Chapter Five

❦

The next morning she went back to being herself. She was stiff and cold, which made him moody and brooding. They didn't speak, until the next day when he took it upon himself to repair her roof.

It took a week for Conn to fix it. While he worked on it, he discovered something about his landlady. Miss Eleanor Austen was so softhearted, she fed cream to all the stray cats in the neighborhood.

He had been right above her, working with some glass sealant when he heard her chattering away. He looked down and saw her puttering around the kitchen, gathering bowls and filling them with cream from the bottles he'd seen the milk wagon deliver.

Every day the cats came up the fire escape and sat there until she opened the window. Then they huddled near her feet, whining and crying until she placed the bowls on the floor.

Afterward she would tie red and green Christmas ribbons with little brass bells around their necks and open the window. Four cats stayed after that first morning, curled up on her sofa. Five others left, but from what he could see, they came back at the same time every day.

She began to talk to him the second day. By the third, she fed him sandwiches and coffee. They sat at her table and talked about the building, about her grandfather, and she explained about the lease and Andrew Austen's dream.

Conn had liked the old man and thought him fair. But Conn's first impression of his granddaughter had been that she was completely unpredictable and unreasonable. He never did understand her.

Until now when he knew her better.

While he worked on the roof he learned her routine. Kept watching her when he should have been working harder. She was tall and lean and had an efficient manner about her. But he'd seen her do the strangest things.

She was an odd mixture of logic and illogic. He supposed that wasn't her fault. She was a woman. But watching her try to put together one of her grandfather's telescopes had been something he wasn't likely to forget. She sat in the middle of the floor, with all the parts spread around her while she kept muttering that nothing fit. She stuck to it for three days.

In exchange for supper one night, he put the pieces together in an hour.

It was after that he had found himself thinking about her. At the strangest times. Every night he lay in his bed staring at the ceiling and wondering what Miss Eleanor Austen looked like naked.

He listened to the tap of her shoes across the wooden floors. But it was the soft padding of her bare feet late at night that made him sweat like he had before his first fight.

She was a night owl like he was, which surprised him. He'd have never thought it. Somehow he had imagined her rising at the same exact time every day, going to bed at the same time every night, eating the same breakfast, the same dinner, the same supper in polite little portions that for him would be one mouthful.

She ate like a horse. He had never seen a woman who could pack away food like she could. She ate it with perfect manners. She just ate almost as much as he did.

After the third night of sleeplessness, Conn was in a foul mood. It was late afternoon. He was working on the gymnasium's account books and making a mess of it. Nothing added up. He was just adding up a column again when a loud racket echoed up the stairwell.

Bam! Bam! Bam!

He ripped his door open and scowled at the third-floor landing. "What are you doing now?"

She held a Christmas tree by its top and dragged it up another three stairs.

Bam! Bam! Bam!

He didn't ask if she wanted his help. He simply took over. Muttering, he picked up the tree and walked upstairs.

She hadn't moved and was still on the stairs below.

He stood outside her flat for a minute, then leaned over and glared down at her. "You want to open this door, or do you want the tree out here?"

She grabbed her skirts and ran up the stairs. She fiddled with the key for a moment, then shoved open the door.

She blocked the doorway. "Thank you. This is far enough. I'll take it from here."

If she hadn't have moved, he would have walked right over her. "Where do you want it?"

For just a moment it looked as if she were trying not to smile.

"There." She pointed toward a bucket filled with sand.

He carried the tree over to it and stuck it in the wet sand. The tree was too big, too crooked, and it tipped over.

He picked it up again. "You need to buy trees with straight trunks."

"Do I? I have always felt a perfect Christmas tree was unimaginative. I think the bend in it gives it character."

"Trees don't have character."

"Well, I think this one does."

He struggled until he finally got the thing to stay put. He stepped back and eyed the tree. It was exactly right. Straight as possible.

"You know . . ." she said. "I think it needs to be tilted toward the right."

"I thought you wanted a crooked tree. What happened to its character?"

"Just because it's a little bent, doesn't mean I don't want it *standing* straight."

He turned around and stared at her. "Then, why didn't you buy a straight tree?"

She waved a hand in the air as if to dismiss him and began to drag a wooden trunk across the floor by its leather handle.

He walked over and picked up the trunk. "Where?"

"Just set it by the tree."

He put the trunk down and the tree slumped to the right again. Half an hour later she was finally satisfied. He thought it still looked lopsided. But she was happy.

He had tied the tree to a line of rope that he wrapped around the stem of a wall lamp. A hurricane wouldn't move that tree.

She began to pull out glass ornaments from the trunk

and handed them to him, commenting on each one and how it held some memory for her. Some made her laugh. Some made her drift off toward some distant place. But with each one he saw a little bit more of her true self.

Lost in his own thoughts, he stood there, looking at the glass ornaments but not really seeing them. She was humming Christmas carols and hanging decorations on the fir tree.

She stopped humming "Jingle Bells" after a few minutes and glanced at him over a shoulder. "Don't you want to help?"

He looked down at the ornament, then shrugged, "Sure." The next thing he knew he was decorating the first Christmas tree he'd done since his grandmother died.

A few hours later they finished the tree. Together. It sparkled with strings of electric lights with colored bulbs shaped like fruit. Tin birds in gilded cages hung from the branches along with paper chains and popcorn balls. Fine blown-glass ornaments from Germany were scattered all over while golden angels with porcelain faces looked like they were flying from branch to branch. Paper St. Nicholas likenesses hung from satin ribbons, and clay animals from Noah's ark were everywhere.

It was the best tree he'd ever seen, even if it was crooked. And when he stood from it and really took it all in, he realized that they had accomplished more than simply creating a stately looking tree from a fir that at first reminded him of a hunchback.

The most valuable thing they had accomplished had nothing to do with Christmas trees, crooked or straight.

Conn felt as if they were old friends. Nellibelle and

him. Who would have thought it possible? He could have never imagined them talking and laughing as they had.

Now she stepped back, sipping steaming coffee from a thick mug she held with two hands. "It looks lovely." She turned to him. "Now it feels like Christmas."

"You like Christmas?" He asked, thinking she was like him and didn't do much celebrating since they lived alone.

"Don't you?"

He shrugged. "I hadn't thought about it much. I did as a kid. But not in years."

"You should be ashamed. Everyone needs some bit of Christmas around them." Something caught her eye, and she looked past him. Her face lit up like the tree. "Oh, look!" She raced over to the window. "It's snowing!"

He joined her at the window, and for a few minutes they both stood silently watching the snow fall. As he stood behind her, the snow lost his attention.

He was looking down at her. At that shiny black hair he knew went clear to the backs of her thighs. Her straight nose, white skin, and bright pink cheeks. Her brows tilted upward at the ends and gave her normal expression a kind of exotic look.

There was an easiness about her—something he'd learned about her and liked. He'd had a good time tonight. He never even looked at his pocket watch, never looked at her clock. He wasn't bored, and it was almost two in the morning.

He watched her face, intrigued by what he saw. Her thoughts were there. Plain as day. She was completely lost in the pleasure of something as simple as falling snowflakes. She looked about sixteen.

She must have felt his stare because she turned and smiled up at him. He felt as if he'd taken a punch in the gut. Her smile was so powerful, he was certain it could knock him right out of the ring.

He thought about that moment a lot afterward. After he'd left and after he was in bed. And for years he would remember that smile, that wonderful joyous smile, as the one moment in his life when he saw how truly beautiful a woman could be.

Chapter Six

∽◦∽

She found the hole in the floor the very next morning, when she was trying to find one of the cats. The hole was underneath her rag rug and was about the size of a dime—just big enough to see through.

She pushed the cat out of the way and pressed her face to the wooden floor. There it was—his apartment. She shifted a little to try to get a better view.

Someone pounded on her front door, and she shot up so fast the cat shrieked. She stared at the door.

"Nellie?" He knocked on the door again.

She swiped a strand of loose hair from her face, brushed off her dress, and walked to the front door. When she opened it, he was standing there all covered in flakes of fresh white snow. He looked like a human mountain.

"Have you been outside yet?"

She smiled. "No, but you have."

He laughed that same deep wonderful laugh. "How could you tell?"

She stepped back. "You want some coffee?"

"Sure." He stomped the snow from his shoes, then shook his head, sending snow from his shoulders like a dog. Then he came inside, pulling off a pair of great shaggy gloves that made his hands look like paws.

She poured him a mug of steaming coffee and turned to hand it to him.

He was looking at the Christmas tree. "It looks as good in daylight as it did last night."

"It does." She watched him take a long drink that should have burned his mouth, but it didn't seem to bother him. "What were you doing outside?"

"Shoveling the walk."

"Is there that much snow?"

He nodded, took a drink, then stared at her for a moment. "The streets are starting to fill with sleighs."

She had moved to the window and was peering out. It looked as if the world outside had been dipped in sugar.

He stood behind her. She could feel the heat from his body and smell the wet leather of his heavy coat.

"Are you doing anything today?"

"No."

"I thought you might like to see the city. There's a sleigh just below the window."

She pressed her cheek to the old windowpane. Sure enough. There was a sleigh and a team tied to the front post. "I'd love to." She smiled up at him, and they both stood there for a second, neither saying anything. It was uncomfortably intense, so she looked away because it made her itchy for something more to pass between them. "Give me five minutes."

"Sure. I'll be downstairs." Then he left.

Eleanor raced across the room, pulled out a metal vacuum bottle, and filled it with hot coffee. She sealed it and then stuck it in a sock the way her grandfather always had. She grabbed it and tucked it inside a basket with some apples and a wedge of cheese, then she grabbed her coat, hat, and gloves and was down the stairs in a couple of minutes.

At the second-floor landing she slowed down so she didn't look like some silly old woman racing down the stairs. He met her inside the foyer and opened the door.

There was nothing like New York City when it was cloaked in a thick layer of fresh snow. He helped her into the sleigh and climbed in the other side. The seats were soft, and there were some wool blankets inside. She tucked one around her legs and feet, and straightened in the seat just as he snapped the reins.

The sleigh lurched forward, and they were off. The steel runners swished over the snow and the harnesses tingled. The horses trotted in a muffled clip-clop until he gave them the freedom to take off. A second later they were going so fast the sleigh bells hardly had time to jingle.

They passed other sleighs filled with people chattering and laughing like they were. Some people were singing Christmas carols and sleighing songs, and Conn began to sing.

She smiled and looked at him. He finished his song . . . if you could call it a song. Her cats sounded better. "It's a good thing you're a boxer and not a singer."

"I'm not a boxer. I'm a retired boxer." He grinned at her. For the next hour, he told her about his life as a boxer. They talked about everything while they drove all over the city.

The red and brown houses of Harlem were capped with snow. Manhattanville in its hollow looked as if it were peeking out from a thick, fluffy white blanket. Sleighs went up and down the wide boulevards, and the red shawls of work women flashed like cardinals in the snow.

Their noses turned red, and they sipped steaming coffee when the air turned colder. Sleighs dashed throughout the city, and at the intersections people shouted Merry Christmas! Miniature avalanches fell from roofs and awnings and onto the sidewalks below. People ducked and ran, but no one seemed to mind being doused with fresh snow.

He took her to lunch at an Irish tavern where the novelty of the day was to guess the weight of the owner's pig. Eleanor's guess was off by a hundred and fifty pounds. They sat by a toasty wood fire talking while they drank coffee mixed with rum. Lunch was spicy lean corned beef and cabbage. She loved it and ate as much as Conn did.

When they walked back outside, a mountain of snow had been formed along the curbs because the snow plows had been by. The ten-horse teams lumbered down the streets while the workers shoveled sand from carts behind the plows. One team turned the corner. The horses were frosted with a coating of frozen sweat and snow, and icicles hung from their harnesses like gems.

After the plows passed, the snow was piled in mountains along the roadside, where children bundled in mufflers threw snowballs at anyone wearing a large hat. A group of kids had made an ice slide in the banks of snow by the curb.

She and Conn watched them play for a few minutes. The boys would run halfway down the block, leap on the snowbank, and slide down it standing up, their arms out wide to help them keep their balance.

Before she could blink, Conn was running down the street and onto the snow. His height and weight made him slide even faster, and people stopped and watched, cheering him into a perfect landing. He turned, swept his hat off his head, and made a bow. She was laughing so hard when he joined her she could barely speak.

He made some stupid comment about a man's sport while they walked toward the sleigh.

"A man's sport?" She repeated, her hands planted on her hips.

He turned back just as she began to run down the sidewalk. She went over the bank and pressed her ankles together, and held onto her hat. She slid down the icy snowbank to a round of whistles and applause.

Conn was staring at her with an open mouth. She marched back toward him, her chin high and feeling more than smug.

"Where'd you learn to do that?"

"I was raised in New York, too. And if you'll remember, I've had more years of practice than you." She hopped up into the sleigh, pulled the lap blanket over her, and said, "Well, are you going to stand there all day or are we going to go sleighing?"

He muttered something about bossy older women that made them both laugh.

Snow was in the air. It began to fall a few flakes at a time, slowly at first, then faster and heavier. A light wind near the river carried clouds of snow in whirling eddies. Sparks from the potbellied woodstoves flew from trolleys and tin chimneys, and disappeared as if they were gobbled by the falling snow.

The trees of Central Park were covered in snow, making it a fairyland right in their own city. The Egyptian obelisk poked up out of the snow like a giant icicle. All the statues were dusted white and KEEP OFF THE GRASS signs leaned at cockeyed angles.

They parked the sleigh and walked down a covered path where children were having a snowball fight. She gathered up a handful and hit Conn, knocking off his hat like the kids from across town.

He spun around, completely surprised, then he slowly walked toward her, revenge on his face. She laughed and taunted him, and then turned and ran as fast as she could.

He tackled her in the snow and rolled with her down a hillside, tumbling like children and laughing. She tried to smear his face with snow but he pinned her to the cold wet ground. He grinned down at her. "Cry uncle?"

"Never."

He rubbed snow in her face and watched her squirm and shout.

"That's not fair! You're bigger than I am."

"I'm bigger than everyone." He grinned down at her. He seemed like a giant against the gray sky, and she understood where he had gotten his name. There was snow in his hair and all over his face. She slipped a hand out from under his and swiped the snow off his eyebrows and chin.

He mimicked her motion and brushed the snow off her face with a tenderness that didn't fit his size. But when he was done, his hand cupped her cold cheek. His smile faded. His look turned intense. He stared down at her mouth.

An instant later he was kissing her. She was forty years old and until this very moment Eleanor had never been kissed with an open mouth.

The first thing she noticed after the shock passed was that their lips fit together perfectly. His mouth was warm and a little wet from the snow, and she felt heat rise from somewhere deep inside of her, a place and a shivery feeling she never knew existed. His tongue played along the line of her lips, then scandalously slipped inside.

Oh, but this was better than her dreams.

Her hands moved to his shoulders. His hands held her head.

He kissed her eyes and nose and cheeks, then moved to her ear. He whispered her name, then pressed his hips harder against her thighs.

"I want you Nellie . . . I want you. Can you feel how I want you?"

She moaned his name.

His mouth was at her ear again and he chanted her name in barely a whisper. It was the most erotic thing in the world.

His lips skimmed her neck and jaw and lips. He kissed her brow, and then he was whispering in her other ear, as chills went down her whole body. "Marry me," he said.

She froze. "What?"

He pulled away and looked down at her. "I asked you to marry me."

She flattened her hands against his shoulders and pushed hard. "Let me up."

"Hey, what's wrong?"

"Let me up." She bucked up against him, and he sat up, his knees still straddling her legs.

"Now." Her voice sounded gritty and cold and distant. She turned her head away and closed her eyes. She was such a fool.

"Nellie? Stop. Please." He tried to turn her back to face him.

She held up a hand to warn him away. She thought

she might easily just crack in two. She squirmed out from under him, then stood and turned her back to him.

Her legs felt like wood. Still she trudged through the powdery snow and picked up her hat, whipping it in the air to shake out the snow.

He was standing stiffly when she turned around. She could see he did not understand. "I'm sorry, Conn. I'm sorry about this, about everything."

"Don't you understand that I care about you? I want you in my life, and I want to make your life better."

She just shook her head, unable to tell him how impossible this was. She was too old, just too, too old for him. People would laugh behind their backs and she loved him too much to expose him to any pain. He couldn't seem to see how useless the idea was.

When she had turned twenty-one and was a woman, he was thirteen and had hardly left his childhood. Yet she knew he wouldn't understand. She was the one who had to remain sane. She was the one who had to say no.

He walked toward her. "There must be something I can do. Something to make you admit you care."

"I do care."

"Then, why won't you marry me?"

"I can't."

"Tell me what I can do."

Her face felt twisted and tortured, and tears burned in her eyes. "You can't do anything."

He held out his hand for her. The look in his eyes was almost pleading. He obviously couldn't see how impossible marriage would be for them.

"I'm forty. You're thirty-two."

He jammed his hands in his pockets and stared at the

ground. His voice was so very quiet. "That doesn't matter to me."

"But it should. And it matters to me." She began to walk backward toward the park path. Putting distance between them.

He looked up. "Please, Nellie."

"I'm sorry, Conn."

"I'll give you everything you need."

"You can't give me what I need. No one can."

He stood there looking as empty as she felt.

"Tell me what it is, and I'll try."

"Eight years. I need eight less years." Then she turned and ran away.

Chapter Seven

❧❧

Snow kept falling and falling. Conn stood at his window trying not to think so he wouldn't feel. Snow and ice had whirled down so rapidly that it obscured buildings. Wind drove blinding clouds of it around street corners and made the snow stick to the buildings, frosting everything.

He didn't know how long he stood there. He'd watched the storm whip up even stronger, and at the height of it you could hardly see out the windows. Sometime ago night had fallen and with it the slowing of the storm.

But to him, time meant nothing now. He wasn't used to losing, especially something that meant so much to him. He wanted her in his life. He wanted to grow old with her and have babies and laugh and cry and love her.

And he'd made such a mess of things.

He wondered if he had taken one too many punches. There had to be a reason he would do something that stupid. He shouldn't have rushed her. He'd frightened her off.

The whole thing was so damn silly. It didn't matter

what their ages were. He paced his flat, and then heard
the patter of her feet above him.

He stood there staring up at the ceiling. He heard her
crying. At first he thought it was one of those cats, but
the longer he listened the louder she was.

His jaw tightened, and his hands clenched at his
sides. Everything was out of his reach. After a few
more minutes he crossed over to the window and
pulled it open. A blast of icy air and snowflakes
hit him. He didn't care. He stepped out onto the fire
escape, and quietly walked up to the fourth level.

There was a dim light coming from the bedroom. He
squatted down and looked inside the frosty glass.

She sat in the middle of her convenient bed, surrounded by mangy cats with the bright Christmas
bows. Her face was buried in her hands, and her shoulders were shaking with her sobs. It liked to break his
heart in two.

If he hadn't been certain she cared before, he was
certain now.

She loved him. He could tell, especially when she
wasn't very good at hiding her feelings. She sat there
looking like nothing but one big heartache. He knew,
because that was how he felt. Aching and empty.

But now watching her sitting there with her heart
broken, crying so pitifully was almost more than he
could take. It was so stupid. She was too stubborn to
see how very wrong she was.

A gust of freezing wind hit him and ruffled his hair.
Inside she was huddled in a blanket and had tear
streaks running down her face. He stood and turned,
then went quietly down the metal stairs. He went back
inside his window, not caring that snow was all over
the floor. He didn't think he could feel anything, even

the cold. It couldn't affect him. He was already frozen inside.

He lay down on the bed, and soon he was crying, too. Tears just ran down his temples and into his hair. His chest was tight, and it hurt.

He closed his eyes and lay there until it passed, his arm slung over his eyes. When he opened them, only hard reality stared back at him. For the rest of his nights, he would have to lie to himself. He had no choice but to pretend that he didn't know she was just one floor above him.

December seventeenth, the evening of Sally Waverly's Christmas wedding, came all too quickly for Eleanor. It was one of those evenings when the air turned blue with cold, and breathing it was sharp and painful and made you long for the lush feeling of a warm summer night.

She dressed in a deep green silk dress with a fitted jacket trimmed in jet that was the same color as her hair. She piled that thick wad of hair up on top of her head in a loose knot, stuck in some hairpins, then walked across the room, her heels tap tap tapping. She got her kid gloves, her woolen coat and scarf, threw them on, and moved toward the door.

She plucked her velvet hat off a peg near the door and stood before the oval wall mirror. Raising her chin, she held the hat just so—one hand on the back and one holding the brim, then set it on her head at a perfect angle. She took the hat pin from between her teeth and jabbed it through her topknot as she ran down the stairs.

And right into Conn.

"Hey there, Nellibelle. Slow down." His huge hands

grabbed her shoulders, and she stared up at the same face she dreamed about. The man she had watched through the hole in the floor.

She grew as stiff as a street pole. "I'm sorry."

He leaned against the wall and gave her a look that started at her head and stopped at her toes. "You're all gussied up."

"I have somewhere I have to be in"—she paused and looked down at her watch pendant pinned to her lapel—"in fifteen minutes."

"Where?"

"United Methodist Church." She paused, then added, "For a wedding."

He just watched her, as if she hadn't said that word. As if he hadn't ever asked her to marry him. No emotion showed on his face. He just turned and started down the stairs. "I'll get you a cab."

"That's not necessary. I'll take a cable car."

"You'll never make it across town in fifteen minutes."

"But—" She raised her hand to stop him. The front door closed.

She crossed the entry and opened the doors, then stepped outside, intending to tell him not to do her any more favors.

He stood there all tall and gallant, holding the door open to a shiny black cab.

She looked from him to the carriage driver, then decided to avoid an argument and went ahead and got inside.

She leaned toward the window to the driver's seat. "How much is it to go to—"

Conn leaned inside the door. "Put your purse away." His loud deep voice blocked out hers.

"Mr. Donoughue—"

Conn handed the driver a gold coin. "Get the lady to United Methodist Church in fifteen minutes."

"You got it!" the cabdriver said, and he snapped the whip before Eleanor could protest.

She sat there inside the warm, roomy coach, half annoyed and half grateful. Something made her turn and look out the oval window in the back.

Conn Donoughue began to shrink, smaller and smaller the farther away they went, until he was only a black dot no bigger than her thumbnail.

She turned around, then leaned back and closed her eyes, telling herself that he was just a dream, one that with time would finally fade away.

It was cold when she left the wedding reception, a bouquet of Christmas lilies held loosely in her hand. So very cold that the twilight had turned a frozen blue. Above the sidewalks, the telephone lines crackled in the cold.

The air was different; it seemed to be alive. Her breathing was labored, and she could have sworn there was ice inside her chest.

She kept walking, listening to the crunch of her boots in the icy snow. She stopped for a second and looked down at the bridal bouquet. She didn't coddle to superstitions. She'd even tried to give the flowers away, but everyone laughed at her.

She tossed the bouquet in a dumpster, then wrapped her arms around herself and just stood there for a long time. She would not be marrying anyone. She had lost her opportunity.

For the first time tonight, she understood what Conn had meant. Sally was twenty, youthful and pretty and full of life. The man she married was forty. But no one could have doubted their love. It was on their faces every time they looked at each other.

No one seemed appalled at the age difference. Old men frequently married younger women. So why did it bother her so that Conn was younger? She looked deep inside herself and knew that she was scared. It was her. Not anyone else. She had lived without love for so long that she had made herself into what she thought she was—an old maid.

But she hadn't been old with Conn. She'd felt alive and young and so very happy. What a foolish woman she was.

She tilted her face upward and took in the night sky, which was filled with so many stars it seemed impossible for the streets to be dark. She wondered what it was like out there where the stars sparkled and the moon glowed silver or orange.

If she were the moon, would she be able to watch the world below? Could she spend her life watching everyone else live and love? If she went somewhere else, would she feel as she felt here—a loneliness that made life sometimes seem almost insurmountable?

It would be so marvelous to just go soaring off into the sky until you were nothing but a tiny bright dot. Away. Far far away from everything. Far away from Conn Donoughue.

By the time she had walked another cold and icy block she was crying, sobbing hard painful tears that froze on her cheeks and chin and made her nose feel like an icicle. And when she got home and climbed up those stairs, she stopped on the third floor, wishing for something that could never be.

Half an hour later she climbed into her cold bed. What

had she done? She had given up what she wanted. She gave up her future.

It seemed as if she had lived her whole life between cold sheets and dreams. She wanted so badly to take back the years. She wanted to take back the moment she looked into Conn's strong face and said no. She wanted the chance to live part of her life over again. The part she had wasted, and the part she had thrown away.

Chapter Eight

❦

Four days before Christmas, Eleanor was in the kitchen making a huge pot of fudge so she could drown her sorrows in something wicked. She heard a thump above her and looked up. One of the cats was on a glass panel and crying down at her.

"How did you get up there?"

She wiped her hands and walked around the room. The cat followed her, crying the whole time. She went to the window and opened it and called him. All he did was cry harder and harder.

He was stuck up there.

She grabbed her skirt and climbed out on the fire escape. She went up the ladder and scrambled onto the roof. "Here, kitty. Come here."

The cat just cried and sat there.

After a few more tries she began to scoot over the roof. The moment she got near the cat, he leapt up and ran past her. Like a fool she tried to grab him and missed.

She slid in the snow and ice. She tried to grab something. Anything.

Oh, God she was going to die! She screamed as loud

as she could. Panic seized her so hard, she couldn't breathe.

A second later she felt nothing but cold air. She grabbed out again, and her hands closed around the icy gutters while momentum slammed her against the bricks. Her shoes scraped at the building, looking for some kind of footing.

There was none. She just dangled there. Her hands ached, but she hung on.

"Nellie!" It was Conn's voice.

"Don't move!" he hollered.

"Do I look that stupid!" she screamed back. She glanced over her shoulder as best she could and saw Conn running across the street.

She gripped the gutter more tightly. Her arms hurt like the dickens. She didn't know how much longer she could hold on.

Then she heard a clanging. It was the fire wagon.

She peered over one shoulder again and saw Conn Donoughue driving the wagon, a line of shouting firemen running after him.

He'd stolen the wagon. For her.

She smiled a little. Suddenly her arms didn't hurt anymore. She wasn't scared. She knew she would be safe.

The crank of the extension ladder made a squealing sound. The ladder crawled up the side of the building.

"Hang on, Nell!"

As if she would let go.

Conn climbed the ladder two rungs at a time. Then his arms were around her. She just held onto him and closed her eyes.

He carried her back down, whispering things that didn't really register because she was so thankful to be in his arms again. She could make out some words. Strange words like crazy and love and stupid along with a few choice curses. She could feel his racing heartbeat. The air was cold, yet his face was dripping with sweat. They reached the wagon and he got down, then strode toward the gym door.

"You can put me down now."

He was silent.

"I can walk."

"Be quiet."

She frowned at him. "I'm not hurt."

"Not yet."

"Are you threatening me?"

"I said, be quiet."

"I won't be quiet. I can speak whenever I choose. You are not my lord and master, you know. I realize that you just saved me from an awkward predicament, and I'm very grateful, but that doesn't give you the right to tell me what to do and not do. I'm my own woman. An adult. So don't think I'll just cower and be meek and submissive just because you tell me to. In fact, I don't know who you think you are—"

He kicked open her door with such force she did shut up.

He slammed it closed with an elbow. He lowered her legs to the floor and cupped the back of her head with his hand.

"This is who I am." His mouth came down on hers.

She was so surprised, she just let him kiss her. Then it was too late. She kissed him back. Kissed him with every hidden emotion in her lonely heart.

His tongue slid inside, and her breath caught just like before. Her heart pounded in her ears. She gave herself up to the passion and desire, all those things she had only imagined before.

He pulled her closer, kissed her longer and deeper, and held her so tightly she didn't have to hold on to him. Her toes barely touched the floor. She could feel his hard body against hers. She wanted more. She wanted to climb inside of him and feel everything he was and everything his kisses offered her.

She heard a low and earthy moan. It was her own voice.

He broke off the kiss so abruptly, she staggered back against the door.

He was angry, and his face showed it. "You need a goddamn keeper. If you even think about climbing on one more piece of furniture or get near that roof for any reason, I swear I'll—" He cut himself off and drove a hand through his hair.

He jerked open the door, then scowled back at her. "I don't know what I'll do, but if I were you I wouldn't test me."

He slammed the door behind him.

She stared at the door for a moment, then raised her fingers to her lips. She crossed the room to her sofa and plopped down on it. She grinned, then gave a short joyous laugh that on anyone younger would have been called a giggle.

"Oh, my," she sighed. "Oh, my, oh, my, oh, my. Be still my heart."

And then she began to really laugh.

Someone knocked on Conn's door that night. He was still trying to decipher his accounts. He threw back the chair and threw open the door.

Nellie stood there holding a plate. "Here." She held out the plate. "It's fudge."

He stepped back from the door. "Come inside."

She crossed the threshold as if she were stepping into hell.

"I'm not going to eat you."

"You're still angry."

"I'd like to wring your neck. How the hell did you get on the roof. And why?"

"I was saving one of my cats."

"The little black one?"

She nodded.

"That damn cat goes up there all the time."

"I didn't know that. I thought he was stuck and scared."

She was such a softy. "Why didn't you come to me?"

"I didn't even think to go to you. I just reacted."

He turned to keep from grabbing her and kissing the breath out of her. "We're friends, too, Nellie. We became friends first. Just because you have some idiotic idea about our age difference doesn't mean I have stopped loving you. It doesn't mean I'm not still your friend."

"I'd like to be your friend."

"I'd like you to be more."

"How much more?"

"I already asked you once. I won't ask again."

"Oh." She stared at her hands. "You don't want to marry me anymore. I understand."

"That's not true. I do want to marry you. I just won't be the one who asks."

She stood there a long time. When she raised her head, there were tears streaming down her cheeks.

"You know pride is a crazy thing. It can actually

make something completely unimportant seem to be the most important thing in the entire world." He pulled her into his arms and buried his face in her hair, knowing he was lying, knowing that he would ask her to marry him every single day of his life if that's what it took.

She muttered something against his chest, but he couldn't understand her.

She tilted her head up and looked at him. "Well?"

"Well what?"

"Will you marry me?"

He stood there for a moment. "What about our ages?"

"I was wrong. I was very wrong. I think I was just so scared, too scared of what I was feeling." She tightened her arms around him. "I used our age difference as an excuse."

He kissed her long and hard and with every ounce of passion and love he felt. "God, how I love you, Nellie."

Chapter Nine

❧❦❧

They were married Christmas Eve morning at a small neighborhood Presbyterian church. Since he was Catholic and she was Methodist, they settled on Presbyterian. It was also the first place Conn found that would marry them in less than twenty-four hours.

Tony was his witness and Mrs. Edna Waverly stood up for Eleanor. The wedding was small and fast, but it was the happiest moment in his life. His friends gave them a luncheon. Cuba passed out his finest cigars, and Tony made a toast, then Pete said a few words: "Das ist the happiest day for my friends. Vhat God meets, let nein people bury us."

No one understood it.

Cuba stood up. "What the Lord had brought together, let no man put asunder."

"Ja. Das ist vhat I said."

They spent the evening having Christmas dinner with Tony's family, then left to come home. For now, they were going to live on the third floor, where the rooms and furniture worked better for a man Conn's size.

Nellie had been puttering around from room to room.

Conn had a feeling she would just keep on doing so all night unless he said something. "Why don't you go on and get ready for bed."

She just stood there, looking lost and frozen. It was almost as if she had grown roots.

"Nellie?"

She blinked once, then looked at him as if she had just seen him for the first time in her life. She nodded and disappeared in the water closet.

He sat down on the bed, then laid back and stuck his hands behind his head. He turned and glanced at the clock. It wouldn't be long now. After all those nights of lying awake so he could listen to her above him. She was now his wife.

It seemed to him as if he waited forever for her. He glanced at the clock again. He could wait a little longer. They had a whole lifetime. Patience. Just a little more patience.

One of the things those years of boxing had taught Conn was how to be calm and wait for the right moment. He'd learned the lesson well, which was why he never lost. Conn Donoughue was a patient man.

Eleanor brushed her teeth so long she used up half a can of Pepsident tooth powder. She mindlessly brushed her hair a hundred times. Twice. She put almond nut cream on her face and hands, braided her hair three times in three different kinds of braids and then took each one out. And brushed her hair again. She spent another ten minutes dabbing on French perfume and a little talcum under her arms.

Now she stood there, feeling lost and confused and nervous. She went over to her bag and dug around

inside it for a moment. She pulled out a brown bottle of
Dr. Hammond's Nerve and Brain Pills. She took four,
then sat there for another twenty minutes waiting for
them to go to work. Ten minutes after that she decided
Dr. Hammond was a shyster.

She paced the small linoleum floor. Was she supposed to just waltz out there naked? She pressed her
eye to the crack in the door. She was actually getting
pretty good at this.

The lamps were on. She made a face. She just couldn't
walk out there wearing nothing but skin. Forty-year-
old skin.

She looked down at her body. Her breasts pointed
downward.

When did that happen?

Moving in front of the cheval mirror, she squared
her shoulders. Perhaps that helped a little. She turned
sideways. She had a small waist, but her hips were too
rounded and her stomach had a small pouch. She
sucked in a breath. That just made her ribs stick out
farther than her breasts.

She poked her finger into a thigh and watched her
nail sink.

She turned and glanced over a shoulder in the mirror,
then closed her eyes and groaned. She would have to
spend her entire married life walking backward.

She propped her foot on the edge of the claw-foot
tub. Her feet were fine. Of course compared to the iron
claw feet on the bathtub a chicken foot would look
passable.

She did have nice ankles. But she knew that.

She raised one arm up in the air. Turned this way

and that. How strange. She'd grown more skin. It also looked as if she had inherited her grandmother's arms.

She straightened and moved her face close to the mirror. Her breath fogged it up so she inched back a bit. She parted her hair in a few places. She couldn't see any gray hair, so she supposed that was a good thing.

Her hair was long, really long and full. It covered her behind. She smiled, then tried to spread it out so it also covered her arms and her breasts. It wasn't that thick. No one's hair was that thick.

Finally she stepped back, stood directly in front of the mirror, hoping the whole would be better than the parts. She tried to picture how she would look to Conn.

Conn, who had a hard-muscled torso and powerful legs. A rippled stomach.

Conn. A man without an ounce of flab anywhere on him.

Conn, who was thirty-two.

Oh, God, oh, God, oh, God . . . She buried her face in her hands.

What had she done?

What the hell was she doing?

Conn stared at the water closet door. He knew she was in there. He'd heard the water run. And run. And run. He'd pressed his ear to the door after an hour and a half and heard her muttering something that sounded like a religious chant: *Oh, God, oh, God, oh, God.*

He didn't know that much about Methodists. He was Irish Catholic, though he hadn't been in a Catholic church in years. After giving it some thought, he figured what she was doing was penance, like Our Fathers and Hail Marys. Perhaps she was too embarrassed to do it in front of him.

He sat back on the bed, happy that he was Catholic. Even if he hadn't been to confession in over ten randy years, his penance wouldn't take this long. He stared at the door, then muttered, "Hell, the devil's penance wouldn't take this long."

The door cracked slightly.

Thank you, God. He shot to his feet.

"Conn?" She was whispering.

He frowned. "What's wrong?"

"Nothing."

Nothing? he thought. She'd been in there since ten. It was after midnight. His patience had disappeared forty-five minutes ago.

"Would you mind turning down the lamp. I'm well . . . uh . . ."

"Sure! Yeah! Okay!" He leapt across the bed and snapped down the gas key.

The lamplight turned dim and golden. He had to admit it was more romantic and kind of nice. Made him feel like slowing down a little.

He turned back, his mind on what was to come. He winced. That was a bad pun.

She was still hiding behind the door.

"How's the light?"

She poked her head out. Just her head.

Her hair was down. Long and straight and thick. The kind of hair he could bury his fists in while he was loving her all night long.

"Don't you think it's still a little too bright?"

He looked from her to the light, then back to her. "You want it off."

She nodded.

He turned the light off. Anything to get her out of that room and into the bed.

He sat back against the headboard. She shuffled across the room. He felt the mattress dip from her weight. He resisted the urge to rub his hands together.

He lay there waiting.

She sat there not moving.

He sat up and gently cupped her shoulders with his hands, which felt twice as big as usual. He slowly pulled her back down on the bed. She was so stiff, she felt like she had been starched.

He leaned over and gently kissed her. He took his time, moving real slow. He didn't deepen the kiss, just tasted her lips over and over. Her hands slid around his neck. He pulled her into his lap.

Her robe was so thick he couldn't feel her body. He deepened the kiss and moved his hand lower, untying the belt to the robe and slipping it off. He slid his hand to her breast.

What the hell was she wearing? He rubbed his broad palms over the cloth.

Flannel pajamas. She was wearing flannel pajamas on their wedding night. He took a deep breath and said, "Sit up, sweetheart."

She popped up so fast, she almost knocked him in the chin with her head. He kissed her some more, deeply with his tongue and lips. He kissed her neck and ears and brow, and then returned to her mouth. He could die in that sweet mouth.

She wasn't so stiff, so he took a chance and rolled over with her so she was lying on top of him. When she finally moaned against his mouth, he slid his hands slowly up her back, rolling the pajama top up with it.

He had it off of her so quickly, he almost shouted with triumph.

He put his hands on her back again, seeking her warm soft skin.

She had on long woolen underwear.

He sat up and ran a hand through his hair. She was watching him as if she were a cornered animal waiting for him to pounce.

"You're nervous."

"How could you tell?"

"Sweetheart?"

"Hmm?"

"Please tell me what are you wearing?"

"Clothes."

"Layers of clothes, right?"

"Uh-huh."

"How many layers?"

"Just a few more."

"If I promised to go slowly and be gentle will you take off the long underwear?"

She unbuttoned it, and he felt her squirming out of it.

"Anything else?" he asked calmly.

"A cotton shirt. Should I take it off, too?"

"Yes."

"Okay, I'm done."

"Anything else?"

"A corset cover."

"Is that the thing with all the tiny buttons?" he asked.

"Yes."

"Will you take it off, too?"

She did so.

"Anything else?"

"An undershirt."

"And?"

"A shift."

"And?"

"A camisole."

He watched her for a long time. Then kissed her. He raised his head. "Nellie, I can't love you with all those clothes on. Don't be frightened. It's a beautiful way of loving. I promise."

She stood then, and he heard clothes falling to the floor. He wondered what else she had been wearing. Then she was in his arms and kissing him, holding him.

His wife.

She was so beautiful. He told her over and over.

He touched her whole body, and loved her with his hands and mouth and his body. She was everything he'd ever fought for and the one thing he would never lose.

Her name was a prayer on his lips, his name a whisper of love from her.

And when he was deep inside her, loving her tenderly and gently, it was good,—so very, very good. He cried when he felt her passion explode, because he was so in awe that she loved him and was his.

They loved all night and most of the morning. It was late Christmas afternoon before they got up. She tried to hide her body in the bright daylight.

He chased her, pulling off her clothes until she stood naked before him.

She had trouble looking at him. "My body is old," she mumbled, looking embarrassed and ashamed.

"Not to me. You are the most beautiful woman I have ever seen."

"But I'm not perfect. I'm not young."

He walked over to her and placed his knuckle on her chin and tilted her face up. Her eyes met his. "No, but

your body's got something else that's better than per-
fection, my beautiful wife."

"What?"

"It's got character."

And she burst out laughing.

Epilogue

❧

New York City, Christmas Eve, 1905

Giant Gymnasium still sat in the belly of New York, except now there were two entrances—one for the gentlemen and one for the ladies. There was also a separate smoking room. This Christmas, like the last seven, there were holly wreaths on the doors, one with red ribbons and one with green, and garland was draped on the fire escapes.

In the rear alley where carriages used to park there was now a brand spanking new Pierce Arrow sedan that still had pine needles scattered in the back from this year's Christmas tree. Inside, the lobby was still huge, but there was a homey wood stove with a basket of pine cones next to it, and Christmas music played on a Victrola with the RCA dog painted on the horn.

The message board was no longer there, because a large black telephone switchboard sat in its place. Behind the lobby was a small office, where Mrs. Nell Donoughue took care of the gymnasium books.

Up the stairs, the family home was now both the third and fourth floors, with an inside staircase that connected the floors. High above the fourth floor, the ceiling was still glass and two telescopes sat on their bases in the center of the main room.

Conn Donoughue stomped up the stairs, his huge arms filled with brightly wrapped packages. He shook the light snow from his shoulders and walked through the front door, stepping around cat toys and a scattering of children's mittens.

He set the packages down by the crooked tree and turned around just as his five-year-old son hollered, "Catch me, Daddy!"

Adam Donoughue leapt off the tall oak cabinet, bounced on his mother's new brocade sofa, and flew toward his father with his arms spread like an eagle.

He smacked into his father's chest with a thud. But his father would catch him; he always did.

Conn carried his son into the kitchen, where there were small hand prints of fudge on the table, the ice-box, the walls, and his wife's face, and where nine cats with Christmas bows tied around their scrawny necks played under the work table.

Three-year-old Julia sat in her mother's lap, her small hands cupping Nell's cheek while she gave her a kiss. "Happy Chrith-muth, Mama."

"What's this? No happy Chrith—muth for your father?" Conn gave her a mock frown.

Julie looked up with a very serious face that looked exactly like her mother's. She planted her fudgy hands on her waist and frowned at him, scolding, "Not Chrith—muth, Daddy! It'th called *Chrith-muth*!"

He leaned down and planted a loud smooch on her small face, then bent toward his wife. "I believe it's not only Christmas, now, is it?" He kissed Nell and tasted

chocolate and love and everything that was important
in his life. "Happy Anniversary, Nellibelle."

"Ah, mush!" Adam screwed up his face. "Yuk! I'll
never kiss a girl!"

Conn looked at him. "I'll remind you of that someday, son."

And later that night, when the children had been
tucked into their beds in their rooms on the fourth
floor, Conn stood one floor below, in the their bedroom
and pulled his wife into his arms. "Happy Christmas,
Nellibelle."

Then he started to kiss her.

Above him, someone whispered, "Ah, mush!" Then a
small giggle that sounded like his Julibelle sounded from
the ceiling. He snapped his head up and saw one small
eyeball, just like his son's, peering down at them from a
small hole he'd never seen before. There was some whispering, and second later, he saw his daughter's eye staring
down at him.

"Go to bed! Now!"

Two pairs of feet scampered over the floor above.
He looked back down at Nellibelle. "Just how long has
that hole been there?"

"Oh, let's see . . . Not too long," she said.

"How long?"

"About eight years."

Then she slid her arms around his neck and laughed,
that joyous, wonderful laugh. And once again, Conn
Donoughue saw the Christmas gift he'd always loved
the best. He looked into his wife's smiling face and
saw how truly beautiful a woman could be.

New York Times bestselling author JILL BARNETT is incurably romantic, from her first job at Disneyland to marrying her first love. A native Californian, this award-winning author of twelve novels and short stories is called "the master of love and laughter romance." Her books have been critically acclaimed in the *Dallas Morning News, Detroit Free Press,* and *Library Journal,* and nominated for the prestigious Golden Choice and Rita Awards by the Romance Writers of America. She has received Reviewers Choice, Readers Choice, and Career Achievement Awards from *Romantic Times* and a starred review (books of unusual merit) from *Publishers Weekly,* who praised her work as "hilarious! A ray of summer sunshine."

There are over three million Jill Barnett books in print. Her novels have been published in nine languages, audio and large-print editions, and have earned her a place on such national bestseller lists as the *New York Times, USA Today,* the *Washington Post, Entertainment Weekly, Ingram, Barnes and Noble, B Dalton,* and *Waldenbooks.* Be sure to look for Jill Barnett's latest release, *Wonderful,* at your favorite bookstore now.

CLASSIC WINTER ROMANCE
TO READ BY THE FIRE

Also Available from Signet

WINTER FIRE
BY JO BEVERLEY

A CHRISTMAS KISS,
AND *WINTER WONDERLAND*
BY ELIZABETH MANSFIELD

REGENCY CHRISTMAS WISHES
BY EDITH LAYTON, EMMA JENSEN,
SANDRA HEATH, BARBARA METZGER
& CARLA KELLY

Available wherever books are sold
or at penguin.com